I Didn't Think You Existed

I Didn't Think You Existed

Hazel Ro

www.urbanbooks.net

Urban Books, LLC
300 Farmingdale Road, NY-Route 109
Farmingdale, NY 11735

I Didn't Think You Existed

ISBN 13: 978-1-64556-236-8
ISBN 10: 1-64556-236-0

First Trade Paperback Printing August 2021
Printed in the United States of America

10 9 8 7 6 5 4 3 2 1

Distributed by Kensington Publishing Corp.
Submit Orders to:
Customer Service
400 Hahn Road
Westminster, MD 21157-4627
Phone: 1-800-733-3000
Fax: 1-800-659-2436

This book is dedicated to my loving and dear mother,
Hazel "Faye" Chamberlain.

Chapter 1

Tiffany

My three-bedroom, ranch-style home was just the way I liked it—clean, cozy, and peaceful. After a long and hectic day, I'd rushed home to my place of safety and serenity. Now after washing and putting away the dishes from dinner, it was finally time to relax. The only thing that awaited me was a nice, hot bubble bath to soak all my cares away. I'd already begun to run my bathwater filled with scented salts and oils. Then, afterward, I planned on curling up in my queen-sized mahogany bed to finish the latest novel by my favorite author, Carl Weber. First things first, I needed to pour myself a glass of chardonnay to assist in my unwinding.

As the water ran, I turned on my Pandora to the Lalah Hathaway station. I thought about how I couldn't believe I was about to give all of this up. David Allen, the man I'd had a long-distance relationship with for the past three years, finally asked me to marry him, and I'd gladly accepted. The weird thing was that I always thought I would have a completely different feeling about it. For some reason, I had thought that whenever that special someone God had created specifically for me entered my life, I would know without a doubt that he was the one. However, with David, I still had a ton of reservations.

We'd met three years ago in one of my favorite restaurants. My best friend and I needed a girls' day out, which included pigging out on some good ol' Southern cuisine at St. Louis's own Sweetie Pies. It didn't matter how many times I went there, I never grew tired of their food, especially since no one came close to making collard greens and cornbread like my mother except them. It had grown to be my home away from home, and I couldn't wait to get there.

When we arrived, the restaurant was filled with nothing but women, except for one lonely man sitting off by himself at a table in the corner. That in itself made me curious, but my growling stomach told me to just sit down and enjoy my meal. My best friend had other plans for me though, seeing that I had been single well over a year before that day.

"Tiffany, girl, he's kind of cute. You should go over there and introduce yourself to him," she suggested while waving me in his direction.

"Keisha, why are you always trying to play match-maker? First of all, he's not my type. And secondly, I'm sure he has to be with one of these women in here."

"Look, if he were with someone, then why is he sitting all alone? And there's nothing wrong with a simple introduction. Besides, you won't know if he's your type unless you get to know him."

Physically, I wasn't attracted to David. He was a lot shorter than I liked. Based on my eye test, he appeared to be between five foot eight and five ten, and even that was a stretch. His complexion was a caramel brown, and I was more into dark chocolate. He was also a little on the pudgy side, which was all right, but not my taste. I didn't want to come across as shallow, but I also felt that a person had to be at least a little attracted to whoever they were pursuing. None of that stopped Keisha, however. She was determined to hook me up by any means necessary. After I'd begged and pleaded with her to leave it alone, we still found ourselves enjoying the rest of our lunch in Mr. David Allen's presence.

We learned that he drove a tour bus on a weekend women's retreat, which explained why he was the only man in a roomful of women. He said they were from Dallas, Texas, and would be in St. Louis for the weekend. His conversation was cool, and he really didn't seem that bad of a guy, but still, he wasn't the guy for me. Not to mention, I'd never dated someone long distance or even someone his age, for that matter. David was twelve years my senior, although he didn't look a day over 35.

We finished up our small talk and lunch, but I was still starved from trying to eat daintily instead of totally pigging out. That was when David caught me by surprise.

"So, Tiffany, do you think I can call you or even see you again sometime?"

Before I answered, I looked over at Keisha, who gave me the evil eye and kicked me underneath the table. After a couple of moments of contemplation, I figured that a simple phone call would be all right. Especially after realizing how much I missed conversing with the opposite sex.

"Well, I guess a phone call wouldn't hurt—"

"Great! I plan on taking the ladies to the Galleria Mall and then to the riverfront, but I can give you a buzz sometime after that."

"Sounds good," I said with a partial smile on my face. I gave Keisha the same evil eye she'd given me before.

David called around eight that evening. There was no denying my nervousness, because I hadn't conversed with a man in that way in a long time. So that I wouldn't come across too forceful or anxious, I allowed him to take the lead, and let things flow naturally from there. To my surprise, it turned out to be one of the best conversations I'd had with a man in a long time. David had the greatest sense of humor, and I laughed the entire time. We actually stayed on the phone until three the next morning like a couple of high school teenagers. Neither of us wanted to let the other go, to the point that we both fell asleep on the phone.

Needless to say, he turned out to be a really good guy who I didn't mind hanging out with whenever he came into town. Little did I know he would come that very next weekend just to see me, then the weekend after that and the weekend after that. We started to enjoy each other's company so much that he visited me twice a month, and I, in return, visited him in Texas twice a month. That was all of three years ago, and now, only one month ago today, he'd asked for my hand in marriage.

I was overjoyed, to say the least, at the mere thought of being married, although it would require me relocating to Texas. He'd already made it very clear that St. Louis wasn't somewhere he could ever consider home, so I would make the sacrifice and move there instead. Even though I still had my inhibitions, I decided to go along with the whole idea. In my mind, I felt I wasn't getting any younger with 40 approaching only two years away. Not to mention the fact that my family had grown to adore David. Besides that, I was also ready for a change and new scenery with the recent loss of my mother. Everything here reminded me of her and kept me in a state of depression. So I needed to do something drastic, and moving to Texas was definitely drastic.

With all of that in mind, I assumed any jitters I felt were because I was leaving my comfort zone. I tried to talk myself into believing that anything I felt unsettled about would reveal itself once I was there with him. In the meantime, I laid my head back in my Jacuzzi-style bathtub and began to talk to God.

"God, I'm so scared and confused. I truly need to hear from you. Please talk to me and tell me if David is the one for me before I make what might be the biggest mistake of my life. I mean, I love him but . . . Wait, there really shouldn't be a but, huh? Anyway, God, please talk to me, even if it may not be what I want to hear. Please tell me what I need to hear."

That was the very last thing I could recall before I was awakened by a loud, thunderous sound. My eyes shot open wide, and my body trembled, frightened and shaking from the now ice-cold water. Thinking that someone had to be inside of my home, I jumped out of the tub, wrapped my bathrobe around me, and grabbed my bat from my hallway closet. Slowly, I began to search the house.

No one was there, and I giggled at myself when I realized it must have been a bad storm outside. Even after all these years of living alone, the slightest noise still scared the hell out of me. I went and looked out my window to see how bad it was outside, but oddly enough, I saw nothing but the dry ground. Walking toward my master bedroom, I felt completely puzzled. Things were strangely just as quiet and peaceful as before, other than the sound of the water that dripped from my bathroom faucet.

Right away, tears began to stream down my face as I remembered the last thing I heard with the exuberant sound. The voice that now replayed over and over again in the back of my mind said, *David is not for you.*

Chapter 2

Terrence

I pulled my black Cadillac Escalade up to my four-bedroom, three-bathroom home and sat there, sinking my head back into my plush leather seat. It had been such a long day. Actually, all my days were long. They normally started around three in the morning, when I had to get up to be at my first job with the Texas Department of Transportation. After that, I would race to my second job by three in the afternoon at North Dallas High School, where I coached and mentored the varsity football team. By the time I finished up with practice, games, and all of my paperwork, it would be around eleven at night. I wouldn't make it home until well after midnight. Then if all went well, I could try to hit the sack no later than one in the morning, only to be up by three to do it all over again. That was if all went well.

However, it had become a normal routine of arguing with my wife, Patricia, once my feet hit our living room floor. Night after night, I would come in and immediately be hit with, "Who is she? Why is she making those comments on your pictures? Why can't you just delete her?"

Needless to say, Facebook and other forms of social media had started to take over her mind as well as ruin our marriage. If it wasn't that, then she stressed me about our kids. Biologically they were hers, but I'd stepped up to the plate the minute we began dating since their father was such a deadbeat. The boys needed a man in their lives, and whether they liked it or not, I was it.

The oldest was Kendall. He was 20 years old. He'd dropped out his first year of college and couldn't seem to find a job. Patricia made excuse after excuse for him, but I knew good and well it was only because he couldn't seem to pass a drug test. Then there was Keith. He was 16 and seemed to have a good head on his shoulders, although he came out of the closet a few months ago. Now his only goal in life was to be a model, in a men's magazine, no less. So as one would expect, there was always some type of drama that I had to come home to.

Patricia and I had only been married for the past two and a half years, although we'd known each other for at least eight. Things actually started off great between us. We always laughed and talked, went on dates, and not to mention, had some of the wildest sex you could imagine. But as crazy as it sounds, all of that seemed to change the very minute we said, "I do." After the wedding, we started to go out less and less. Our conversations became voicemails or text messages. And the sex . . . well, let's just say there was always some type of excuse, whether it was a headache, the boys might hear us, or her very favorite, that time of the month. Either way, I wasn't getting any, so that combined with our daily arguments had started to become more than a notion.

For the life of me, I couldn't understand why she wasn't happy. She hadn't worked in the past year since her last job relocated. Besides that, she didn't have to worry much about money since I brought in decent income to support us with my two jobs. I purchased this house just for her and the kids and made sure there were two luxury cars available for our leisure. Although we weren't rich by a long shot, we lived a good, modest life, and she had nothing to want for.

Even with all of that, Pat still wasn't happy. Her only focus was on who I might be flirting with on social media. She bypassed all my suggestions like getting a part-time job, writing a book, or better yet, furthering her education. Instead, every night, I came home to her in flannel pajamas, a scarf or bonnet on her head, and her laptop on her lap as she surfed Facebook.

That was the very reason I now sat in my truck contemplating going to a hotel for the night. There was no way I could stand another night of arguing over something I wasn't doing. All I wanted was a hot bath and a peaceful three hours of sleep, but even that seemed too much to ask for. A few more minutes passed before I decided to go inside and face whatever fate I was dealt for the night. That was until my phone started buzzing across the center console of my truck. I looked down and let out a huge, aggravated sigh. "Damn, here we go again."

Terrence, where are you? Why aren't you home yet? We need to talk about this chick Sasha who's been commenting all over your pictures on your Facebook page! Who is she, and where do you know her from? I want you to delete her!

I barely finished reading the text before I realized that I'd started my ignition. It didn't even matter where I went as long as I was far away from Patricia and her nightly antics. I turned off my cell phone and drove toward the nearest Best Western.

"Tonight, I'm going to get some rest even if it kills me. God, please help me."

Chapter 3

Patricia

Terrence hadn't answered my calls or texts, and it was driving me crazy. He should have been home by now, and I started to feel like I was losing my mind thinking that he might be with her.

"Who in the hell is Sasha anyway? And I swear you'd better not be with her right now, Terrence Montgomery, or you'll have hell to pay!"

Pacing back and forth, I dialed his number again only to hear that his voicemail was now full. Not being able to leave a message pissed me off even more. If I knew where to start, I had the right mind to go out there and look for him, in pajamas, bonnet, and all. Instead though, I shot him yet another text, making sure he knew I meant business whenever he finally decided to come home.

You need to get home, Terrence! I'm not playing. You're going to tell me who the hell Sasha is, or you won't hear the end of it from me! I promise that!

Throwing my phone down on the bed, I thought back to the day we first met. I could tell he was younger than me, but he was extremely sexy, so I bypassed the age difference. His skin was dark and creamy, his body was built like a professional athlete, and he had so much swag that it made me crave to know more about him. I'd learned that he was somewhat down on his luck at the time, after losing everything from his previous marriage, but I didn't care. I could help pick up the pieces while training him to be the perfect man for me. We'd both worked extremely hard to get us to the point we were now. It took some doing, but we did it together, and here we were. Of course, we weren't completely where we desired to be, but we were comfortable, and that was all I could have asked for—until now.

I had no idea where things started to go wrong between us though. Our relationship used to be so good. We enjoyed one another and had fun building a life together. Then out of nowhere, it all seemed to change. Terrence tried to say it was I who'd changed. However, I didn't see it that way. In my eyes, he wanted to keep up the exact same behavior after we'd married as before, and I no longer felt like I had to. The facts were that I was ten years older than him, and my days of having sex anywhere or satisfying him orally all the time were over.

Also, being a Southern man, he was accustomed to those Southern women before me who believed in catering to their man's every need. Well, I was far from that. In case he hadn't noticed, I had two boys I needed to devote my time and attention to. I was the one who had the responsibility of forming them into good, well-rounded black men. I was all they had, and they were with me before him and would be here long after him if it ever came to that point. So if that meant I'd changed, then so be it.

I, on the other hand, felt that the distance between us was because of the lack of attention and affection he gave. He always worked. Then if he wasn't working, he was tired. Then if he wasn't tired, he was with those damn children at the school. There was always something else that took priority over me. He didn't take me out anymore. He didn't send me flowers or anything. And when it came to intimacy, any thought of foreplay was nonexistent. The whole act was all about him getting his and then rolling over to go to sleep. I felt like I didn't even know my husband anymore. In fact, we barely saw one another or even talked.

Basically, if I wanted to find out how things were with him, I had to go to one of his many social media accounts and stalk those. That, however, would lead to an argument because of his many so-called female friends. It seemed like every day several new ones were added. They made comments on everything, liked his pictures and statuses, and even posted pictures to his page with hardly any clothing on. These women obviously didn't give a damn that he was married, and I wouldn't stand for it. It was all so disrespectful, yet in his eyes, I was the one overreacting. He said it was only social media and I was reading way too much into things. His concern was more with me getting a job or going back to school, which I would only do when I was good and ready, not a minute before. The whole point of getting married was so that the man would be the head, so I took full advantage of that philosophy. Not to mention, I needed help with these boys, which I had to admit, Terrence was great with. His only flaw was that he was still somewhat a youngster himself and needed a little guidance in being the perfect man and husband for me.

Chapter 4

David

"Dammit!" What in the world had I done? And how on earth was I going to tell Tiffany that I didn't want to get married or have her move to Texas—all within the next few days? True enough, I'd grown to love her, but marriage for me was plainly out of the question. I absolutely loved the freedom I had as a single man, or better yet, an unmarried one. The more I continued to think about it, I wasn't ready to give that up—not for Tiffany or anyone, for that matter.

As I thought of it, I didn't understand why she had to go and push this whole marriage issue anyway. In my mind we had something great going with the long-distance thing, so I failed to understand why she wanted to go and mess things up. It was as if, all of a sudden, she started to harp on marriage over and over again, so much so that I practically felt my hand was being forced in the matter. Day in and day out, all I heard was, "David, I'm not going to be your girlfriend forever," or, "If you love me the way you say you do, you'll make an honest woman out of me." She even went biblical by reciting that verse from Proverbs that says, "He who finds a wife finds what is good and receives favor from the Lord." Yeah, I wasn't a deeply spiritual guy at all, but I knew that verse backward and forward now as much as I started hearing it from her.

Despite my true feelings, I didn't want to lose her or what we shared. So without thinking, I did the only thing I felt there was left for me to do. Just over a month ago, I had the bright idea to go ahead and ask for her hand in marriage—in front of her entire family at that. *Damn.* Now that I thought about it again, that had to be the dumbest thing I'd ever done in life. My thought was that I could merely give her the proposal and a ring, and that would be that. I was sure that was all she wanted anyway, to be able to show off to her friends and family. Then, afterward, I planned on us having a very long, extensive engagement until I figured out my next move. That was what I came up with because I was willing to do almost anything to keep Tiffany. She was really a wonderful woman with a lot going for herself.

But now that the ball was rolling, I realized how stupid it was, because I didn't want to get married or need her all the way here in Texas with me. There was still so much that she didn't know and probably would never understand. Sometimes men had to do the unthinkable for their daily survival, and there was no way Tiffany would agree with that. With that in mind, I had to find a way to stop her, and I had to do it sooner rather than later.

Tiffany was an extremely determined woman though, so it would be extremely hard to sway her. She was not the type to accept the word no without some type of explanation. In her world, what she wanted she got, and that was that. I only needed to come up with a clever way of making her think she was getting what she wanted, without actually having to give it to her.

Chapter 5

Tiffany

Despite the answer I'd received from God, the day had come for me to start my new life in Dallas, Texas. It wasn't that I didn't believe God or fully trust in Him, but I guessed my own personal desires far outweighed my better judgment. Not only that, but St. Louis had become so mundane to me that I desperately longed for a change of atmosphere.

David, surprisingly, didn't seem as enthusiastic about today as I'd thought he would. He'd been acting so strange and distant for the entire past week that it made me quite nervous. Keisha continued to suggest that I shouldn't read too much into his strange behavior though. She said that he probably had the same insecurities as I did, seeing that this would be new to both of us. Still, something in my gut said things just didn't feel all the way right.

Giving a look around my beautiful home one last time, I picked up my cell phone and called my fiancé, hoping that his disposition had changed.

"Hello?" he answered, still with the same dryness in his voice that had been there all week.

"Hey, baby! I'm about to hit the road in a second. I can't wait to see you and start our new journey together!" I said pleasantly while trying to hide my fear and anxiety.

"Uh, actually, I won't be there, baby. Um, a trip came up last minute, and you already know that I really can't afford to turn it down."

"Are you serious, David? I know money is a little tight right now, but you couldn't turn down one trip this once? I mean, this is a really big step for you and me, yet you're deciding to go on a trip?"

"I know, I know, but this is my only means of income. I can't just turn down trips like that. So, look, how about you wait, and come here when I get back instead?"

I paused and wondered if God was trying to get His point across yet again. Even if that were the case, I felt it was way too late for me to back out now. Everything was already in place for the move.

"David, I can't do that. I'm scheduled to start my new job on Monday morning. What am I supposed to do, call them up and say, 'Hey, I can't make it'?"

"Why are you so damn stubborn, and why does everything always have to be your way? Would it really kill you to wait until next weekend?" he asked with his voice in a raised tone. "I'm sure your job can find a replacement for one week!"

I pulled the phone away from my ear and looked at it with the side-eye since he wasn't standing in front of me. I didn't know what was going on with him, but he was starting to push me to call off the move, the marriage, and any dealings with him altogether. The only thing standing in the way was the fact that I'd already quit my job and scheduled Keisha to take over my lease to my home. Everything was in place, so whether he was there or not, I was making this move.

Closing my eyes, I took a deep breath and tried to soften up before I spoke. "David, honey, please tell me what's wrong. This is a huge step for both of us, but you act like you're upset with me and resent me coming there.

I thought you wanted this as much as I do. You did ask me to marry you, remember?"

"Look, I do want this, baby. I just have a lot on my mind," he said in a much calmer tone.

"Well, I hate to put more on your mind, but at this point, I really need to know. Do you still want to marry me, David? Do you still want me there with you?"

The phone fell silent for a moment or two while my heart almost thumped through my chest. I feared what he was thinking or what was about to come from his mouth. A few more moments passed before he finally answered.

"Tiff, yes, I still want to marry you. It's like you said. This is a huge step for the both of us."

Letting out an enormous sigh of relief, I tried to adjust my approach. "David, trust me, I'm sure we both share the same fears, but it's not going to help if we start taking things out on each other. Now it may not have been my desire for you to have a trip on the day that I'm coming there, but I guess I understand. We both have to try to make the best of the situation."

"You're absolutely right, babe. Hey, how about I leave the key under the mat for you and you let me know when you've made it, okay? I'll also text you the code to the security system."

"All right, sounds good to me."

"Good. I'll see you when I return."

"Okay and, David, I love you."

There was that deadened silence that brushed over the phone again. Then, moments later, he struggled to say, "I love you," back and told me to drive safely. That was the extent of it, which made me more afraid of what I was in store for. I only hoped that everything would somehow turn around and magically work out for the best when I arrived. Right now, I wasn't very hopeful.

Chapter 6

Patricia

I couldn't recall the last time Terrence had upset me to this magnitude, but I was steaming hot. It had been an entire week and he still hadn't explained where he'd been or who he was with the night he didn't come home. All he did was stroll up in here the next night, take a shower, and go straight to sleep without uttering a single word. To repay his behavior, I decided to sleep in one of the guest bedrooms until he chose to come clean. There was no way I was about to lie next to a liar and a possible cheat, so sleeping in separate rooms was beginning to become the norm in the Montgomery household.

Today was his day off, and I could smell the aroma of the breakfast he was preparing downstairs in the kitchen. I actually would have loved to sit down and have a nice, pleasant meal with my dear husband, but of course, that was out of the question. Instead, I darted downstairs, still in my pajamas, to see if he was ready to talk to me face-to-face.

"Good morning." I crossed my arms and stared at him as he placed everything neatly onto his plate. It all looked and smelled amazing, and since he was a great cook, I was sure it tasted the same. When I thought about it, I was glad to have a husband who cooked and enjoyed doing it as well. My mouth damn near started watering as I eyed the scrambled eggs, hotcakes, cheesy grits, and fresh fruit on his plate. However, I tried my best to remain focused on the matter at hand. Terrence didn't look up once or return my morning pleasantries. He simply walked over to the refrigerator, filled his glass with crushed ice, and poured some orange juice into the glass.

"I said, 'Good morning,' Terrence," I repeated, watching him walk over to the kitchen table with his plate and glass in his hands.

My blood really boiled when he opened his newspaper in front of his face like I hadn't said a damn thing. Next thing I knew, I pranced over to him and snatched the paper right from his hands.

"Woman! What the hell is wrong with you?"

I threw my hands in the air, amazed at what I had to do to finally receive some type of response. "What's wrong with me? You're what's wrong with me, Terrence, walking around here like I don't even exist. And you still haven't explained where you were a week ago when you didn't come home. Oh, and by the way, have you noticed that your wife hasn't been sleeping in the same bed as you, or do you even care?"

"Look, first you need to lower your voice and talk to me with some respect. Then maybe I'll answer your questions," he said matter-of-factly while putting the paper right back in front of his face as if the conversation were already done.

I snatched it again though to make sure he knew we were far from finished with this. "I'll talk to you with some respect when you behave like a loving and respectful husband and not some damn gigolo."

"Gigolo, huh?" He laughed while taking a sip of his juice. "You're funny, Pat."

"Just tell me, Terrence, where were you, and who were you with?"

"Now would you really believe me if I said no one? Because in your mind you already have it made up that I cheated on you, right? With uh, Sasha, I think is the name?"

"Please don't antagonize me, Terrence!"

"I'm not. I literally want to know; would you believe me if I said I hadn't cheated?"

I looked at him and wanted to smack the little smirk off his face as he waited for an answer. I would never admit that he was right about not believing him. So I lied. "Of course I would believe you if that's the truth."

"All right then. I wasn't with anyone. It was extremely late that night. I didn't feel like arguing like we normally do, so I went to a Best Western to get a good night's rest."

Part of me wished I could believe him, but something inside told me there was more than what he was letting on. "Best Western, huh? Really? Even when I'm sure you saw me calling and texting, you couldn't respond?"

He inhaled and exhaled before answering. "You and I both know that, had I responded, we would have ended up in an argument, Pat. All I wanted was rest!"

"Wow! Rest. Is that what we're calling it now? Neglect your wife and kids and have me worried to death all because you needed some damn rest?"

"Woman, stop it please. Your only concern was if I was with another woman. And by the way, Sasha is an old college friend, nothing more, nothing less. But I'm sure you won't believe that either."

"You know what? I'm so glad you're making light of all of this."

"I have to just to remain sane. I have to."

I leaned against the island and looked at him for a moment or two, observing his nonchalant and cavalier behavior. Despite all our recent arguments, for the first time, I became fearful for my marriage. So much so that I quickly spurted out, "Terrence, I think we need counseling."

"Counseling? You have to be kidding, right?" he said through a forkful of his meal.

"No, I'm not kidding. I'm dead serious. Honey, it's something that's been on my mind for a while now."

"Pat, have a seat please."

I hesitated while still leaning against the island until he repeated himself.

"I asked you to have a seat, Patricia."

Slowly, I took the chair across from him and looked him square in the eyes, waiting to hear what he had to say.

"Now I agree that lately we've done more arguing than loving, but to suggest counseling is a bit farfetched to me. In my opinion, marriage counseling means that there's a fault on both our ends that we need to reconcile, and I just don't find that to be true. I work hard to take care of this family, and maybe if I had your support instead of accusations, things might be different. So my answer is no. I won't fit counseling or anything else into my already-hectic schedule. But maybe personal counseling for you might not be such a bad idea. Maybe someone else can get through to you where I can't. I honestly believe you have way too much idle time on your hands, which brings about all this negativity. But since you won't hear me, maybe you will hear it from someone else."

I was downright offended and hurt by his response. It was unbelievable how he basically portrayed himself as almost perfect while making me out to be the bad guy. In his little mind, all I needed to do was go back to work or school and things would suddenly be good between us again. Well, I didn't believe that. In fact, I didn't even bother replying to what he said. Rather than addressing him any further, I hopped up, shoved my chair underneath the table, and ran back upstairs to the guest room. Until things were right between us, this was how it would have to be. And I didn't plan on seeing anyone's counselor alone!

Chapter 7

Terrence

Counseling. I shook my head and laughed to myself at the mere thought of it while I finished my breakfast. Patricia, the kids, our marriage—all of it had started to take a real toll on me. Every day, there was something new, and no real sense of peace and happiness was anywhere in sight. I didn't want to quit or give up on our marriage. I prided myself on being a man who took care of my responsibilities. I'd also never failed at anything in life before, and I didn't want to start now. But this entire situation had begun to change me. It changed my beliefs, my outlook on love and relationships, and even my faith. All I wanted was to be happy, and basically, I wasn't. My usual care and concern about my marriage slowly diminished, and I hated this feeling.

It didn't matter to me that I hadn't been intimate with my wife, kissed her, held hands or anything in quite a long time. On top of all of that, as quiet as it's kept, finances had become a major problem in our household. Everything was so much easier when she was working and contributing to the household as well. But, for the past year since she'd been laid off, I'd struggled to make ends meet being the only breadwinner in the house. Even our nest egg of a savings that I'd established when Patricia received her pension had started to dwindle.

Every time I turned around, Kendall was in some kind of trouble and needed to be bailed out. He stayed in fights with the law, and we'd poured out thousands already to keep him out of jail. Then I had to figure out how I was about to pay for yet another college tuition bill without taking out student loans for Keith, who I prayed wouldn't follow in the footsteps of his brother. And to add fuel to the fire, Pat's latest hobby had become buying unnecessary things from Amazon because she had nothing better to do.

They left me drained mentally and financially to the point where I had very little left for my own two biological children, Kiara and Tiara. They were twins and the joys of my life. They were my reason for being, and most times I wished their mother and I could have had a real family. I just wasn't the man I should have been or what she needed when she got pregnant with the girls. I was in the world doing all sorts of things that I had no business doing instead of at home, taking care of my family. I could now acknowledge that I'd lacked the maturity she needed in a man, let alone a husband, to help her raise two children. So we divorced, and she found someone who could do for her what I didn't. I did have weekly visitations with my girls though, but only at her parents' home. Patricia and their mother hated one another, and she didn't want my obnoxious wife around our children. I couldn't say I disagreed either based on their initial meeting.

Pat behaved horribly that day. What should have been a peaceful dinner in hopes of blending our families turned into a Pat bragging session. She showed off her ring every second and boasted how she was the wife while my ex was nothing more than the baby momma. I was completely embarrassed by it all and still found myself apologizing to this very day to my children's mother. Of course, Pat didn't see anything wrong with her behavior or that my girls weren't a part of our lives like her boys were. My life was nonexistent while I bent over backward for hers. She even had the nerve to say that she didn't care for little girls anyway because they were too fast and hot at too young an age.

The more I reflected on it all, the hotter I became. That was the very reason I couldn't wait to get dressed and head to my new favorite pastime to release some stress—the casino. True enough, it was a little early in the morning to go, but with my schedule, I had to sneak it in when I could. I'd hit pretty good the other day when I went with an old college buddy, so with the day off, I figured I'd try my luck again. Just the thought of doubling or tripling my money made me smile. I needed to hit much bigger this time around and was determined to do just that.

I washed my dishes, cleaned off the table, and headed upstairs to the master bathroom to shower and get dressed. Patricia must have heard me, because she shot out of the room and bolted downstairs with the speed of lightning. She even made it a point to let me know how upset she was by shoving my shoulder with hers without a word as she passed. Unbothered, I rolled my eyes and continued in motion to prepare for my mission for the day. Until I walked away from that blackjack table with enough to pay at least a couple months' worth of bills, Pat was the least of my worries.

Part of me also looked forward to meeting someone new, beautiful, and interesting, like Lisa. There were always single and even married women who lurked around looking for good conversation and attention. Lisa was one of the single ones, and we'd just happened to hit it off the night I went. She was extremely easy on the eyes and a great conversationalist. She was a breath of fresh air from my problems here at home. I hoped she'd picked up on my hint of being there today and showed up herself. I didn't have any thoughts of cheating on Patricia with Lisa, because that wasn't my style, but I also didn't think there was anything wrong with a little harmless flirting here and there.

As I put on my dark denim jeans and a soft blue button-down shirt, I admired my reflection in the mirror. I loved how the color looked against my dark skin, and I hoped that Lisa would feel the same. After I finished dressing, I made sure my bald head wasn't too shiny and that the hairs in my full beard were perfectly in place. Then I sprayed on one of the new colognes I'd purchased, Burberry Touch. It gave a clean and fresh scent with just the right hint of spice. It wasn't strong and overpowering but proved to turn heads as I walked by. One final check in the floor-length mirror and I felt like I was ready to win on the blackjack table and with Lisa. That was until I caught a glimpse of my ring finger.

I looked down and realized I hadn't removed my ring once since I married, but today was different. It might have been wrong of me, but since I'd been accused of being a gigolo, I may as well look like one. Pulling off my ring, I threw it on the nightstand drawer and walked out without a second thought.

Chapter 8

David

My stomach turned flips ever since I'd gotten off the phone with Tiffany, and this feeling was sure to last until I figured out what to do. Sitting at my mother's kitchen table while she prepared breakfast for us, I watched as she moved gracefully around the kitchen, putting a little dab of this here and a little dab of that there. It always amazed me how she took so much pleasure in making sure that everything was perfect for me, her only son. My mother took care of me in such a way that I was sure no other woman on this earth would be able to. It made my soul and growling stomach happy.

As my thoughts slowly drifted back to Tiffany, I wondered if maybe that was likely the very reason I was so fearful of committing to her. Well, that and a couple of other reasons that I was sure she would never understand. Of course, I was much further along in age than she was and probably should have been ready to settle down. If I actually planned on settling, then the person would have to be an extraordinary woman. That wasn't to say that Tiffany wasn't that woman, but then again, I wasn't 100 percent positive that she was.

On the flip side, I also knew that I didn't totally measure up to the man she desired either. When we met, she had quite a long list of must-haves, which I basically didn't have. So what started off as a little embellishment on my behalf to get her attention has now led us here. I hated this entire situation altogether and knew that had I only been straight with her upfront, we wouldn't be in this predicament. I'd thought that in time, though, I could take care of things before it was too late. But here we were, and it was definitely way too late. Now I desperately needed to find a way to tell her the truth about everything without her hating me in the end.

My mother's deep, raspy voice interrupted my thoughts as she made her way to the table with our plates. She set them down, and everything looked so good that I took my time deciding where to begin.

"David, I worry about you so much, honey," she began before I was able to put my fork to my mouth. I'd actually had a feeling some sort of lecture was coming the minute her eyes spotted my overnight bag when I came through the door.

"Momma, I keep telling you there's nothing to worry about. I'm good."

"Now how can you sit there and tell me there's nothing to worry about when you're barely working and can't keep enough money to take care of your financial responsibilities? Oh, and don't think I didn't see that bag with you, too. You're staying the night again, huh?"

"Momma, look, I didn't come over here to get fussed at or criticized, all right? I hit a small rough patch, that's all, but I'll bounce back. I always do. And yes, if it's all right with you, I would like to stay the night here. Well, more like a few nights."

"A few nights? David, what's going on with wherever you've been laying your head? And where have you been staying anyway? You know, as your mother, I think I have the right to know these types of things."

"Momma, do we really need to discuss this right now? Can't we just enjoy our breakfast quietly and peacefully?"

I asked firmly while shoving a forkful of eggs into my mouth.

"Well, I don't see a better time to discuss things than now, and I certainly plan on enjoying my breakfast either way. But tell me what's going on, David. My guess is that you must be shacking up with some woman and made her mad, so now she's put you out, huh?"

"Wow, it seems to me that you already have it all figured out, so why are you bothering to ask me?" I shot at her.

"Now you wait a minute. Don't go taking that type of tone with me. All I'm trying to say is that you need to stop giving these women that type of control over you. At your age, you need your own place so that no one will be able to throw you out whenever there's a disagreement."

I put down my fork and took a sip of juice while choosing my next words carefully. "I'm sorry for my tone, but nobody has thrown me out of anywhere, all right? I just need a week or so to myself to relax and straighten some things out. I hoped I could do that here."

"David, honey, you're always welcome here but—"

Before I knew it, I'd cut her off, because I really didn't feel like hearing whatever was on the other end of her statement. "Then there's no need for us to finish this conversation, right?" I tried to persuade her to change the subject or quiet down as I put another forkful of her cheesy scrambled eggs into my mouth. I should have known that she wouldn't leave well enough alone though. She kept right on going whether I wanted to hear it or not.

"As your mother, I want the very best for you, David. I want you to have a good, stable job instead of contracting these trips here and there. I want you to have a home of your own and a wife and kids—a family, honey. Can you blame me for that?"

Although she expected a response, I didn't bother to answer only because I really didn't know what to say. For a few seconds, there was this deathlike silence that filled the room other than the clanking of our forks hitting our plates. Then suddenly she finished her thoughts as if they'd popped right back into her head.

"And if you ask me, I think that if you're going to be in this trucking business, then it should be yours, not working for someone else."

Her words were unbelievable to me. Now she sounded exactly like Tiffany. Tiffany always pushed for me to stop contracting and become my own boss. She even went so far as to say that she would invest in it as well as handle all of the administrative duties. The only problem was I didn't share that same passion that she and my mother did. Sure, I loved driving, but I was comfortable and content driving for others. It allowed me to have a sense of freedom without being tied down with all the extra responsibilities of ownership. Besides, normally I stayed busy, but as of late, business had become a little slow. It seemed like for the past few months the trips just weren't coming around as they had when I first started. Therefore, I did whatever was necessary with business and my personal life until everything got back on track. My only problem was that I never planned for Tiffany to relocate here during the process.

Although I'd missed the last couple of minutes of my mother's interrogation, she clearly hadn't noticed. She'd talked the entire time and now awaited my response to whatever question she'd just posed. "David? David? Are you listening? Did you hear me?"

I snapped out of my daze and tried to gather my thoughts. "I'm sorry, Mom. I must have missed whatever you asked. What was your question again?"

"I asked when you planned on getting yourself together."

I was about to make up something in order to appease her when Tiffany's name ran across my cell phone as it vibrated on the table. I didn't know which would be the better option—answering my mother's question or answering Tiffany's text. I decided on the latter. When I motioned to my mother that I had to take care of something on my phone, she turned her lips up as if I'd lied to avoid her question.

More than likely, she probably felt I was trying to dodge her continued questioning, and she was right. I simply wasn't in the mood to discuss David getting his life in order with anyone, not now and especially not with my mother. Besides, since I wouldn't be there when Tiffany arrived, the least I could do was respond to her text. My eyes took in the words on the screen as I moved from the kitchen to the living room.

Hey, honey! I just wanted you to know that my trip is going smooth so far. I should get there sooner than I expected! I still wish you could be there when I arrive, but as I said, I understand and I love you!

Glancing over the text several times more, I tried to decide what to say in return. I was glad that she was fine and safe, but I still knew I'd made a huge mistake by allowing her to come here. I needed to fix things quickly, so I swallowed the huge lump in my throat and responded.

Hey, sweetie! It's good to hear that the trip is going well. I wish I could have been there too, which is why I think we should change plans a bit. Why don't you get a hotel room until I return? It will be a little inconvenient, but you shouldn't have to move into the house alone. I should be there with you. I want to be there with you.

After I typed the last word, I took a deep breath and then exhaled. It was almost as if a weight had been lifted from my shoulders. And now as I waited for her response, I prayed she would see things my way. Of course, Tiffany wouldn't be too thrilled by my suggestion, but hopefully she'd agree. That way, I would have a little more time to think the rest of all of this through. Keeping her out of that house might actually be easy, but the far more difficult task would be to get her moved back to St. Louis.

A couple of minutes went by, and still there was no reply. Maybe she was so focused on driving that she hadn't checked my response. Or maybe she was so upset that she couldn't find the words to say to me. Either way, I started to sweat bullets from the mere anticipation of her reply. A few moments later my phone started to vibrate in my hand, and I slowly prepared myself for what might be the worst argument Tiffany and I had ever had. However, my eyes bulged when I looked down and saw the name that scrolled across the top of my phone.

"Leslie." I knew before I even answered exactly why she was calling, and I didn't feel like dealing with her at all. Instead, I let the phone ring until it went to voicemail. Admittedly, I felt bad about all of this, but I was only doing what I needed to with her and Tiffany. She called again and again and yet again until I finally decided to bite the bullet.

"Hello?"

"Thank you for answering, David. I know you've seen me calling over and over. Now tell me why the hell my account is short seven hundred dollars!"

"All right, look, I know you're upset, but the truth of the matter is I needed the money. It's as simple as that."

"You needed the money? But you couldn't have the decency to ask me for it, David?"

"Leslie, it was an emergency, so I did what I had to do. Baby, I planned on telling you, but it just slipped my mind."

"Emergency, huh? And what type of emergency required seven hundred dollars?"

"My mother needed some help with something, and I couldn't turn her down. But I'll return it when I get paid from my next trip."

"Yeah, right, David, just like the three hundred dollars last week and the five hundred a couple of weeks ago. Listen, I know you've hit hard times, but there's no way in hell I'm going to keep supporting us alone. If you don't have a trip next week, I think you need to go and find a real job! If you don't do that, then don't come back to my house. And as for my bank account, the ATM machine is officially closed. Did you hear that, David? C-l-o-s-e-d."

I heard a beep in my ear and finally saw Tiffany's name pop up. Lord knows at this point I didn't feel like hearing her response to my text after this call with Leslie, but there was no way that I could leave her hanging.

"Look, Leslie, let's talk about all of this later, all right? I have another call coming in that I really need to take."

I didn't give her the chance to agree or disagree or yell anymore. I just switched right over to Tiffany and attempted to change my now-sour tone to joy. "Hey, you."

"David, what is going on? Why are you suggesting that I go to a hotel for an entire week? I thought we already discussed this."

Damn. She hadn't even said hello. "Baby, we did. But the more I thought about it, I feel like it isn't fair having you move in all alone while I'm not there. I really should be there when you arrive at your new home, our home."

"Well, I won't argue with that, David, but you chose to go on this trip, so what's done is done. Anyway, my savings is withering with having to pay all my final debts off before relocating. I can't afford to go and lie up in some expensive hotel for an entire week."

"You won't have to worry about that, all right? I had them pay me half the money upfront for the trip, so I have seven hundred bucks to put your beautiful self in any hotel you like until I return. How does that sound?"

The phone fell quiet for a few moments. I hoped that was because she was considering my motion until, moments later, she shot that dream down.

"Look, as much as I would like for you to be home when I arrive, you're not. And I can't go to a hotel. Better yet, I won't go to one. I really want to get settled at our place so that I can focus all my attention on starting my job on Monday. I hope you understand that."

My mind raced. This woman wouldn't budge one bit, and I didn't know what else to say. I figured I'd just have to stay with my first plan, which now I wasn't so sure of after my conversation with Leslie. Anyway, little did Tiffany know we only had around a month before we would both need to find new living arrangements.

"All right, all right, sweetheart. Yes, I completely understand."

"Good."

That was it. That was all she left me with before hanging up in my face. I sat there in my mother's living room and tried my best to figure out how to take care of this with her. Once I took care of this, I could make things better with Leslie and then my mother. So now I was more determined to get Tiffany back to St. Louis, even if that meant breaking up with her altogether.

Chapter 9

Tiffany

Man, was I seething after I hung up in David's face. I couldn't believe him, and once again, I was left totally confused by his actions. He'd become so puzzling within the last month that I almost didn't know who I was about to marry. Even though I didn't want to face the truth before, I had to finally listen to what my gut was telling me—that something definitely wasn't right. Immediately, I thought back to my prayer and hearing God's voice letting me know that David was not for me. Part of me wondered if this was yet another sign of whatever God was trying to protect me from. *How could I have been so stupid and naive?* All types of thoughts began to run through my mind as I instructed my phone to dial Keisha.

She answered on the first ring. "Hey, girl! I know you haven't made it there already."

"No," I said plainly with a weakened voice, trying not to give in to my tears.

"Tiffany, what's wrong? You sound like you've been crying."

I'd already started to pull off to the next rest stop because my eyes were filling fast, and I knew I shouldn't drive with watered-down eyes. "It's David. Keisha, something's not right. I'm sure of it!"

"What do you mean? Did you all have another argument?"

"No, not quite. But I don't understand him or the sudden weird behavior that he's had for the past month."

"Did something else happen?"

"Well, I texted him just to let him know that the trip was going well, and that I should be there in no time . . ." I paused to take a deep breath.

"And?"

"And he shot me a text back saying that I stay in some hotel until he returns from his trip. Now all of a sudden he feels the need to be home when I arrive."

"Wait a minute, Tiff. I don't see what the problem is. You wanted him to be there, right?"

"I know, but the problem is, why would he suggest this now? Completely out of nowhere, he wants to waste money for me to stay in a hotel. That doesn't sound strange to you? Not to mention that he's not thinking of how inconvenient and inconsiderate that is when I need to be preparing for my new job on Monday."

"I'm sorry, girl, but this time I really think you're overreacting. Maybe, just maybe, he realized how inconsiderate it was of him for taking that trip in the first place and not being there when you arrived. Maybe this was the only way he could think to try to make things right."

I started to think that Keisha could possibly be right. Maybe I was overreacting because I was pretty much expecting for things to go wrong. "I don't know, maybe you're right."

"I am right. I think you need to calm down and make the best of the trip. I promise you two will work everything out and be back on track when he returns."

"Thanks, Keisha. Thank you so much for calming my nerves and helping me look at things totally opposite of what I'm feeling. You're always there for me when I need you, girl."

"Hey, that's what friends are for. Now stop stressing, finish your trip, and get excited about starting your new life in Dallas . . . as Mrs. Tiffany Allen!"

After the reassurance from Keisha, once again my spirits were lifted. In deep thought, I replayed the last thing she'd said over and over again in my head.

Mrs. Tiffany Allen. Mrs. Tiffany Allen.

It didn't have the ring to it that "Tiffany Tate" had, but "Tiffany Tate" also didn't have "Mrs." in front of it, so the last name Allen would have to do. Thinking about David again and my reaction to his request, I started to feel that maybe an apology was in order. With that in mind, I instructed my phone to dial my fiancé's number. I giggled a little because when he asked me to marry him, I took out his name and put My Fiancé into my phone. I dialed once, then twice, then after the third try, I finally decided to leave a voicemail.

"Hey, David, it's me. I wanted to apologize to you for the way I reacted earlier to your suggestion. I realized that you were only trying to make things right, and I guess I overreacted. Please forgive me. But I do hope you understand why I'd rather go straight to the house instead of a hotel. Anyway, can we just try to make the best of all this? Call me back when you can. I love you, David."

Once I hung up, I realized that, although I'd said the words, I wasn't sure this time if I meant them. I always felt that when you truly loved a person, there was a certain level of trust that came with that love. For the first time, I had to admit to myself that I didn't fully trust David. Although it somewhat made sense that he was probably as nervous about marriage as I was, I still believed there had to be more to this. I didn't know.

Maybe I only felt this way because things were in such shambles right now. Instead of dwelling on the matter, I tried to make myself believe that once I settled in and he came back from his trip, everything would be all right. I had to convince myself of this because I had nothing to go back to. I had to make this work.

Chapter 10

Terrence

After about an hour-long drive, I finally entered my new home away from home. Walking in, I inhaled the aroma of cigarettes and cigars, and I looked around. It was amusing to me that no matter what time of day I came, everything was always the same. The room was always packed with people of different ages and ethnicities, but we were all there for one common goal—to hit it big. The slot machines buzzed and chirped as everyone talked, which made it hard to hear even if the person stood right next to you.

I walked through, looking around, just to get a feel of the atmosphere before picking my game of choice. It amazed me to see so many elderly people on walkers and canes there to try their luck also. Who was I to judge though? We could all use a little extra cash in our pockets. Soon after, I decided that I wanted to stick with my usual and play blackjack. However, before I found a suitable table, I was on a bit of a different mission. My eyes surveyed as much of the space as possible to see if I could spot Lisa. True enough, I had a pocketful of cash and hoped to win some more, but somehow my trip wouldn't be complete unless I bumped into her.

After I hadn't located her beautiful face anywhere in the room, I decided to get back to the more serious matter at hand: to make sure I doubled or even tripled what I'd come in with. I walked over to what had become my favorite table with my favorite dealer. Jasmine had a lot of spunk and personality, which kind of livened things up for me. She must have seen me coming, too, because a big, bright smile crossed her face as she invited me to join the other four people already there. I also knew that Jasmine was a little infatuated with me, which I found sweet and adorable, so I obliged her invitation. Not to mention, the other tables were way too jam-packed for my liking.

"Hey, Terrence. How are you today?" she asked with a smile as bright as the sunshine.

"Good, pretty good, Jasmine." I smiled back at her and then nodded my head at the other gentlemen there. "But I hope to be a lot better once I leave your table."

"Don't we all?" the heavyset man next to me said with a strong, deep voice, and we all laughed in agreement. It was funny how our common money goals kind of made us a small happy family. At least while we were at the table together.

As Jasmine dealt each hand with grace, I concentrated hard and watched each card closely. Lady luck herself must have definitely been on my side, because in no time I was up $400 on top of the couple hundred I'd started with. I felt like things had gotten off to a great start, and pretty soon I'd be ready to up the ante.

I played the next few hands with the same intensity as I did the very first, and it amazed me how well I'd done. Winning was such a wonderful feeling that I completely ignored my cell phone in my pocket when it rang. Of course, I had a strange theory that it was only Patricia anyway. Knowing her, I figured she'd probably found something on social media that she wanted to interrogate me about. There was no way, though, that I would walk away from this table for her nonsense and allow her to mess up my lucky streak. Every hand got better and better, and I felt on top of the world, even with the continued interruption of my phone. After all my luck on the table, I felt my current high couldn't get any better. That was until I heard a soft, sensual voice in my ear. There was no need for me to even turn around, because her lovely scent had already introduced herself. The person I'd wanted to see had arrived.

"Well, hello, sexy," she whispered.

I couldn't afford a distraction, but she was a very pleasant one, so I welcomed it without hesitation. "Hello to you, beautiful. I was hoping we would cross paths again."

"Well, I'm glad I was able to make your dreams come true."

Everything about her was sexy. Her skin was flawless, her aroma was sweet, and her body was practically every man's fantasy. She was casually dressed, yet there was still a hint of sex appeal. She wore some very form-fitting, ripped jeans, a simple peach one-shoulder top, and peach strap-up sandals. Her accessories were also the perfect touch to her attire. She was absolutely beautiful to look at, and I loved her company. In fact, I enjoyed her so much that I hadn't noticed I'd lost my last three hands.

I continued to try to focus, but Lisa had all of my attention. Slowly but surely, that lucky streak of mine started to fade away hand after hand. The huge winnings I once had were now right back down to the $200 I'd started with. I quickly became disgusted and especially embarrassed that she witnessed it. Then, before I knew it, I played that money along with the other $900 in my wallet and lost it all. Instantly it was as if all the air had been let out of me, and I felt deflated. She must have sensed that my enthusiasm was gone, because she rubbed her hand across my back to soothe my woes.

"Hey, why don't we go over to the bar and you let me buy you a drink?"

"Lisa, I can't do that. I should be the one buying you a drink."

"Trust me, it's okay. C'mon."

It was hard to look at Jasmine directly, so I gave her a quick nod to say goodbye and walked away with Lisa. My phone still buzzed continually, which irritated me more because I wondered why Patricia couldn't give whatever it was a rest. Lisa and I then found a couple of seats at the bar and ordered our first round of cocktails.

"So how can I cheer you up?" She gazed at me while rubbing her hand up and down my shoulder.

"Oh, it's that obvious, huh?"

"Yes. But it's all right. See, the way I look at it is, you can always come back and try your luck again. There's always an opportunity to win."

"Yeah, that's true. But I was kind of hoping to win today!"

"Honey, everybody in here is hoping to win today and every other day they come in here. You're not going to win them all."

"But I was up big and just couldn't seem to walk away."

"I understand, but I'm hoping I can make you feel better," she offered again and smiled as she brushed her leg against mine.

Lisa had to know she was a huge turn-on, and I couldn't help but imagine doing all kinds of things with her in my mind. All of that had to wait, however, because I had become extremely irritated with Patricia.

I excused myself from Lisa for a minute and pulled out my cell phone, ready to give her a piece of my mind. But after I read her numerous texts, I realized she'd been trying to reach me to inform me that my father was at our home. Moving a few more steps away from Lisa, I hurried up and dialed Patricia back.

"It's about time, Terrence."

"Look, I was taking care of some business, all right? Where's Pops?"

"He's downstairs."

"Okay, great. Just tell him I'm leaving right now and I'll be there shortly. And can you please go ahead and fix up the guest room for him? Let him relax until I get there."

"No, Terrence, I can't fix up our guest room because there's no way he's staying here."

"What the hell are you talking about? That's my pops, and you're trying to tell me he's not welcome to stay in my home? Where I pay all the damn bills?"

"What I'm saying is that this is my first time ever laying eyes on the man. Me and the boys have never met him, so he's a complete stranger to us. I don't feel comfortable with a stranger staying the night at my home."

"Wait a minute, are you in some way trying to suggest that my father would do something to you?"

"Terrence, you're going to hear what you want to hear, but please hear this: your dad is not staying in this house. You're going to have to get him a hotel room," she demanded.

"Pat, you're a real piece of work, you know that? You get upset with me over some nonsense that you make up in your own head, and now you're trying to take it out on my pops."

"Look, this is not nonsense, Terrence. It's not my fault I never met your dad or any of the other members of your family. If I can recall, it was their decision not to come to our wedding."

"No, they weren't going to come to some shotgun wedding that they didn't agree with."

"Shotgun wedding, Terrence? Are you for real right now?"

"Just tell him I'm on my way. He and I both will go and stay at a hotel."

I hung up in Patricia's ear to get home as fast as I could. I'd forgotten all about Lisa until making it to the parking lot and inside my car. I felt extremely bad about it and made a mental note that I had to make things up to her next time, if there was a next time. Then again, maybe this interruption was meant to block me from doing something I didn't need to do with her in the first place. Either way, I felt horrible leaving her there all alone, but my father came first.

Driving as fast as I could, I bobbed and weaved through Dallas's heavy midday traffic. I was furious and prayed that I wouldn't put my hands on my so-called wife. That wasn't my style at all, but she had a way of pushing a person way too far. All I wanted to do was grab a couple of things, get my pops, and go. I prayed hard that things would go exactly that way.

Chapter 11

Patricia

Furious was not the word. Maybe enraged, irate, or raging was more like it. Terrence could not make me believe that he had no idea whatsoever that this man was coming here. A man I and my children had never met or known anything about. A man who thought he was about to stay an entire weekend in my home. No, it would not happen. Not over my dead body. There was no way I would allow it, and I didn't care one cent how Terrence felt about it.

I tried my best to calm down, but the more I thought about it, I couldn't seem to get past how selfish Terrence had become. How on earth could he think that it was perfectly fine for a complete stranger to lay his head in our home without consulting me? I didn't care if it was his father. It just wasn't right.

I thought about how Terrence hadn't seen let alone talked to this man in the almost three years we'd been married. Before the wedding, they'd communicated quite often, but it seemed as if something changed the minute he and I announced our engagement. Sure, there were members of his family who didn't agree with Terrence marrying someone older with two children, but they simply needed to get over it. Terrence was an adult, and it was his decision, not anyone else's. We proved that by going right along with our wedding as planned without one member of his family or friends being present. I'd made him realize that if they didn't want to share in our joy, then it was their loss and not his. And that was that.

Now all of a sudden, after all this time, his father showed up here like they'd just spoken yesterday. Well, I wasn't having it, even if Terrence and I had to fight tooth and nail about it. *Come to think of it, he'd also better guess again if he thinks he'll stay at a hotel with him.* There was no chance in hell he would stay another night away from this house. I planned on making damn sure that leaving his wife and kids home alone was not about to become some nightly routine.

My cell phone rang in my hand. I had been anticipating their call and what they had to tell me. "Hello?"

"Hey, I did as much as I could today, but something must have come up before I was able to ask everything that you wanted."

"It's all right. Something did come up, but I can't discuss it right now. Anyway, you just keep on doing what you do, and as I said, I'll make sure you're well taken care of for this."

"Sounds good. But, Patricia, I have to ask, are you sure you really want to go through with all of this? What if things actually turn out the way you're expecting them to?"

"Then I will have all the answers I need."

"But then what?"

"Look," I said before I took a deep breath and continued, "I haven't quite thought that far, but we have to do this. Please don't try to back out on me, because there's no turning back now."

"Don't worry, I got you. I only wanted to make certain that this is what you really want."

"It is. But we'll need to finish this later, all right? I think my husband is home."

I ended my call and quickly ran downstairs to find Terrence greeting his father with a warm embrace. He had the biggest smile on his face, almost like a kid who just saw Santa Claus or something. I, on the other hand, failed to understand what all the love was about when his family clearly disrespected us in such a major way by not attending the wedding. Why wasn't he still as upset about it as I was?

"So, Pop, you met Patricia, but did you get a chance to meet the boys?" he asked.

"Uh, no. It's only me and Pat here, but I can't wait to meet them. I'm sure they're some great kids. What about the twins though? Will I get a chance to see my granddaughters, too? Hey, maybe we can grab them and then all go out for dinner somewhere."

This man was a real piece of work. Terrence was far too googly-eyed to notice it, but I sure did. Some nerve his father had to make that kind of suggestion. Terrence had to know that was not about to happen with the twins' hateful mother involved. I watched with my lips turned up as he gave his father a half-smile when he suggested it. Then, to add insult to injury with his comment, he was "sure my children are some great kids." *Well, he's damn right they are, and he would have already known that had he been around all this time.*

On top of it all, where the hell did he get off calling me Pat like we were bosom buddies? I'd had enough of this already with this mini family reunion. I needed to talk to my husband, and I needed to talk to him now.

"Terrence, I hate to tear you away from your father, but do you think I can speak with you upstairs for a moment?" I asked in the sweetest tone I could muster up.

He didn't even bother to answer my question. Instead, he shot me a mean glare and headed upstairs toward the bedroom. Of course, I followed right behind him. This talk would happen whether he wanted it to or not. Once inside the bedroom, he wasn't discreet or anything. He left the door wide open and talked as loudly as he wanted.

"What is it now, Patricia?" he questioned with folded arms as if he had the nerve to be fed up with me.

"What is it? You already know why I called you up here, Terrence. How could you think it's perfectly fine for him to stay here?"

"Are you seriously asking how I think it's fine for my own father to stay in my house?"

"Your house? Really? The last time I checked, we shared the same last name and this was our home!"

"Yeah, maybe the same last name, but when was the last time you contributed a dime to any of the bills in our home?"

"Oh, wow, here we go with that again. You're the one who said you were fine with me not working when my job relocated, Terrence."

"You're right. I did, Pat. But I thought you would do something like further your education or even start a business, not stalk me every day, all day about nonsense."

"Oh, so now I'm stalking my own husband?"

"You may as well call it that."

He grabbed his overnight bag from our master closet and started to pack it. I jumped in front of him though to stop him. "What are you doing? Where do you think you're going?"

"Move out of my way, Patricia. I already told you that Pop and I would stay at a hotel."

"No, you're not. Why do you have to go? Why can't you just put him up in a hotel and come back home?"

"Because I want to spend time with my father, that's why. Do you really think I'm going to let him come all the way here and not spend time with him?"

"Why should it even matter, Terrence? Not he nor anyone else in your family had the decency to come to our wedding!"

"Is that all you can come up with? That was almost three years ago. Besides, did you really expect anyone to come to a wedding that was thrown together at the last minute?" His large hand pushed my small frame to the side as he continued on his mission.

"Terrence, I'm begging you not to leave, all right? We have things we need to discuss."

"So we'll discuss them when I return. But this weekend I'm staying wherever my father is."

"We are your family, Terrence, me and the kids."

He stopped briefly and shot a look that almost made me question if that were still the case. Then he moved from the closet to the armoire and got a few things from there and headed back downstairs like he didn't care about anything I'd said. I didn't know what to say or do at that point.

When I walked back downstairs, his father stared at me for a few moments before speaking, as if he were trying to figure out the right words to say. "Pat, I heard everything while the two of you were upstairs. Please, let me apologize for barging in on you all like this. I thought it would be a welcome surprise and finally give us the chance to try to get to know one another. Also, if it matters, I'm sorry that I didn't attend your wedding. I didn't agree with things because I thought Terrence was rushing into everything. It was nothing against you or the boys. Now although I am highly disappointed that you prefer that I don't stay here, I still respect you as the woman of this house. I pray that one day we'll finally get to be family."

He extended his right hand, and I had no other choice but to oblige. Bashfully, I looked away as I extended mine also. A second later, Terrence motioned to him, and they both left without another word. I didn't know what I felt more at that moment: ashamed of myself or hurt by my husband. However, one thing I felt for sure was fear. For the first time in my marriage, I was afraid that Terrence might not return through those doors.

Chapter 12

Tiffany

The air became hotter and stickier the closer I got to my destination. My GPS had informed me that I was only twenty or so miles away from good old Texas, and all of a sudden, I started to have mixed feelings about my arrival. I'd started to feel what felt like a million or so butterflies in the pit of my stomach. There was no doubt that I was nervous about the unknown of my new life, but I tried my hardest not to let it consume me.

"Think positive thoughts, Tiff. Think positive thoughts," I repeated over and over.

I figured I should probably give David a call and make him aware that I'd made it safely, but for the moment, I decided against it. Despite my apologetic message from earlier, I still wasn't in the mood to talk to him. He acted so strange about everything, and it still didn't sit well with me. Regardless of what Keisha or anyone else said, I knew for myself that something more was going on. Besides that, I just needed a quiet moment to embrace my new surroundings. No distractions, no questions, or anything, just me and the friendly land of Texas.

My heart started to beat a little faster when a few minutes later I saw a big green sign that read, WELCOME TO TEXAS. DRIVE FRIENDLY, THE TEXAS WAY. After spending my whole life in St. Louis, it was hard to fathom that I'd finally made such a huge leap. Yet here I was, and those butterflies became worse when I realized that there was no turning back. This was now my new home.

I stopped at the first gas station I saw to fill up my gas tank. Once I arrived at David's, there was no coming back out until it was time to start my position at the school. I wanted to move everything inside of the house and into its proper place so that I could kick back and relax. My challenge, however, would be redecorating David's bachelor pad. I promised myself I wouldn't completely redo everything, but I needed to make it feel like home for me and make my presence known. Hopefully he wouldn't mind. It shouldn't be too bad anyway, because I'd left all of my larger items in St. Louis until we became more comfortable with our living arrangements.

Heading inside to purchase my gas, I was immediately met with huge smiles, hellos, and "How are ya's" in some of the sweetest Southern tones. Everyone was so nice and friendly that it instantly took away my fear. It probably wouldn't have seemed like much to anyone else, but it was everything to me. In my eyes, first impressions were lasting ones, and the simple kindness of the strangers in this gas station practically made me feel like Texas was where I belonged. I grabbed a few snacks and drinks, then paid for those along with my gas before I settled back into my truck. Once I was situated, I entered David's address into my GPS again. At last feeling a sense of comfort and relief with my decision, I smiled to myself for the remainder of the ride.

"All right, Tiff! Here you go. There's no turning back now."

A little less than thirty minutes after leaving the gas station, there I was, pulling up to my new home. I'd been to the house several times before throughout our relationship, so I didn't feel completely out of place there alone. Pulling into the driveway, I sat for a second to take in the house and my surroundings. I loved how beautiful the landscaping was, and already I imagined where I would plant a bed of red roses. Roses were my mother's favorite flowers, so I had to have them nearby as a way to feel her presence.

The excitement started to grow within the more I looked forward to going inside my new home, so I didn't waste any further time in the car engulfed by daydreams. I had to unload everything from my truck, which I was sure would take a little while, so the sooner I began, the sooner I'd finish.

As I exited my car, an older African American woman who watered her lawn next door quickly approached me. With the tons of things on my to-do list, I wasn't in the mood much for small talk, but I figured I would bite the bullet and grin and bear it. I knew how important first impressions were, and in the event that I needed her assistance one day, I had to be nice to my new neighbor. She toddled over to me in her flowered housedress and slippers with the water hose in one hand and a cane in the other. Her gray hair was pulled back in a small bun, and she had a small pair of reading glasses dangling on the tip of her nose.

"Excuse me," her little voice trembled. "Excuse me." She continued to inch her way closer toward me until she was sure she'd caught my attention. "Can I help you?"

"Uh, no. No, ma'am," I offered. "Thank you, but I'm fine."

"All right, but just so you know, no one is home at the moment."

Although she came across a bit pushy, I appreciated how she looked after the house in David's absence. We all needed more neighbors like her to help control the crime rate. Usually, people feared being labeled a snitch if they told what they saw, but I could tell, not this lady. It was obvious that she was the neighborhood lookout, ready to report anything that looked odd or suspicious. I quickly answered her though, so she'd know that this was now my home as well.

"Oh, yes, I know that no one is home. However, David is expecting me. Thank you very much for your concern though. We appreciate it."

After that, she didn't say anything for a few seconds. She only stood there watching me as if trying to figure out what to say. Then she spoke up again. "Look, if you want to leave your name with me, young lady, I can let them know you came by. I don't feel comfortable with—"

There was that damn pushiness again. My mind tuned out the remainder of her words as utter annoyance kicked in. I figured David must have forgotten to tell her that he was engaged now and that I was moving in with him. It clearly must have slipped his mind with all that was going on. The only thing that was strange to me was that she said she would let "them" know.

"Who in the hell is 'them'?" I said to myself. I remembered that David's sister once lived here with him, but as far as I knew, she'd moved out at least four months ago. Assuming that perhaps that was the "them" of whom she spoke, I decided to ignore the comment. I figured that maybe the old lady was senile and just couldn't remember a damn thing. One thing was for sure though—in order for us to get along, she would have to mind her own business when it came to my and David's affairs.

I interrupted whatever her next words were. "Uh, no, ma'am, alerting David really won't be necessary. As I said, he's already aware that I am here." Then I stuck out my hand as a friendly gesture for a handshake since it seemed we'd gotten off to a weird start. "Forgive me, I never introduced myself. I'm Tiffany . . . David's fiancée."

The little old lady never told me her name in return or shook my hand. Instead, she pulled her glasses down farther, frowned at me in a perplexed manner, and questioned, "Fiancée?"

"Yes, ma'am! David and I are engaged, and I relocated here from St. Louis. Unfortunately, he had a trip today, so I'm stuck moving all this stuff in alone. That is unless you want to help," I said playfully, hoping to somehow get this lady to crack a smile.

The strangest thing happened next, however. Without another word to me, she threw down her water hose and hobbled as fast as she could into her home. I wasn't exactly sure what I said wrong, but whatever it was, she didn't care for it all. I tried my best not to think anything of it as I finished unloading my things, but it was hard tearing myself away from her odd reaction. I was almost tempted to go and knock on her door. However, I didn't want to start any confusion. All I wanted was for things to go as smoothly as possible, especially with this being my first day here without David. So I tried to brush off the strange encounter as much as I could but made a mental note to address it with him as soon as we spoke.

Hoping to get things started on a better note, I put the key he'd left underneath the mat into the doorknob and opened it. Things were just as I remembered them from my weekend trips here. Everything was clean and very classy, just the way I liked, so that in itself set my mind at ease. I wasn't used to a man who decorated his home or even kept it up in this manner, and it made the thought of living with him much easier.

Looking around, the only thing I planned to address were the pictures of his sister around the home. There didn't appear to be many, but I hoped he wouldn't have a problem with packing them away. When he and I first met, he shared with me that she'd gone through a very ugly divorce and needed somewhere to stay. He said that because he traveled a lot, along with the fact that she was a flight attendant who also traveled, it made the decision easy for both of them. They'd shared the home up until a few months ago, when David said she'd gotten engaged and moved in with her fiancé.

Thinking about it, I loved the relationship they shared. He always talked about her and how close their bond was. Unfortunately, I hadn't had the opportunity to meet her yet because she was always gone whenever I came, but now I couldn't wait. I looked forward to the day I met my soon-to-be sister-in-law along with the rest of my in-laws. Those were the kinds of things that had been prolonged by our long-distance relationship, but now there was surely no excuse. I would finally get to meet everyone, except for his mother, of course. He'd told me that she passed away years ago. With that in mind, I prayed she was looking down from above and giving us her blessings.

By the time I made my way to the master closet to see how I would fit my things in with his, my phone started to flash his name across the screen.

"Well, speak of the devil," I answered.

"Wow. I take it from the sound of your voice that you're in much better spirits than when we talked earlier."

"Yes, I am. Like I said, I guess I was overreacting. But I realize that you were only trying to make things better for my arrival, David, so thank you for that."

"There's no need to thank me, baby, but you're right, I was only trying to make things better. So I take it that you're safely inside the house?"

"Yep! I've been here for at least a half hour now and just unloaded my things from the truck."

"A half hour? Why didn't you call when you first got there?"

"David, because it's been a long day, and I wanted to get settled in the house first and take everything in. Oh, but I better warn you, I had a pretty strange interaction with your nosy neighbor next door."

"A strange interaction?" he asked with a hint of nervousness in his voice. "With what neighbor? Please don't tell me you got into it with Mrs. Smith."

"I won't say I got into it with her, but she's a very pushy old woman. She told me that no one was home and that she could take a message for me. But I politely told her that wouldn't be necessary because I was your fiancée who relocated from St. Louis and—"

Before I knew it, he cut me off and started yelling at me like a maniac. "Tiffany, you told her that? You told her you are my fiancée? Why on earth would you do that? That's none of her business."

"Wait a minute. Calm down, all right? What's the big damn deal?"

"The big deal is that I don't need my neighbors in my business with what's going on inside of my home and my personal life."

"Well, I think it's a little too late for that with Mrs. Smith. She seems like she's already very much informed."

"Listen, you just shouldn't have done that, Tiffany. Not at all."

A deafening silence invaded the phone call. I didn't know what I'd done wrong, and it seemed as if he wouldn't say anything more about it from his quietness. I wondered why something like our engagement was supposed to be such a huge secret to some old biddy next door. Or why it would be a secret to anyone, for that matter. Then, after a moment longer, he finally spoke.

"Hey, I'm sorry, but I really have to go. Look, I'm also sorry for yelling at you, okay? It's just that I don't like for the people I live around to know my personal business."

"I understand, David," was all that I could get out because deep down I felt it had to be way more than what he let on. Other than our goodbyes, neither one of us said anything more after that.

That quickly, the unsteady, sour feeling I'd felt earlier had crept its way back in. I sat for a moment on the side of his bed in the master bedroom and contemplated what I should do. No matter how much I thought about it, I had no choice but to suck it up and attempt to make the best of things. I'd already given up so much in St. Louis and had nothing to return to. Texas was now my home whether I liked it or not.

Trying to shake off my uneasiness and get back on task, I looked at the clothes inside the closet. "Wow, his sis really left a lot of things here."

I didn't want to be rude, but if I were to feel any better about this entire situation, I had to make this my home too. I went through the house and found a few empty containers. Then I turned on his radio and started to neatly pack her things in order to make room for mine. As I packed them away nice and neatly, the thought of this being a huge mistake filled my mind.

Out of nowhere, tears streamed down my face. At that point, I did the only thing I knew to do. I talked to God as best I could. I asked Him to take away this insecure feeling and replace it with peace. I told Him how sorry I was and that I should have listened to His voice from the very start. But now that I was here, I asked that He would have grace and mercy upon me as well as cover me with His protection.

"In Jesus' sweet name, I pray. Amen."

Chapter 13

David

Dammit! Although I thought I'd made sure everything else was under control, Mrs. Busybody Smith was the one factor I'd forgotten all about. All I could think about was the damage she would cause if she ran her mouth to the wrong person. She could destroy everything for me, not only my relationship with Tiffany. All I needed was a little more time to do damage control and get Tiffany back to St. Louis. My intent surely wasn't to hurt her but simply to have things back the way they were, because there couldn't be a worse time for her to be here. The perfect time may have never come, because I still had way too many things in my life that I needed to get in order.

Why couldn't you just be happy with the ring, Tiff? Any other woman would have been focused on planning the wedding of her dreams and not worried about relocating right off. "Damn!" If I didn't think of something soon, things were sure to get worse. Something told me that Mrs. Smith was going to dig and dig until she found out exactly who Tiffany was.

I also knew that Tiffany was not about to let things go with that crappy explanation I'd given her. Knowing her as well as I did, I was positive she was still concerned about the way I reacted to her interaction with Mrs. Smith. I wanted to call her back, but I figured that might do more harm than good. Anyway, I had no clue what to say to her to convince her that I wasn't hiding anything. I sat there a few minutes longer trying to contemplate my next move until my phone began to buzz.

"Damn, Leslie! Why are you calling now? What the hell do you want?"

Thankfully, it stopped before I decided to pick up, but seconds later it started right back . . . then again and again. Mental exhaustion took over as I laid my head back on my mother's recliner in her living room and closed my eyes. Something had to come to me quickly or everything that I had set in place would be ruined.

Then suddenly it dawned on me. If only there were some way to get Tiffany to hate Texas. If I could do that and basically make it her decision to go back to St. Louis, then she wouldn't hate me in the end. If she didn't hate me, then there would still be a possibility for us to be together. If things could go right back to the way they were, then all would be well again in my world with her, Leslie, and my mother.

That was it. This was the plan I'd been waiting for. I would make her hate everything—the weather, the people, the traffic, her job, absolutely everything. Then I knew for sure she would be right back on the expressway headed back to her hometown, and I could go back to business as usual.

"I'm sorry, baby, but right now this is the way things have to be."

Chapter 14

Terrence

Right up until the last ten minutes or so, I had been having a wonderful time with my father. Despite how things started off when he first arrived, the rest of the weekend had been a breath of fresh air and exactly what I needed. In fact, it was almost scary that it hadn't bothered me once that Patricia and the boys weren't around. I enjoyed life without them, and things were so comfortable that I started to think I could get used to it. A small part of me wasn't completely sure if that was what I wanted though. I was trying my best to stick with it for better or for worse, but that had become much easier said than done. I didn't want to leave her with two boys to raise on her own but, in reality, that would ultimately mean sacrificing my own happiness.

For a few moments, I sat on my hotel bed and took deep breaths in and out. Finally, I admitted to myself that I was no longer happy in my marriage. No matter how much I tried to talk myself out of those feelings, it was the truth, and it crept up on me from the deepest crevices of my mind, making its long-awaited appearance. The ugly truth was that I wasn't happy, and for the first time, I contemplated ending my marriage.

"God, what is wrong with me? What am I doing? I'm a man, and I'm supposed to be able to tough these hard times out. But Patricia just isn't making that possible.

Isn't she supposed to be my comfort, my peace, my support, my helpmeet?"

I hung my head low and thought about her, hoping to spark an old flame through positive thoughts. The crazy thing was I'd become irritated by the mere thought of my own wife. She hadn't crossed my mind all weekend, and now that she had, not one pleasant thought came to the forefront of my mind. I didn't miss her. I didn't long to see her face, kiss her lips, or feel her touch. The only thing that I did think of when it came to her was the type of deviousness she might be up to.

The fact of the matter was I knew my wife well enough to know that whenever she became this quiet, trouble definitely brewed on the horizon. She confirmed that for me when a text came over my phone saying that she needed me home immediately. Hearing the shower cut off in the bathroom, I stepped into the hallway of the hotel to call her. There was no way I was about to let my father hear yet another argument between me and this woman.

"It's about time you called, Terrence. We haven't heard from you all weekend. You do remember that you have a wife and children at home, don't you?"

Pacing back and forth in that hallway, I became more and more agitated by the second. I could have kicked myself for even bothering to call her back, because I already knew what it would be.

"Hello? Don't you hear me talking to you? Don't you have anything at all to say?"

I knew that I needed to answer, but I wasn't about to address her questions. In her text, she'd stated that there was some type of emergency, and that was all I was focused on, nothing else.

"What's the emergency, Patricia?"

"Oh, I see. So you're just ignoring everything I asked you, huh? Is that what we're doing now?"

Rubbing my hand across my forehead, I closed my eyes tightly to stop the ache that threatened my frontal lobe. "Look, Pat, you said there was an emergency, so that's what I'm calling about. If there's nothing going on, then I'll see you after I get back home, and we can talk then."

"Fine, Terrence. Fine," Patricia huffed with a brief pause to gather her thoughts. "Your son has gotten himself in trouble again, and he's been arrested. I need you to go with me to get him out of jail."

"What? What did he do this time?" I rolled my eyes, feeling like this was a never-ending story with this kid.

"I don't have the full story yet, but I don't want my baby sitting in some jail cell overnight."

"Look, regardless of what you want, that's probably exactly what he needs. If we keep bailing him out every time he gets in trouble, he'll never learn. And we just don't have the money to keep doing this. Let him spend a night there, and see if that can shake some sense into him."

"What in the hell is wrong with you, Terrence? I'm not about to let him stay there. First of all, he's a smart boy who has made some bad choices, that's it. So he doesn't need any sense shaken into him. Secondly, I don't care how much it costs. We're going to get my baby."

"That's just it, Pat. He's not a baby anymore. The boy is twenty years old, and it's about time you take his mouth off your titty."

"Terrence!"

"Yeah, I said it, and I'm going to say this also: if we bail him out this time, then it's going to be time for him to leave my house," I said calmly and clearly to make sure she got the point.

"Wait a minute. What do you mean, leave your house?"

"Exactly what I said. Now let me explain things to my father so that I can pack up and leave. I'll meet you at the police station in the next hour."

My infuriation with her and this situation wouldn't allow me to give her a chance to say another word. I was fed up with Kendall and planned on putting him out once and for all. There was no way that he and I both would be under the same roof any longer. If I had to sacrifice, then so would she. Ultimately, she would have to choose between me and him.

Almost three hours later, we pulled up to our home. I was exhausted and pissed, to say the least, but ready to stick to my guns. I fully meant everything I'd said and wasn't about to back down under any circumstances. As they hopped out of her car and quickly went inside, I eyed them and followed right behind. There was no way I was about to allow him to get comfortable, and I was ready to get this all over with.

When I stepped in, Kendall was nowhere in sight, and just that fast, his mother had gotten comfortable on the living room sofa and turned on the eleven o'clock news.

"Where's Kendall?"

"He went upstairs. Terrence, please don't start in on him. He's had a rough day as it is."

"He's had a rough day?" I repeated in utter disbelief. She had a nerve. "Please tell me what he's done to have a rough day besides get himself in trouble yet again and wait for us to come and bail him out."

"Look, he feels bad enough as it is, and all I'm asking is that we both sit down and talk to him in the morning. Is that too much to ask?"

"You're damn right it is. Kendall? Kendall? Come down here please."

He came downstairs. As usual, he trudged along with no real sense of urgency, and the sight of him alone pissed me off even more. There he stood with sagging pants, a large shirt, and no haircut in probably the last three weeks. Of course, I believed that a person should never be judged by looks alone, but we had to take responsibility in the way we presented ourselves as well.

"Yes?" he said with rolling eyes, hating to be there as much as I did.

"Yes?" I said back and crossed my arms as I waited for him to finish.

He huffed and leaned his head back as if he were irritated. "I mean, yes, sir?"

"What do you have to say for yourself today?"

He shrugged his shoulders. "Uh, I guess I'm sorry."

"Was that a question or a statement?"

Patricia stood up. "Terrence, please leave him alone," she jumped in.

Ignoring her, I continued, "Look, Kendall, you are twenty years old, a grown man now. I have provided for you the entire time I've known your mother with no real thanks or appreciation from you or your brother. Neither of you even show me the respect I deserve, but I won't start on that. My point is you won't get a job to contribute anything to this house. You hang out with your deadbeat friends getting high all day. You don't try to help your mother or brother with anything. You dropped out of college. Quite frankly, I'm sick of it all, and I want you to pack a bag and leave my house tonight. I really don't care where you go, but you won't be under my roof another minute. Once you've found somewhere to stay permanently, you can pick up the rest of your things."

Instead of giving me a response, he looked over at his mother.

"Terrence, stop it," Patricia yelled and then turned to her son. "Kendall, honey, go back upstairs. You don't have to go anywhere, all right?"

"Stay out of this, Pat. He's leaving my house tonight." I started toward him and grabbed him by the arm to pull him down the stairs.

Grabbing his other arm, she wailed, "No, he's not. He's my son, and I'll say when enough is enough."

"Your son, huh? Well, how about you and your son go live with his father? Oh, I forgot. His father lives with his mother." I released my grip on his arm and looked him square in the face, man to man. "Kendall, you need to do as I said. I'll give you an hour to leave."

"I don't care what you say, Terrence. I'm not letting you do this. I'm calling the police."

"The police? On who? Me? All right, well, go ahead and call them."

Chapter 15

Patricia

If Terrence thought he was going to put my child out of our home without a fight, he was sadly mistaken. I dialed 911 as quickly as I could.

"911, what's your emergency?"

"I need the police at my home immediately. My husband is trying to put our child out on the street with nowhere to go."

The operator took my name, number, and address and informed me that the police should arrive any minute. Terrence didn't look like he cared one bit, but his attitude was sure to change once the authorities showed up.

From that moment, the house had an eerie feeling in it. Terrence sat nonchalantly on the living room sofa and flipped through the television channels as if nothing were going on. However, I ran back and forth from Kendall's room to the front door as I waited for the police to arrive. I could tell that Kendall was nervous and panicky too, but I continued to assure him that I wasn't about to let anything happen to him. I made sure that he knew he was my first priority and not Terrence.

Coming back downstairs once again, I finally saw the flashing red and blue lights from the police car through the window. Soon after, two officers knocked at our door. To my surprise, Terrence continued to sit there.

I hurried to open the door. "Hello, Officers. I called you all because my husband is trying to put our child out without anywhere to go."

"How old is your child, ma'am?"

"He's twenty, Officer, but—"

Both officers smirked at me. One of them responded, "Uh, ma'am, your son is considered an adult. Is your husband home so that we can speak with him?"

I pushed open the door to show him sitting on the sofa.

"Uh, sir, do you think we can talk to you for a second?"

Terrence grudgingly got up from his comfort and made his way to the door. I listened carefully to hear what he would say to them.

"What's going on, sir?" they questioned.

"Nothing's going on, Officers. I have an unruly son who continually gets in trouble, doesn't want to work, and doesn't contribute to our home, and I feel it's time that he left. He's an adult, and I no longer want him here."

"Well, I can assure you that we understand. However, it is pretty late, sir. Does he have somewhere to go?"

"That I don't know. He has a father, grandparents, and tons of friends, so I'm sure he can stay at anyone's home for the night."

I wasn't able to contain myself any longer, so I butted in. "No, he's not going anywhere. His home is right here, Officer, and better yet, I want my husband arrested."

"Arrested?" Terrence shouted. "For what?"

"Officers, I want him arrested now for putting a minor in danger."

Terrence looked as if he wanted to put his hands on me. I could see the anger deep within his eyes.

"Ma'am, first, please calm down. Now like we said, your son is considered an adult, and this is your husband's home."

"Well, this is my home too, and I'm saying that he's staying."

"How the hell are you going to demand anything when you don't pay one dime into this house any more than that kid of yours does?"

"I don't care what's paid. My name is on the deed just as well as yours is, Terrence."

"Sir, look," the officer said, directing his attention to Terrence. "It doesn't look as if any of this is going to get resolved tonight. To avoid any further conflict, why don't you stay somewhere else for the night? You and your wife can try to figure this out in the morning."

"Wait, why should I have to be the one to leave my home, Officer? Besides, nothing will change in the morning. I will still want him out."

"Officer, I agree he should leave. I don't feel safe having him here with me and my children. I mean, you see for yourself how angry he is."

"You don't feel safe, Pat? Really?"

"Again, sir, why don't you just pack a bag and leave for the night? We think it would be best for everyone involved."

Terrence was furious and looked as he if could kill me. He went upstairs while the officers and I waited downstairs. Twenty minutes later, he came down with a couple of bags thrown across his shoulders. He didn't even look at me. He simply shook the officers' hands and left.

I wasn't sure where things had gone completely wrong, but I stood there in tears as the police prepared to leave. I was so torn. On one hand, I wanted my husband back, but on the other, I wanted my son to stay. Needless to say, if it came right down to it, I'd choose Kendall over and over again. Terrence would simply have to understand.

Chapter 16

David

Nearly three weeks had passed, and I hadn't been able to say anything to change Tiffany's thoughts on Texas at all. As a matter of fact, from the sound of it when I spoke with her, it seemed she loved it more and more each day. I thought she loved it so much that it didn't bother her anymore that I still hadn't returned home since she moved in. Once I was able to speak with Mrs. Smith and get her out of my business, I'd told Tiffany that yet another trip popped up, and I couldn't afford to pass it up. I told her it was another long trip, almost two weeks long, but that it would pay extremely well. Of course, I could sense that she wasn't happy, but she never said a word. Instead, she only told me to be safe and that she'd see me whenever I returned.

I thought for sure my absence would put a sour taste in her mouth. I'd even been extremely short and nonchalant, and whenever we talked, I tried to be as negative as possible. Yet, nothing I said or did swayed her to go back home. She loved the house, the neighborhood, her job, and basically her life in Texas overall.

On top of all of that, my mother reminded me over and over again that I said I would only be at her home for a few days. Now that it'd been almost a month, she hounded me every day about my departure date. Not to mention, she also drilled me every single chance she got about work. What was mind-blowing though was that she even had the nerve to suggest I pay her for staying there. That was definitely out of the question, and I was utterly shocked she would go there.

Then, as the added cherry on top, Leslie called me damn near every second of the day. Her words continued to ring in my ears like a record stuck on repeat. "When are you going to replace the money, David? Don't even think about asking for another dime, David, because you're not going to get it. And I swear, you'd better have a stable job by the time I return, David." I'd never been so irritated hearing her voice on my voicemail. It was all such a headache and had become more than a notion to deal with.

Still, as far as Tiffany was concerned, I wasn't exactly sure what to do. I could either continue with my attempts to get her to leave on her own, which realistically might not ever happen, or the other option would be to break down and tell her the truth. I had already enacted in my mind how I could do it, too. I would buy her a dozen long-stemmed roses, which she'd love. I would take her to one of her favorite restaurants and then take her somewhere we could enjoy some nice drinks and live music, which she also loved. It would be a night she would never forget.

But then, after we arrived back to the house, I would sit her down and explain to her that I loved her more than she knew, but neither a marriage nor a committed relationship was what I wanted anymore. She would be angry, or more so hurt. But hopefully, the entire night would lessen the blow. All I knew was that whatever I decided, it had to be done within the next week. Any longer than that and the crap would surely hit the fan. If I didn't get this done, and fast, then it would destroy things with Tiffany and me, Leslie and me, and possibly my mother and me.

My most dire issue now after having Leslie on my back was the fact that I needed some more money and another place to stay. This was something I had been thinking about because I refused to pay my own mother for a place to lay my head. Also, if I was going to go all out for Tiffany to let her down, then I needed a way to finance it. After taking some time to think about it all, I believed I knew just who to contact.

"Hey, Sonya! How have you been?" I asked, trying to sound ecstatic when I heard her voice on the line.

"David? David Allen? Really?"

"What? Aren't you happy to hear from me?"

"Well, I don't know, let's see. You asked me out for dinner only for me to find out at the end of the meal that it was my treat. Then you took me to some ratchet motel instead of your house. Then, against my better judgment, we were intimate, and you were done in no more than two minutes. Then you rolled over and went to sleep only for me to wake up to a damn note that said, 'Had a great time. We should do this again soon.' Now you call weeks later, and I'm supposed to sound happy to hear from you? Honey, you're lucky I haven't seen you out anywhere, because you and I both would definitely be getting arrested. So what the hell do you want, David?"

It was time for an Oscar-winning performance, so I put on the most sincere voice I possibly could. "Look, I've been thinking a lot about you since that night. Sonya, you don't know how sorry I am for being a real jerk. I don't know what was up with me, and all I can ask is that you give me the opportunity to make it all up to you."

"What kind of fool do you take me for, David?"

"No, sweetie, I don't take you for a fool at all. Actually, you're one of the most intelligent and classiest women I've ever met. To tell the truth, maybe that's what was wrong. See, I've never been with a woman like you, and I really didn't know how to handle it. That night, I basically treated you like all the average women I've dealt with in the past. That's because I didn't know any better. I realized that I was in over my head, which is why I wrote the note and bounced. But, Sonya, I've been kicking myself ever since. Can you please let me make it up to you?" I asked while having to hold myself from laughing at my own dramatics.

She paused, and I could sense that she was still very hesitant. "I don't know, David. That was such a messed-up thing to do. You were a real creep for all of that, and I shouldn't even be talking to you right now."

Mustering up all the fake emotion I could, I begged, "I know, I know, and again, I'm so very sorry. Please, please forgive me and let me make it up."

She became quiet, and I could tell she was considering my offer. My only problem was that I needed some cash and somewhere to stay tonight, so I had no time to waste and needed her to say yes. I had to say something in order to get into her good graces.

"Sonya, I know I've called you out of the blue, and that's unfair of me. I was one hundred percent a jerk, and I'll apologize a million times for that, but I swear I haven't been able to get you off my mind. If I'm being completely honest, I didn't know how to approach you again, but it's weighed on me heavily, so I had to take the chance to reach out. If you just give me one more chance, just one, I promise to make things right. I promise to make things the way they should have been that night. You deserve that much, baby."

"I still don't know, David. I'm really not in the mood to go out tonight—"

"Okay, that's even better. We can have a quiet evening alone. Just the two of us."

She was quiet again. This time I didn't say anything either because I didn't want to seem as if I were pressuring her, so I patiently waited for her response.

"Okay, David, I guess it wouldn't hurt if you came here. We can start over. Talk and get to know each other again."

"Wow, that sounds great to me," I shouted with exuberance for added effect. "See, I knew you were something special. To give me another chance after how badly I behaved? You are amazing," I said, thinking more along the lines of naive or gullible.

"Yeah, well, just be prepared to do exactly what you said and make that first night up to me. I really would like to meet the gentleman I thought you were."

"I will and you definitely will. You won't be sorry, I promise."

"All right, well, I'm trying to finish up with cooking, so why don't you come over around seven or eightish?"

"Sounds like a plan. I can't wait to see you again, Sonya!"

"Sure. Okay."

We hung up, and I patted myself on the back for my win. Of course, I still had to figure out a way to get some cash from her as well as get her to allow me to stay a few days, or weeks even. With her giving me another chance so easily after being the creep I was that first night, I figured it might be a piece of cake. That thought alone gave me a bit of hope. *Who knows? A night or two with her may be exactly what I need to relieve my mind of all the drama I have with all the other women in my life.*

Chapter 17

Terrence

Patricia must have come to her senses, because she'd blown up my cell phone for the last couple of hours. Little did she know the past three weeks alone in a hotel felt amazing. There were no arguments about social media, other women, or children. To ensure that my mind was completely free of distractions, I hadn't even gone to my job at the school because I needed a mental break. Besides that, I didn't want to take my negativity out on the boys on the team. They were like my own sons, and I didn't want them seeing me all messed up like this.

I felt bad that I hadn't at least called or texted to check on my family. It still blew my mind that my own wife had me put out of my own home for her spoiled-ass kid. Maybe I had this marriage thing all messed up or something. In my mind, I'd always thought a husband and wife were supposed to be a team and stick together through thick and thin. Any decisions that affected our household should have been agreed upon by both of us. In the end, I would have the final say since I was the head of that household, but with Patricia, I clearly wasn't the head of anything. She proved to me over and over that those boys came first over everyone in her life, including me. This was something I thought about day and night while being here at the hotel. However, that time was the final straw for me. Yesterday, I actually went and spoke with my attorney about drawing up divorce papers.

The bills must have started to come in also, which was one reason that would explain her continuous phone calls. I toyed around with the idea of answering or calling her back but figured it would serve her well to make her sweat a bit. If she truly knew her husband, she would know that there was no reason for her calls, because I was a man who prided himself on taking care of his responsibilities.

Money was becoming a little tight, though, and I had to pick and choose what got paid and what didn't. With that said, I'd bypassed the mortgage payment for the past month since I wasn't in the home in the first place. I'd always been on time, so a month wouldn't be a big deal. Besides, I planned on picking right up with the payments once things settled down and I knew exactly where she and I stood. It might have appeared a little childish of me, but it served her right anyway.

Nonetheless, I decided not to answer or call her back. As a matter of fact, I went ahead and did something that I wouldn't normally do. I turned my cell phone off to avoid talking to Patricia, but mainly so that I could fully enjoy the beautiful woman who sat in front of me at present. Since I hadn't gone to school in the evenings, it freed up some time for me to visit my favorite spot. I tried my best to keep a handle on things, but somehow I seemed to end up at the casino almost every other night. The bills along with my newfound enjoyment definitely took their toll on my pockets a bit, but having the chance to see Lisa made up for it big time. In fact, these past two hours of her company had been a welcome distraction from my situation at home. Although I'd pretty much had a great time with her, she must have sensed some irritation from me.

"All right, so what does a girl like me have to do to get you to enjoy yourself?"

"Oh, trust me, I'm enjoying myself. Being here with you is enough enjoyment within itself."

"Wow, that's really sweet of you, Terrence." She smiled at me, then looked away with a distant stare. When she faced me again, she looked as if something serious had crossed her mind.

"Uh-oh, what just happened? Now you're starting to seem like you're the one not having so much fun."

"No, no, believe me, it's not that at all. I guess I'm wondering where all of this is going. I mean, for the past several weeks we've seen each other almost every other night. We've had amazing conversations, and I've enjoyed myself more than I have in a long time."

"So what's wrong with that? I thought we were two people merely having a good time."

"Don't get me wrong, we are. I guess I'm a little ready to take things a step further though, if you know what I mean."

I knew good and well what Lisa meant, but I hadn't even desired to go there with her. When all of this first started, the thought surely seemed like an option I could entertain. However, regardless of my status with Patricia, I didn't want to complicate things further by cheating. Aside from that, after being with Lisa these past few weeks, I'd noticed that she seemed way too forward for my liking. She took the chase out of it all and made me wonder, if it was that easy for me, then what about the other men she'd come across? Her eyes looked at me as if to say she was ready. I didn't have a clue how to break it to her without hurting her feelings.

"I didn't scare you, did I?" she joked playfully.

"No, you didn't. Maybe more caught me off guard, but I'm not scared."

"Caught you off guard? Really? Now don't tell me you haven't thought about it."

"Honestly?"

"Of course."

"No, I haven't. I've simply been enjoying you. Lisa, I don't want to rush or complicate things."

She began to fidget around, and I could tell how uncomfortable this conversation was for her. "What exactly do you mean by 'complicate things'? How?"

"Well, it's just that I like and respect our friendship that we're building. I don't want to destroy that by moving too fast."

She gave me a weird frown, and then I noticed her phone vibrating. Actually, I noticed it long ago. It had buzzed back-to-back so much that I would have sworn it was my wife calling her. That was exactly how my phone rang before I'd turned it off. It made me so suspicious that I wondered if maybe she had a man she hadn't told me about.

"Wow, it looks like someone's trying hard to reach you."

"Yeah, I guess they are."

"Do you need to take that? There must be some type of emergency."

"No, trust me, she doesn't want anything."

"She, huh?"

"Yeah, a friend of mine who always has some kind of drama going on."

"Oh, okay."

From that point, things seemed a bit awkward between us. She was more focused on her cell phone, and I wanted to go lie down in my room. I was sure that if I told her that, then one of two things would happen: either she would think I was a complete lame for turning in so early, or she might try to invite herself to join me despite what I'd just said.

"Is everything all right?" I asked.

"Uh, yeah. I guess I'd better take this or else she'll continue to call."

"All right, well, don't let me stop you. I'm a little tired now anyway. I think it's from the alcohol."

If I were psychic, I'd have been rich because she did exactly what I thought she would. "Would you like some company? I could help you relax and unwind."

"That sounds nice, very nice, Lisa, but I'm not sure I would be good company tonight. I'm pretty beat. My eyes would probably be shut before I hit the bed good."

I could tell she wasn't thrilled with my answer, but she didn't press the issue any further. We gave each other a hug, and that was that. I hadn't lied though when I said I was beat. I was so tired that I hadn't turned my phone back on to deal with the hundreds of messages I was sure Patricia had left. I figured I would deal with it in the morning.

Chapter 18

Patricia

"What the hell is going on?" I screamed.

Terrence had clearly turned off his phone, and she hadn't answered hers either. I was paying her to set him up to see how far he would go, and she had the nerve to ignore me? I knew they were together, too, and the thought of them doing more than talking made me sick.

"Who does she think she is? It's a damn shame you can't even pay people to do right."

Finally, my phone rang, and her name flashed across the screen. If I could have, I would've wrapped my hands around her neck through the phone. "What are you doing with my husband, Lisa?"

"Wait, what?"

"You heard me. He turned his phone off, and I've called you over a hundred times and you didn't answer. So what were you all doing? Were you screwing my husband?"

"You know what, Patricia? You're not paying me enough to call me a ho, all right? And the answer to your question is no. I haven't done anything with your husband other than talk. He's been a perfect little angel, although I'm not exactly sure why."

"What the hell is that supposed to mean?"

"It means you have a good guy on your hands. Why on earth are you going through all of this? The man probably never has cheated on you and probably won't, so all of this is pointless, Pat."

I heard the words coming from her mouth, but I still didn't believe them. My husband wasn't this perfect man she'd described. He'd changed a lot toward me, and then there were all these women he claimed were only friends on his social media. He had to be involved with one of them, and I would find out what he was up to one way or another. I ignored the last couple of minutes of whatever Lisa had said.

"So where is he now?"

"He went back to his hotel room. He said he was tired and went to go to sleep. Even after I suggested that I go back with him, he turned down my offer. So again, your husband is not cheating on you."

"Yeah, well, maybe you're just not his type. I should have found someone curvier, someone well-endowed," I poked at her.

"Look, I'm not going to be insulted by you any longer. Consider your last payment the final one. I don't want to have anything else to do with you or this situation."

"Oh, no, ma'am! Don't you dare think you're going to quit on me like that. I'm not done yet."

"Well, it really doesn't matter to me whether you're done. I am. I promise to do the best thing I can for you, which is pray for you. You surely need lots of it, Patricia. And just a word of advice, if you don't get yourself together and stop looking for something that's not there, you will lose him in the end." She hung up after that, and I felt like I could explode at any minute.

"Lose my husband? Who does she think she is to tell me that I would lose my husband? I know exactly what I'm doing, and I don't need you, Lisa, to get it done. I'll find out what my husband is up to on my own."

I didn't care what time it was. I tried to reach Terrence repeatedly again. He still had his phone off, and I had to admit that it killed me on the inside. Despite what Lisa said, I couldn't help but wonder what he was doing, and if he was with someone else. Being mentally and emotionally depleted, I climbed into our bed and curled up under the covers. All of this nonsense with him affected me in such a drastic way. Suddenly, an overwhelming amount of tears ran down my face, and I couldn't seem to get control of them. I tried to get them to stop, but they wouldn't. I loved my husband. I missed my husband. As much as I tried to let go of what Lisa said, it was now branded into my mind. She was right. If I kept this up, I would lose my husband, but the jealousy consumed me, and I wasn't sure how to stop. Lying there, I curled up into a fetal position and bawled my eyes out until I couldn't cry anymore. The last thing I remembered was calling out Terrence's name and pleading for him not to leave me.

Chapter 19

Tiffany

David called yet again, but this time, I didn't answer. My mind was much more fixated on the dream I'd had the past three nights. I wasn't one to remember my dreams often, but when I did, they were always signs or warnings, or some way that God Himself communicated with me. This dream was one that I didn't quite understand though.

It was the same one every single night. In each one, it seemed as if I was getting married. Everything was beautiful, from the venue to the flowers to my dress, absolutely everything. It all looked like something from a fairy tale, and my heart was overwhelmed even as I reminisced over the dream. What I didn't understand was the man who awaited me at the altar. In each dream, it was not David. This man was someone I didn't know in the dream nor in reality, but I almost felt as if I'd known him forever. That was how comfortable and safe he made me feel. He was tall and dark and had an extremely nice build, but his most incredible feature were his eyes. They were so dark and intense. When he looked at me, it was as if they pierced right through my soul. I could practically feel our love for one another, and it always left me with the warmest feeling inside.

God, what are you telling me? What does this dream mean for me and David? And who is this mystery man? Please, God, talk to me. I don't want to make another decision, not another move, without you.

God was trying to tell me something. It may have seemed strange, but the dream left me that much more unsettled when it came to David and me. Yet it somehow gave me peace with this unknown man.

My attention went to my phone as David called yet again. Part of me wanted to answer to see what would come from his mouth this time, but the other part of me couldn't take another lie. It had been a month since I'd relocated here, and he still hadn't returned home. First, there was another long trip that lasted two weeks to take a group of teens to a football tournament. Now there seemed to be a week-long trip that popped up out of nowhere. It wouldn't be a problem if he were actually being honest. But something deep down continued to tell me that he wasn't. I hadn't put my finger on it yet, but David was lying about something. Our calls were always short and direct. He always sounded as if he made up things as he went along. He wasn't the man I'd been with this entire time, or maybe I had no idea who he really was. Either way, I had seen way more of him when I was in St. Louis than I had since I'd been here, and it was no longer sitting well with me.

Several times, it crossed my mind that maybe there was another woman. I wondered if he lived with her, but if that were the case, then why would he hold on to this house? Also, why would he have asked me to marry him or allowed me to go through with relocating? He should've known that he couldn't keep lying forever. I didn't want to believe that David would do that to me, especially since he knew everything that I'd lost, but there was no other way to explain it. I even snooped around the house a bit, but there was nothing that proved he was with someone else.

The only thing that did seem strange to me was the number of things his sister had at the house. After I packed her clothing and the pictures away, I thought that would be it. But then I saw jewelry, perfumes, and personal papers. It was almost like she still lived there. That made me think back to his nosy neighbor, Mrs. Smith. She still gave me the strangest looks every morning when I left for work. She would never say a word to me, and I still pondered over what she'd said the day I moved in—that she would leave them a message for me. Maybe his sister still lived there, but why wouldn't David just tell me that so that we could get our own place? Why would he lie about something like that? If she did live there, he could easily use that address while residing somewhere else with someone else.

Since I only had a brief time alone in the library during the second half of my day, I decided to do a little digging. With all the new technology out these days, I could easily find out if David had another address. While I hated to stoop to such levels, I needed answers that I was sure I would never get from him. I typed his full name and Texas into the Google search bar to ensure the right person came up. Information for at least five different David Allens popped up on the screen. I picked the one that had his age, and lucky for me, it showed an address. The information that was displayed wasn't the address where I resided, but I was certain it was an address I'd seen before. I couldn't recall at the moment if I saw it on a piece of mail at the house or what, but I remembered that street before. Without any hesitation, I printed the page and hurried to answer my phone as he called.

"Hello?"

"Well, damn, I thought you would never answer. I've been calling you all day."

"Oh, hi, David," I answered a bit dryly.

"'Oh, hi, David'? What's with you?"

"Nothing, but where are you, David?" I asked, preparing myself to hear what he'd come up with this time.

"What do you mean where am I? I told you already. I had to drive a football team to their tournament."

"Really? I thought the football tournament was the trip you just came from."

"Oh, well, this is, uh, a smaller team that had a tournament as well."

"David, why do I feel like you're lying to me about something?"

"Tiff, please don't start. I don't have a reason to lie to you about anything. Now I don't know what's got you all messed up, but whatever it is has you believing things that aren't true. Is it Mrs. Smith again?"

"No, it's not her. Besides, what would she say anyway that would suggest you're lying about anything? And speaking of her, why does she always look at me like I'm crazy or something? What does that old lady know, David?"

"She doesn't know anything. I keep telling you that she's old and senile. That's the only way to explain it. Baby, please listen. I am not lying to you about anything, okay?"

"All right, but when do you plan on coming home?"

"Look, if you just let me finish up this trip, I'll be home in three days tops, and I'll make all this up to you, okay?"

"Yeah, okay, whatever."

Our call ended with the same disappointment that had lingered since I'd arrived in Texas. I'd answered in the hopes that I would receive some type of answer to make me feel better after giving him the cold shoulder. I hoped that, for once, I could depend on him to be honest with me about something, anything, but even that was too much to ask. You can bet I wouldn't hold my breath on this "three days" crap either. Something told me that the answers I needed lay within the four walls of this unknown address. So, I promised myself, if I didn't see him in exactly three days as he said, whoever's house this was would definitely find me on their doorstep.

Chapter 20

David

There was no question that I hated lying to Tiffany, but I felt like I had no choice. I still wanted her to love me after all was said and done. But I only had about another week before I had to get her out of that house and back to St. Louis. So, more and more, coming clean and telling her I didn't want to get married was my only option. Of course, she would be hurt and have a million questions, but it was something that had to be done.

If only I knew what put doubt in her mind all of a sudden, I could handle it. Just the other day it seemed like she was fine with my absence, but all within a few days she'd flipped out and accused me of lying to her. This new revelation caused me to become somewhat agitated because I thought I'd covered all my bases. My gut told me that Tiffany knew something, and whatever that was, it definitely had me shook.

"Dammit." I could have kicked myself for getting into this predicament in the first place by asking her to marry me. My thoughts traveled back to that very day. She'd been talking so much about marriage, and her family kept bringing the subject up, that I got the bright idea to ask . . . right in front of them, too. All I really wanted to do was shut her up, but the minute I proposed, it was like she went full speed ahead with planning our future together. If only I could understand why she couldn't just be happy with things the way they were, because they seemed perfect to me. Anyway, I couldn't keep putting off the inevitable, but every time I rehearsed the breakup in my head, my mouth wouldn't form the words that it was over.

As I sat on the sofa and flipped through channels while thinking of the best way to break things off with Tiffany, I heard the jingle of Sonya's keys when she unlocked the door. I'd sent her out to grab some items that I needed, and she'd obliged grudgingly. It was only a ploy to provide me with the time and space that I needed to make that call to Tiffany.

"Hey, you," I said when she entered. She didn't say anything back, and I could have sworn she slightly rolled her eyes as she walked past me. "You need some help?" I asked while secretly hoping she said no. I'd become so comfortable on the couch that I didn't feel like moving.

"Oh, no, David, please don't be a gentleman by helping me," she answered.

Immediately, I hopped up and walked into the kitchen after detecting the sarcasm in her voice. I felt that things were going good so far, and I didn't want to take any chances of messing them up.

"I'm sorry, you're right. You shouldn't have to tell me to come and help you. I guess my mother has me a bit spoiled," I joked to lighten things up a bit.

She continued to put the groceries away without acknowledging anything I'd just said. Once we were finished, she walked out of the kitchen without saying another word. I could sense something was wrong but had no idea what it could be. In my eyes, things were going great.

When I arrived over here yesterday evening, she'd prepared an amazing meal, we watched a couple of movies on Netflix, and then, of course, I attempted to take things a little further. She shot the message back loud and clear though that she'd meant exactly what she'd said about getting to know one another again, and she stopped me before things got hot and heavy. It didn't bother me, however, because it wasn't my true mission in the first place. I brushed it off and made up something to be able to stay the night. My aim now was to find the perfect moment to hit her up for some cash and stay a few more nights.

Her quietness gave me the impression that something was wrong, so rather than continue to watch television, I walked into the bedroom, where I found her sitting on the edge of her queen-sized bed. Sitting down next to her, I placed my arm around her shoulder. In order to get what I came for, I had to remove the memory of the creep she thought I was from her mind.

"What's wrong, Sonya? You know you can talk to me, right?" I said softly and lightly squeezed her to my chest.

She was quiet for a few moments until she finally spoke. "David, I had a great time with you last night, but I need you to know that I'm not the foolish and naive woman you must think I am."

I practically choked at her comment. "What do you mean, foolish and naive? I think you're far from that."

She pulled back, moved away, and then faced me. "Well, I told you before you came by that I wanted to get to know you. Yet even after the evening went well, you tried to take things further. David, I'm not on that page with you yet, especially after last time. Then you asked if you could stay the night because you didn't feel like driving home, and on top of that, you got up this morning and asked me to pick up all of these things for you as if you live here. It just seems like you're the same low-down person from before, and I'm not with it."

Think, David, think, I said in the back of my mind, because she was more intuitive than I'd thought. Somehow I had to convince her that she was wrong about me.

"Sonya, I'm sorry. I told you that I'm far from the creep I portrayed myself to be before, but I just don't know how to act with a woman like you."

"What do you mean, a woman like me, David? And you're a grown-ass man. I'm sure you know the right and wrong way to treat a woman."

"All right, I do, but honestly I haven't been with someone who has herself together like you in quite a long time. So please forgive me for enjoying myself too much and getting too comfortable with you too quick. Like I told you, you are a beautiful, intelligent, and amazing woman, and I would never take advantage of that." I scooted a little closer to her. "I like you, Sonya, a lot, and I'm just thankful for the chance to get to know you better. I want you to know me too."

"Can I ask you something, David?"

"Sure."

"You're in your early fifties. Don't you want something real? A wife and a family one day? Or do you want to keep playing around from woman to woman? Because that's not where I am in my life right now. I'm not casually dating with no desired outcome."

Now that caught me completely off guard, and I wasn't sure how to answer. I could have sworn when we first met that she'd told me she wasn't in that chapter in her life where she desired to be married or even in a fully committed relationship. If I recalled correctly, I clearly remembered she expressed that those types of relationships took more time and energy than she could give. She hadn't even wanted anything too complicated. So now it puzzled me that she'd flipped the entire script, basically like every other woman I knew.

I didn't get it. Why couldn't these women simply enjoy the time we spent together instead of all this marriage, wife, and commitment talk? They almost made it seem like there was some huge privilege to being married or like we'd be damned to hell if we didn't get married. In my eyes, marriage was nothing more than a piece of paper for someone to be able to get all your belongings whenever you left this thing called life. I didn't see the whole honor in it the way they did, and I guessed that was why I felt the way I did. Rather than say that though, I had to keep in mind what I was here for. So just like with Tiffany, I told Sonya what I thought she wanted to hear.

"I do want to get married, but I don't want to feel as if I'm settling either. I have to know that the woman I will spend the rest of my life with will be able to satisfy me in every way possible."

I placed my hand on top of hers and caressed it. She looked up at me, and her eyes said everything I needed them to say at that moment. It was time that I made the move I was sure would secure everything I wanted from her. I looked deep into her eyes and then placed my lips against hers.

To my surprise, it was one of the sweetest kisses I'd shared with anyone in quite a long time. Tiffany and I really didn't kiss at all. To think about it, I couldn't say that we ever shared a kiss like this with one another, and I didn't know who was to blame for it. All I knew was that when Sonya kissed me back, it felt good. Her lips were soft and tender, succulent even. I didn't want it to feel that good, but it did. That very moment almost made me regret my hidden agenda altogether.

She stood up and then straddled me. We kissed more, then more, and even more. It was as if we didn't want to let each other's lips go. She started to unzip my pants, and I was amazed at how aroused she had me. I wanted

Sonya and I wanted her bad. I closed my eyes, lay back on the bed, and let her take full control of what was about to happen. As much as I didn't want to admit it, Sonya had me in the palm of her hands. I could tell she wanted me just as much as I wanted her, and what happened in the past was nothing more than a memory.

Laying her body down on the bed and climbing on top, I couldn't wait to feel her warmth. As our bodies slowly became in tune with one another, I entered her treasure. I let out a weighty sigh of relief when her moisture surrounded my manhood. Immediately, I started to feel things I hadn't felt in a very long time with a woman. As her legs gripped my waist, her love was so passionate and sincere. In that moment, she almost made me want to be honest and true to her. With each and every stroke, I wanted more and more of her.

Out of nowhere, a vision of Tiffany crossed my mind. Then a second later it was Leslie. I didn't know what was going on or what had come over me. The two women's faces flashed back and forth from one to the other. Sonya's cries of passion to me let me know that she was enjoying every minute of it, but I was being haunted by Tiffany and Leslie. Trying to shake them off, I began to pound my weight on her forcefully to somehow erase the sight of the two women.

"C'mon, dammit, c'mon," I yelled.

"Oh, David, please don't stop," she begged me.

Sonya's sweetness made me stroke faster and harder as the sweat dripped from my body onto hers. I continued to thrash myself inside of her, hoping to find relief from my subconscious. Instantly, I saw my release in sight as Tiffany's and Leslie's faces slowly faded from my mind. Sonya's helpless body lay there in pure pleasure, while I, on the other hand, wondered what the fuck had just happened.

Chapter 21

Tiffany

North Dallas High School had basically become my home away from home, especially since David wasn't around. I'd come to love my position as the head counselor and evening librarian more than I could have ever imagined. Although there was a lot to absorb rather quickly, all of the staff were very sweet and extremely helpful, which made adjusting go a lot smoother. I especially enjoyed working with the children, too. They always kept me laughing and reminded me of my youthfulness. It dawned on me that unlike in St. Louis as a librarian, this job gave me a sense of pride that I didn't get there. True enough, I enjoyed my career and made a decent income doing it, but here, I felt more like I was giving back and making a difference in the lives of the children. Anyway, it left me highly fulfilled, so it didn't bother me at all when Mrs. Williams asked if I could stay and go over some paperwork for her.

Mrs. Williams was the principal of the school, and the little that I'd learned about her so far, I absolutely loved. She had an immensely sweet spirit, and I could tell that she loved her staff wholeheartedly. Not to be fooled though, I saw that she was also a no-nonsense leader who didn't take any mess from anyone. She was definitely a woman who had it all together, and being around her inspired me to up my game.

So far, I'd learned that she'd been married for the past fifteen years and had three beautiful children with her husband, Todd. She seemed like a very spiritual woman, because she always found a way to introduce God into any conversation. Yet, she was down-to-earth with the best personality. She was at the same time refreshing and motivating to be around.

It all made me think about something my mother used to tell me. She would always say to surround myself with like-minded people to the person I strived to be. That topic mainly came up whenever Keisha was around. It wasn't that my mother didn't love Keisha. In fact, she'd loved her like one of her own. Keisha and I had been friends since grade school, but my mother would some-times point out that Keisha was content with her life exactly the way it was. She was single, hung out all the time, and didn't mind that she worked a job she didn't care for, day in and day out, contently until retirement. She didn't see beyond the here and now or have dreams that she aspired to reach. I didn't knock my girl, though, because whenever I needed someone to have my back, she was always there.

As of late, it just seemed like we were on different wavelengths and she couldn't understand my desire or quest for more. I remembered she once told me that I already had a perfect life, so why burden myself trying to chase after dreams that may never come to pass? Mrs. Williams was the complete opposite, however. She pushed her staff to do better, reach for more, and make a difference somehow in every morning meeting. She told us every single morning that we had the best job there was being an influence in the children's lives. But she encouraged us to never stop there. She said there was always more to life available to us and it was up to us to go after it. My thoughts shifted to David and how

I'd felt like I made one of the worst mistakes of my life, but my new career and meeting Mrs. Williams was the turnaround I needed at this point.

A few students started to stroll into the library after their last classes. I helped them find books for their assignments and answered any questions they had before starting on Mrs. Williams's documents. She'd brought the files into the library earlier while I was on the phone with David. I hated that she'd found me on a personal call during work hours, but it didn't bother her at all. I'd even gestured that I would get off, but she politely wrote me a note that she had to hurry to a meeting and left. Now as I sat there with all this paperwork in front of me, I still couldn't take my mind away from those dreams. Most people would probably think I focused way too much on a dream, but deep down, it was much more than that. For me, God was speaking to me, but I only wished I could get a clear understanding of what He meant.

Then there was that phone call with David. I truly hated the direction we were headed in. I'd tried my best to hang in there simply because of feeling like I'd invested too much already into us and the relationship, but the fact of the matter was I was not happy. Instead of calling Keisha as I would normally, I thought about what Mrs. Williams would do in this situation. I was positive that she wouldn't play these back-and-forth games with David like I was doing. With that in mind, I made up my mind that I would no longer accept his going on another trip without us having a face-to-face conversation. If he wanted to be with me, then things would absolutely have to change from this point on, or it was going to be all over.

Chapter 22

Tiffany

"Hey, you're still here? Don't you have a fiancé to get home to?" Mrs. Williams asked as she rushed into the library to pick up the files she'd given me.

"Yeah, well, I really wish that were the case, but no, I don't. My fiancé drives buses as his profession, and he's away on a trip."

"Oh, I see." A hush came over the room for a moment or two until she asked, "Is everything all right, Tiffany?"

Deep down, I was thankful she asked. She had no idea how much I needed someone to talk to. I attempted to go into the conversation with ease because I didn't want to seem too eager to pour my heart out to a stranger. "Well, not quite."

"Do you want to talk about whatever's bothering you? I'm done with all my meetings for the day and have some time to talk."

"You mean it wouldn't be a bother?"

"Oh, no, not at all, and I promise that whatever we discuss will be strictly confidential."

"Well, I . . . I really don't know where to begin."

"Wherever you like, Tiffany. Now what's wrong?" She pulled up a chair and sat down facing me.

I fidgeted around for a few seconds before I started, "Mrs. Williams—"

"Oh, please, call me Monica. Mrs. Williams seems so stuffy and, girl, I'm far from that," she said with a chuckle, I assumed to try to ease the tension in the room.

"Okay, Monica. Well, you and your husband have been married for fifteen years, right?"

"Yes, we have, fifteen beautiful years."

"Well, how did you know that he was the one? I mean, did you pray about it? Did you receive a sign from God? How did you know for sure that this was the person you wanted to spend the rest of your life with?" I sat with my eyes and ears focused on her, eagerly awaiting her response.

"Oh, well, of course I sought God as I try to do with any decision in my life. But as mediocre as this is going to sound to you, it's the truth—I just knew."

"Really? You just knew? No doubts or second-guessing yourself?" I asked, feeling a bit deflated by such a simplistic response.

"Yep, as simple as that. Of course, there was some second-guessing before the wedding, because we are all human, but I knew that he was the one I wanted to go through life with from the time we first met. So I sought after God, and He confirmed for me what I already knew inside, and well, the rest is history."

"Wow."

"Tiffany, are you asking me this because you're not sure if your fiancé is the one?"

"You want me to be completely honest with you?" I asked, almost bypassing her response because I couldn't wait to unload what I'd held in all this time.

"Yes, please."

"When he asked me to marry him, I kind of knew that he wasn't, and then God confirmed it for me."

"Wait, God confirmed that this man was not the one you should marry and you're going to marry him anyway?"

"Yeah, well, I mean, we've been together three years, and I've invested so much. Plus, I'm getting closer to forty, and most of my friends are married with families, and well—"

"Oh, Tiffany, honey, those are all not reasons to go into a life-altering event like marriage, especially if you've heard from God on the matter. Honey, going against His will for you can bring about so much unnecessary pain and heartache in the long run."

"Trust me, I know, because now he's acting totally opposite from before he asked me to marry him and before I relocated here. I moved out here alone, and he's basically been on trips ever since. We barely talk more than five or ten minutes when he does call. It just seems like he's not being honest about something, but I can't put my finger on what it is."

She reached over and wrapped her arms around me when she saw a tear begin to roll down my cheek. "Tiffany, I haven't met your fiancé, but it doesn't sound right that he didn't help you move here or hasn't been home since, especially if he didn't advise you of that before you moved. He could very well be busy, but I have to ask, are you sure he doesn't have another family somewhere? Some men are good for doing that nowadays—living double lives and all."

"I don't know," I managed to say between tears. "I'm not sure what to believe anymore."

"Well, I will say that whatever is not right will eventually reveal itself. I only pray that happens sooner rather than later. As a matter of fact, do you mind if I say a quick prayer for you?"

I shook my head no, and she held both of my hands as she began to pray. I thought about how Monica was truly godsent. She comforted and encouraged me as the friend I needed right now. I thanked God during her prayer that

He allowed us to cross paths. Then when she finished up, we both said, "Amen," and she gave me a warm and tight hug.

"Tiffany, please promise me that before you make any decisions regarding your future, you'll sit down with this man and discuss his true intentions for you. I really wouldn't suggest you marry him if you know for sure that's not who God has for you. But it's also not my decision to make. So if you are still planning on going through with this, you need to go in with a clear mind and a clear heart. But let me also say that you are God's best, so there's nothing wrong with waiting for His very best for you."

She hugged me again, and we both prepared to leave for the evening. I replayed everything in my head on the drive home. She was right on so many levels, especially that I never should have gone against God's will for me. He told me exactly what I needed to hear. I didn't listen, and now I was the one paying the price for that. What stuck with me even more was that she said there was nothing wrong with waiting for His best for me. Somehow I knew that whoever this was in my dream was God's best, not David. Maybe that's what He wanted to reveal to me, that He had someone so much better in store once I let things go with David.

Before making it to the house, I stopped and picked up my favorite bottle of wine. Then when I arrived, I went inside, locked the doors, and turned on the alarm system. I'd already had dinner while I reviewed Monica's files, so all I looked forward to was a nice, relaxing bubble bath and several glasses of wine. I lit the candles that I'd placed around the bedroom to make it cozy as well as give off the scent of lilac throughout. Then I turned up my Luther Vandross Pandora station, slipped out of my clothes, poured my first glass of wine, and headed into our master bathroom.

The atmosphere became more relaxed while I let the tub fill up with bubbles. When I felt it was just enough to drown my emotions, I dipped my toe in to make sure the temperature was just right. The hot water covered my body as I sank in and instantly drifted away. The music, candles, and wine all did the trick as I laid my head back and closed my eyes. It felt absolutely amazing, and no one, not even David, could mess up this moment of ecstasy for me. At least, that was until thirty minutes later when David's sister stood over me with a gun pointed directly at my head.

Chapter 23

David

Sonya slept peacefully with her head on my chest, and as I looked at her face, she almost appeared angelic. She was beautiful in every way, even without makeup on and her hair tousled to-and-fro. It almost started to bother me a little that my intentions weren't totally true, but I kept trying to force myself to stay on track. My focus had to remain on the money and having somewhere to lay my head, so there was no way I could allow a moment of good sex to throw me off task. Besides, I knew for a fact that she wanted more than a mere "friendship with benefits" type of relationship, yet that was all I could really offer. Attempting anything serious with her was not something I could add to my life at the moment or anytime in the near future. I had way too much going on already with the women who were present in my life, and adding her to the mix would only make matters worse.

Speaking of the women in my life, I still couldn't seem to pull my mind away from the visions I'd had of Tiffany and Leslie or the significance of seeing them both in that moment. It wasn't like either of them knew about the other, yet there they were intermingled in my thoughts. It continued to spook the hell out of me as I lay there trying to make sense of it all.

Then, a second later, Sonya shifted her naked body in her sleep, which quickly took my thoughts away from them as my nature started to rise again. I couldn't deny this feeling that I felt with Sonya. Needing to savor the moment, I closed my eyes and tightened my arms around her as the warmth of our naked bodies consumed one another's.

Things were so tranquil and peaceful until I suddenly heard my phone begin to buzz across the nightstand. After it buzzed more times than a couple, I wiggled myself from underneath Sonya to look at it. It was Leslie. What on earth could she want right now? I hadn't expected to hear from her until a week from now. I figured she might still be upset about the money I took from the account, but I doubted that she'd call this time of the evening about that. I was almost tempted to answer, especially since she'd called several times after back-to-back. I had no idea what she wanted, but I wasn't in the mood to deal with her. Right now, I preferred to devote my time and attention to Sonya and only Sonya. Tiffany, Leslie, and even my mother would all have to wait.

Chapter 24

Tiffany

My heart raced at a fast and unsteady beat as I watched the eyes of David's sister. She had the gun pointed directly at me in one hand and her cell phone in the other. I tried my hardest to get out of the bathtub, but every time I did, I slipped right back down. The slipperiness from the water along with my trembling body was not the best combination. I attempted to reason with her over and over again, but it hadn't worked at all. She was pissed and looked like she would blow me away at any second.

"I don't know what the hell is going on here, but I want to know who you are and why the hell you are in my house."

"Leslie, please, if you would just give me a second to explain—"

"How the hell do you know my name? Who are you? And you'd better start talking fast."

"Leslie, it's me, Tiffany," I tried to assure her, knowing she should know exactly who I was.

But surprisingly, she looked at me with an even more puzzled expression than when she first got there. I continued to tremble so bad that I could feel urine start to run down my leg right there in front of her.

"I don't know any damn Tiffany, but it seems you sure as hell know a lot about me."

"I'm sorry. I thought for sure David told you about me. I'm his fiancée."

"Wait, you're his what?"

I could damn near see the rage build up within her once the word "fiancée" crossed my lips. It finally dawned on me that there was much more to this story than I knew. Her hand shook with the gun in it as tears rolled down her face. I prayed and prayed some more because, at this moment, my life flashed before my eyes.

"Leslie, please let me explain."

"Explain? Explain what? That my fiancé for the past two years has another fiancée living in my home? Girl, I could kill you and him both, and you'd better damn sure hope I don't."

Instantly, I became sick to my stomach. So many things ran through my mind, but at the forefront was the fact that David was engaged to me and her.

"What? Oh, my God, Leslie, I didn't know," I yelled, on the verge of tears myself. I looked up at her with pleading eyes. "You have to believe me. I didn't know. David had us both fooled. I was just as clueless as you were."

She paced back and forth and still waved that gun around as she attempted to call David again. My entire body shivered from my nerves as well as the cold air in the room. The water in the tub had become ice cold as I sat on the edge of it with fear in my eyes. I didn't know what Leslie planned, but I began to feel like she might not let me out alive. I hoped and prayed she would somehow have compassion and realize that we were in this together. Then she stopped calling David and began talking to herself.

"This pathetic-ass jerk has the nerve to not answer my call. Ughhh!" She let out a loud scream, but I remained quiet as a mouse. "And to think that I thought that Mrs. Smith had lost her mind when she told me David had some woman in my home. I just knew that there was no way that he would do me like that or be that damn stupid. I actually told the old biddy to mind her own business, and this is what I get. Ughhh," she screamed again.

All I wanted was to get out of there alive, but then again, I had nowhere to go. This was a huge, huge mess, and the one to blame seemed to be nowhere to be found.

"Get out of my bathtub right now," she yelled while directing me with the gun.

I hurried up and climbed out, quickly grabbed the dry towel I had lying across the toilet, and wrapped it around me.

"Oh, no, honey, no getting comfortable here. I want you out. Throw some clothes on, get what you can, and get the hell out of my home."

"Wait, Leslie, can't we please just make some type of agreement? I have nowhere else to go. I'm not from Texas."

"Sorry, honey, your ass should have thought about that before you moved out here with a man who don't have a pot to piss in. You should have known that David didn't have a home of his own. This is my house, and I want you gone. What the hell do you think anyway, that we're going to become best friends or something?"

"Please, I'm begging you to have a little compassion for me. I'm as much a victim in this as you are."

"Girl, the more you stand here and the more you talk, the more pissed off I become. I want you out of my home now. And wherever David is, you can go and join him."

"But wait, what about all of my things?"

"Look, I'll throw it all out by the garage tomorrow, and you can swing by and pick it all up. I want nothing else to do with you or David. Oh, and if you find him, tell that fiancé of yours that he better damn sure watch his back because this ain't over by a long shot."

"Leslie, please don't do this. I'm begging you. I had no idea that you and David were engaged. He lied to me like he's been lying to you. He told me that you were his sister," I pled with her.

"Listen, I said I want you out of my home. I don't care about David lying to you. I don't care about you being a victim. I don't care about your things. And I definitely don't care about you not having anywhere to go. Get the hell out now before I really lose it on your ass."

I threw on the same clothing that I'd just taken off when I got there. I grabbed what I deemed valuable and most important and left. Leslie didn't hesitate when she slammed the front door right behind me. At that point, I didn't have a clue what to do, but I needed to get away from her house as quickly as possible. Throwing my things into my truck, I slid inside and started the ignition. Unable to think clearly, I only drove to the next corner before I pulled over in a daze. I tried my best not to cry, but the tears flooded my face like a river. I was hurt, angry, confused, and I felt so stupid for allowing something like this to happen.

"God, why? Why did this happen to me? I mean, I've made some bad choices. I should have listened to you from the beginning, but why this? Now I'm sitting here with nothing and nowhere to go. I don't have a home. I have no savings left. All of my belongings are stuck in her house. God, why? You said you would never leave me or forsake me even in my own stupidity. You promised to be there," I whimpered as I cried uncontrollably.

The tears wouldn't stop flowing as I tried my best to think about what I should do. I had nowhere to go and no one to call at this hour. Suddenly, my thoughts turned to the one person whose fault all of this was. I began to dial David's number over and over again. Every single time, I received that annoying recording that his voice mailbox was full. I assumed it was more than likely from Leslie who was still trying to reach him as well. It was like he was nowhere to be found and had all of a sudden dropped off the face of the earth. Yet and still, I planned on finding him no matter what it took.

As my mind became slightly clearer, I remembered that address from earlier. With no regard to how late it was or who he might be laid up with, I planned on making him face me whether he wanted to or not. I put the address in my GPS and headed in the informed direction.

The thought of how drastically my life had changed in less than thirty days consumed me. If only I had listened to God's voice. I asked Him and He told me, and I chose not to listen. The tears continued. My head pounded harder and harder the more I thought about Leslie and her gun. And my heart ached. All I truly wanted at that very moment was my mother's shoulder to cry on. As my thoughts shifted to her, the tears became stronger. I felt completely confused and all alone, even to the point where I didn't even feel God on my side. It wasn't right to feel this way, but I did.

Feeling as if I had nothing else to lose, I picked up my speed. I was determined to get to David, and the way I felt at that moment, there was no telling what I might do. The only thing for sure was that I intended on making Mr. David Allen pay for all the pain I felt at that very moment—every last bit of it.

Chapter 25

Terrence

"Look, Terrence, it was wrong for me to call the police on you. I realize that maybe I handled things inappropriately, but I had to do it. There was no way I could let you put my baby out with nowhere to go. Anyway, I'm really hoping you call so that we can talk about all of this. Baby, I'm still your wife, and I miss you like crazy. I love you, and I hope you still love me. Please come back home."

The phone went mute at that point, and once again, I clicked delete. That had to be the hundredth message I'd received from Patricia with the same ol' message over and over. She was sorry.

I'd tried and tried my hardest to put myself in her shoes. I thought about if I were the wife and mother and she were the husband. It was true that I loved my children just as much as she loved hers. However, there was still no way I would've chosen them over her. Hell, if she really thought about it, I was choosing her over my girls now. Besides, the man is supposed to be the head of the household. There shouldn't have been any opposition to whatever I decided. That son of hers needed a little tough love, yet she was determined to treat him like a baby. There was no way I could win in this type of situation. With that in mind, I needed to continue to think long and hard about my next move, regardless of how much Patricia begged and pleaded for me to come back.

Pulling up to the school, I parked in my designated space assigned for the head football coach. I had already shot Principal Williams a text message to inform her that I would stay the night here at the school. Lucky for me, I had a boss who was extremely kind and showed compassion to all her staff. She knew that my situation at home wasn't the best right now and told me that if I ever needed anything at all to let her know. So from time to time, when I didn't want to pay extra money out of my pocket for a hotel room, I would stay the night here at the school. It was pretty close to my other job, and since I was always here long after hours, it only made sense. The cots here weren't as comfortable as a five-star hotel bed, but I didn't have to dole out five-star hotel cash either.

I walked into the coach's office and tried to make things comfortable for the night, but my phone started buzzing again. I was positive it was only Patricia leaving another message because everyone else I knew was more than likely asleep at this hour. Patricia should have been doing the same, but I was convinced she was trying to make this a miserable night for me because she was, in fact, miserable herself. Well, she needed to think again, because my phone was about to get turned off, and I was about to get some real rest. We would have to deal with things in the morning.

Chapter 26

Tiffany

The house was huge and dark except for the one small light that lit up only half the front porch. Although it was late, it still didn't look as if anyone was home. I expected to see the flicker of light from a television set or some form of life on the inside, but there was nothing. It almost looked abandoned. I didn't even see David's car out front, which made me suspect that I was way off track about his whereabouts, but I had to be sure. Even if he wasn't here, I had to know whose home this was. A thousand things circled through my mind. Was this another home he shared with yet another fiancée? Did he have children I didn't know about? Was he really a truck driver away on a trip? Was his real name David Allen? After all the lies he told, nothing seemed too farfetched at that point. I wondered exactly what kind of lies he'd told on this side of town as well.

I sat another five minutes before I pulled together the nerve to walk up to the door. For the most part, I wanted to start my car up and drive off as fast as I could, but I also knew that wouldn't give me the answers I desperately sought. It was far easier to leave, but a small part of me was determined to know who resided at this address. The small part won, and I exited my truck, walked up to the porch, and rang the bell. A couple of minutes passed by, and there was no answer. I almost walked away but decided to ring the bell just one more time. A couple more minutes went by, and still no one appeared. Deciding to give up, I turned around and headed back down the steps.

Suddenly I heard a small but stern voice question, "Ma'am, can I help you?"

Turning around slowly, I found a short, older woman dressed in a flowered housedress with a bonnet on her head. I looked her up and down for a few seconds before I opened my mouth to say anything. She was the female version of David, so I knew without a doubt that this had to be his so-called deceased mother.

This low-down, dirty, lying-ass bastard.

I really didn't know what to say to her, being shocked that she was, in fact, alive. "Uh, I'm so sorry to come by here so late, ma'am. I was looking for David . . . David Allen."

"David, huh? And who are you?"

"Um, my name is Tiffany. I'm an old friend of his."

She looked puzzled and confused all at the same time. It almost seemed as if she were trying to make out my face without saying too much.

"Well, honey, I'm sorry. David isn't here, and I'm not sure when he'll return. He may not return too soon, either. My son is kind of a fly-by-night type of guy if you know what I mean."

Her words almost cut like a knife because I knew very well what that phrase meant. Basically, in so many words, she was telling me her good-for-nothing son was untrustworthy and unreliable.

"Okay, and yes, I know what you mean. Again, ma'am, I'm so sorry for coming to your home at this hour. It's just that I've been trying to reach David and . . . and . . ."

Before I knew it, the tears streamed down my face, and I was unable to speak, thinking of all the lies this man had told.

"Oh, honey, why are you crying? Look, why don't you come in and get yourself together before trying to drive? I'll even try to reach David for you."

We went inside her home, and it was the complete opposite of the outside. It was warm and cozy and decorated beautifully. I immediately noticed all the pictures of David throughout the living room at all different ages. It made me angrier with him that he'd never shared this part of his life with me in the three years we'd been together. It also showed me how sad and disrespectful this man was to lie about his own mother being deceased. I couldn't even come up with a good reason for him to lie about something like that.

"All right, honey, now c'mon and have a seat and get yourself together."

She gave me some tissues and rubbed my back. Her nurturing spirit reminded me of my own mother, which brought on even more sadness.

"So I take it you and David are pretty close?"

I wasn't exactly sure how to answer her. Was I supposed to tell her about our engagement? Should I share that we'd been together for the past three years? Or should I explain that I hated him for lying to me and practically destroying my life? Needless to say, I decided against the latter. This was between me and David, and I thought it would be classless to involve his mother any more than I already had.

"Uh, we're just really good friends. I had something important to share with him, and since this was the last address he'd given me, I thought I'd come by."

"Well, David doesn't live here, honey. He was here a couple of days ago. Told me he needed to stay with me for a few weeks, but then he just up and vanished. David does that a lot, ya know. I can't seem to settle that son of mine down. Anyway, I haven't heard from him, but I'm sure he's all right, because like I said, he goes through this all the time, especially when he's not working."

"He's not working?"

"Oh, no. David hasn't worked in months." She went into the kitchen while she kept talking. "He keeps telling me that business is getting slow because of the weather, but I'm not so sure about that. Anyway, I keep telling him to start up his own truck-driving business, but he won't listen to me." She came back in carrying two coffee mugs with her. "Here's some tea to try to calm your nerves. Now what is all this crying about?"

I didn't know what to say, so I threw out the first thing I could come up with. "Um, someone passed away. Someone we grew up with."

"Oh, I'm so sorry to hear that. But did you say someone you and David both grew up with? You look quite a bit younger than him."

"Uh, yeah, blame it on good genes, I guess. People always tell me I look a lot younger than I really am," I continued to lie.

"Oh, I see. Well, let me see if I can reach him for you since you came all this way, especially so late."

"No, please don't. You know what? I think I'll just keep calling him until I reach him myself. I shouldn't have disturbed you this time of night by popping up here."

"Honey, are you sure?"

I didn't want her to call because I had no idea what to say to him. I wanted to curse him out bad. I mean, that ghetto, ratchet, hurt-you-to-your-soul kind of cursing out. But there was no way I could do that in his mother's home. I was a lady and would remain one even in this situation. It would all just have to wait.

"Yes, ma'am, I'm absolutely sure. Again, I'm sorry for disturbing you."

"No, it was good to finally meet one of David's friends. You two are just friends, right?" she pried.

It was at that point that I really wanted to break down and tell her everything. She seemed to be such a sweet and kind woman, and she needed to know what a lousy son she had. How could she have raised someone so pathetic? Someone who lied, cheated, and played with the lives of innocent women like this? I prayed silently that my mouth didn't take off and have a mind of its own, because if I got started, there would surely be no turning back.

"Um, uh . . ." It was the only response that I managed to come up with.

She looked at me again with a baffled expression. I wanted to tell her everything, but I also knew that was her son, and regardless of what I said, she would still take his side.

"Yes, ma'am, David and I are only friends."

"Well, that's a shame, because you are such a sweet young lady. I'm from the South, and I can tell when someone's been raised right, with manners and all. And David, well, he sure could use a good woman like you in his life. Are you married by the way?"

Her statement alone confirmed that she had no idea about me, Leslie, or any other woman he might be involved with. He was such a horrible man. How could he have not one but two fiancées and his mother hadn't known about either of us? It was then that I knew it was best I hadn't seen him tonight, because I wanted to hurt him. I wanted to hurt him and then throw him in a ditch where he belonged.

"No, I'm not married, but David and I are only friends." That was all that I could get out through gritted teeth. "But, Mrs. Allen, I really hate to run off, but I better be leaving now."

"Yeah, it is pretty late. Do you have far to go?"

I tried my best to fight back the tears that threatened to fall at the thought of having nowhere to go. I wasn't sure if she was about to invite me to stay, but I prepared my lips to decline before her question was complete.

"I have a bit of a drive ahead, but I will be all right."

"Well, I have more than enough room if you want to stay the night, and then maybe we can reach David in the morning. I can cook you a good breakfast, too, before you head off."

"Thank you so much for the offer, ma'am, but I have an appointment first thing in the morning, so I better get on my way."

We both stood and walked to the front door. Before I knew it, her small frame reached up and hugged me real tight. It was one of those loving hugs that only mothers gave. Little did she know it was definitely what I needed at that moment. After she told me to take care of myself, I damn near ran to my car to avoid any further eye contact. I didn't want her to see my tears any more than she already had. I hopped in my car as fast as I could as my chest heaved up and down uncontrollably. I was so overwhelmed by everything that I couldn't even think straight.

Needing to leave his mother's home as quickly as possible, I tried to think of where I could possibly go. I drove off fast, still hurt, still confused, still shocked, still everything. I drove for miles in no particular direction, just wherever my car and God led me. And as I drove, I talked to God again.

"God, please. Please take control of this situation. Give me somewhere safe to stay, to dry up my tears, and please heal my broken heart. I should have listened to you from the very start, but I promise to never go against your will for me again. I give my life over to you, Lord. I trust you."

Then it suddenly dawned on me. I turned my car around and headed to the one place where I found total peace.

Chapter 27

Terrence

Looking at the clock on the wall, which now read one thirty, I struggled to fall asleep. I should have drifted off long ago since I would have to get up soon, but I couldn't seem to find any sense of comfort on the cot I'd pulled out. It was hard and cold, absolutely nothing like my bed at home. Actually, just the thought of sleeping on it pissed me off even more. Had it not been for Patricia and her craziness, I could have been home in the warmth and comfort of my own bed.

I tossed and turned a few minutes longer with my eyes shut tight, trying to force myself to go to sleep. But before I was able to get into a deep sleep, I heard a loud noise in the hallway of the building. At first I figured it was perhaps the building settling, so I brushed it off and closed my eyes again. That was until I heard the noise again.

This time I was sure someone was there, so I grabbed a steel rod that I kept near the cot and slowly crept out the door into the hallway. Walking slow and steady, I crept down the right side. We hadn't been known to have break-ins, but I figured it was some neighborhood hoodlums, especially since we'd gotten new laptop and desktop PCs last week.

Continuing to move slowly, I looked for shadows and listened for any little sound while staying low until I could sneak up on them. Then I heard some noise come from the library. I could have sworn that the library door was locked when I first got here, but now it was open wide, so the computers were what they were after.

Waiting to hear something, I stayed quiet and low until I decided I would try to reason with whoever this was. I hoped and prayed I could get through to them and that they wouldn't take from the children in need here. This school was the only positive thing in most of these children's lives.

"Whoever's there, why don't you come out so we can talk? I can help you. You really don't have to steal from the children." At that moment, I still didn't hear anything. They were as quiet as a mouse, and I couldn't tell where they were in the library. "C'mon. As I said, I can help you, and that way I won't have to turn you in to the authorities."

Still there was nothing until I suddenly heard a book fall from a shelf on the left side of the room. I started to head that way, but I could tell that, as I approached that side of the room, the intruder crept toward my side of the room.

"Are we really going to play this game? If you turn yourself in now, you will be in much less trouble than if you don't." I walked closer to where I heard the book drop and looked behind me to cover all bases. "C'mon," I said slowly, trying to reassure them that they were safe.

"Please don't hurt me," a woman said with a soft and trembling voice.

I turned to face her. I had no idea who she was or why she was here, but she was beautiful, and there was no way I could hurt her. Putting the rod down slowly, I kept my hands in her eyesight to let her know everything was all right and she was safe with me. For a second or two, we both stood there looking at one another. I tried my best to figure her out, because she didn't look like she was homeless or a thief. So, finally, I decided to try to ease the tension in the room and get to the bottom of who this beauty was. I gradually extended my right hand to her.

"Hello. I'm Terrence Montgomery, the head football coach here at the school."

She didn't reach out her hand, and for a second, she didn't respond. Then a moment later, she spoke with a bit of sarcasm in her voice. "Head football coach, huh? I haven't seen you before, and what are you doing here this late at night anyway?"

I chuckled at her questioning because she asked it as if she belonged here and I didn't. "Well, I could ask you the same thing. By the way, you still haven't told me who you are."

"Tiffany," she said firmly. "Tiffany Tate."

"All right, Ms. Tate, now that we're finally getting somewhere, what are you doing here in a school library this time of night, or morning I should say?"

"Look, I don't want any trouble, all right?"

"And I'm not here to give you any trouble, but as a staff member of this school, I have to find out what you're doing here and how you got in."

I wasn't sure what button I pressed, but all of a sudden she started crying.

Chapter 28

Tiffany

My tears gushed down my face, and I felt like I couldn't control them even if I wanted to. This man probably thought I was insane by my behavior, but this entire situation with David had my emotions all over the place. I'd given up everything to be with him, and I couldn't believe this was how he repaid me. Then there was Terrence or whatever his name was. *What is he doing here? I thought I would have the entire school to myself to gather my bearings until in the morning.* Now I'd made a complete fool of myself in front of a total stranger.

I wished I could just blink my eyes and he would disappear, but that would have been way too good to be true. Through tear-filled eyes, I saw the shadow of his large, muscular frame begin to walk toward me. I didn't move away, and as he inched closer, I felt him put his arms around me. I practically melted inside of his massiveness and laid my head on his chest. If I hadn't known better, I would've sworn he was made of steel. It was crazy, because I didn't know this man from anywhere, yet I felt totally comfortable at that very moment.

"Whatever it is, it's going to be all right, I promise," he said, holding me close and rubbing my back.

I didn't even try to dispute what he said, although I felt very unhopeful at the moment. Still, I allowed myself to find a small sense of solace in the peacefulness of his presence. His body was warm and strong as he held me. I felt his heart beating at a relaxed and steady pace. I also recognized his scent of Kenneth Cole's Mankind and had to admit that he wore it well. At once, I realized that if I didn't pull away, my vulnerability would surely lead me into some deep, deep trouble. I pulled away as I wiped my eyes.

"I'm so sorry. I . . . I . . ."

"Hey, it's all right, you have nothing to be sorry about. If anyone should apologize, it's me. I didn't mean to treat you like you're some criminal, but you have to understand where I was coming from."

We stood there for a bit as we snuck quick glances at one another. I assumed that he was trying to figure out what to say as I did the same. It was strange, but I really wanted to know more about him. That was until I saw the silver band around his wedding finger. Immediately, I knew he was just like David and all the rest. Here he tried to console me and pretended to be this sincere and caring man when he had a wife somewhere probably wondering where the hell he was at this hour.

I became infuriated all over again, so much so that I finally shot back, "Look, if you don't mind, I really just want to be alone before it's time for school to start."

"Uh, okay, but can you at least tell me how you got in here? And if it's shelter you need, I can help you find a women's shelter that's probably not so bad."

I let out some much-needed laughter at his comment. "Listen, despite the looks of it, I'm not homeless, all right? Well, I mean, I am, but . . . Anyway, if you need to know, I'm the school's new counselor and librarian, and I have my own key."

He threw his hands up as if to say he surrendered, I guessed sensing that now I had an attitude. "Okay, okay. Well, although this was probably the craziest way for two people to meet, I guess I should welcome you to the school. I'm glad you're here."

Folding my arms, I rolled my eyes and shot him a look that said, "I just bet your ready-to-cheat behind sure is glad that I'm here."

He continued, "So maybe this wouldn't be the best time to ask what you're doing here or what has you so upset, but if you need someone to talk to, I'm here for you."

There he went pretending again that he had good intentions and that he cared about me. I swore all men must have read from the same book of lies. If it weren't for the different tones of their voices, I could probably close my eyes and not be able to tell who I was speaking to.

"Who said I'm upset? And why would you think I would talk to you and tell you all my personal business if I was, anyway?"

"Look, it's clear as day that something's going on from your swollen and bloodshot eyes, and I'm only offering to be an ear, all right? I think sometimes we all need someone who's neutral and nonjudgmental to talk to when we need it."

"Well, thanks but no thanks. I don't like to confide in complete strangers." I made my last statement like I hadn't just cried a river on this poor man's shoulder.

He gave a confused look probably because he'd thought the exact same thing. However, I assumed he finally took the hint when he walked away without saying another word to me. It'd never been like me to come across so mean and hostile to someone, but I blamed David for it all. He was the cause of the disgust and bitterness that I felt deep inside. He was the one who made me feel like I never wanted to deal with another man again.

When I thought about it, it was funny, because I could remember when I'd told Keisha how I would never allow myself to be a part of the Bitter Women's Club, yet here I was. I'd allowed one man to turn my heart cold, hard, and very bitter. From that very second, I vowed not to open it up anymore, not for anyone, including this Terrence fellow I honestly wished to know more about.

Chapter 29

David

"Someone has really been trying to reach you all night, huh?"

Sonya looked at me with a very suspicious expression on her face. She was right though. My cell phone had been in overdrive all night long. I'd taken glances at it here and there, and it seemed as if Tiffany, Leslie, and even my mother all tried to get in contact with me. I felt like Tiffany and Leslie could wait, but I needed to check on my mother quickly, and that was exactly what I told Sonya.

"It's my mother. I need to call and check on her and make sure she's all right. She's never called me this much unless something was wrong."

I hopped up with urgency and went inside Sonya's master bathroom for some privacy. I didn't even bother looking at any of the texts that were sent, but instead dialed my mother immediately. She answered on the very first ring.

"Mom, what's wrong? Is everything all right?" I asked in a panic.

She was calm though, and had a very cynical tone in her voice. "I had a visitor last night, David. A very pretty young lady who said she was looking for you. She claimed she wanted to tell you of someone's passing, but I could almost tell she was lying straight through her teeth. So who is Tiffany?"

I was lost as to why my mother asked me about Tiffany. How had Tiffany even located her when I lied and said my mother was deceased? All of a sudden, my heart started to beat a little faster as I dreaded to find out what Tiffany had revealed. The phone fell silent for a moment or two as my thoughts ate away at me.

"Did you hear me, David? Who is Tiffany, and why do you have these women coming by my house at ungodly times of the night?"

A million things swirled through my head as my mother yelled in one ear and Sonya yelled in the other, wondering if everything was all right.

"David? David? Is everything all right with your mother?"

I peeked out of the bathroom and put my finger up as if to say to give me a second. My mother was talking nonstop.

"David, I don't appreciate you leaving here and not telling me where you are, and then out of nowhere some random woman comes by. You are a grown man, and you really need to start acting like it. I'm not about to allow you to start disrespecting my home. Next time, I won't be so nice about it all."

"Mom, Mom, all right. Calm down, please. To be honest with you, I have no idea how Tiffany even knows your address. I don't know what she wanted or why she came by, but I can assure you that it will never happen again, all right? Now as for my whereabouts, you are right, I am a grown man. I don't have to disclose where I lay my head, Momma."

"Oh, you don't? So you think you can just come in and out of my house as you please, but not tell me where you are when you're not here?"

"Mom, all I'm trying to say is that where I am is not important. As long as you have a way to reach me, that's all that matters, and you always have a way of reaching me. Honestly, if my coming there from time to time bothers you that much, then I really don't have to. I don't have to ever come by." I said it loud enough for Sonya to hear. This argument with my mother was the perfect opportunity to ask Sonya for a place to stay.

"David, don't you dare take that tone with me. I'm the one who gives you money when you need it, a place to stay when you need it, and I cook and clean for you like I'm your wife, but from this day forward I'm done. If you're such a grown man, then try acting like it. Grow up and take care of yourself, or find you someone who will do it for you."

I was stunned when I heard the phone disconnect in my ear. My mother had never been that upset with me or talked to me in such a manner. Everything was all messed up, and I still had Tiffany and Leslie to deal with. Thinking about it, I was positive that things were more than likely over with Leslie and me. All we did was argue, as of late anyway, and I was tired of it. And Tiffany, well, I hated the thought of hurting her, but she crossed the line by going to my mother's house. True enough, I'd lied and told her that my mother was deceased, but that still didn't give her the right to dig into my personal business. She especially had no business going there. At last I'd found my exit with her and decided to take it. Pulling up her name in my phone, I shot her a quick text.

Tiffany. I got a call from my mother that you stopped by her house. All right, so I lied, and I guess you're happy that you found out the truth. But that still gave you no right to go there. I can't begin to tell you how rude and disrespectful that was to show up to someone's home who knows nothing about you, especially at that time of night. What is wrong with you? You know what? Forget it. I really hate to do this, but you've basically left me no choice. I don't think we should go through with getting married. Actually, I don't think we should even continue a relationship. I'm sorry, but it's over.

A sudden sense of relief came over me as I typed the last word. I shouldn't have done things this way, but honestly, she left me no other choice going to my mother's home. I still wanted the best for her, but this was the way things had to be. Preparing myself for the onslaught of calls and texts from her wanting answers, I decided to block her number for a while, at least until I felt the coast was clear. I figured it would be best for everyone involved.

My only focus now was Sonya, and I couldn't wait to get back to her. I went back into the bedroom and found her fast asleep again. Slowly, I started to kiss her body in the most random places—her nose, belly button, inner thighs, and then her lips. She squirmed around but in a good way. She was very much tuned in to my advances, which made me excited in return. My head found its way between her legs, and now she was fully awake with both hands atop my bald dome as she held it tightly. She moaned and her breathing became heavier. I'd done my job right, and ensuring she was pleased was the only thing that mattered at that time. Taking care of her intimately would surely secure her taking care of me in the long run. It was a win-win situation, and these arguments with my mother, Leslie, and Tiffany were all a part of history. *Goodbye and good riddance.*

Chapter 30

Patricia

It felt like my eyelids were glued shut as much as I'd cried during the night. I'd been calling Terrence in between my twenty-minute catnaps only to receive his voicemail every time. Now the morning sun glared in my face as I sat on the edge of my bed and contemplated what to do next. I was determined that my husband wouldn't leave me without a fight. Even though the clock on the nightstand reflected the early hours of the morning, it didn't matter to me what time of day it was. I grabbed my cell phone and dialed my pastor. Thankfully, he answered on the second ring.

My voice was weak as I hoped to get right to the point and avoid all the pleasantries. "Pastor Jones? Hi, it's Sister Montgomery."

"Oh, Sister Montgomery, to what do I owe the pleasure of speaking with you on this beautiful morning?"

"Well, I was hoping that I could come by the church and speak with you. It's kind of a personal matter."

"I see. Well, I would need to get you over to my secretary to check my schedule, but I can tell you right off that I'm quite booked for the next couple of weeks."

"A couple of weeks? Pastor, I can't wait that long. My marriage depends on it." I prayed he could sense my urgency and desperation.

"Your marriage? Now wait, try to calm down, Sister Montgomery, and tell me what's going on."

Although I would've preferred to discuss matters in person, I told Pastor Jones all the grimy details of my marriage that had occurred over the past few months. I even shared how our intimacy had diminished into thin air. Then I concluded with the night the police came by and that I hadn't heard from or spoken to Terrence since.

"So please, Pastor Jones, you have to help me get my husband back. I don't want my marriage to be over."

"Okay, try to calm down, please. Now did I hear you correctly? You said you called the police on him?"

"Yes, but that was only because he was trying to put Kendall out." I immediately started defending myself.

"Wow. I really don't know what to say. Are you sure there was no other way you could've handled things without getting the police involved?"

I looked at the phone sideways because it almost sounded as if he were blaming me for my husband's departure. It was like he hadn't heard anything else I'd said about Terrence not spending enough time with me or the boys, or the fact that he wanted to put my son out on the street that night. If he weren't a pastor, I would've had the right mind to put him in his place, but I kept my composure because I needed his help.

"No, Pastor Jones, there was no other way. I only wanted the police to calm him down. I never wanted my husband to leave," I lied, knowing good and well that I was the one who suggested it.

"Okay, Sister Montgomery, so how do you think I can help you all with this, especially if he's not in the home?"

"If you can just call him, please. Call him and make him realize that a man's place is home with his wife and children. Explain to him how he's going outside of God's will by not being here with us."

Pastor Jones hesitated for a moment before he released a breath that was laced with uncertainty. "Sure, I can do that. But you do know that you also have to take responsibility for your actions too, don't you, Sister Montgomery?"

There he went again! He acted as if he needed to put me in my place instead of just doing what I asked. *Lord, please don't let me say anything out of the way to this man of the cloth.*

"Uh, yes, I know that as well, Pastor. But I can't fix things with my husband if he's not here and won't answer my calls. I really need you to help me get him home. Then I can do the rest."

"I'll tell you what—I will give Brother Terrence a call to see what I can do. I won't make any promises to you, but I promise I will give it my best shot."

"Thank you. Thank you, Pastor Jones. That's all I'm asking. If he would just come home, I will talk to him and fix this. I will be the perfect wife from here on out." The phone was silent, almost as if the pastor was at a loss for words. "Pastor Jones? You still there?"

"Yes, I am. However, your last statement . . . Don't try so hard to be the perfect wife, because none of us are perfect. Just be the best wife you can be for your husband."

"Thank you again, Pastor Jones."

We hung up, and finally I had begun to feel some sense of hope. I didn't care what Pastor Jones said. I planned on being the perfect wife to Terrence. I would do whatever he needed . . . within reason. There was no way I'd ever let him leave again, and I damn sure wouldn't stand by while another woman took him away from me.

After thinking about it a little while longer, I decided to have my father, brother, and best friend call Terrence too as reinforcement. I figured that if Pastor couldn't get through to him, then one of them would. There was no way possible he could say no to all of them. So I talked to all three, and they all assured me they would give him a call.

Now I was at peace. I decided I wouldn't call Terrence myself anymore. I would simply wait for his return, when we would make everything right again. In the meantime, I decided to run to the mall and purchase something nice and sexy for him. We hadn't been intimate in quite a while because I always used sex as a way of punishment. But if he came home—no, when he came home—he'd never leave our home or bed again. Deep down, I hoped he didn't get used to it though, because it wasn't something I enjoyed on a regular basis.

While getting dressed, my mind wandered back to when Terrence and I first met. Back then, we couldn't keep our hands off one another. However, I was younger then, and I only did what I needed to get my man. Once we got married, there was no reason to place so much importance on sex. But seeing how things were so out of control, it was time to switch that up a little. I figured if he didn't upset me, I would break down and pleasure him at least once or twice a month, but nothing more.

Chapter 31

Terrence

Normally, I wouldn't have been here for these morning powwows with Monica and the rest of the school staff, but I went ahead and decided to take some time off from the other job. I had more than enough compensatory time to use, and right now, my main priority needed to be my home life. I also wanted to take this opportunity to devote more time to my team instead of being away from them. The young men at this school needed as much positivity in their lives as they could get, and I wanted to be there for them. Plus, helping them gave me a sense of fulfillment, especially since it didn't seem as if I could play that role in the lives of Kendall and Keith.

While Monica spoke to us, my thoughts went to how Patricia never wanted me to discipline the boys or even suggest anything beneficial to them without her approval. She always made it a point to remind me that she was their mother and I was the stepfather. At least, that was until one of them needed something. Thinking of them made me begin to think of my own kids. It broke my heart that I couldn't really be there in the lives of my girls the way I wanted, all because of Pat's actions. The more I thought about it all, I realized how much of a mess my life was, and it basically started with my marriage to her. All I really wanted was peace and happiness and to take care of my family, yet I didn't have any of that.

However, looking over in our new counselor and librarian's direction, I hoped that would change.

Even after only a couple hours of sleep in a school library and cleaning up in the girls' locker room, Tiffany was still amazingly beautiful. I sat directly across from her, trying my best not to look her way, but it didn't seem to be working. I wasn't exactly sure what it was about Tiffany, but she had my full attention, and I wanted to know more. I didn't want to seem intrusive or anything, but I was more so curious as to what had her down or who had stolen her beautiful smile away. The more I caught small glances of her, the more I wished there were something I could do. I wanted to encourage her, uplift her, put a smile back on her face where it belonged. But I also knew I had to find the right moment. I didn't want to come across too eager or pushy because she very well may tell me where to go. Instead, I only wanted to be her friend because it seemed she needed one, and I could sure use one myself.

Before I knew it, Principal Williams told us to have an amazing day before ending the meeting. I really hadn't heard much of what she said, but I was confident that I hadn't missed any pertinent information. Usually, her meetings were more about encouraging us to find ways to encourage the children, sort of a ripple effect, and she was right on point with it all.

Tiffany got up from her seat, bypassed the donuts, bagels, and coffee that were set out for us, and went directly into the hallway. I got up and followed right behind her.

"Hey, good morning, you."

She looked behind her as she kept walking as if I hadn't said a word.

I put a little more pep in my step to try to catch up with her. "Hey, I said, 'Good morning.'"

"Look, I'm sorry, but I'm really not in the mood this morning, okay?"

"Yeah, I can see that. You want to talk about it?"

"No."

"I'm a really good listener—"

She stopped walking, turned to me, and looked dead into my eyes. "I said no. I'm not in the mood, I don't want to talk, and I just want to be left alone. Is that too much to ask?"

I could see the pain in her eyes from whatever she was dealing with. It was strange, because I hadn't even known this woman twenty-four hours yet, but I wanted to be there for her. I wanted to be the one to take away her pain.

"Hey, I'm sorry. I didn't mean to be so aggressive or intrude on your privacy. I can leave you alone if that's what you really want, but just so you know, my offer from last night still stands. I am here if you need to talk. By the way, if you don't mind me saying it, you're way too beautiful of a woman to walk around not smiling, but that's just my opinion."

Nothing I'd said seemed to move her. She simply kept her mean mug on and walked away. If only she knew I was even more intrigued by the resistance. I fully prided myself on being a man, and men go after what they want. So her cat-and-mouse game was cool with me if that was how she wanted to play it.

Finally, I looked at my phone, which had buzzed a couple of times during the meeting. I figured it was only Patricia, so I hadn't bothered until now. To my surprise, there was a missed call from her father as well as Pastor Jones. I wondered what they could possibly have to say to me, so I went directly to my office to listen to the voice-mails. Closing my office door, I entered my password.

"Hey, Terrence! It's your father-in-law. I was hoping to catch up with you. I wanted to see how you were doing and possibly schedule some time to have lunch. Give me a call back as soon as you get this. You have my number. Take care."

I deleted his message immediately after listening to it. "Lunch, huh? Yeah, that will be the day that I take time out of my schedule to have lunch with you," I muttered to myself.

His phone call was nothing more than a failed attempt to interfere with my business with my family. The man had never really liked me. In fact, every time Patricia involved him or any of my in-laws in our affairs, they made me out to be the Big Bad Wolf and her the victim. Once, her father even suggested that things could be better between us if I stopped bullying his daughter and grandchildren. Bullying? He had to be kidding me. I was the one who cared for his daughter and grandchildren the best way I could with no help from anyone in that household or him. I was the one who brought home a steady income, while they always shelled money out. Yet I was the bully. It was all garbage to me, which was the very reason I had no intention of calling him back or scheduling any type of outing with him. If her father was any indication, then I guessed she'd put the pastor up to his phone call as well. I started to delete his message without listening, but I was too curious to hear what he had said.

"Brother Montgomery. Hello there, this is Pastor Jones. Long time no hear or see, young man. I haven't seen you at the church or heard anything from you lately, so I thought I would call and check on you. And I guess I have to be honest. Sister Montgomery did call and ask me to give you a buzz. I never heard her like this before, which was very worrisome to me. She's extremely concerned about the state of your marriage, and from the things she shared with me, so am I. Now she made some poor choices, but you guys cannot work things out with you outside the home. A husband's place is inside the home with his wife and kids. You all need to be communicating and praying together so that you can get through this troublesome time. I would even go so far as to say it would be best to come in and have some counseling with me. Anyway, I hope to hear back from you so that we can talk and I can pray with you one-on-one and share some helpful Scripture with you. Be blessed, Brother Montgomery."

I deleted his message too, and once again I was completely outdone. This woman even had the pastor involved. To add insult to injury, he added his two cents in on what my role was as a husband and head of the house. Wow, what a load of crap. I was curious to know exactly what she shared about what she'd done to bring us to this point. He'd stated that she made some poor choices, but I wondered if that included her decision to call the police on me. Either way, it was funny to me how people always divulged the things you'd done wrong, but never their own faults. In this case though, I couldn't see where I'd done anything wrong. I'd only made the right and necessary decisions for my family. Who could blame a man for that?

I had to think long and hard about my next move, especially if I leaned toward divorce. Deep down, I wished that there were some way we could fix things, only because I didn't want to be a failure in another marriage. But with the way I felt about everything, we were surely headed in the opposite direction. I sat there allowing my thoughts to take over. Looking down at my wedding band, I reflected on the day we took our vows. I took so much pride in becoming her husband and being the man for Patricia that I should have been for my children's mother. This ring and our vows meant so much to me, and now I wasn't so sure what it actually represented.

Patricia and I didn't have a marriage or a union anymore. This situation has turned into one big heap of chaos that I didn't believe could be fixed, no matter what her father or Pastor said. Besides, even if there were some way we could possibly settle all our differences, I was no longer sure that I wanted to.

My head started to ache, which let me know I was stressed out. With that in mind, I decided to do what I felt made the most sense. Until Patricia and I could get back on track, I removed my wedding band for good and placed it inside my desk drawer. It had become nothing more than a constant reminder of our turmoil as well as my failures as a husband and a man.

Instead of continuing to dwell on my marital troubles, I turned my thoughts back to something more pleasant. For me that was Tiffany. I had to find a way to help her through whatever she was going through, and I was dead set on doing that—whether she liked it or not.

Chapter 32

Tiffany

The last school bell rang, and I prepared myself to transition from counselor to librarian. The entire day had been a bit of a struggle for me ever since I'd left the morning meeting. Once I got to my office, I saw that I had a text message from David. To top off everything else he'd done, that no-good-ass jerk had the nerve to break up with me because I went by his mother's home—the mother he'd said was deceased. He couldn't even be a man and tell me that he had another fiancée. He wouldn't come clean about every last one of the lies he'd told. He only said it was over, and that was it. I guessed I would have been asking for too much for him to face me like a man. I thought about how I'd always tried to never feel hate for anyone, but I felt that way toward David right now. And it wasn't that I was so torn up about not being with a pathetic-ass man like him. It was more that I'd ever put a single ounce of trust in him from the start. Despite what my gut had already told me, I tried my hardest to believe in him. I thought we could make it work. Now here I was left feeling like a complete fool.

I didn't want to cry again. In fact, I told myself that I wouldn't shed another tear over this good-for-nothing jerk. But I had to admit, I was sad and confused and wasn't sure what I needed to do. Never in a million years would I have thought I'd end up in this predicament—a grown woman without a place to call home or any sense of what to do to rectify the situation. I knew for sure that I couldn't continue to live in the library, but I needed some time to find a place. Even if I returned home to St. Louis, there was nothing to return to. I'd lost a lot simply trying to be with who I thought would be my husband. It was all such a huge mess.

On top of all of that, I had yet another dream in which I married this mystery man. I almost felt like God was teasing me in a sense as He continued to show me what my heart truly desired without actually having granted it to me.

Stopping by the girls' restroom, I threw some water on my face before going into the library. I was able to cover up my sadness throughout the day as the counselor. Basically, I stayed closed up inside my office and only saw two children. But as the librarian, I knew it wouldn't be that easy. There were definitely more students who always needed help, so I had to get myself together. After I splashed a few handfuls of water on my face, I dried it and went into the library. There were already a few students inside, and as I looked at my desk, I saw Mrs. Williams sitting there, waiting for me. She spoke first in her normal chipper tone.

"Hey, Tiffany, how are you?"

I attempted to adjust my tone and demeanor to match hers so she wouldn't notice my sour mood. "Hey, Mrs. Williams. I mean, Monica." I quickly corrected myself when she turned up her nose at me for being so formal.

"So again, how are you?"

"I'm good," was all that I could manage to say.

"Are you sure?"

"Of course. Why do you ask?"

"Well, I glanced at you a couple of times during this morning's meeting, and I saw you in the cafeteria at lunch, and you seemed a little distant and withdrawn."

I was at a loss for words. I wondered whether to tell her the truth or continue to lie about my situation. Her opinion of me mattered though, and I didn't want her to look at me as a foolish woman for having believed half the things David said.

I remained silent for a moment and then suddenly said, "It's David."

"We can talk about it if you want."

"I want to, but I don't know how without crying a river of tears. Lord knows I don't want to do that anymore, especially not in front of the children."

"All right. How about once you close up the library this evening you come to my house with me and have dinner? You can tell me what's going on then as well as get a nice home-cooked meal."

"That would really be nice, Monica. I could definitely use that."

"Good. I'll come back to the library later and you can ride with me."

She gave me a hug and left. I started to feel somewhat better. Although I didn't want her to look down on me or pity me, I felt relief that I had someone to confide in about all of this. I started to do some busywork while the students worked with their tutors until a few moments later when I had another visitor pop up. That feeling I felt after Mrs. Williams left instantly turned bitter when he walked up to the desk. For the life of me, I couldn't understand why he couldn't give it a break. I didn't want to be bothered with him, or any man for that matter.

"Hey, you."

"Hey," I said in a very dry tone while I continued to look at the papers in front of me and hoped he'd get the hint.

"I wanted to check these books out for some of my players if that's all right."

"Sure, no problem." It came out in the same monotone way as before. I almost wanted to look up and see his expression, but I also didn't want to give him the idea that I was interested in anything he had to say.

I went through the routine of checking out the books, and the entire time it was quiet. He stood there and watched me as I did my work. I had to admit that I was shocked, because I was positive he would have tried to encourage me, make me smile, or something of that nature. Since he hadn't, I hurried to finish up and give his books back. But then he just stood there gawking at me.

"Um, is something wrong?"

"No, not at all."

"Well, I'm done with your books."

"I know."

"Okay, so why are you still standing here?"

"Just trying to find the right words to say."

"What do you mean by that?"

"I want to make you smile."

I rolled my eyes and neck, completely exasperated with his presence. "Here we go again. Is that why you came in and got all these books? Just so you can start this with me again?"

"No. The books are really for my players. Seeing you though was icing on the cake."

Okay, Mr. Head Football Coach. He scored one with that unexpected compliment. I thought he would spew more happy-go-lucky rhetoric at me, but the compliment, while unwarranted, was surprisingly welcomed. One thing was for sure, the man was absolutely charming. I tried my best to fight it, but before I knew it, he finally got his wish.

"Uh-oh, wait a minute. Could that be a smile I see?" He chuckled, then all at once he picked up his books and started to walk away.

"Hey, wait a minute. Where are you going?"

"Back to my office. Why do you ask?"

I shrugged and fanned my hands outward. "Uh, well, I mean, you finally make me smile and then you leave? Just like that?"

"I got my wish, so that's it."

My mouth hung wide open and so was my nose. At long last, he had my complete attention, and it meant nothing to him. I tried not to let it upset me all over again, but it seemed he'd just played me, like all the others. With that thought in my mind, I put my head down and went right back to my busywork. That was until he caught me off guard again.

"All right, look, would you like to grab something to eat when you close up this evening?"

Once again, I was left speechless. Although I'd already arranged to go to Monica's, I was extremely curious about this man. Then I wondered if I should even bother going there with him. My mind shot back to our initial meeting, and the only thing that stood out was the wedding band on his finger, which was now conveniently gone. I was positive one had been there, so I couldn't help but wonder if he was playing some type of game with me. Besides, I knew deep down that I had no business letting my guard down with anyone this quickly after David. So as much as I wanted to oblige him, I went with what made the most sense.

"I'm sorry. I don't think that would be a good idea."

"Why not? I have to eat. I'm sure you have to eat, so what's the problem?"

"Can I ask you something first?"

"Shoot!"

"Didn't I see a ring on your finger before?"

He looked at me a few moments, and I pretty much knew his answer without him saying a word. However, I still waited for him to respond. "I'm married."

"Yet you've been flirting since we met, and now you're asking me out to dinner. I swear, all you men are exactly the same."

"Look, wait. Maybe I have been flirting, but I can't help that. You're an extremely attractive woman, and I'm a man. But please believe that my intentions are sincere. I asked you out to eat because we both have to eat and I figured you could use someone to talk to. But only if you want to. No pressure."

"What about your wife though? Why are you not going home to eat with her? And if I said yes, would she know that you're taking me out and listening to all of my problems? I'm sure she wouldn't be too thrilled about that."

"If I need to explain now rather than later, it's not the best time between my wife and me, which is why I removed my ring. I've been living in hotels for weeks now, which is why you found me sleeping here at the school last night. So there you have it. I promise, I'm not trying to play any games with you or lead you on. I just have to get more clarity in that part of my life. But I really didn't think all of that mattered only to grab a bite to eat. I mean, at least give me some credit. I was honest with you about being married."

I hesitated for a second and wondered if he was being sincere. It all seemed harmless, and he was honest about being married. But as I thought more, I wasn't so much afraid of his intentions, but instead my own. As he stood before me, I couldn't deny that there was a mutual attraction between us, and I was in an extremely vulnerable state.

"Look, I'm sorry, all right? I guess I'm just a bit cautious with men right now. My last relationship didn't end on the best terms."

"I see."

"Anyway, I would love to take you up on your offer, but I'm having dinner with Mrs. Williams this evening. Maybe some other time."

"That's fair. Are you staying the night at Mrs. Williams's?"

"I doubt it. She has a husband and children. I can't invade on her family like that."

"All right, well, how about I leave my number with you and you can call me when you return? I can even get you a room for the night so that you can at least have a good night's sleep instead of staying in this stuffy old library."

Everything he said sounded wonderful, and my mind had already gone into daydream mode about a long, hot bath and being curled up in a nice bed for the night. Then beyond my better judgment, I asked, "What about you?"

"What about me?"

"I'm sure you could use a good night's sleep also, seeing as how we both slept here at the school."

He cracked a slight smile and his sex appeal, charm, and the fact that he smelled amazing sent chills through my body. Yep, I'd reached a new point of desperation as I flirted with this married man while awaiting his response.

"You're right. I could. Maybe I'll get a room too. I'll just play it by ear."

"Okay. That sounds like a plan."

We stood there and looked at one another. He almost seemed as if he didn't want to leave, and I didn't want him to. I wasn't sure what it was about him, but his presence gave me a sense of peace and tranquility that I needed. In that moment, I did make a promise to myself that I would completely respect his marriage. No matter how intrigued I was, I wouldn't disrespect the next woman, no matter their situation. No lie, though, I couldn't help the fact that I wanted to know more about

Coach T, as the students called him. As we continued staring each other down, it became apparent that we both wanted to say something. However, we left well enough alone.

"I look forward to hearing from you when you return," he said.

"Sounds good."

"Enjoy your dinner with Principal Williams."

He walked off, but his aroma lingered around my desk. I kicked myself the minute he left because of the thoughts that swirled through my mind. *Lord, why can't this man be single? And please give me the strength not to let all of my guard down in his presence. He is married, and I want to respect that. But please, God, be with me. I'm only human.*

Chapter 33

Terrence

Walking back to my office, I was happier than I'd been in quite a while. Although I could tell that Tiffany was still on guard with me, I'd slowly but surely chipped away at the wall she'd built up. I wasn't sure yet what was going on with her, but from a couple of things she said, I figured it more than likely had to do with a man. Whoever it was, though, I felt had to be a real jerk to let a woman like her slip away. But I was glad he did because now it gave me an opportunity to give her hope again. I wanted to prove to her that there were still some good and decent men out here. Of course, she might be a little skeptical, especially from the expression on her face when I mentioned I was married. But I was going to find a way to prove that not all men were the same.

Instantly, I began to wonder just how much longer I would have that title—married. Divorce was constantly on my mind. Not to mention the overwhelming peaceful feeling I'd had since I hadn't been at the house. I wasn't all stressed out by the constant arguments I used to have with Patricia. I hadn't been upset from busting my tail working two jobs, only to come home and see everyone lounging around. I felt free and really didn't care about my home life or marriage anymore. I was still trying to pay the bills as best I could, but only because that was simply a part of my manhood and character. Regardless of our failing relationship, I'd provide as I was supposed to until the day that I was no longer obligated to do so. As of now, I took my happiness any way I could get it, whether it was temporary or not.

Being somewhat curious, I logged on to my Facebook account from my office computer and immediately typed the name Tiffany Tate into the search bar. It was somewhat of a common name, so I hoped there weren't a thousand Tiffany Tates I'd have to search through. To my surprise, she popped up in the first three, I assumed because we worked together and had a mutual friend in Principal Williams.

Clicking on her page, I went directly to her pictures. Her beauty shined through in each one, and I couldn't get past the smile on her face, which enhanced her beauty even more. Being nosy, I looked around for pictures of her and a man, and there were only a couple. I hurried to click on them to enlarge them in order to get a better look at the guy.

There was definitely no hate inside of me, but at first glance, it seemed like he wasn't her type. Not that I actually knew what her type was, but they appeared to be a fairly odd couple. I tried never knocking the next man, but the brother wasn't physically fit, wasn't a great dresser, and in all honesty, was a very average-looking guy. I guessed that could be looked at as a positive thing on Tiffany's behalf because it showed she wasn't all caught up in looks. Yet it shocked me a bit because Tiffany seemed like a little above-average type of woman. They simply didn't complement one another at all.

I clicked out of her pictures and scrolled through the rest of her page. Surprisingly enough, I learned that she was quite the artsy type. She'd posted about singing and spoken-word poetry, and more recently dabbling in writing. Then I saw how she hoped to one day write an entire book and become a bestselling author. I loved that she had dreams and aspirations, and I became even more intrigued by this woman. We had so much in common, and I couldn't wait to share with her my passion and love for the arts as well.

I also wanted to share my future desires with her—my love for cooking and my dream to one day have my own restaurant chain. Patricia was the only one who knew anything about it, but she suggested long ago that I wake up and stop dreaming. She'd always said that although I was a damn good cook, I needed to focus my energy on a legit career and not on some pipe dream. Only it wasn't just some silly hobby. It was my passion and one that I wanted to pursue. I planned to start off small, but then eventually I hoped to own my own restaurant chain with businesses around the globe. Patricia listened to me talk about it all the time but felt we would lose money before making some, and it was too much of a risk for a man with a wife and children to care for. She didn't want me wasting my time with it at all.

Little did she know, however, I'd been cooking for school events and the football games and even catered some small events for the staff outside of school hours as my schedule permitted. Monica even became so involved, after I'd shared with her how Pat didn't support me, that she allowed me to use the home economics room for my personal kitchen. It was the one thing that allowed me to be creative as well as relax in my zone. If Patricia knew, she'd be upset that I still played around with the idea of my own business. I just wished that as my wife she could see how important this was to me and encourage me in the pursuit of my dreams.

I could have gotten lost in Tiffany's Facebook page alone, but a few minutes later, I decided to shoot her a friend request and then log off. I wanted to make reservations at my favorite dessert bar. She'd mentioned having dinner with Principal Williams but hadn't said anything about dessert. The place I planned on taking her had a real grown and sexy feel to it. Most nights they had a live band and the best chocolate martinis. Then I planned on booking two suites at my favorite five-star hotel. Of course, I'd be shelling out a lot of cash that I needed to save right now, but I wanted to live a little after being suffocated by Patricia and her antics. Furthermore, I was positive that Tiffany was worth it.

After I made all the reservations, I cleaned up so that I could look and feel my best. Not to be cocky—well, maybe a little—but Tiffany would be accompanied by an above-average guy tonight. I also wanted to pamper her and make this night unforgettable. I could sense that she needed it, and I was definitely going to be the one to make it happen.

As I finished up everything in my office, I glanced at my phone and saw that I received a notification from my Facebook account that Tiffany accepted my request. Although I'd sent the request in the hopes that she'd accept it, I didn't believe that she would. She seemed to be extremely private and cautious in the way she handled her personal affairs. For those reasons alone, I thought for sure she would deny my request, but since she hadn't, I figured that I must have been winning her over. I beat my chest a bit as I thought, *another brick down, Tiffany Tate, and only a few more to go.*

Chapter 34

Patricia

Terrence always begged me to stop smoking for as long as I could remember. He felt it was unladylike and hated how it lingered in my clothes and hair. I'd tried a couple of times just for him, but it never lasted long. Lately, I found myself smoking more and more because of our situation, to the point where I was on the last one of my second pack already. Not only was I on my second pack of cigarettes, but I was also on my third glass of wine as I paced back and forth, wondering why no one had heard from Terrance, including me. I'd already spoken with my father and Pastor Jones hours ago. They both had the same report. They'd left messages for him to return their calls. Yet no one had heard back. I assumed that he would at least have the respect and decency to call the pastor back, but that wasn't the case. It was never like Terrence to be so disrespectful, so something more was going on with him.

Not only that, but as I flipped through the morning's mail, I saw letters from our mortgage company that we'd missed our last payment and needed to become current as soon as possible. "Wow, Terrence, not only did you leave, but you stopped paying the mortgage, too?"

I wanted to scream at the top of my lungs at my husband's carelessness. Not only was he out there doing God knows what with God knows who, but he was proving that he no longer cared about the well-being of his family. Terrence had gotten completely beside himself, and it infuriated the hell out of me. Even still, I wanted him back home so that we could try to get things back in order.

I tried my best to stay away from social media because I always seemed to get stressed whenever I looked at it, but Terrence left me no choice. If he wasn't going to call, I had the right to check his page to try to find out what was going on with him. I dreaded it because he would have a million likes, comments, or even new friends from no one but females—single and thirsty females at that. Terrence couldn't seem to realize that what I'd said was true. These women today were extremely desperate and couldn't care less that a man was married. Marriage no longer meant a thing, and they couldn't wait to sink their claws into a man who looked halfway decent.

I went directly to his account, and as I thought, there were women, women, and more women. I looked at the hundreds of likes on his pictures. I saw females commenting, Hey, handsome, or Looking good, Mr. Montgomery. I'm jealous of the wife. *Well, yes, tricks, you should be jealous, because he is mine—all mine.*

I decided to make a few comments under their comments. Just to shake things up, I replied, Yes, he is very handsome, isn't he? Love you, baby! and Yeah, you'd better be jealous of his wife, because she doesn't share! He'd be upset, but I didn't care at all. I'd told him time and time again that he needed to check these tricks about what they said on his page or delete them. However, he would always have the audacity to say that they were only friends and I was the one who needed to stop being so insecure. Well, I was going to show him insecure since that was what he thought I was.

I went on to look at his new friends. I'd already seen some of their faces before, so I really wasn't concerned.

Then there were others who didn't look like much to be worried about. But then I came across someone named Tiffany Tate. I'd never seen her face, and I had to admit that she was attractive enough to actually be his type. I clicked on her page to get a better view and find out more about her.

"Oh, so she's your coworker, huh? I've met all of your coworkers, so why haven't I met her? Well, let's see if she's single or married. Oh, engaged, huh? Well, you'd better be, and you'd damn sure better stay far away from my husband."

I was just about to click off her page until I saw a post pop up from none other than my husband. I was completely stunned for a moment as I looked at that screen. Reading the words in front of me over and over again, I began to boil on the inside.

Thanks for the add, Tiffany! Glad I was able to make you smile today!

"Glad you were able to make her smile? Are you kidding me, Terrence? You have a whole wife and kids you haven't been concerned with for weeks, but you're somewhere making some heffa smile?" Pissed wasn't the word for what I felt at the moment, and my face was damn near beet red with the anger that raged inside of me.

I logged out of my account and found myself attempting to log into his. I didn't know his password, but nothing was about to stop me from figuring it out. I tried everything. My name, his mother's name, his children's names, and nothing worked. I almost gave up until it dawned on me. I was positive it was his grandmother's name, the one who had raised him and whom he adored. I typed her name nice and carefully, and bingo, I was in. After deciding on exactly what I would say, I began to private message each female friend I thought he might have some speculative dealings with.

Hello! Some of you may know me and others may not, but just to make it clear, I am Terrence Montgomery's wife. Yes, his w-i-f-e. I would appreciate if you all would respect me and his page, or simply face being deleted. We all know that he is fine as hell and extremely charming. But also know that he is very much married, happy, and all mine.

I signed off and felt damn good about what I'd just done. Terrence would be ready to kill me once he found out I'd hacked his page, but I would just have to deal with it when we crossed that bridge. A huge smile came over my face as I imagined all those women reading my message—all except for Tiffany Tate, that was. I purposely hadn't sent Tiffany a message because I had something very special in mind for her. Since my husband was making her smile, I wanted to see this smile when I showed up to the school to meet her face-to-face. In fact, we would all see who would be smiling then.

Chapter 35

Tiffany

Monica came into the library right as the last student left. I had to admit that I was extremely happy to finally come to the end of this workday. It had been long and stressful, to say the least. Now I looked forward to a nice meal with her and her family as well as being able to get some things off my chest. I needed someone to talk to about my situation, and I was happy that she had a listening ear.

Although I didn't want to come out and say it, I also looked forward to seeing Terrence afterward. Certainly, nothing could ever happen between us, not that I was ready to get involved anyway, but I was still happy he was here for me. He seemed like a very genuine guy, and I could appreciate that. Actually, I was thankful for all the kind people God had placed in my life as of late. Besides David, He'd put some wonderful, sincere people in my life who had my best interest at heart. I realized though that I had to look at David as a blessing as well. He'd served his purpose for the three years we were together, and he'd definitely shown me what I did not desire in a man. When I thought about it, I desired a man more like Terrence. There was still a lot I had to learn about him, but he already seemed unlike any other man I'd ever met.

"Hey, almost ready?"

I jumped, startled out of my fantasy and back into reality. "Yep. I'm signing off of my computer as we speak, boss."

"Wait a minute, that's a look I haven't seen all day. You're smiling, too. Did something happen that I need to know about?"

"Oh, of course not. It's just Terrence. I accepted his friend request on Facebook right before logging off."

"Terrence? Wait, you mean Coach T?" she asked with a look of curiosity.

"Yeah, Coach Montgomery."

"Is there something you're not telling me?" she asked as I detected the inquisitiveness written all over her face.

"No, Monica, there's nothing to tell. That man is married," I tried to remind her and myself while hiding my smile at the mere thought of him. "He's just been really kind to me, and I appreciate it. The same way you've been kind."

"Yeah, but I ain't as fine as he is." We both laughed as I gathered the rest of my things.

"Well, I hadn't quite noticed that," I lied.

"Girl, stop it. You wouldn't be human if you didn't notice how nice looking that man is."

We fell out laughing that time as we walked out the door. Monica was right though. I felt better than I had all day. Better than I had the past couple of days. She gave off good, positive energy, which I surely needed. But my sudden good vibes also came because I would see Terrence later, and I couldn't wait.

Monica didn't hesitate once we got inside her car. I'd hoped this conversation would wait until we were in front of some good food and several glasses of wine, but she saw to it that that wasn't the case. I looked at it as a good thing though, because if we talked about it now, then we could speed up dinner. That way I could get to Terrence sooner than expected.

"All right, so tell me what's going on with you. What's had you so upset?"

"I really don't even know where to begin. Things are such a mess, Monica."

"Is it your fiancé? Has he come home since the last time we spoke? Or is he just not acting right overall? Because I can tell you, all men get a little crazy and nervous at the thought of marriage, like their life is suddenly ending or something. Or is it you? Have you finally decided that he really isn't the one?"

"Well, I didn't have to decide anything. And no, he hasn't come home since the last time. Actually, the man doesn't even have a house to come home to."

"What in the world do you mean by that?" she said, glancing over at me while trying to keep her eyes on the road. "I thought you moved into his house."

"Nope. I came to find out that I moved into her house!"

"Wait, who is her? Girl, maybe we need to wait until we have a glass of wine for this."

"How about a whole bottle each?"

"Wow, Tiffany, I have so many questions."

"I'm sure you do. Anyway, the other night, once I left the library, I went home . . . or at least what I thought was my home. I ran some nice bathwater, dimmed the lights, and lit candles, turned on music, and prepared for a nice, relaxing evening. But after I got in the tub and closed my eyes, I had who I thought was his sister standing over me with a gun pointed to my head."

"Oh, my goodness. What?" she screamed and almost slammed on her brakes. "Tiffany, what in the world did this man get you involved in? See, I had a strange feeling. Something wasn't adding up when you were telling me about him. I knew there had to be more to it!"

I couldn't hold back my tears as I relived what happened that night. I suddenly felt that maybe it wasn't such a good idea to discuss it, but I had to finish telling her.

"Yeah, well, there was definitely way more to it, and I hate that I couldn't see it myself. I feel so stupid, Monica."

"Oh, honey, don't feel that way. You have to believe that everything happens for a reason, good and bad. There's a reason you dealt with that jerk. There's a reason you relocated here to Texas. And there's a reason everything is happening the way it is now. In due time, trust me, God will reveal it all. But wait, if she wasn't his sister, who was she? His wife?"

"No, at least not yet anyway. She was his fiancée, and the house I was in was hers. Not his, but hers!"

"Wow. I really don't believe this, Tiffany."

"She had that gun pointed directly at me, and from the look in her eyes, she wouldn't have hesitated to pull the trigger if I didn't do exactly what she said."

"What was that? What did she say?"

"She wanted me out—out of the tub, out of her house, and out of her life."

"But didn't she see how this wasn't your fault? That he is the liar and the cheat and both of you all were taken advantage of?"

"None of that mattered. She didn't care about any of that. She only wanted me out. She basically let me throw on my clothes, grab what I could, and that was it."

"But what about the rest of your things?"

"I don't know. She said she would put them outside this morning and I could come by and get them if I wanted. I planned to just chalk it all up as a loss and start fresh though. I don't want a constant reminder of David or his sister/fiancée."

"Aw, Tiffany. So what did you do after that? Please tell me you went hunting that jerk down."

"I couldn't. I have no idea where he is, and I still don't know my way around Texas like that. I did, however, have an address to another house. I thought that maybe that was his real home, so I went there."

"And what happened? Was he there?"

"Nope. It was his mother's home—the mother he said passed away a long time ago."

"Oh, no. The man lied about his mother still being alive?"

"Yep, and I couldn't believe that I disrespected someone's mother by going there so late, but I was desperate, Monica. I had to have answers. Anyway, I apologized to her and made up some silly reason as to why I came by. I tried to make it seem like an emergency."

"I still can't believe all of this, Tiffany."

"Me either. I feel like, what did I ever do to deserve this? All I wanted to do was try to love this man and start a life with him."

"But you can't start a life with the wrong one. You have to look at this as God saving you from a lifetime of heartache and pain down the line by having this happen now."

"I know, but it still hurts. I have absolutely nothing now. I can't go back to St. Louis because I let go of everything there, and I don't even have a home or anything here. To be honest, I slept in the library last night because I had nowhere else to go or enough money to get a hotel room."

"Oh, Tiffany, why didn't you call me?"

"I don't know. Pride, I guess. I didn't want to bother you and your family with my drama, especially not that late at night."

"Honey, that's what friends are for. I'm not just your boss. I'm your friend."

As she said that, we finally pulled up to her home. We both got out, and she came over to the passenger side and gave me a big hug. She held me tight for a while, and I definitely needed it. It almost felt like my mother's arms wrapped around me, and I laid my head on her shoulder and cried as long and as hard as I possibly could. I wanted to get all my pain out at that very moment because I promised myself that, from that point on, I would not allow myself to feel anything when it came to David again.

She pulled away, wiped my tears, and grabbed my hand to go inside her home. I realized that Monica was right that everything happens for a reason. God had placed her in my life for this very specific reason.

We went inside her home, and I was amazed by its beauty. It was practically a mini mansion compared to what I lived in. It had vaulted ceilings and dramatic entryways. Its decor was modern yet classic and elegant. I wasn't sure why I was so shocked, because it was exactly what someone would picture when meeting her.

What I loved most, however, was the pure joy and love you felt within it. As soon as we walked in, her husband, kids, and even the dog all ran to fill her with an abundance of hugs and kisses. I stood there in so much awe as I daydreamed of the day when that would be my reality.

After the hellos, she introduced me to her husband, Todd. He was exactly what I would've pictured as well. He was tall, physically fit, and very clean cut. Between them both they made the perfect-looking black couple, and I simply couldn't take my eyes off of them. Her two little ones were beautiful also, two boys named Austin and Dallas. All four of them made the picture-perfect family, including their dog, Ashes. I surely didn't want to be envious of her, but it was hard not to be.

Todd took her things out of her hand. "C'mon, you two, while dinner is hot. I made some spaghetti and meatballs, catfish, and Caesar salad. Then for dessert, I whipped up one of my famous apple pies."

"Monica, a man who can throw down in the kitchen is definitely a keeper," I joked, trying to take my mind off our conversation in the car.

"Girl, why do think I snatched him up?"

She and I gave each other a high five, and we all laughed as I looked over at Todd and saw him blushing from cheek to cheek. We gathered around the table, said grace, and stuffed ourselves on his delicious food. I turned down the apple pie though because I didn't need my hips to spread any more than they already had. After the meal, Todd took the boys downstairs to his man cave while Monica and I finished talking. She grabbed a bottle of wine from the fridge and two wineglasses. I followed her into their family room, and we curled up on the sofa.

"So, Tiffany, I still can't get over what happened to you."

"Yeah, me either. I never imagined David would do something like this to me, and I can't help but wonder how long he planned on keeping up this whole charade."

"There's no telling with a man like that, honey. They just lie, lie, and lie until they get themselves caught. They should know that everything comes out eventually. Anyway, I only wish I could be a fly on the wall when his sister/fiancée finally comes into contact with him."

"Yeah, she told me to tell him that he'd better watch his back, and I got a feeling she just might use that gun on him for sure."

We laughed at the thought, but I knew how serious something like that was. People got hurt or lost their lives on a regular basis these days over affairs.

"Well, you know I'm not letting you sleep in that library anymore, right? You'll stay right here until you get everything squared away."

"Oh, no. I couldn't intrude on your family like that."

"There's no intrusion, and I won't accept no for an answer. There's a guest room on the lower level with its own bathroom and kitchen, so you'll have as much privacy as you need."

"I don't know. I don't mean to sound ungrateful, but I really don't want to put my problems off on anyone else, so please just let me think about it."

"Of course, but at least stay tonight."

My head lowered because I'd have to come clean about my plans for after I left here. I took another long swig of wine before I told Monica the deal with Terrence. "Actually . . ." I paused and tapped my wineglass with my finger because I was afraid of what she might think. "The coach insisted on getting me a hotel room tonight since my stay at the library wasn't the best last night. He thinks I should have a good night's rest."

She looked at me skeptically before she leaned forward and placed her hand atop my arm. "Okay, so what's up with that, Tiffany? Are you sure there isn't something you're not telling me?"

"No, not at all, and trust me, nothing's going on. He found me at the library late last night. I don't know why he was staying there, but I guess he thought I was a burglar or something. Anyway, things didn't start off so great because I really gave him a hard time, but I kind of eased up on him this evening. He seems like he's a very genuine guy."

"Oh, yeah, the coach is a great guy, and he was more than likely at the school because of that wife of his."

"Really? What's up with her?"

"I try to stay far away from the lady anytime she's around, but she just seems rather mean and insecure. She's always hounding Coach about something when the man does everything possible to take care of her and the children."

"How many children do they have?"

"He has none with her, thank goodness, but he has two of his own and she has two. If it's not her boys getting into some kind of trouble, then it's her and her shenanigans. He's even talked about divorce a couple of times before but never goes through with it. I think he'll feel a bit guilty about leaving her to fend for herself and two boys. And although I don't wish divorce upon anyone's marriage, I personally think it would be the best thing for him."

"Wow, it makes me look at him through a totally different lens. At first I thought he was just another man trying to have his cake and eat it, too. His kindness, though, has really made me reconsider my first thoughts. But for obvious reasons, I guess I was on the fence about the type of man he really was. My judgment in men hasn't been the best."

Monica waved her finger jokingly. "Nope, I doubt it." We laughed and then she turned serious. "Listen, Coach Montgomery is definitely one of the good ones though. As you can see, he's very attractive, he's intelligent, athletic, a superb cook, and so much more."

"Wait, did you say a superb cook?"

"Hell yes! The man could have his own business if he wants, but he's listening to that wife of his who doesn't think owning a restaurant is a good career choice."

"Really?"

We were quiet for a second while taking sips of our wine, and then she blurted out, "Are you going to tell me now what's going on with you two? Because I'll find out eventually."

"I told you. Nothing at all. He offered to get me a room, and after the last couple of days I've had, I agreed. Of course, he's very attractive, but I don't want to cross the line with him being married. I've been there and done that whole thing. Anyway, I'm not in the right frame of mind to think about anything with anyone after all this mess."

"I know, I know. I was only asking. I surely wasn't trying to suggest that you get down with a married man. I guess I'm just ready for the coach to have a good and decent woman in his life. And I want the same for you. Both of you need it and deserve it. But like you said, I agree that you do need to take some time for yourself and clear your mind and heart from this whole situation first."

"Yes, exactly."

We sat there for another thirty minutes talking about men, relationships, and possibly which direction I should go from there. She told me that if I didn't take her up on the offer to stay there, she would give me an advance in my salary to get an apartment or townhome of my own. Either way, she said she was not letting me go back to St. Louis.

I had to admit that I loved being around Monica. Her spirit was so calming and soothing. She told me she'd been that way since the very day she invited God into her life. It suddenly made me think about my own personal relationship with God. There was a time when I was way more faithful and committed to my faith by going to church and studying my Word regularly. But somewhere I'd fallen off. Everything else in my life somehow became more important, including David. As I sat there, I saw Monica's mouth moving, but I didn't hear the words coming from it. My mind was focused on what I needed to do to get my relationship back right with God.

The conversation kind of died down on its own when she suggested that she get me back to the school to Terrence. I didn't argue because I really liked the sound of that. I quickly shot him a text to let him know that I should be back soon.

"Tiffany, before we go, I hope you don't mind if I say a quick prayer for you."

"Oh, no, not at all. I actually think that would be great."

We stood from the couch, she grabbed both of my hands, we bowed our heads, and she began to pray. "Dear Heavenly Father . . ."

Chapter 36

Tiffany

Terrence opened my door, took my hand, and led me into a dessert bar called the Chocolate Factory. He said it was his favorite, and he was thrilled that he could take me there. As he walked a couple of steps in front of me, I watched him closely and admired his broad shoulders and the confidence within his glide. I was so thankful that I'd gotten a dress from Monica so that I could complement him and his attire. He had on some dark denim jeans with a crisp cream-colored button-down shirt and a cashmere camel-colored blazer. Terrence was so well put together, I thought as my eyes glided up and down his muscular frame. Not to mention, his blemish-free chocolate skin looked sweet enough to eat. This man was so handsome and debonair that I was proud to be the lady on his arm for the evening. He seemed to be everything a woman could possibly ask for, so much so that I almost feared what I might allow to happen if I enjoyed myself with him a little too much. He was married, but I was also a single woman again who'd been hurt and needed to be rescued. Mr. Montgomery seemed like just the man who was capable of doing the job.

When we approached a table for two in the back of the bar, he pulled out my chair for me to sit down. I tried my best not to show my enthusiasm, but I was ecstatic to be out with such a pure gentleman. David was a jerk without an ounce of chivalry or romance inside of his body. I never even looked forward to dates with him. He never opened my door, held my hand, or pulled out my chair. I couldn't place all the blame on him, though, because I was the one who put up with it. He'd learned how to treat me from me, so it was practically my fault that I'd let him believe that crap was all right. For a long time, I wondered what kind of woman had raised him, but after meeting his mother, I couldn't even place any blame on her. That nonsense was all because David was a low-down, good-for-nothing jerk. I'd made up my mind that my days of dealing with men like him were over. I deserved better, and I would no longer settle for just saying I had a man. Any man I chose to have in my future would definitely know what I liked and would have to cater to my needs and desires.

I sat down, then Terrence took his seat and ordered two chocolate martinis from the waitress. Looking around, I could see exactly why he was so in love with the place. It had such a laid-back, sexy vibe that you instantly fell in love with it. But the live band was what did it for me. When the current performer announced the next performer as Ms. Lalah Hathaway, I became even more ecstatic. After the day I'd had, it was turning into a night I'd never forget.

Terrence looked over at me with a sweet tenderness in his eyes that I hadn't seen from a man in a long time. "You know, you look amazingly beautiful this evening."

"Why thank you, Terrence. So do you. I mean, you look quite handsome, that is."

"Thank you. Didn't I tell you this place was the best? I love coming here."

"Yes, it's very nice. You must bring your wife here a lot, huh?" I blurted out without thinking. I didn't even know why I'd brought up his wife, and I could have kicked myself for doing it. After what Monica told me, I was sure that she was probably the furthest thing from his mind. I wanted her to be.

"Nope. We don't go out together much. We went out all the time years ago, but not anymore."

The look on his face dampened, and I tried to think of something quick so the mood wouldn't turn completely sour. "Did you know that Lalah Hathaway would be here tonight? I love her voice. She's actually my favorite female artist."

"You're kidding. I love Lalah too. And I think I heard something a couple of weeks ago about her coming, but I'd forgotten all about it. I guess it seems like we picked the perfect night," he said while gently massaging the top of my hand.

I started to feel a tingle on the inside as I imagined his strong hands on other parts of my body. I didn't know what he had in mind, but I needed him to stop. *Saved by the waitress.* She came and set our drinks down in front of us. From that point on, Terrence and I chopped it up about anything and everything that came to our minds except for his wife and my ex. The conversation was so light and free flowing. We laughed and talked and laughed and talked some more. It went without saying that I was having the time of my life, and I believed he was too.

We were on our third martinis when he ordered a couple of cupcakes for us that were absolutely amazing too. Ms. Hathaway had already performed a couple of her more upbeat songs before they brought a chair out to the stage. The band softly began to play her remake of "Angel" by Anita Baker. I grooved right there in my seat as I closed my eyes and allowed her melodic voice to drift me away. Suddenly, I felt Terrence's hand take mine, and then he led me out to the dance floor. He pulled me close to him just like last night when he comforted me in the library. Once again, I felt safe and protected by this man. Not to mention, his scent damn near made me moist inside. I had a million things that ran through my mind as I prayed to myself that I wouldn't let him have his way with me. Lord knows I wanted to. I was desperately in need of a man's touch, and I wanted him to be the one to fulfill my every desire.

I was so nervous that I almost pulled away. My thoughts haunted me as I imagined Terrence doing much more than holding me inside his strong arms. I wanted to be caught up in his strength and his mild tenderness. We swayed from side to side as the warmth of his body devoured mine. The intensity between the two of us practically drove me insane when I heard his baritone voice speak softly in my ear. Usually it was strong, powerful, and commanded attention, but this time there was a gentleness about it. It was low and sexy, and I liked it. I liked it a lot.

"This is nice. Isn't it, Tiffany?"

I was so caught up that I was almost unable to speak. "Um, yes. Yes, it is," was all that I could manage to get out.

He held me tighter. If I didn't know any better, he almost acted as if he never wanted to let me go. I wouldn't be upset one bit if he didn't. The song was over, but somehow the two of us remained on the floor as we moved to the tune in both of our heads. We were so in sync until we heard Ms. Hathaway say, "Let's give it up for the beautiful couple on the dance floor."

Terrence and I opened our eyes and burst out laughing after we realized we were the only ones left on the dance floor, moving in complete silence. It was hysterical, and we couldn't stop laughing about it.

"Now see, I think I need to get a picture of this, because I'll probably never get a chance to see your smile this big again."

Once we got back to the table, he pulled out his cell phone, and we both leaned in for a quick selfie. Lalah finished up her set as I summoned the waitress for a glass of water and he got a shot of something stronger. It was starting to get late. However, I didn't want the night to end, until he reminded me of the hotel room.

"Hey, it's getting late, so why don't we get out of here and go get checked in?"

"Uh, sure, that sounds good! But do we have two rooms or one?" It slipped out from nowhere. I could have kicked myself.

He looked at me, and I gave him a look back that said I hoped it was only one. He didn't utter a word, though. He grabbed my hand and led me outside. The valet hurried to bring the truck, and there was total silence during the ride there. I wondered if he was as nervous as I was, because there was no denying the chemistry between us.

Finally, he glanced over at me. "Tell me, Tiffany, why were you so sad last night? That is, if you don't mind me asking."

I really didn't want to talk about the whole issue with David, and I had hoped he wouldn't bring it up, but I knew he'd want some type of explanation. "Honestly, Terrence, I'm engaged—or was engaged, I mean—and things ended last night."

I could feel his hand grip mine a little tighter as the silence came over us once again. I imagined he tried to think of what next to say after I gave such a nonchalant answer.

"Oh, okay. Well, I hope I'm not prying, but exactly what happened? Because in my eyes, a man would have to be a complete idiot to let someone like you get away."

What he said made me smile, but I wondered what he saw in me that was so amazing, and why David couldn't see it after three whole years together. "I could say the same about you. Any woman would have to be out of her mind to let someone like you get away."

We both smiled when "Angel" suddenly started to play on the car stereo. That was when we both burst out laughing again as we relived our dance. Terrence and I knew it would become something we'd always share and remember.

He pulled up to the hotel doors to let me out while he went to find somewhere to park.

All right, Tiffany, you were way too forward at that bar. This man is married, and you need to respect that. You cannot share a hotel room with him, and you definitely can't sleep with him.

I kept telling myself that until he finally walked up, and we went inside. I heard him tell the front desk clerk that he had two connecting suites for the night. My heart kind of sank a little, but I also knew it was nothing but God who was saving me from myself. Terrence grabbed our keys and our things, and we hopped on the elevator up to the thirteenth floor. Our joint rooms were 1307 and 1309.

"Were you ready to turn in, or could you stand to have a nightcap with me?"

I was relieved that he asked, because I longed to be in his presence a little longer. "Yes. I would love to have a nightcap with you."

"All right. How about we make ourselves comfortable in our rooms, and I'll knock on your door in, say, ten minutes or so?"

"Sounds good."

I got to my room, closed the door, and hopped on the king-sized bed. Immediately, I punched and kicked it as if I were having a tantrum.

"God, why on earth are you doing this to me? How could you send me the perfect man, right now, and he's . . . he's married, for crying out loud?"

I sank my face into one of the oversized pillows while I tried to fathom what I'd done to deserve this madness.

Chapter 37

Terrence

Pacing around the floor for a few minutes, I questioned why the hell I'd suggested a nightcap. I wanted this woman in every way imaginable. The problem was I'd never cheated on Patricia and couldn't believe that I considered doing it now.

Damn Patricia. I felt like if all this nonsense hadn't happened with her, then I wouldn't be here right now possibly about to do the unthinkable.

I pulled out my cell phone, which had vibrated for what seemed like the millionth time. I figured it was nothing more than texts from Patricia or Facebook notifications from people who'd liked the picture I'd posted of Tiffany and me. To my surprise, it was female after female who'd either called or sent inbox messages, and they all seemed quite upset. I looked closer to try to figure out what was going on when I read the mass message that Patricia sent to all the females on my friend list.

"What the hell! Really, Patricia? Really?"

I didn't want to hear her voice, but I couldn't help myself. I immediately dialed her number, and she didn't hesitate to answer on the first ring.

"What the hell is wrong with you, woman?"

"Who is she, Terrence, and are you screwing her?"

"What? What are you talking about now?"

"The picture you posted on your Facebook page. I believe you said something like, 'Having a great time with a great coworker.'"

"Are you seriously asking me about a picture with a coworker when you just hacked my damn account and sent messages to my friends? What is wrong with you? What on earth would possess you to do such a thing? Was calling the police on me not enough?"

"I had to do it. You won't bring your ass home, you're staying out, hanging out with new coworkers, and from the looks of it you haven't been paying the mortgage. And you still didn't answer my damn question. Are you screwing her?"

"You know what? You seriously better hope I don't, Pat."

I hit the end button and threw the phone down as hard as I could. I hadn't been this upset in a long time, and my blood was boiling. I was totally serious with her, too. After all the shenanigans she'd pulled lately, it would serve her right for me to get pleasure elsewhere.

I went to the bathroom to take a quick, hot shower before going to Tiffany's room. I had already made up my mind that whatever happened, happened, and I wouldn't feel guilty about it at all.

Twenty minutes later, I found myself staring at Tiffany in a long silk black nightgown and robe. She looked radiant, and it assured me even more of what I wanted to take place.

"I'm sorry it took so long."

"I was starting to think you stood me up or something."

"No, never. I just had something going on with my wife."

"Oh, really? You want to talk about it?"

"She's the last thing I want to talk about. I'd much rather talk about you. I want to finish our conversation from the truck."

"About David and me? Can we not please? I don't want to think about that man, let alone talk about him."

"All right, that's fair. No wife and no ex-fiancé."

It was quiet for a moment or two, so I went over to the minibar and poured us glasses of wine. I figured that would loosen us both up, and I definitely needed it. She had already made herself comfortable on the love seat when I went over to join her.

"So what brought you all the way here from St. Louis?"

"I told you already. I relocated to be with David. He asked me to marry him, and since he didn't want to relocate to St. Louis, I made the move here."

"Man, that's a major transition to pack up your entire life only for the man to up and leave a month later."

Dammit, I could have kicked myself when I saw the expression on her face. She looked like she would burst into tears at any given second. And we'd just promised not to discuss my wife and her ex, yet here I had pried and coerced her into the conversation anyway.

"It sounds so pathetic hearing the words come from your mouth."

Oh, crap. I should've left well enough alone, but we were already in the thick of things now. I saw that tears threatened to spill from her watery eyes, so I shifted my body closer to hers and put my arm around her. "Look, what's done is done, and there's nothing wrong with crying if you need to. I just want you to get it all out, because you're right, you don't need to waste any more tears over someone like that."

She dabbed her eyes with her fingertips as I continued to cocoon her in my arms. "I know. I just keep thinking about how foolish I was to give up everything for him."

"I don't think it was foolish at all. At least not when it comes to true love. And I'm sorry, I didn't mean to sound so insensitive about everything. I only meant that you must have really been in love with him to make the sacrifices that you did."

"Yeah, well, that's the crazy thing about it. I wasn't. I mean, I loved him. At least, I loved the person I thought he was, but I was never in love with him. Somehow, I simply made myself believe that one day it would suddenly happen. That I would fall head over heels in love with him and we would live happily ever after."

"But why? Why would you leave your life to come to a whole new state and start all over for a man you weren't in love with?" I asked, looking at her with the most puzzled expression. I could sense that she hadn't planned to share this much information with me by the uncomfortable look that graced her face, so I tried to make her feel as comfortable as possible.

"It's somewhat of a long story."

"I have plenty of time for you."

With a huff, she explained, "I had come to a point in my life where I felt marriage was the next step, and David was available, and he asked."

It sounded as if she thought she'd had no other option. Why in the world a woman as beautiful and intelligent as she was would allow herself to think something like that was beyond me. "Please explain that some more."

"If you listen to everyone who knew me back home, they would say I had it all. I had a beautiful home, a nice luxury car, a great career with a very nice salary, and two degrees. In everyone else's eyes, I was this confident woman who had everything going for herself. Some people would even dare to say there was a bit of arrogance about me, while others would say they would die to be in my shoes. Little did any of them know I was this lonely and broken woman inside. I wasn't totally as happy and fulfilled as I portrayed myself to be. The material possessions didn't do it for me. My job didn't. Hell, not even the money. I also felt like I was longing for more, and I thought that maybe it was because I didn't have a husband and family. Then after dating David for those couple of years and he asked me to marry him, I somehow thought he could provide what I'd been missing."

"But I guess I'm asking, why him? You're such a beautiful woman inside and out that I'm sure you could have any man of your choice. Why settle for someone you weren't absolutely in love with and someone who clearly didn't love you enough to be honest with you?"

"I don't know. Maybe I thought I could change him. Or maybe I thought I could change me. I really don't know. It's just that I saw how happy my high school friends were in their marriages and families, and I wanted to feel that same sense of completeness they felt."

"Well, I'm here to tell you that things are not always the way they appear to be on the outside."

"What do you mean?"

"Sometimes it's just easier for people to put on a huge facade like everything is great instead of being completely honest. You don't know what's actually going on with your friends in their marriages behind closed doors, only what they told you or let you see."

She put her head down like she was deep in thought. I wanted to inquire, but I also didn't want to pry any further. I waited for her to speak again.

"Can I ask you something?" she questioned hesitantly.

"Shoot."

"You and your wife—"

I jumped in before she finished her question. "Tiffany, when I think about it, my wife and I never should have married. We don't have real love for one another, or even a friendship for that matter. Even our intimacy was shared as strangers. As crazy as it sounds, Patricia and I have never shared true intimacy with one another the way that two people in love do."

She gazed into my eyes with a look of utter shock and disbelief on her face. "I guess I don't understand. How is that even possible? How can you be married to someone and not have shared intimacy with them?"

"The same way you would have married a man without being in love with him. I don't want you to get me wrong. I do care about my wife. She's a good person and an amazing mother, but a not-so-good wife. We got married for all the wrong reasons. She's older than me and wholeheartedly desired a husband, but more so a father for her children. Me, on the other hand, I felt an obligation to her because she was there for me when I hit rock bottom. Neither one of us married for love or being in love with each other. I guess we both thought that in time everything would fall into place and the love would come, but unfortunately for me, it still hasn't."

"Can I finally ask you a question?"

"Sure, go ahead."

"Why are you here with me instead of at home talking with her and trying to work things out there?"

"Because we don't talk anymore. All we ever do is argue. Every time we're in each other's presence, it's either dead silence or an argument. For once, I just want to be at peace, be happy, and have a good time with someone."

"Hell, why bother even staying married then? I mean, I'm not an advocate for divorce or anything, but I also feel that life is much too short to be anything but completely happy."

"One reason, I guess, is that it's what everyone else expects of us—to be this happy, loving couple. And the other reason is that I just don't want to fail again. I feel like I've already failed with my children's mother. I don't want that feeling again. Plus, having to start all over is not as easy as it seems."

"I guess I understand," she said, putting her hand on top of mine. "But just know that your peace and happiness is worth more than having to start over or what others think of you."

"Now wait, I thought I was supposed to be here for you tonight, but you are here for me more than you'll ever know."

I held her hand and massaged it softly. Looking into her eyes, I studied her and knew that we both desired the same thing. My heart started to pump a little faster. My mind told me not to do it, but my body led the way. I took my hand from hers and then gently stroked the side of her face while I gazed into her soft, beautiful eyes. A second later, I leaned forward and pressed my lips against hers. To my surprise, she didn't even try to pull away. I kissed her a little harder, and she kissed me back. At once, it seemed as if all my thoughts of Patricia had slowly but surely slipped away from my mind. Standing up, I took Tiffany's hand and led her over to the bed. She was totally in sync with me just like at the chocolate bar.

I laid her beautiful body down and prepared to climb on top of her. I wanted Tiffany in the worst way possible and couldn't wait to explore her curves or the unknown. Her skin was soft and smelled like fresh rose petals. I could sense her nervousness, so I took my time to let her know she was safe. Continuing to kiss her softly, I slowly moved my way down to her breasts. They were succulent, and her nipples let me know they were ready to be caressed. I glided my tongue around them, at times sucking and at times biting. She moaned so soft and sweet as she held on tight to me. Kissing and licking down her body, I'd finally made my way to her treasure. I immediately inhaled the sweetness of her moisture and was more than ready to taste her.

"Terrence? Wait."

I'd heard her voice, but I knew my ears had to be deceiving me. "Baby, what's wrong? If it's protection you're worried about, I—"

"No, no, it's not that at all. We can't do this."

I struggled to pull myself away from her as I sat on the side of the bed, and she crawled up on the side of me.

"Terrence, I'm really attracted to you, maybe a little too much. But I've done the whole side chick thing in my life before, and that's not where or who I am anymore. I need more than that, and I deserve more. I want someone who only wants me, and I don't ever want to be with another woman's husband just to have love. I wouldn't want someone to be with my husband if I were married, and more importantly, it's not right in God's sight. And I'm just trying to do better in my life. I'm sorry."

"What do you mean you're sorry? You don't have a reason to be. We both knew that this wouldn't have been the right move. Maybe we should just call it a night."

"Can you still just stay the night with me?"

I looked at her and knew that she needed me as much as I did her. We pulled the covers back on the bed, curled up next to one another, and I simply held her in my arms.

Chapter 38

Tiffany

I closed my eyes tight as I thanked God for saving me from myself. I wanted Terrence more than he knew, but not in that way. I could tell that he felt the same, and I sensed that we both felt disappointment and relief at the same time. I allowed my body to snuggle a little closer to him while I took in his scent. His eyes were closed. However, I knew he hadn't fallen asleep just yet.

I softly whispered in his ear, "Thank you, Terrence."

It took him a moment to respond, but when he did, it seemed as if it were hard for him to get it out. He almost seemed a bit choked up. "You don't have to thank me," he said.

A few more minutes went by as we both lay there in silence. It must have been hard for either of us to fall asleep. I heard him say my name. "Tiffany."

"Yes."

"Tell me something that you've never told anyone else. Tell me your dreams and desires."

"My dreams and desires, huh?"

"Yes. If there were one thing in the world you would do that no one else knows about, what would it be?"

"You promise not to laugh at me?" I turned to face him.

"Sure I wouldn't," he said, but I could tell he was already chuckling on the inside.

"All right, here goes. My dream is to one day be a *New York Times* bestselling author."

He immediately started to crack a smile, and I sat up and playfully hit his arm.

"See, you promised not to laugh."

"All right, all right, forgive me. But I'm only laughing because I already knew that from your Facebook page. I just wanted to hear you say it. What kind of books would you write, anyway?"

"Novels about love and romance. For once I want to read a book where the two people fall head over heels in love with one another without having to go through a ton of hardship first. I want to write about them building a life and family together and basically having it all."

"Do you really think that's possible in real life, though?"

"I do. If the two people love one another enough, I believe they can have everything their hearts desire."

I made myself comfortable again lying under him as we both stared at the ceiling. I almost drifted off when I heard him say something.

"*I Didn't Think You Existed.*"

"What? What are you talking about?"

"The title for your first book. *I Didn't Think You Existed.*"

"Terrence, that actually sounds amazing."

"And you have to promise that, no matter when, I will get the first autographed copy."

"I can promise that. As long as you promise that I'll get a free meal at Montgomery's Barbeque and Soul Food restaurant."

"Wait, what? Now how did you know about that? I never told you."

"You didn't, but Monica did. She told me what a great chef you are."

"Yeah, but—"

"No buts. Remember, we can have everything our hearts desire."

Terrence kissed me again, and this time I didn't stop him. There was no way I could deny the chemistry between us, and we both needed one another. As he pulled my body on top of his, we promised that whatever was going to happen would happen, and it would remain there in room 1307. That was our pact . . . as we began to make love.

Chapter 39

Terrence

"Hey, there's something I need to tell you," I said to Tiffany after we'd left the hotel, gotten into my truck, and headed toward the school. It pressed on my mind whether I should even involve her in this, but after last night, I knew that I had to. I felt I owed it to her to be completely honest.

"Is something wrong?"

"Yes and no. See, before I came into your room last night, I had a pretty heated argument with my wife."

"You didn't tell her you were with me, did you?"

"All right, don't get upset, but I posted the picture I took of us at the chocolate bar last night on Facebook. It was a dumb decision on my part, but I guess I just got caught up in the moment. I was having such an amazing time, and I wasn't thinking and, well, she saw it."

"Oh, no, Terrence, why didn't you tell me this last night?"

"Because I didn't want to think about her, let alone discuss us, like you with your ex. Tiff, she had me so angry because after seeing the picture, she'd hacked my Facebook account and sent a mass message to all of my female friends."

"What?"

"Yeah. So we argued. She asked who you were and if I was having sex with you, and I told her that she better damn sure hope that I didn't."

"How could you do that? I mean, from what you've told me, your wife doesn't seem too stable. What if she comes after me or something? I already have enough on my plate with this entire mess with David and his other fiancée."

"I know, and I apologize, but trust me, you have nothing to worry about. My wife might seem a little crazy right now, but I don't think she's that crazy. Plus, her issues are with me, not with you."

"I don't know. Women can become really crazy, psycho even, when it comes to matters of the heart."

We were extremely quiet in my truck after that for a little while. I had no clue what to say, and I guessed neither did she. I wondered if what she said was true though. What if this whole situation *had* made Patricia psycho? Of course, I'd read and seen on the news about situations where the woman snapped on a man, but I never imagined it would happen in my own home. Thinking of the mess I may have placed Tiffany in, I took her hand and tried to make her feel secure.

"Look, you don't have anything at all to worry about. I won't let anything happen to you. I promise." I glanced at her so she could see the sincerity and seriousness in my face.

"This is none of my business, but maybe you should go home to your wife and try to work things out with her."

"What? Why would you say that? Especially after last night?"

"Because you owe her, your marriage, and yourself that much. I think maybe you all need counseling or something to get to the root of all your problems."

"She did mention something about counseling, but I was completely against it. You really think so?"

"I think you should at least try. I feel like that way, if things don't work out, then you will be able to say that you didn't give up before you gave it all you had. Or that you didn't give up because of someone else being involved. Don't you think your marriage deserves that?"

"I don't know. I've been going over and over it in my head for weeks now, and I haven't been able to come up with any clear direction. On one hand, I do feel the same as you, that I should give it my best shot. Then, on the other hand, I wonder if it's at all worth it. I feel like if I stay, I would only be sacrificing my true happiness just to live a lie."

"Hey, all I'm saying is to try."

What Tiffany said made total sense. I'd gone back and forth in my own thoughts about my marriage with Patricia. Though it was wrong, the questions that were now on my mind about whether my marriage could be or should be salvaged had nothing to do with Patricia and me. I decided to ask the real question that plagued my heart. "All right, say I took your advice. What would that mean for us?"

"What do you mean?" She glanced at me and must've seen my need for her, so she placed her hand on my thigh reassuringly. "Terrence, we're still coworkers and friends. That's not going to change. And I promise I'm going to be there for you as much as you have been for me these past couple of days. I'm not going anywhere, no matter how crazy your wife seems to be," she said with a slight chuckle.

Her last statement really made me feel some type of relief. Although I dreaded the thought of going back home, she was right. I had to at least try. It made me feel a lot better to know that she'd agreed to remain in my corner. I didn't want things to end on such a bland note, so I tried to think of a much more positive topic of discussion for the remainder of the ride.

"Hey, so tell me your favorite dish."

"Um, okay. I love pasta, any kind," she answered eagerly. It seemed she was as happy to move away from the subject as I was. "Once I get established here, I plan to find a nice Italian restaurant with really good drinks."

"No, you won't, because Montgomery's isn't open yet. But I will make you some pasta and bring it over. We can have a nice, quiet dinner at your place."

"I guess you forgot that I don't have a place."

"Damn, I guess I did. But look, don't worry about that either. I know some people, and I can make a few calls and get you into something by the end of the week. It won't be some shack, either. I got you."

"But I don't have that kind of money right now."

"Stop worrying, woman. I said I got you. And before you say it, I'm not taking no for an answer."

She smiled at me as we pulled up to the school. Before I let her get out of the truck, I pulled her closer to me. "Tiffany, I don't know why we met right now with so much craziness going on in both of our lives, but I'm a firm believer that everything happens for a reason. Somehow, maybe the Man Upstairs knew that I would need your friendship and you possibly need mine."

"You almost sounded exactly like Monica when you said that."

"It's true. For a while now, I've been going back and forth with no real direction, but you've helped me these past couple of days more than you know. I guess what I'm trying to say is I'm grateful that we met."

I kissed her forehead and gave her a hug. I knew that once we got out of the truck, I would have to face my future with Patricia. The thought of that alone was a scary one, but I also knew it was exactly what I needed to do for all of us.

Chapter 40

Patricia

How could he do this to me? How could my husband be so damn careless and disrespectful? It wasn't enough that he had hundreds of female friends on his social media who didn't give a damn about our marriage, but now he posted a picture with one of them. And someone he worked with, on top of that. I'd been up all night, pacing the floor with my mind on 1,000 as it went in all different directions. I'd called Terrence repeatedly after he hung up on me, but of course he didn't answer. I'd been on and off his social media accounts to see if he'd posted anything else, but still there was nothing. I couldn't help but continue to look at that picture of him and that tramp, Tiffany Tate.

"Who do you think you are taking pictures with my husband? Smiling and grinning like he's your man. Well, he's not. He's not yours. He belongs to me, dammit. Me," I yelled.

I went to her page yet again. I'd probably seen her pictures and posts at least a million times between last night and now, but I didn't care. I had something in store for her and Terrence, something that neither one of them would ever forget. First things first, I decided to make a quick last-minute call to my hairdresser. Marcus was one of the best in the business, and he would take good care of me and give me exactly what I needed.

"Hey, Ms. Pat," he said in his usual upbeat and sassy tone. "What can I do for you?"

"Hey, Marcus. I need a huge favor. This is pretty last minute, but I need to come in and get my hair cut."

"Now you know it's not time for your ends to be clipped. I have your hair on a schedule, sweetie."

"You don't understand. I don't want my ends clipped. I want all of my hair chopped off."

"What?"

I had a feeling it would be tough to get Marcus to do what I wanted. I had long, flowing hair that went past my shoulders, which he'd maintained for the last couple of years. It would be a fight with him. But after I got to the shop and told him what's been going on, he'd understand and cut my hair as short as I wanted it to be.

"Look, I can explain everything when I get there. I even have a picture of how I want it cut, so can you please squeeze me in?"

"All right, honey, I guess I can. Do you think you can make it here within a half hour?"

"Yep, sounds great. I'll see you then."

Chapter 41

Tiffany

Making myself comfortable inside my office, I threw my iPod earbuds in and opened up my laptop. My email had over a hundred unread messages, but instead of reading any of them, I logged in to my Facebook account. Instead of looking at any of my notifications, I went straight to Terrence's page. There it was looking back at me: the picture we'd taken at the chocolate bar. Although I hated that he posted it for the world to see, a smile immediately adorned my face. This man was amazing, and I couldn't help but wonder if he was the mystery man in my dreams. I'd gotten the same feeling being with him that I'd gotten every time I envisioned the unknown man.

Suddenly, the song "Comfortable" by HER began to play on my iPod. Thinking of how comfortable I'd quickly become with Terrence, I allowed the words to send my mind drifting away. Swaying back and forth in my seat, I sang aloud, reminiscing of being inside his arms on the dance floor. I could still smell his scent, feel the warmth of his Herculean body next to mine, and just like last night, I never felt as safe with anyone as I did with him.

"Someone must have had a good time last night," I heard faintly over the music in my ears as I looked up and saw Monica peeking in the door.

I was so embarrassed that she'd caught me in a vulnerable state that my fair complexion was almost beet red. I snatched the earbuds out and nervously smiled back at her as she entered all the way. "Yeah, I guess you could say I enjoyed myself last night," I said as she took one of the seats across from me that was normally designated for the children.

Despite knowing there was no way around this conversation, I hated that she'd made herself comfortable. In the back of my mind, she was still my and Terrence's boss. And even though he was having problems, he was still a married man. I simply didn't want her to get the wrong impression that I'd gone against everything I'd said yesterday, although I had.

"So?"

"So what?" I was somewhat bashful at the thought of telling her too much about what happened between him and me.

"How was it? Dessert? The hotel? How was it all? I've been dying to find out."

"I don't know. It was good, I guess," was all that I allowed to come out as I shrugged my shoulders and hoped she would leave it there.

"Good, you guess? Girl, that smile across your face and the way you were just slow dancing in your seat says far more than, 'Good, I guess.' Now are you going to spill it or what?"

Knowing there was no way around it, along with the fact that I really did want to confide in her, I got up and closed the door to my office before telling her everything. "Okay, okay. It was amazing, Monica, absolutely amazing. Terrence was the perfect gentleman from the start. He was charming, smooth, and so damn sexy. The atmosphere was great, his vibe and energy were on point, and the conversation was nothing less than stimulating. It was the best date I've probably ever experienced. We had such a great connection."

"Date? I thought it was just two coworkers grabbing some dessert."

"Did I say date?"

"Uh, yeah, I think that's the word I heard."

We both started to laugh until she asked the one question that I'd hoped she'd forgotten all about. "I have to admit that I'm extremely happy you were able to get out, relax, and enjoy yourself, especially after all that you've gone through with David. You needed this. And I don't mean to pry, but I have to ask, did the night end at the dessert bar?"

Taking a deep breath in and exhaling, I looked at her before I answered. My eyes were set on hers, but in the back of my mind, visions of Terrence and me sharing intimacy played over and over again in my head.

"Tiffany? Tiffany? You still there?" she called, snapping me out of my daze.

"Oh, I'm sorry. What I will say is that what Terrence and I shared last night was innocent, pure, and the most beautiful experience shared by two people who needed each other most in that moment."

She gazed at me with her hand clutched to her chest and her mouth open as if she were watching some sappy Lifetime love flick. "That sounds beautiful. I guess the only question left is, now what? How do the two of you plan to move forward as simply coworkers and friends knowing that you all have this connection? Especially because that wife of his is not about to let him go anywhere."

"Yeah, don't I know it. And the crazy thing about is I suggested to him that they seek marriage counseling."

"You're joking, right? After what I told you that woman has put him through? After the definite chemistry the two of you have? You actually suggested counseling?"

"Yes, I did. Call me crazy, but if Terrence and I were to ever have anything outside of a friendship, I want it to be because he's absolutely positive that there's no hope for his marriage and that he truly wants to be with me. I don't want to be the cause or reason for someone getting a divorce. I can't handle that."

"Listen, I get it. I'm not trying to tell you to be his side chick or anything, but the man who just stopped by my office before I came in here is a man I haven't seen in quite some time. He was happy, smiling, and I could almost see a sense of hope in his eyes. Not to mention coming in here and seeing you in the best mood I've seen you in since we met. Now I'm not saying that there's no hope for God to fix his marriage, because I know that's not true, but I also believe that everything happens for a reason."

"Yeah, I believe that too, but this has to be right. That means Terrence trying to do everything possible to fix his marriage before calling it quits."

"All right." She put her hands up as if she surrendered. "I still think you might have sent him right back into a web of destruction, but that's only my opinion. Anyway, I have a meeting coming up soon, so I'll check in with you a little later." She got up and began to walk toward the door.

I nodded my head to acknowledge that I'd heard her, but my eyes and attention were now focused on what was on my laptop screen in front of me on Facebook.

"Oh, my goodness. Oh, my goodness. I can't believe this."

"What? What is it, Tiff?"

Shaking my head in disbelief, I tried to calm down enough to get my words out. "It says that Carl Weber has a movie coming out based on one of his books, and he's looking for people to put together VIP events in different cities."

"That's amazing. I've read several of his books, and he's a great author. I'm positive a movie will be just as good. But what has you so moved by that?"

"Oh, I'm sorry. I should explain. See, I've always had this crazy dream of one day writing a book and being published by none other than Carl Weber. In fact, I actually just shared this with Terrence last night. Wouldn't it be amazing if I could meet him and put on the event here in Texas?"

"Girl, it sure would. I had no idea you were interested in being a writer. So what are you waiting for? What do you need to do? Call him? Email him? Hurry up."

"Okay, okay. It says to just shoot him a message, but I don't know anyone here in Texas yet. I wouldn't even know where to have the event, and I don't know the first thing about putting together something like this."

"Don't worry about that. You've got me here, I'm sure Terrence would help, and this has God's name written all over it. He's placed this connection right in your lap. So do it and let Him figure out the rest. Remember what I just said. Everything happens for a reason."

"All right, I'll send Carl a message and then go to Terrence's office to tell him all about it. Maybe I can even get him to cater the event."

"See, now you're thinking. But I guess I should tell you that Terrence isn't here. When he stopped by my office earlier it was to tell me that he was leaving. He said he needed to go home and handle something with Patricia. My mind is now telling me it has something to do with marriage counseling."

My heart sank as soon as the words came from her mouth. Not only did I want him to be the first person I shared the news with—other than Monica, of course—but I also couldn't believe I'd actually suggested counseling to him, especially after last night. Not wanting Monica to see how messed up I was about him not being there, I simply shrugged my shoulders. "Oh, okay. I'll just tell him some other time."

She stood there for a second or two examining me, then left quietly. I tried to keep my excitement about the whole Carl Weber thing, but now my mind was more focused on Terrence and Patricia. If they were able to work things out, it would have to be something I would have to accept, no matter how much it felt like I was falling in love with him.

Chapter 42

Patricia

Exactly thirty minutes later, I walked into Marcus's shop and headed straight to his chair. "I'm ready when you are," I said, skipping the girl talk and hoping to get right down to business.

"Ms. Pat, now what's all this talk about cutting your hair off, honey? Are you having some type of *Waiting to Exhale* moment that I don't know about?"

"Call it what you want, but I call it doing what I have to do to keep my husband and marriage intact."

"All right, who is she?" he asked, already knowing it had something to do with another woman.

"This trick." I held my cell phone out to him. "She's trying to sink her claws into my damn husband, but over my dead body."

"Oh, no she ain't."

"Oh, yes she is, and if Tiffany Tate is who he wants, then that's who he'll get—in me. I want my hair cut exactly like hers."

"You know that once we do this there's no turning back. Are you absolutely sure you want to do this?" He waved his shears in my face.

I looked at the picture on my phone again and then back at Marcus. "I'm positive."

"Then sit down, girlfriend, and let's do this."

I didn't think it would be that easy talking Marcus into it. I'd had long hair all my life, and because of him, I'd never once considered cutting it. He might have been gay, but he was still a man and always told me that men love long, natural hair. However, as of late it seemed my husband liked just the opposite, so it was time I officially became a part of the short-hair club. Of course, it would be a huge adjustment and take some time getting used to, but if it meant getting his attention again, I was more than up for the challenge.

Marcus made the first snip, and as I saw my long tresses fall to the floor, I almost wanted to pass out.

"Are you all right, girl?"

"Uh, yeah, I'm okay." My breathing was heavy, and I could feel the anxiety building.

"Look, I can stop right here and just add layers to your hair. We don't have to cut it all off, and I'll make it look as beautiful as ever."

"No, no. I've come this far, and I want to go through with it. My marriage depends on it," I confided in him as a small tear slid down my cheek. "So please, let's just hurry up and get this over with."

"If you say so. Here goes."

A short time after, he spun me around in his chair, and I stared at the woman in the mirror. I didn't even look like my usual self.

"So? What do you think, girl? Did Mr. Marcus work his magic or what?" He turned his lips up while waiting for my response.

"I don't know what to say. Did I really just do this?"

"You did, but you look fabulous if I do say so myself."

"Question is, will my husband like it?"

"If he doesn't, then he's the fool. And let me tell you something anyway." He spun me around to look me square in the eyes. "Your hair doesn't make you the beautiful woman you are, and you have to know that for yourself. If your husband can't see the diamond you are, then it's his loss. You hear me?" He lifted my chin with his hand like I was 6 years old to make sure I'd heard him clearly.

I only shook my head in acknowledgment because nothing seemed to come out when I parted my lips.

"Now go and get out of here. You go home and throw on some sexy lingerie, whip that man up a good meal, and then give him the blowjob of his life. You'll make his eyes, his stomach, and his manhood happy, and that, my dear, will keep his heart happy. He won't be running to little Ms. What's Her Name. Trust me."

Marcus laughed at his own words as I hopped out of his chair and planned to do exactly as he said. I was going to make every inch of Terrence happy.

Getting into my car, instead of going straight home, I decided to head to the school first. I wanted to give everyone a little peek of the new me, especially Tiffany Tate. Then I planned to go to my husband's office and give him a little taste of what would be in store for him once he arrived home. The thought alone brought to my memory how much he loved excitement, spontaneity, and the possibility of being caught. It really wasn't my thing because I'd much rather be in the privacy of our home and in our bed. However, being intimate in public places had always been much of a turn-on for him.

Looking at the time displayed on my dashboard, I wasn't exactly sure whether my husband would be at the school this time of the day. Terrence normally went there in the evenings to coach those little boys after his first job. However, call it intuition, but something in my gut told me he would be wherever she was. I smiled from ear to ear at the thought of both of them seeing my new hairdo.

Pulling up to the school, I realized I hadn't been there since Terrence started coaching. He'd begged me and the boys to come to his first game, saying it wouldn't look right if his family wasn't there to support him. I never understood why he even wasted his time at this place with these children. It wasn't like he needed it. He already had a great-paying job that supported our home, and the income from this was only change in our pockets. I felt like this school and these children did nothing more than take time and attention away from our family. On top of that, now I had little Ms. Thing to add to the distractions. The thought of her alone made me fume, and when I spotted the car I'd seen on her Facebook page, I couldn't help myself. Right there in broad daylight, I hopped out of my truck, went over to the car, and keyed scratches all over the back of it. I made sure there was no way she would miss it, and it made me bubble over with laughter.

"Yeah, you messed with the wrong wife, Ms. Tate."

Then it was time for my next mission. As I headed in the direction of my husband's office, I walked down the halls of the school, portraying a ton of confidence with my new hair. I stepped heel to toe like I was America's Next Top Model on a runway. I waved at the children, the security guard, and some of the staff I could remember. But as I strutted to my destination, I bumped into his boss, Principal Williams, who came out of the main office. Her mouth dropped wide open as she looked at me.

"Hello, Monica. Long time no see," I greeted her as if we were old buddies.

"Uh, uh, Mrs. Montgomery? Uh, hello," she said, hugging me. It was one of the fakest hugs ever, because this woman didn't like me one bit, and the feeling was mutual. She kept staring at me, though, as if she'd seen a ghost.

I fanned off her greeting. "Oh, Monica, please. We're so much better than that. Call me Patricia," I said as she continued to gawk at me. I tried to act surprised, like I didn't know exactly what she thought. "Oh, you must be shocked by my hair."

"Uh, yeah, I am. You look . . . you look—"

"Younger? More vibrant? I know, right? I had no idea that cutting my hair would be so exhilarating. That's why

I decided to see if my hubby was here so I could show it off to him. Is he anywhere around?" I asked, itching to catch him and Tiffany together.

"Uh, actually no. I mean, he was here this morning, but he left."

"Really? He must have had to get to his real job," I said, noticing a frown come across her face.

"Well, I don't know about getting to his real job, but he told me that he had something to take care of at home," she stuttered, still staring in awe. "You don't know the whereabouts of your own husband?" she asked, poking at me while at the same time picking and choosing her words carefully.

"I do know his whereabouts, and like I said, I wanted to surprise him. So I guess I'll be heading home too then," I answered with that same fake smile plastered across my face, trying hard not to let on that her response pissed me off.

I couldn't help but wonder what my husband was doing home this time of the day and not working one of these jobs. Especially since it seemed we needed the money given the missed mortgage payment. He had some real nerve hanging out all night and then not going to work to take care of his responsibilities. It was childish and careless, to say the least.

As I was about to dismiss myself from Monica, I suddenly heard the sound of heels hitting the floor. Without having to turn around, I knew it was none other than her.

"Hey, Tiffany, let me introduce you to Coach Montgomery's wife."

I turned around slowly to finally look my nemesis in the face. Part of me was relieved that she wasn't somewhere with Terrence, but then the other part wanted to haul off and slap the hell out of her for being with him yesterday. Instead, I smiled and extended my hand.

"Mrs. Montgomery, this is our new counselor and librarian here at the school, Ms. Tate. Tiffany, this is Coach T's lovely wife."

"Yes, Ms. Tate. How wonderful it is to finally meet you. I've heard nothing but wonderful things about you from that husband of mine."

She tried her best to mumble a hello while shaking my hand in return, yet I followed her eyes, noticing how she couldn't seem to take them off my hair.

"Oh, and what a coincidence that you and I have the exact same hairstyle. Great minds must think alike. I was getting so tired of having to deal with my long hair that I just went and had mine cut. I think my stylist did an amazing job, don't you? I can't wait to show my husband."

"Uh, yeah, I'm sure he'll love it, Mrs. Montgomery."

I finally heard her speak. Her voice was just as irritating as it was staring into her face. Now that my job was done and I let her get a glimpse of me, it was time for me to go and find the man I called my husband.

"I'd better go. Monica, it was so good seeing you again. I'll really have to arrange a time to have you and your husband over for dinner so that we can catch up with one another. And, Tiffany, you and your significant other are welcome to come as well. I would love to get to know you better. How does that sound?"

"Uh, sure, it sounds good, Patricia," said Monica.

Tiffany simply nodded her head, looking as if she were still in a state of shock.

"Okay, great then, it's settled. I will see both of you ladies soon. Toodles."

I walked away, cracking up on the inside with laughter. They were both stunned and didn't have a clue what to say. I figured if the two women reacted that way, then I was definitely in for a treat with Terrence.

Chapter 43

Tiffany

"Oh, my God, Tiffany, did you see that?" The look on Monica's face was just the same as mine.

"What exactly was that? I mean, the woman practically looked like my twin. Our complexions, our hair, and thinking about it, I believe I have that exact same outfit on one of my Facebook pictures. That was creepy."

"No, that wasn't creepy. Honey, that was a scorned wife on a mission, and I would say it's Mission: Get Rid of My Husband's Mistress."

"But that's just it. I'm not his mistress. I'm the one who told the man to go home and work things out with her, remember?"

"Yeah, but she doesn't know that. All she knows is that her husband just spent some time with his new very attractive and very single coworker instead of being at home with her."

"Well, I need to call Terrence."

"No, let me. The last thing any of us needs is for him to go confronting her saying what Tiffany said."

Monica picked up the receiver of the phone on her desk while I took a seat. All I could think about was what happened between me and him last night, and what could happen if she ever found out. I watched Monica hang up and dial his number a couple more times until she finally filled me in.

"He's not answering. His phone keeps going to voice-mail." She took a seat on the edge of her desk.

"Now what?" I hopped up and started pacing around. "What if this woman has really lost her mind? I mean literally lost her mind. She already thinks I'm sleeping with him. She went and got her hair done and clothes like mine. Who knows what else she's capable of doing?"

"Listen, calm down. If there's one thing I know from conversations with Terrence, her bark is much worse than her bite. I'm sure once she gets home, Terrence will handle everything," she tried to reassure me.

At first it was helping. I started to calm down and tried to refocus my thoughts on the news I was coming to tell Monica before Patricia had completely thrown me off. At least, that was until there was a knock at her door.

"Come in," she called out.

Our head security guard, Officer Campbell, poked his head inside. "Hey, boss. I'm sorry to interrupt, but it seems Ms. Tate has some damage done to her truck. It looks like someone has keyed some scratches on the back. I found these two boys out of class and in the parking lot, but they are swearing they had nothing to do with it."

"Yeah, but I'm more than positive who did have something to do with it." She looked at me as I practically read her mind. All signs pointed right back to Patricia Montgomery.

Chapter 44

Terrence

After making it home, I looked around the house. No one was there, not Patricia or the boys. I figured they were out somewhere with their friends as usual, but it was a bit strange not finding Patricia there, especially at this time of day. Until she returned though, I decided to cook us both a nice breakfast. It was something I hadn't done for us in a while, and I thought the gesture might make our conversation go a lot smoother. She was probably still upset from our phone call last night.

While I waited, I decided to turn my cell phone completely off. I didn't want any distractions once she made it here and we started talking about possibly attending marriage counseling. I still couldn't believe I was actually considering it. Everything inside of me had already said there was no working through our issues. Not to mention, I just didn't love her the way a husband should love a wife. Yet the more I thought about what Tiffany said, the more I was convinced she was right. I had to at least try this so that I wouldn't feel guilty if and when I decided to walk away.

Sitting down at the table, I grabbed the morning paper and tried to catch up on current events. But before I knew it, I heard Patricia barging through the front door. Oddly enough, she didn't say a word to me when she walked into the kitchen. However, I knew why when I removed the paper from in front of my face. Nothing could describe the horrific look I had when I saw my wife standing before me. I could not believe my eyes. My mouth fell wide open as I looked at her from head to toe. She was basically the spitting image of Tiffany. Her hair was cut exactly like Tiffany's, and she had on a dress exactly like the one Tiffany wore on her profile picture on her Facebook account. Even her makeup, which my wife never wore, resembled Tiffany's. Suddenly, what Tiffany said about love making people go psycho made total and perfect sense to me.

"Patricia? What's going on?"

"I think I should be the one asking you what's going on. How was your night last night with your little mistress? You two must have been out pretty late. Is that why you're home at this hour and not at work?"

I tried my best to keep my cool and understand where she was coming from. True enough, I would have been upset too if she suggested to me that she was going to be unfaithful with another man—if I cared that much.

"Look, let me go ahead and apologize to you right now. The things I said last night were all out of anger, and I never should have said them—"

"Well, in my eyes it's a little late for an apology, and it still doesn't negate the fact that you were out with another woman last night instead of being home with your wife and kids," she yelled at the top of her lungs.

I was livid at the way she was talking to me. The last thing I needed was for this woman to push me further to the point of no return. Once again, I tried my best to play things cool and deal with her delicately.

"All right, now you need to calm down and listen. I said I was wrong for what I said, how I said it, and maybe even for being out with Tiffany in the first place. But if you're going to go pointing the finger and placing blame anywhere, why don't you start with yourself and how you've been behaving lately?"

"How I have been behaving? I guess you think it's perfectly fine for a husband to neglect his wife and kids to hang out with some single coworker."

"Let's be straight. I haven't neglected you all one bit, and you know that. But I think my actions are more than justified when you do things like continually accuse me of cheating, hack my social media account, and let's not forget that you called the damn police on me."

"More than justified, huh? Well, I think I'm more than justified too when you go around not acting like a married man and you try to throw my child out on the street like this isn't his home too."

"You know what? We're not getting anywhere like this. I don't know what I was thinking. I actually came home hoping we could reach a happy medium, but you are determined to see things your way. So go right ahead, Pat. Everything can remain exactly how it is between us."

I got up, pushed my chair away, and started walking toward the front door. In my eyes, I'd tried and that was that. There would be no counseling or working things out. In fact, she would be lucky if there would still be a marriage to fight for, because divorce was now running rampant through my mind. I'd already spoken briefly to my lawyer before, but now it was time to take action.

"Where do you think you're going? We're not done here!" She jumped directly in front of me and ran to cover the front door with her body.

"Move away from the door," I said calmly.

"No, I'm not moving until you go back and sit down, Terrence, so that we can finish this."

Before I knew it, I grabbed Patricia by the arm and looked her square in the eyes. "What in the world is wrong with you? Have you completely lost your damn mind?"

"Oh, so something's wrong with me? I'm your wife and the mother of your children. You haven't been home with us for weeks, and then you go hang out and play around with some . . . some tramp. And I'm not supposed to be upset about it? You basically threaten to sleep with her last night, and I'm not supposed to feel some type of way?"

The more she spoke, the more I felt anger and rage bubbling up inside of me. If I didn't regain my composure quick, something would end up happening that I would truly regret. I took a step back from her and the door and began to speak.

"Patricia, have you forgotten I haven't been here because you called the police on me? Huh? Do you even realize that all of this has nothing to do with Tiffany or any other woman because we've had issues for a very long time now? And just so you know, if I wanted to sleep with someone, I would just do it. I don't have to make threats about it. In fact, I could have done it long ago and didn't have to wait until Tiffany came along. Oh, and speaking of Tiffany, I don't know what's with you coming in here looking like *Single White Female* or something, like the woman's twin, but you didn't do a good enough job. You only made yourself look crazier than what I already thought."

The next thing I knew, she started to do the exact thing she'd always done over the years: play the victim. I watched her as she forced tears from her eyes.

"Look, I just want my husband back. I hate acting all crazy like this with you, but I was desperate, baby. I thought that she was what you wanted, so I thought if maybe I made myself look more like her, you'd want me back. And no, I haven't forgotten that I called the police, but you have to understand why. I was only protecting my son. But, honey, I miss you, and I need you back at home . . . with us."

I was torn about what to do. On one hand, I really wanted to call my lawyer to have him draw up divorce papers immediately. But then I had Tiffany's voice in the back of my mind when she told me to do all I could to fix things. However, when I looked at Patricia, a realization came to me. As she stood there not looking anything like herself while bawling her eyes out, I felt numb to it all. I didn't feel the sympathy that she wanted me to, and I really didn't have much to say to her. I wanted so badly to understand my wife, but I kept feeling like there was no reasonable explanation for all of this. I felt she was her own worst enemy and the only way we could ever get back on track was if she came to grips with that. I could sense she wanted me to have sympathy for her, needing me to hold her and reassure her of our bond, but I couldn't. I had no words and, worst of all, no feelings for her.

All I could seem to get out was, "You're right about what you said before. We need counseling."

She looked at me with a world of hope filling her eyes. "Really?" she said, wiping tears from her eyes. "You really want to work things out? Does this mean you're coming back home?"

"At this very moment, I don't have much left in me to say to you. To be totally and completely honest, I don't even want to be near you. But I also know we seriously need to address if and how we are going to move forward, because things can't go on like this. I'll agree to counseling, and we'll have to see what happens then. I'm going to leave now, and I really can't say when I will be back, but once you've made an appointment for the counseling, you can text me the information. I promise I'll be there. Then if we can come to some type of understanding, I'll come back home. Until then, please don't call me, and don't have your family and friends contact me either. Just give me some space."

As she stood there in disbelief, I walked up close to her to get one last thing off my chest. "Let me say this once and one time only. You'd better not ever go into my social media account again. This will be the last time you get the chance to embarrass the hell out of me the way you did yesterday, because next time I won't be so nice. I mean that."

I walked to the front door and this time left, leaving her exactly where she stood in the middle of the living room floor, looking as pathetic as she probably felt. My only goal at that point was to call Tiffany. I needed to hear her voice and get whatever sense of comfort she could give.

After I turned on my cell phone, the alerts began sounding one after the other. From the looks of it, I had several voicemails and text messages, mostly from Monica and Tiffany. Something had to be extremely important, so instead of calling, I raced over to the school to find out what was so urgent. As I bolted in and out of traffic, all types of things ran through my mind. Was something going on with Monica? Or maybe something was wrong with Tiffany. I even started to wonder if maybe she was trying to stop me from suggesting counseling with Pat. But that didn't make sense, because Monica had been trying to reach me too. I couldn't get there fast enough, and all of thirty minutes later, I barely stopped my truck as I hopped out and ran inside the building.

I tried to find Tiffany first. After I went to her office and then to the library and still hadn't found her, my heart and mind began to race, and I started to get nervous.

Where are you, Tiff, and what's going on?

I went inside Monica's office and tried to steady my breathing as I spoke with her secretary. "Hey, uh, is Monica in there? I really need to speak with her."

"Go right in, Coach Montgomery. She's actually been trying to reach you."

When I walked through her door, I was able to breathe much easier after seeing Tiffany sitting in one of the leather chairs across from Monica's desk.

"Terrence," Monica said, "please tell me what is going on."

I wasn't sure what she was referring to, but whatever it was had her and Tiffany extremely upset. "What do you mean what's going on? What happened?"

"Didn't you listen to any of your messages or read your texts?"

"No, I didn't. I'd just had a huge argument with Pat, so when I noticed the number of messages from the both of you, I raced right over here."

"Oh, so you've seen her, huh?" she asked with her hand on her hip and lips poked out.

"Yeah, I saw her, but I don't understand. What's wrong?"

"Coach, are you saying you didn't notice the uncanny resemblance between your wife and Tiffany?"

"Oh, of course I did, but when did you all see Patricia?"

"She was here earlier. I ran into her coming out of my office when she first got here. She claimed to be looking for you, but I got the funny feeling she was here more so for Tiffany, to reveal her new look to her."

"You can't be serious. What did she say? What did she do?"

"What she said we can pretty much deal with. She's harmless in that case. But we do have the right mind to believe she may have keyed Tiffany's car. We just haven't figured out how she knew it was hers."

"Dammit." I took a seat in the other chair next to Tiffany. I wanted to hold her hand, but I wasn't sure if it would be appropriate in front of Monica. "Social media is how she knew. I'm sure of it. Facebook has practically been her life lately, and that's where she finds out all of her other information. Tiffany, I'm so sorry for this, and I'll take care of any damages to your truck."

Leaning back, I buried my head in my hands. "I just don't know what's come over Pat. I mean, we're having our issues, but I've never seen her act this crazy before. I would have been far more cautious with my actions had I known that Patricia would take things this far."

"I don't know. I think that getting a little beside yourself because of issues with a spouse is understandable. However, making yourself up to look like another woman, flaunting yourself around in front of your mate's boss, and keying someone's car is on a whole other level. And the crazy thing is, it almost seemed like she took pride in her actions. Now you know I don't like getting involved in others' personal affairs, but if you don't mind me suggesting it, Patricia may need to see someone."

"Like a therapist or something?"

"I really don't think it would hurt."

"I don't know. Maybe I'll examine that option more after we go to counseling and I can try to make some sense of all this madness."

"You still plan on going to marriage counseling with her?" Tiffany spoke for the first time since I'd entered the room. She caught me completely off guard, and I didn't know how to answer her. The very minute the words came from my lips, she looked at me as if I'd betrayed her, which confused me even more because I'd only entertained the idea because she'd offered it. I couldn't wait to get her alone to see what was really going through her mind.

I turned my attention back to Monica. She appeared to have more to say.

"Coach, I sincerely hope that the counseling can help you bring some type of resolve to this situation. I can't have your wife coming up here unannounced and showing out the way she did, especially not in front of my staff or any of the children. It also causes concern for your safety and Tiffany's. I hate to say this, but next time, I will definitely have to get security involved."

"No, Monica, please," I begged more for the sake of my employment than for Patricia. "There won't be a next time. I'm going to fix everything and make absolutely clear to her to never set foot in here again."

"Good. Now that that's settled, I really need to get to a meeting with one of the other teachers. You and Tiffany are more than welcome to stay here in my office if you need to talk."

She patted my shoulder as she got up to leave. Over the years, Monica had proved that she was not only a good boss but an amazing friend. I was more than grateful for her and sincerely took her advice to heart. Maybe Patricia did need someone to talk to, one-on-one, outside of the marriage counseling. I made a mental note to look into that later. Right now, though, I had to fix things with Tiffany.

I looked at her and took her hand. Thankfully, she didn't resist and held mine. "Tiff, I really don't know what to say other than I'm so sorry about all of this."

"So you're going home with her? You're still going to go to counseling with her and pretending like everything is all right?"

"Wait a minute, isn't that what you suggested I should do?"

"Yeah, I did, but that was before she came up here like some crazy woman. She's insane and completely unstable, Terrence."

"Her actions seem a little off-the-wall, but she's not normally like this. And it's like you said—I have to do everything I can now so that I'll have no regrets later."

"I guess," was all she said, putting her head back down. I could almost read her mind when the silence attacked us.

"Listen, my only goal is simply to see if she and I can cohabitate together, but that's it. We are far from being husband and wife, and that's a long ways off if it even becomes that."

"I'm sorry. I'm definitely not trying to make you feel guilty about your decision. She's your wife, and I don't have a right to feel one way or the other about what you need to do for your family."

"Trust me, it's all right," I said, interrupting her apology because there was no need. Then I stood her up and held her tightly in my arms. I wanted to make sure she realized how much I didn't want to let her go. "Hey, I'm going to get you that same room you had last night at least for a few more days until we figure out your living arrangements."

"Thank you, but that's all right. I took Monica up on her offer to stay with her and her family. I just don't feel like being alone right now."

"You don't have to be alone. I'm here, and I promise I'm not going anywhere."

I held her some more to make sure she knew I meant every single word coming from my mouth.

Chapter 45

Tiffany

His arms surrounded me, and I felt as safe as I did last night on the dance floor. It was crazy to feel this way so soon, but my heart already loved this man, and I didn't want him to let me go. Suddenly it hit me that maybe I did understand Patricia more than I ever realized.

As Monica and I talked when Patricia left, trying to make sense of her actions, she told me to try putting myself in Patricia's shoes and imagine how I would respond. I tried to tell myself that there was no way I would go to the lengths that she did, but I couldn't say that for sure. Monica even said herself that she couldn't say how she would react if it were Todd. We all reacted to things in different ways, but there was something about matters of the heart that made us all go insane. I just prayed that Terrence could deal with her and not get hurt in the process.

Slowly, I pulled away from his embrace and walked a few steps away from him. "As much as I want to say yes, it would be best if I didn't."

"Why? Because you're afraid of what might happen again?" he asked, closing the gap between us.

I swallowed the lump in the middle of my throat while trying hard not to give in. "Terrence, because of what shouldn't have happened last night or ever again. You have so much that you need to address first, and you and I giving in to temptation will only complicate things."

"Or it might confirm that you want me just as much as I want you."

His lips made their way next to mine, and before I knew it, our tongues intertwined. My nipples stood at attention as the warmth of his body immersed mine. Somewhere in the back of my mind lingered the words, *we shouldn't do this,* but they never exited my lips. Instead, the excitement and intensity grew as his hands began to massage my breasts through my blouse. Our breathing became heavier as Terrence commenced to unbutton my blouse and I undid his pants. He picked me up, sitting me on the edge of Monica's desk. Then somewhere in the middle of it all, my mind reminded me of exactly where we were and what we were doing.

"Terrence, wait." The words slowly and softly came out as if I really didn't mean them. I imagined that he hadn't heard them as he continued to kiss his way toward the center of my breasts. I struggled to say it louder, and this time I demanded his attention.

"Terrence, please stop."

All at once everything ended, and he stood paralyzed in front of me, appearing as if I had crushed him. Feeling his ego may have been bruised, I attempted to soften the blow.

"I'm sorry. I want this as much as you, but not here and not after everything that happened today with your wife. You need to get that straight first."

I longed for him to say something, anything in fact, but he only fixed his pants and left. My mind raced a million miles per minute, wondering what I'd done and what to do next. But as I buttoned my blouse and did my best to gather my thoughts, it all settled at the fact that I was falling in love. Only problem was, it was with a man who belonged to another woman.

After the day I'd had, I couldn't wait to get to Monica's house. She'd already told me that Todd cooked again and afterward I could take a long, nice bath in her Jacuzzi tub in the guest room. My heart was set on it, too. I simply wanted to lay my head back, close my eyes, and talk to God. I could talk to God anytime, but there was something about when I had that quiet, relaxing, intimate time with Him. I truly needed to hear His voice on my life and what direction it was headed in. I also needed to repent for my dealings with Terrence from last night and today. Of course, the damage had already been done, but if he and I were going to continue with any type of friendship and work relationship, then I had to settle this in my mind and my heart.

Chapter 46

Terrence

Only a week had passed by, but it seemed like an eternity since returning to the house with Patricia. At first I planned on staying away until out first counseling session, but my mind and pockets instructed me to do otherwise. Lucky for me, though, she'd been fairly quiet and even pleasant to deal with. I supposed her change in behavior had a lot to do with my being back at home as well as agreeing to the counseling in the first place. Now as I sat next to her on the couch in Pastor Jones's office, I couldn't seem to take my thoughts away from Tiffany. We hadn't spoke at all since what happened in Monica's office. I'd tried calling and texting, yet she never responded, and it seemed like she'd even been dodging me at the school. Even so, once I made it through this morning with Patricia, I had to find a way to talk to her.

"I'm so sorry to have had you all waiting. I ran a little over in my session before yours," Pastor Jones said, finally entering his office. He looked exactly as I remembered, other than his bald head, which used to have a little hair, and his now-gray beard.

"It's all right, Pastor. There's no need to apologize. We're just happy to be able to meet with you today," Pat said, behaving like some perfect angel in front of him. It all made me a little sick to my stomach, and all I could do was roll my eyes.

"And, Terrence? How are you today?

"Oh, me? I'm just fine, Pastor."

"I see." He looked at me, wanting me to say more, I could tell, but he left it right there.

"Well, I guess we'll start with how things are going inside of the Montgomery household."

Pat looked over at me before she began to speak first. I couldn't wait to hear what was about to come from her mouth. "Um, if I can be completely honest, Pastor Jones, things are not at all how I would like them to be."

"Really? Why would you say that?"

"Well, although my husband has actually been home this past week, not much has changed between us. We still aren't living like husband and wife. We don't share a bedroom, we barely say two words to one another, and the intimacy between us is basically nonexistent, not even a hug or kiss. He doesn't even acknowledge our boys when they're around. It's more like we're roommates than anything. I just want my husband back."

I couldn't believe this woman had the nerve to tell the pastor, of all people, that I wasn't having sex with her. I almost wanted to get up and walk out, but I remembered the promise I made to myself and Tiffany.

"Is this true, Terrence? Are the two of you more like roommates than husband and wife?"

"Our living arrangements are as good as they can be for the moment."

"C'mon now. Are you trying to tell me that you live in a house with your wife, but you don't share a bedroom together, let alone have sex, and you're fine with that? I need for both you and Patricia to share your honest feelings in this counseling."

"Look, of course I wish that things were different, but they're just not and probably never will be. It is what it is at this point. Our husband-and-wife relationship went out the window when she called the police on me and had me removed from my home."

Patricia huffed and puffed before trying to defend herself. "Now there. You see his attitude? We could go on living the rest of our lives like this, and it would be just fine for him. But I'm telling you now, Terrence, I can't and won't continue to live like this. Something has to change."

"Something or someone, Pat? And maybe that someone is you."

"Me? You're saying I need to change when you're the one sleeping around with single coworkers?"

"Don't do this," I mumbled to her, hoping the pastor didn't question me about her accusations.

"Why not? Why not do this? Because Pastor Jones is here and you don't want him knowing your dirty little secrets?"

I hopped up and started to head for the door, but Pastor Jones got up with me and grabbed my arm. "Terrence, if you leave now, we're never going to get to the root of the issues. That's what we're here for, right?"

"Sure, but I'm not going to sit here and have her blame me for every single thing wrong in our marriage."

"Okay, so sit back down, and tell me what you think the problem is."

Instead of moving back toward the couch and sitting next to her, I sat in a chair that was closer to the door. "Pastor, the only way I can put it is that my wife has changed. She has way too much idle time on her hands, which is causing all the conflict."

I heard her huffing and puffing again. She rolled her eyes at me from the couch when I made my statement.

"What do you mean by changed?"

"She's not the same person she used to be. When we met, she was much more spontaneous, fun, and carefree.

She was also much more confident and secure in her own skin, not making herself up to look like other people. And since she brought up our sex life, she knew how to satisfy me back then, unlike now."

"And now?"

"I feel like she's insecure, somewhat of a stick-in-the-mud, and her only focus is social media and trying to catch me in something I'm not doing."

"Patricia, what do you have to say to all of that?"

"Maybe I have changed a little, but that's what people do over time, right? They change. They mature and grow. I mean, I have two growing boys to raise into men. I can't be worried about satisfying my husband's sexual fantasies with two sons in the home. And if I seem a bit insecure, maybe it's because my husband pays more attention to his attractive, single coworker than me. Pastor Jones, he took her out, for God's sake, and posted a picture of them together right on social media for all of our friends and family to see. That's not something a married man should be doing. Besides when was the last time you took me out?"

All of a sudden, the waterworks started just like I knew they would. Patricia could win an Oscar for her acting skills. I hoped that Pastor Jones could see right through her the way I did.

"It seems you two have very different views on the same situation. But instead of going deeper into the problems right now, I would like to get you both back to some type of love and care for the other. That way, when you talk about the issues, it will come from a point of compassion and not anger. You will both be able to voice your opinion better as well as understand the other without placing blame. So I want to stop here and allow the tempers to cool down a little. But when you go home, practice kindness to each other up until our next session, even if it's only one kind act a day. Do something to show the other a form of compassion. I also challenge you to write down some things that you still love about the other for our next meeting. We truly need to get back to love. Is that good with the both of you?"

We both mumbled yes under our breath.

"One more thing. Patricia, if you could, limit your time on social media for the next week. Terrence, if you can, limit your involvement and communication with your coworker, okay?"

I let out a laugh as I watched Patricia cross her legs and fold her arms. She almost acted as if Pastor Jones had taken her side on things. However, regardless of how she felt or what he suggested, nothing was going to keep me away from Tiffany. That was the very reason I was happy we were in two separate cars. I couldn't wait to get over to the school, see her face, and tell her everything that happened here today.

"Are you going to meet me at the house?" she made sure to ask in front of Pastor Jones.

"I will be at the house later. Right now, I have some business to take care of," I answered while immediately walking out the door and not giving her a chance to respond. Of course, I could tell she wasn't happy, and the pastor's eyebrows even raised a bit at my response, but I didn't care. I hopped in my truck and headed in the direction where I was sure to find a sense of peace and happiness.

All of twenty minutes later, I poked my head into Tiffany's office to see if she was inside. Luckily, I caught her fully engulfed in whatever she was looking at on her laptop.

"Hey there," was all I said, first trying to judge her current disposition.

Her eyes looked up at mine, and her face began to crack somewhat of a smile. "Hi, Coach Montgomery, how are you today?"

"Seriously? Coach Montgomery?" I questioned her while walking in and shutting the door behind me.

"Should I call my colleague and the head coach of the football team here anything else?"

"I don't know. Maybe Terrence, or baby, or even daddy would sound better rolling off those pretty lips of yours." Before we knew it, we both burst out in laughter as I went around her desk to give her a hug. "It looks like someone is in a better mood and talking to me now, huh?"

"First of all, I'm in a great mood. Secondly, I never stopped talking to you, Terrence. I just figured I needed time to think about things, and you needed some time as well to yourself with your wife. Speaking of which, how are things going between you two anyway?" she asked with a hint of distaste in her voice.

"I don't know. It's like every time I think my wife can't shock me any more than she already has, she does something else to outdo herself."

"Really? What happened this time?"

"Well, this morning was our first meeting with the marriage counselor, who just happens to be her pastor. Anyway, in his efforts to get to the root of our problems, she bypassed everything that she's done and blames you."

"Me? Are you serious?"

"Dead serious. Every other word from her mouth was something in regard to my 'single coworker.' Not once did she take blame for any of her actions."

"I can't believe this. You and I haven't known each other long. Hell, I haven't even been in Texas that long, and it sounds like the two of you had issues way before I moved here. Does the pastor know that?"

"Trust me, I tried to voice all of that, but she's still trying to imply that all of our problems started when you can into my life. Tiff, I agreed to this counseling because I saw exactly where you were coming from, but I don't think it's going to help. I still feel the same when it comes to Patricia, and nothing is going to change that. In my mind, my marriage is already over, so I'm pretty much just going through the motions."

"I hear you, and I can't believe I'm about to say it, but I still believe you need to do this."

"Maybe you're right, I guess. Our next session is next week. Get a load of this—he suggested that she remains off social media and that I have no contact with you for the next week."

"Which you're clearly not going through with because you're here right now."

"You're damn right I'm not going through with that. No one is going to tell me who I can and can't be around, not Patricia or her pastor."

She looked at me as if she had no idea what to say, and we were both quiet for a minute or two, allowing things to sink in.

"But enough about me and my marital problems with Pat. You mentioned you're in a great mood when I first came in."

"Oh, yeah." Her eyes lit up as soon as she started to speak. "So much happened the day your wife came here that I never had the opportunity to tell you. My favorite author, Mr. Carl Weber, is releasing a movie based on one of his books. Well, he posted on Facebook that he was looking for people who could host VIP events before the movie in cities that he couldn't make it to. So Monica encouraged me to send a message, and he selected me to put together the event here in Dallas."

"Get out of here. Are you serious? I'm not much into reading myself, but Patricia has read all of his books. I've heard all about him. I'm so happy for you."

"Thanks. I'm really excited and nervous all at the same time since I just moved here and don't know a lot of people."

"It's okay. I've got your back, and I'm sure Monica does too. We'll help you with whatever you need."

"I'm glad you said that, because I was hoping to have Montgomery's Barbeque and Soul Food as the caterer for the event."

"Are you serious right now or just pulling my leg?"

"Totally serious. So will you?"

"Hell yeah, I will. I would be honored." I walked to her side of the desk again and did the one thing I wanted to do most since first entering. Taking her hand, I stood her up so that I could wrap my arms around her waist. Despite what had happened a week ago in Monica's office, she didn't hesitate to hug me back. She smelled sweet enough to eat, and I began to have visions of doing just that. I wanted to taste every inch of her, and I got the feeling that the feeling was mutual when she softly whispered in my ear.

"Terrence?"

"Yes, baby?"

"I need you . . . all of you."

"Baby, you got me . . . all of me."

Our lips finally met, and it was what I wanted and needed most. I didn't get this feeling with Patricia, not now or possibly ever. At that very moment, I'd made up my mind that I would go through only one more counseling session, and that was it. I was no longer going to delay my happiness, and at present, that was right here with this woman.

Chapter 47

Patricia

"Now do you understand why I'm so afraid for my marriage, Pastor Jones?" I asked, staying back in his office when Terrence left.

"I will admit that there's some cause for concern, but not just on Terrence's part."

I looked at him and started to wonder if he was taking up for Terrence because they were both men. Did they automatically share some type of male brotherhood that went without words?

"All right, go ahead and blame me for everything just like my husband," I spoke sarcastically.

"Pat, have a seat. Now listen, I'm not blaming you for everything. Terrence has done his share that I'm not in agreement with as well. But in order for either of you to get somewhere with this process and your marriage, you have to admit your own wrongdoings. It starts with yourselves first."

I folded my arms and crossed my legs while he spoke. I was trying to hear what he said, but I couldn't seem to tear my mind away from Terrence and Tiffany. In my mind, she was to blame, and nothing was changing that, not even Pastor Jones's words.

"Can I propose something to you, Patricia? And you can make a decision on your own."

"Yes, that's fine," I answered in a dry, uninterested tone.

"Why don't you try to go back to work, even if it's part-time? Show Terrence that there's more to you than surfing social media. I bet it will make you feel good as well that you're not so dependent on him."

"I don't know. I mean, Terrence is fine with me not working right now, and being home gives me more time with my boys."

"Be honest with yourself, Pat. Terrence is not okay with you not working, and those boys are practically men. Why are you so afraid of going back to work?"

"I'm not afraid," I shot back in my defense. "I just really don't know what it is I want to do anymore. Before my last employer relocated, I wasn't happy there. I was only going through the motions because I'd been there over ten years, the pay was decent, and it offered benefits. But now that I have some type of freedom, I don't want to go back to being depressed every day just to collect a check."

"But are you truly happy right now? Not working, depending solely on Terrence, and with your marriage in shambles?"

"No, I guess not."

"All I'm trying to say is stop putting your happiness in the palms of Terrence's hands. Now I'm not pushing for you guys to get divorced. God created and honors the covenant between a husband and wife. But what I am saying is the two of you can't survive like this—angry, arguing, no intimacy, no friendship, no praying. So what I need for you to do is start focusing on Patricia again. Start loving yourself again, working out, eating right, taking yourself on a date, all the things that make you happy. And trust me, before you know it, Terrence will see a whole different Patricia. Hopefully, for his sake, it won't be too late."

"Maybe you're right, Pastor Jones," I said softly, not actually wanting to admit it to myself.

"I am right, and if you don't know what type of work you want to do right now, that's okay. Consider going back to school and taking some classes in a field that you do want to go into. All right? Sounds like a plan?" he asked while standing me up and wrapping his arms around me.

"Sure, sounds like a plan."

I walked out of his office and got inside my car. He'd said so much that made sense, but for the life of me, I couldn't take my mind away from Terrence . . . or Tiffany. The truth of the matter was I despised that woman for even coming into my husband's life, and I wanted her to pay one way or another.

Chapter 48

Tiffany

"All right, you have the location, the food is taken care of, tickets are designed and printed, and we've set up everything at the movie theatre, so I think you're all good, Ms. Event Planner." Monica seemed just as excited about the event as I did.

"Yeah, it's crazy how everything came together so smoothly. Monica, I pretty much owe that to you and Terrence. You all have helped me more than you know."

"Girl, it was my pleasure, and I'm sure Terrence feels the same. By the way, has he mentioned anything to you about his marriage counseling sessions? He's been pretty quiet about it, and I didn't want to come right out and ask."

"Yes, he told me all about it. They had their first one about a week ago, and the next one is tomorrow I believe. He said things went exactly how he thought they would. Patricia basically blamed him for everything wrong in their marriage, the problems that she claims didn't start until he met me."

"What? I swear, that woman is out of her mind. She and Terrence had issues way before you ever came into the picture. But I guess she has to blame someone to help her sleep better at night. I just wish Terrence would decide if he's going to stay or leave and act accordingly. I hate to say it, but I blame him for a lot of this as well. It's time he made a decision."

"I think he was close to making one before I encouraged him to try this, so I guess I am involved in this entire mess even if I don't want to be."

"You were only doing what you thought was right. Terrence is a man, and it's his life and his family. He should have fixed this a long time ago. If only I knew why he stayed when he's clearly not happy. I mean, if it's the boys, I'm sure they can work something out."

"I don't think it's that. In fact, I know it's not that. Terrence doesn't want to fail or have to start all over again."

"Really? Is that what it is?"

"He really hit rock bottom after his first divorce, and now that he has everything back in place, he doesn't want to go through that again."

"I guess I understand, but no amount of money or things will ever outweigh his happiness. Plus, I just believe that sometimes we have to let go of some things to gain others."

"What exactly do you mean?"

"Well, being with the wrong person can hold you back instead of push you forward. Take the whole restaurant idea for example. That's been a passion of Terrence's for as long as I can remember, but he's never been serious about it because Patricia doesn't think it's a good idea. She doesn't encourage or support him, but if she did, who knows where they could actually be in life? If it were me, I would be just as passionate about it as Todd, and if we succeeded, then great, but if we failed, then we failed together. That's a team. That's a husband and wife."

As she made her last comment, Todd called us into the kitchen for the breakfast he'd prepared. It was Sunday, which was kind of a lazy, "lounge around the house" type of day in their household. But instead of lounging, I had other plans I'd been working on, and after the conversation between me and Monica, I knew today was the perfect day to do it. I hadn't told Monica anything about it, only because I wanted to share it with Terrence first. I hoped he was awake. Picking up my cell phone before heading into the kitchen, I decided to text him.

Hey, you, I sent first.

He responded in a matter of seconds, Hey, beautiful. How are you this morning?

Good, about to have breakfast with Monica and Todd. How are you?

Good too, trying to stay low-key and out of the way.

LOL. How about you meet me somewhere? I have a surprise for you.

A surprise for me? Woman, what are you up to?

You'll see. Meet me at the school in about an hour.

Okay, Ms. Tate, see you then.

I hurried to eat, get dressed, and get over to the school within an hour. I was so giddy and could hardly contain myself. I just hoped that this was the encouragement and support that Terrence needed. Thinking about it, I remembered my mother once telling me that the Bible says, "He who finds a wife, finds what is good." So, she'd said, a woman should have the qualities and attributes that exemplify a wife before the man actually finds her. I only hoped this proved to be true.

An hour later, I pulled up to the school and found Terrence sitting in his truck. It was a little difficult getting out of the house at first because Monica kept inviting herself along. But then Todd told her he'd planned a movie day in the house with the kids. That was the escape I needed to get out alone.

Terrence got out of his truck and walked over to mine. "All right, Tiff, what's this surprise all about?"

"Hello to you too, Mr. Montgomery. Now get inside please, and I will tell you when to put this on."

I handed him a blindfold once he got in on the passenger side. "A blindfold? What is going on? What's this all about?" he asked, grinning from ear to ear.

"You will see in about twenty minutes."

We began to talk about a little of everything during the ride: the beautiful weather in Texas, my stay with Monica and Todd, and even Patricia's daily antics since he'd been home. Today, however, I didn't want him to think much at all about Patricia. This would be a day of new beginnings. Shortly after, I pulled up to our destination.

"All right, put this on, and I will lead the way from here."

"Do I really need a blindfold?" he whined. "Can't I just close my eyes?"

"No, Terrence. Now c'mon."

We finally walked in front of what I was so excited about, and I hoped he would feel the same.

"All right, we're stopping, so does that mean we're here and I can remove the blindfold?"

"Yep, go ahead."

His eyes lit up with the excitement I prayed for as I stood in front of a space for rent while holding a sign I had made for him that read, MONTGOMERY'S BARBEQUE AND SOUL FOOD.

"Oh, my God, what is this?"

"It's kind of my way of saying thank you for helping me with the Carl Weber event. You have a lot going on right now in your life, but you're still taking time out to help me, and I couldn't find a better way to say thanks. Now it's only a space for rent that I wanted you to see, but I think it would be the perfect place to start your business. It's close to your home and the school, and the rent isn't that expensive."

"Wow, Tiff, I don't know what to say. I mean, my mind never even went this far. I guess I've kind of been content with cooking here and there. But looking at this right now . . . You've made me believe that this can actually become a reality."

"It can and it will. I believe in you."

Next thing I knew, he picked me up and spun me around until the both of us became dizzy.

"You don't cease to amaze me, Tiffany Tate. I love you."

The words came from his lips, yet I still wasn't sure if I heard him correctly. He must have sensed everything that I was feeling because he stopped, calmed down, and looked into my eyes, saying the words again.

"I love you, Tiffany Tate."

"Terrence, I love you too."

He kissed me over and over and over again. In that very moment, it felt like all my dreams had come true overnight. I loved this man, and he loved me back. It was also at that moment I discovered why God had moved me to Texas in the first place. It was to be found by Mr. Terrence Montgomery.

"Hey, I also wanted to give you this card to say thank you for catering the event. Your payment is in there as well."

"You didn't have to do this. It was my way of helping you because I know how much this means to you. But I guess your novel really will be based on a true story, huh?"

"What do you mean?"

"Well, you said you wanted to write about two people falling in love and all their dreams coming true."

All I could do was smile as I thought about what he'd just said. *My novel really will be based on a true story . . . Terrence and Tiffany's love story.*

Chapter 49

Terrence

I hated being here, sitting next to Patricia, pretending that things would magically get better when we both knew they wouldn't. We were only going through the motions, and it was sucking the life out of me. Especially since the day I'd had with Tiffany yesterday was so amazing.

After going by the building, we went to grab something to eat and then talked in the truck until the sun went down. She had truly become my peace, unlike the hurricane sitting next to me now. I couldn't help but wonder what Patricia was up to, because she'd been as quiet as a mouse and behaving strangely since my arriving back home yesterday. I was sure whatever it was would come out this morning because she'd been fidgeting around like she couldn't control herself.

"Terrence and Patricia, one of my favorite couples. How are you two doing this morning?" Pastor said, walking in, smiling from ear to ear.

"I'm good, Pastor Jones," I responded.

"I've been better," Patricia said, starting things off already.

"It seems like you have some things on your mind, Patricia. Would you like to share?" he asked her.

"Why don't you ask my husband if he kept up his end of the bargain this past week?"

"Oh, you're referencing the tasks I gave you two in the last session. How did that go for you, Terrence? Did you limit your interaction with your coworker?"

"Uh, yeah, as much as I could. I mean, we work together, so of course we would have to have some interaction with one another."

"You liar. You're sitting here lying straight through your teeth to the pastor in God's house. How could you?"

"Pat, if you can, calm down please. Now why are you so positive that Terrence is lying?"

"Because of this."

I watched as she handed him some piece of paper that she'd had folded up inside of her purse. As I glanced at it when she passed it to him, it looked like a copy of the flyer from the event.

"What exactly is this?" Pastor Jones questioned her.

I jumped in to answer instead. "It's a flyer of an event I'm catering for my coworker, which she must have printed from Tiffany's Facebook page. I thought you were supposed to stay off social media for the week, Pat."

"Don't try to change the subject. The point is, you're still dealing with this woman when you need to focus on me and your sons. And this whole catering thing? I could have sworn I told you before that you don't need to entertain this mess. You have a family and responsibilities, Terrence. You don't have time to waste on some fly-by-night hobby that will never support our home."

Her comment punched me dead in the chest, sucking all the wind out of me. Fly-by-night hobby? Was this what my so-called wife honestly thought when it came to my dreams? Instantly, if it hadn't been obvious before, it was totally clear to me now. This woman was not who I needed or wanted to spend the rest of my life with.

"Terrence, do you have anything to say to how Patricia feels?"

"Yes, I do," I said, standing up and looking down at Pat. "Patricia, this marriage is over. I'll have divorce papers drawn up by the end of the week."

With that said, I left her and Pastor Jones sitting there to discuss whatever was left to be said afterward, but as for me, I was done. As I left, I saw that I had several texts from Tiffany. As much as I wanted and needed to talk to her, I couldn't. My mind was all over the place, and I needed some time alone. Instead of leaving my home again though, I planned on going right back there to do the one thing that gave me peace.

During my drive, I started coming up with ideas of dishes that I could prepare for the event, and once I arrived home, I would play around with them to see how they tasted. Of course, I would bump into Patricia whenever she returned, but that no longer mattered to me. From this point forward, I would move around our home as if she didn't exist until this marriage was dissolved.

Surprisingly, the day had been going fairly well since leaving the counseling session. I didn't know where Patricia was or what was taking her so long to get home, but that wasn't my concern. I'd been cooking up a little bit of this and a little of that, and it felt almost exhilarating. Ideas for new dishes were popping into my mind left and right, and it made me believe so much in making my dream a reality.

I was outside standing at my barbeque pit, dancing to some music I had blasting, when I heard Patricia slam the front door. From the corner of my eye, I saw her moving around the kitchen. A few minutes later, she came barging outside.

"Just so you know, there is no Montgomery's Barbeque and Soul Food without me—Mrs. Montgomery. So you go right ahead and play around with this if you want, but I'll be the one reaping the benefits in the end," she yelled. She kicked the grill, and the hot flames almost hit my clothing.

"What the hell is wrong with you, woman?" I followed her into the kitchen where she had dumped everything I'd been working on into the garbage.

"What's wrong with me? Really? You embarrass the hell out of me in front of my pastor, and you're asking what's wrong with me? I swear, you are as dumb and childish as I ever thought. And if a divorce is what you want, then fine, I'll give you that. But I'll make damn sure I leave you as broke as you were when I found you. You'd better believe that, Terrence Montgomery."

I was so hot that I practically felt on fire. I'd never in my life put my hands on a woman, but I damn sure felt like I wanted to in that moment. Instead though, I picked up the phone and dialed her father. He lived less than five minutes from us, and I needed him over here now. If I couldn't talk some sense into her, I prayed that he could.

Ten minutes later he came through the front door, and Patricia ran to him like she was a 6-year-old little girl running to her daddy's arms.

"Terrence, what's going on here?" he asked as she whimpered on his chest as if I'd done something to her.

"I just think that maybe Patricia needs to stay with you for a while so that things won't get any worse than they already have. And if you need to know, we have decided to get a divorce."

"We haven't decided anything, Daddy. This is all Terrence, and I'm not leaving this house because I belong here just as much as he does."

"Pat, try to calm down. Why don't you get some things and you and the boys stay the night at my place? Just one night."

"But why? This is my home too."

"I get that, but why would you want to be here under these circumstances?"

"Because he's my husband, and I love him."

"Honey, why do you still love someone who obviously is no longer in love with you?"

She couldn't answer his question. She only cried harder and harder as she went upstairs and began to gather some things for herself and the boys.

"Terrence, look, I don't agree with what's been going on with you and Pat, but I'm glad you called me and didn't put my daughter in any danger."

I nodded to him as I watched her slowly come down the stairs with her bags. Our eyes met, and I could tell we both felt the same heartache and pain.

"I'll call the boys and tell them to come to my father's, and I'll explain to them what's going on over there."

"We can sit down and tell them together if you want."

"No, they're my sons. I need to do this."

I didn't argue with her any further, but I watched as my wife walked out of our house possibly for good.

Chapter 50

David

I sat in Sonya's living room watching a rerun of *Martin*. He and the rest of the cast were such fools that they had me laughing until my belly ached. Sonya was in the kitchen preparing another amazing dinner for us, and the aroma from it made me hungrier by the second. This had become our daily routine over the last three months. Once she got home from work, she made dinner while I relaxed on the sofa in front of the television set. Afterward, she cleaned up the kitchen, took a bath, and then I would join her in the bedroom.

Things were going good with Sonya in my opinion. She hadn't hounded me about marriage, a family, or getting a job. She seemed happy and content simply having a man to come home to, and I was happy being that man. Sonya was truly a good woman inside and out. She was so good that I really started to wish I could give her what I knew she'd eventually want—what all women wanted deep down. But marriage still wasn't in the cards for me. I didn't feel like I needed to be tied down to one woman right now or anytime soon for that matter. She was the only one in my life at the moment, but who really knew what the future held, especially since Tiffany had crossed my mind a lot lately?

My eyes continued to watch the fifty-six-inch television screen in front of me while my mind traveled back three

months ago when I was an engaged man to two different women. When Leslie found out about Tiffany, she'd
left me a long text, telling me how much of a creep I was
and never to contact her again. She even had the nerve to
make a couple of threats toward me, but I brushed them
off. I hated what had happened, and her words hurt me
to the core, but I was relieved that things were over between us.

At the beginning of our relationship, I felt like Leslie
could be the one. She was perfect. She was beautiful
inside and out, strong and independent, hardworking,
compassionate, and did I say beautiful? She was almost
every man's dream. However, slowly but surely, I started
to realize that I wasn't the man for her. Just like my
mother and Tiffany, she tried molding me into the man
she wanted me to be. She stayed on my back about
getting a steady job and such that things weren't worth it.
I became tired from the pressure of it all, and everything
got old as I struggled to keep up with her overall demands.

Thankfully, her job kept her on the go, so while her
demands were unbearable, her absence softened the
blow. That was the very reason I'd ever asked her to
marry me. With her gone all the time, I was able to live
the life I wanted without having to answer to anyone. I
basically had a roof over my head, money at my disposal
whenever she or my mother loaned it to me, and Tiffany
in St. Louis. It worked out well in my opinion. That
was until Tiffany started talking about having a future
together. I never expected Tiffany to jump the gun the
way she did, but I really should have known better—she
was a woman. If only I'd had the chance to figure all this
mess out before those two found out about one another,
then maybe things would have been different.

I tried to stop by Leslie's a month ago. I simply wanted
to apologize, although I knew more than likely she

wouldn't hear me out. To my surprise, a huge FOR SALE
sign was posted right there in the middle of the front yard.
The first thing I did was go over to Mrs. Smith's house.
She seemed like she'd been waiting for me. She came to
the door with a couple of black leather bags in hand and
told me that Leslie had left them for me when she moved.
I couldn't believe that she up and disappeared like that.
It would have felt better if she'd at least cursed me out or
something. I just didn't want to believe that she hated me
that much to leave my life without a trace. I could even
tell that Mrs. Smith had formed a negative opinion about
me too when I tried to ask of her whereabouts. All she
said was that Leslie was doing better, and then she shut
her front door right in my face. If I only had a chance to
talk to her face-to-face, I could have straightened this
whole mess out, or at least tried to. However, I knew at
that point that it would never happen. With no other
choice, I took the bags and left that part of my life behind
me. I had a strange feeling that she probably damaged
my things and then packed them up nicely to get back
at me. But to my surprise, none of the items were mine.
They all belonged to Tiffany.

I never even tried to reach Tiffany to give her things
to her. I didn't have the heart to face her after the lies
I'd told about my mother and then sending her that final text. So when I arrived back at Sonya's, I put the bags
in her garage and decided to leave that chapter of my
life closed. Although it started to feel that that was easier said than done. Tiffany had been so much on my
mind as of late. I even gave in and attempted to call her a
couple of times but would hang up once she answered. I
didn't know exactly what to say or if she would have listened. I just didn't want to take that chance.

An hour later, Sonya woke me from my daydream
of thoughts when she peeked into the living room and

announced that dinner was ready. Before heading into the kitchen, I tried my best to shake off the thoughts I continued to have of my ex.

"Everything smells great as usual, baby! I can't wait to dig in."

"Well, before you dig in, I was hoping that we could talk."

I gave her a peculiar look, wondering what she could possibly have on her mind. I had become used to the general conversation over dinner like how her day was or how she couldn't wait to be her own boss. Never did she announce that we needed to talk. "Sure, what's up?"

She poured us glasses of red wine and smiled at me before she said anything. I continued to look at her in the strangest way as I tried to imagine what was about to come out of her mouth.

"David, the past few months have been great, don't you think?"

"Oh, yeah, of course they have. I totally agree with you."

"Well, I hope you still feel the same when I say that I think we need to adjust some things, especially with the news I just found out."

She continued to hesitate, but I was about to jump out of my skin with anxiety and anticipation. I chose to ease my way into this conversation she was determined to have. "Uh, what news is that?"

"I guess there's no other way to say it but to just come right out. I think it's time you found some real employment."

I quickly wiped away the beads of sweat that found their way across my forehead. I actually thought she was about to say something else, but this was something I could deal with. "I've been looking for another trucking gig."

"I know, I know, but I was thinking that maybe you could start looking for other positions outside of trucking in the meantime."

"Naw, I don't know about that. You know that trucking is all I desire to do, and besides, it's the only thing that really pays well and allows me the freedom I have."

"Yeah, it pays well when you're working. But, honey, having a trip here and there a couple of times out of the month is not going to help now since I'm . . . I'm . . ."

"You're what? Just say it."

"I'm pregnant."

Before I knew it, my mouthful of red wine shot out of my mouth and right in her direction.

"David!"

"I'm sorry. I didn't know if I heard you correctly."

She began wiping herself off with the black cloth napkin she had across her lap. "You heard me correctly. I went to the doctor today and found out that I'm six weeks along."

"Six weeks? That means there's still time for us to make an alternative decision, right?"

"What the hell do you mean, 'an alternative decision'?"

"I'm only saying that you just sprung this on me, and this is something we need to talk about before doing anything permanent."

"David Allen, if you are suggesting that I abort my child, then you can very well leave my house right now."

"Look, calm down, all right? I'm only saying that we need to think all of this through. Now first off, are you sure it's mine?"

"Oh, my God. Are you serious? You are more pathetic than I thought."

"I'm only asking because, honestly, I didn't think I could have any children."

If looks could kill, I would have surely been dead at that very moment. Sonya pushed her chair away, threw her napkin on her plate, and started to walk out of the kitchen. Before she crossed over into the living room, though, she looked back at me. "I think it would be best if you leave my home."

I heard the words come from her mouth, but I knew she couldn't be serious. I wasn't prepared to go back to my mother's, and I didn't even think that I could anyway. The last time I went there she had the nerve to ask me for my key because she called herself having a boyfriend now. Everything raced through my head, and I had no idea what to do. *A baby? At my age? And now Sonya doesn't want me here.* I couldn't go to my mother's. I had no idea where Leslie was. That only left one other person I could think of.

Grabbing my keys, I ran into the garage and snatched those two black bags. I took a chance of getting cursed out by her too, but under the circumstances, it was one I had to take. If I knew Tiffany, she was a lady with extreme compassion, and well, I needed all the compassion I could get at the moment.

I started out the driveway not even knowing what direction to head in. Ever since that night at Leslie's, I hadn't spoken to her. I didn't know if she had a home, where it was, or even if she had gone back to St. Louis. I was a complete idiot for breaking things off the way I did and not checking up on her. Now she was the one person I would possibly be able to depend on. The more I assessed my situation, the more I knew I had to find her. I had to make things right, and come hell or high water, I was determined to do that. She was my only hope. I figured I would simply drive around until I got the nerve to call her. In the back of my mind, all I heard was my mother reciting how I'd reap what I'd sown. Now I realized that I'd surely been sowing the wrong seeds.

Chapter 51

Tiffany

God is absolutely amazing, was all I thought as I curled up on my living room sofa with a nice glass of red wine and a book by Eric Jerome Dickey. Despite everything that had happened when I first relocated, I now sat in my own home completely furnished, with a true sense of peace in my life. I owed most of this to Terrence. Right after the Carl Weber event, he'd found me a nice three-bedroom ranch-style home to rent with the option to buy. My pockets were still a little tight at that moment, but Monica kept her word and gave me an advance until I was able to get things back on track.

For the last three months, I'd built up a fairly decent savings, and all was well in my world. Things were also going great at the school with my job, and I'd started attending church with Monica and her family every Sunday. I'd considered becoming an official member. I'd even started writing the very first chapter of *I Didn't Think You Existed* in hopes of one day submitting it to Carl Weber. Right after the event, I'd mentioned to him my desire to become an author. To my surprise, he said he would be more than happy to take a look at my project once it was completed. Finally, everything had begun to look up for me, and I couldn't be happier.

The only thing missing was that special someone, but I was no longer in a rush for that anymore either. After the circumstances from everything with David, I felt it was important for me to allow myself the necessary time for my heart and my mind to heal. It would be great to date and have the company of a man, but I didn't want to deal with just anyone. I still had a strong desire to be married, so whoever I chose to date would need to understand it would be with a purpose in mind. We would both have to be on the same page with one another and desire the same goal: a future together.

Unfortunately, the couple of men I'd bumped into weren't looking for anything more than someone to catch sheets with on a regular basis. That was why I generally found myself home, alone, with a book and some wine. Monica even tried to introduce me to a couple of Todd's friends, but somehow they didn't do it for me. They were very nice and all but simply didn't hold the qualities that I desired in a man. Whenever I talked to Keisha, though, she would say how I was way too picky and how I would never find someone if I continued to compare them all to Terrence. In my opinion, however, I felt that not being picky enough was what got me in the situation with David. And of course I compared everyone to Terrence. In my eyes, he was the perfect man—if only he weren't married.

He'd told me months ago that he asked her for a divorce in their counseling session, but nothing had happened as of yet. Patricia was totally against it, and Terrence continued to struggle with taking any action to move things along. I, on the other hand, sat quietly and patiently, waiting in the wings until something official happened, but it never did. He was still even staying in their home—which, he'd told me, was now under foreclosure—and she still had keys, entering and leaving as she pleased. It was all a complete and utter mess that I couldn't seem to pull myself away from.

Thinking about how wrong Terrence and Patricia were for each other sent my mind thinking back to David and how wrong he was for me. Just like Terrence, I wasn't sure why I couldn't see it then, but it was especially clear to me now. We had absolutely nothing in common. He didn't have any dreams or aspirations or anything that I would normally look for in a man. He didn't have a true foundation with God, or anything for that matter. He was simply a decent specimen to say that I had a man in my life. I laughed at how pathetic I must have seemed to settle for that. I was positive he looked at me that way. My friends and family possibly did, and hell, even I did after thinking back on it. I chose not to beat myself up about the situation, though, because now, as I looked around my home, I was more than thankful that God hadn't allowed David or the devil to have any victory in my life. I was a winner, an overcomer, and oh, so grateful to the Man Above. It was just like Monica said: everything happened for a reason. I only hoped that Terrence would come to realize that for himself, and soon.

I thought again how truly amazing God was as a single tear rolled down my left cheek, and this time, I didn't feel any shame in crying. Any tears I cried now were actual tears of joy. I hurried to wipe them away, though, when my phone vibrated on my coffee table. It was Monica.

"Hey, girl!"

"Hey, what's up? I was calling to make sure that you didn't want to go out to dinner with me and Todd."

"Oh, no, I'm good, but thanks for asking. I wouldn't want to be a third wheel, and besides, I'm going to warm up some leftovers and finish up the book I'm reading. But thanks again."

"You know, I really hate this, Tiff."

"What's that?"

"That you're always in the house and not out enjoying yourself. Why don't you think about changing your mind? I can see if Todd's friend is available. He's a very handsome man and has a lot going for himself," she said, teasing me.

"I don't know. I was really enjoying myself already right here, at home with my book and wine, alone."

"C'mon, it's just one little dinner date for maybe an hour or two tops, I promise."

I started to give it some thought. I really wasn't in the mood for my leftovers, and my book could always wait until I got back. Before I knew it, I gave in. "I guess an hour or two wouldn't hurt anything."

"It won't, and it will get you out of the house, enjoying yourself around others and not lying around thinking about Terrence."

"Who said I was lying around thinking about Terrence?"

"Look, I know you and I know him. The both of you are so crazy about one another that it's sickening. But until the coach has this whole situation with Patricia figured out, I won't allow you to waste your time moping over him."

"All right, fine. But I'll drive my own truck because if I don't like this guy, then I'm leaving."

"Deal. If you don't like him, we'll just say you have a migraine or something, all right?"

"Okay."

We hung up, and she texted me the name of the restaurant, the address, and the attire. Luckily, the place was casual enough for me to dress up some jeans with a really nice top and heels, because I still wanted to be comfortable. Thirty minutes later, I glanced over myself in my floor-length mirror before leaving.

"This should be good enough for an hour or two. God, please don't let this guy look like Urkel, okay?"

***

Thankfully, the restaurant wasn't far from my home at all. Even with the evening traffic, I managed to make it there within fifteen minutes. I had my truck valeted and walked confidently into the place. The lights were dimmed low, soft jazz was playing on the overhead speakers, and the crowd was mature and sophisticated, which I liked a lot. After I stood at the entrance a few minutes, stretching my neck while trying to find Monica, the maître d' approached me.

"Are you looking for someone, ma'am?"

"Yes, I'm meeting my girlfriend and two gentlemen here."

"Of course, she already informed me that you would be arriving. Please follow me to your seat."

I followed the very polite and nice-looking man to the table. I figured if Todd's friend looked anything like him, then I just might be having the night of my life. We reached the table, and I couldn't believe my eyes as the maître d' pulled my chair out for me.

"I'm so glad you made it." Monica winked at me.

"Me too." I winked back, letting her know that I was pleased with what I saw in front of me. "It feels good getting out of the house for a bit. Hey, Todd, how are you?" I spoke, giving him a hug from my chair.

"And, Tiffany, this is Todd's good friend, Andre. Andre, this is my good friend, Tiffany."

"Nice to meet you, Andre." I stuck my hand out across the table toward him.

"It's a pleasure meeting you as well," his tenor voice said as he kissed the back of my hand. His lips were soft, but he left the back of my hand a little damp. I hurried to wipe it off with my napkin, then dug through my purse for my hand sanitizer. A second later, we all ordered our drinks and appetizers as we began to make small talk.

I kept stealing glances at Andre only to find him staring back at me. Every time, I smiled a little and then turned away quickly. Monica was right. He was very easy on the eyes, he was well-dressed, and when he spoke, he was extremely articulate. Those were the very reasons I couldn't seem to understand why I wasn't enjoying myself. I kept trying to find something I didn't like about the man, but I couldn't, other than the fact that he wasn't Terrence. As the subject of politics came up in the conversation, I politely excused myself from the table.

"Please excuse me for a moment. I'll be right back."

"Uh, I'll come with you," Monica said.

Todd and Andre both stood as we walked away to the ladies' room.

"All right, what's wrong, Tiff? Andre is attractive, he's nice, educated, and I can go on and on, but you look like you're not having a good time."

"I'm not sure what it is, but he's just not my type."

"Honey, no one is your type other than Terrence, but the man can't make up his mind if he wants you or her, and that's not fair. Now I love Coach T, but I love you just as much, and I want the best for you. And you waiting around while he tries to decide between you and another woman is not the best."

"He's getting divorced," I jumped in.

"Yeah, but when? He declared this divorce three months ago, and nothing has happened. But here you are putting your life on hold for him when, at this point, there should be no question in his mind. Either he realizes how much of a diamond you are, or some other man will, and I think that man might be Andre. So can we please go back out there and give him another chance before we pull the migraine excuse?"

"Yeah, that's fine."

"Good. And smile more at the table, give the man the eye, or do something to let him know you're at least a little bit interested."

"All right, I will." Before we headed back out, however, my cell phone began to buzz inside my purse. I didn't look at the number because I figured it was Terrence. We hadn't spoken much during the day, and he always called before settling in. "I'll be back out in a second, Monica. I'm going to grab this really quick."

She gave me a look as if she knew it was Terrence and to say not to take long. The minute she walked away, I answered with relief, happy to finally hear his voice. "Hey, you," I said the way we always greeted each other.

"Hey, you, back," the familiar deep voice said.

I was totally stunned that this person was on the other end of my line, and I had no idea at all what to say. For the last three months, I'd wondered how I would react if he ever had the audacity to call. I wasn't sure whether I would curse him out or remain ladylike. But now that it was happening, I was at a complete loss for words. Better yet, the only words that did come to mind were not ones a true lady would be proud of saying.

"Hello? Are you there?" David asked.

"Umm, yes, I'm here."

"I'm sure you're surprised to hear from me."

"Surprised isn't actually the word I would choose, David."

"Tiffany, I just want to apologize for every—"

I cut him off mid-sentence. "Look, first of all I'm out having dinner, so this isn't the best time. Plus, I don't know why you decided to call after all this time anyway, but you can save the apology and anything else you have to say. I'm not in the mood for any of it. I'm in a much better space in my life, and I want to keep it that way. So if you don't mind, please don't dial my number ever again. Have a nice life."

"Tiffany, please, please don't hang up. Just hear me out for a second, please."

"Hear you out? Are you serious?" I threw my hands up in disbelief. "Do you realize how much you messed up my life? And then you had the nerve to send me that text that things were over and not to reach out to you anymore? And now you're asking me to hear you out?"

"Look, I understand I was a jerk and messed up with you big time, but I'm only asking for five minutes of your time. Tiffany, please."

One second of my time would have been way too much to give this man, but I couldn't help but wonder what he could possibly have to say to me after the past three months. "What is it, David? What do you really want? Because I refuse to believe that after all this time you're calling just to apologize."

"Well, it is more than that, but I was hoping we could talk face-to-face rather than over the phone."

Briefly, I pulled the phone from my ear and stared at it in utter disbelief. "You're asking quite a lot for someone who I have no interest or desire in talking to in the first place."

"I know, but please just give me five minutes, and I promise to never bother you again. I promise."

It went far beyond my better judgment, but the curiosity killed me. Not to mention there was a sound in his voice, a sincerity, that almost said he was sorry. Or maybe that was what I wanted to believe. Anyway, if I did agree to seeing him, that could free me up from the rest of the evening with Andre. Monica was right with everything she'd said, but while I was single, I was not in the mood to mingle. With that in mind, I took the opportunity to use David as my scapegoat.

I closed my eyes, took a deep breath, and said, "All right, David, five minutes, and I mean just five. You can come over to my home. I'll text you my address. Hopefully, you can be there within the hour, because if not, don't bother coming at all."

"Of course I can, and thank you, Tiffany. Thank you so much. I promise you won't regret this."

As I hung up the phone, I already regretted my decision. However, I looked at it as finally being able to have the closure I'd longed for. I hurried back to the table and tried not to look Monica directly in the eyes.

"Um, I am so sorry, but I have developed a migraine, and I think I'm going to head home."

"I think I have some pills in my purse that should work just fine for that headache. Why don't you try those first?" Monica asked through gritted teeth.

"I don't think that will be the best idea. I've already had a few sips of wine, so I don't want to mix the pills and alcohol. I'm sure I'll feel much better once I get home and get to sleep."

Monica didn't debate the matter any further. Todd looked as if it didn't matter to him one way or the other, but I could see the disappointment immediately all over Andre's face.

"Would it be all right if I walked you to your car?" he asked like the perfect gentleman.

I figured I could give in just a little. "Yes, that would be good."

We walked out, and I handed my ticket to the valet.

"I hope it was nothing that I did wrong, Tiffany." He looked at me as if to say he knew there was no truth to the whole migraine story.

"No, it wasn't, Andre. I'm just not ready to date right now. I just got out of something a few months ago that didn't end well, and I kind of need some time to myself. It has nothing to do with you."

"Trust me, I totally understand. I've been divorced for the past year now, and it's still a little difficult for me to put myself out there. But I'll tell you what—if that migraine ever lets up and you want to give me a real chance, then I'll definitely be honored to take you out."

"Thank you, Andre." We hugged as the attendant pulled up with my truck. Andre helped me inside before he went back into the restaurant.

I drove home with so much on my mind that I really was developing a migraine. Here I was letting down an amazing guy in Andre. I had my good-for-nothing ex-fiancé on his way to my home. And for the life of me, I couldn't get Terrence out of my head while wondering what he may have been up to in his home . . . all alone.

Chapter 52

Patricia

Terrence had fallen asleep on the living room sofa, something I guessed he'd basically become accustomed to doing since I was no longer there. From the looks of it whenever I stopped by, this had become his living and sleeping quarters instead of our bedroom or the guest room.

Not much had changed between us since the whole ordeal when I kicked over the barbeque pit. Ever since then, I pretty much felt nonexistent to my husband and this marriage. Whenever I came by and he was home, I generally found him in front of his computer screen or the television, or sound asleep. We never said much of anything to one another unless it had something to do with the boys, bills, or the house. There was surely no intimacy between us, no hugs, no kisses, and especially no sex. Things went right back to the way they were before we tried counseling, only this time I was no longer in the home.

On top of that, it seemed he'd been making plans for his life that didn't include me and that I knew nothing about. Recently from his social media, I'd read comments about the soul food café he planned on opening. This more than likely involved Tiffany Tate in some way or another. *He might as well think again. Over my dead body.* I didn't care one way or the other if I was out of this house or if divorce was on the table. I was not about to let him move on with her and live happily ever after.

I hated that he was even still friends with the woman. It was like she had some type of hold on my husband and I was the only one who could see it. He seemed excited whenever he talked about her, and she continued to encourage him to get involved with things that weren't beneficial, such as this restaurant. I also noticed from some pictures he'd posted on Facebook that he even started dressing differently when going to work at the school. It was practically like she was his wife and living my life while I was the woman on the outside looking in. I wouldn't have been surprised either if he had her in my home while I was at my father's. I wanted to scream at the top of my lungs and let it all out, but that would have woken him up.

If only Terrence could see my point of view, which he never did, because it was always about Tiffany. Once when we were able to sit down and have a five-minute discussion without arguing, he said how he always felt I was overreacting or making too much of things. His only conclusion was for me to simply get to know her and everything would be all right. Well, I didn't want to get to know her. I wanted her gone and out of our lives and out of my husband's life for good. I wanted my home back. I wanted my life back. And I damn sure wanted him back completely to myself, which was the very reason I now stood before him in my red silk negligee he used to like so much. I felt it was time to stop going with how things were and start taking matters into my own hands. I wanted my husband. Actually, I needed him and all that he had to offer, and tonight was definitely going to be the night.

I'd snuck in the house wearing nothing but my negligee and a trench coat. Terrence slept like a rock, so I knew exactly how easy it would be getting in without him realizing it. There he was lying peacefully on the sofa with the television watching him instead of him watching it. Before making my move toward him, I looked around, and my eyes caught a glance at his cell phone on the coffee table. We were never the type to go through one another's phones, but this would be my only chance to find out how often he talked to Tiffany and what they actually said to one another over texts. Lucky for me, he had the iPhone feature where the device could be unlocked with the owner's finger instead of just by a passcode. I figured it would be a piece of cake since my husband was a pretty sound sleeper.

After picking up his phone, I slowly and gently picked up his right index finger. Terrence was a leftie, but I prayed that wouldn't make a difference. Cautiously, I touched the phone with his finger, but nothing happened to the screen. His body started to fidget around a bit. I was so afraid to get caught that I put the phone back down and decided to carry on with my initial mission.

My body longed for this moment again with my husband. There was no time like the present. I knelt down next to him and placed a soft kiss on his lips just to get an initial response. Our lips hadn't met in so long that they honestly tasted good to me. I wanted to ease my way into things, but my body was extremely eager to feel his touch. I took his hand and rubbed it against my breasts. My nipples instantly found pleasure in the strength of his hand. I kissed him again and again and again. Finally I made an entrance between his lips for my tongue to find its home. I couldn't contain my enthusiasm when he actually started to kiss me back. He took control as he kissed and sucked on my tongue like it was all that mattered to him.

My clitoris became filled with intense excitement, and if I didn't slow the pace, I would cum before we even started. I wrestled my mouth away from his and kissed him all down his body until my lips made its way to his manhood. He was solid as a rock as I imagined him pounding every last inch of his stick inside me. I couldn't wait to grip the head so that he could experience my moistness. First though, I decided to have a little fun. I grabbed hold of him with my mouth and slid up and down to make it as wet as possible. Although I had never been the best at giving oral pleasure, I remembered when he told me that wetness was the key. I assumed I did the job to the best of my ability when I felt his hands grab the top of my head. I really didn't care for the forceful- ness of how he bobbed my head up and down, but I went along with things anyway. We enjoyed one another im- mensely, and I had just climbed on top and started to feel pleasure when he moaned, "Oh, Tiffany. Don't stop, baby."

Tiffany?

I couldn't believe my ears as he whispered the name that sucked all the life out of me. I was so hurt that all I wanted to do was chop off his manhood and leave him crying for Tiffany right there on the sofa. I was stuck in mid-motion when his eyes finally popped open.

"Patricia, what are you doing here? What the hell are you doing? And why are you dressed like that?"

I didn't know what to say. I watched him closely though. Nothing about his behavior said he apologized for his actions. In fact, he shot me a look like I'd done the ultimate wrong.

"Move out of the way so that I can get up, please. I can't believe you. You shouldn't even be here, but you sneak in and try this? You have really lost it this time. And just in case I need to say it so this will never happen again, I'm not interested in having sex with you ever again."

I looked at my husband and still didn't say a word. There was so much anger, turmoil, and frustration built up inside of me, and I just couldn't find a way to release it all. If only I could express the pain I felt, the entire past three months' and more worth of pain.

As much as I didn't want to hear the answer, I couldn't help myself. I had to ask. "Do you still love me at all, Terrence?"

He didn't answer. Actually, he never looked in my direction. Instead, he pushed me aside, went into our guest bedroom, and shut the door. It was that very moment that I realized I had my answer all along. The very day that Tiffany Tate walked into his life, my husband was no longer mine. All of him belonged to her.

Chapter 53

Terrence

God, please tell me what to do. I'm not trying to hurt anyone.

I shut the door of our guest bedroom and leaned against it. I knew exactly what just took place, and I took no pleasure in it at all. So much had happened between Patricia and me that I didn't feel the desire to be intimate with her, especially not the way a husband and wife should be. I didn't desire her and couldn't force myself to act upon emotions that I didn't feel. And saying Tiffany's name, well, I couldn't explain that either. All I knew was that she consumed every part of me, including my thoughts, and it somehow slipped out.

The human inside of me wanted to go back out there and put my arms around Patricia, talk to her, and explain what I felt inside no matter how raw and grimy it seemed. But knowing her, there was no talking about this. She would never fully understand my point of view. In her mind, I would be a cheater, and that would be the end of it. I needed to talk though. There was so much that I needed to get off my chest, but then I thought, *what would be the point?* Our marriage was over, and there was no escaping that. In fact, I wished it could be all over with tomorrow, but deep down, I also knew it would completely destroy Pat. I wasn't trying to do that though. No matter how much I hated her actions, I didn't want to continually hurt her.

I peeked out the door to see if she was still on the middle level. Lucky for me, it appeared as if she'd either left or gone upstairs. Going back over to the living room sofa, I hurried to pick up my cell phone from the coffee table. I had to talk to the one person who had everything to do with the way I felt. I dialed Tiffany's cell number as if my life depended on it. We'd briefly texted earlier, and she'd already told me that she had no plans for the evening. After a few rings, I received her voicemail.

Damn, Tiff, where are you? Maybe she'd fallen asleep. I figured I'd try her again and would hopefully wake her from a nap. But with no such luck, I got the voicemail once again. "Hey, Tiff, it's me. I know it's getting a little late, but I could really use a listening ear right now. Something went down with me and Patricia again tonight, and I don't feel like being here at the house. I was hoping I could stop by for a bit. I'll go ahead and head your way, but text or call me as soon as you get this."

Seconds later, I inhaled the fresh air when I stepped out of the house to get into my truck. It baffled me how people would say your home was supposed to be your safe haven, your place of comfort, and where you felt the most peace. Well, mine was far from any of that, and I always felt ten times better being away. Before I left, I took a look back at the house and wondered if I ever wanted to return, or if this would be it for me and those I called a family.

Taking another deep breath before pulling away, I saw Patricia watching me from the living room window. I could clearly see the pain and confusion written all over her face, and that confirmed for me that a decision had to be made tonight. Both of us were hurting so much, and in return, we were hurting each other. Something had to be done because there was no way we could go on like this.

After about an hour's drive, I started to become irritated that I still hadn't heard from Tiffany. It was so unlike her, because she usually answered my calls within the first ring or two. I couldn't imagine that she was still napping, because that meant she would be awake most of the night. Before calling her again, I decided to make a stop at the gas station not far from her house. That would give her a little more time to call me back so it wouldn't seem like I just popped up.

I couldn't wait to share with her the decision I'd finally made regarding Patricia and me. If anyone would be in my corner, it would definitely be her. She'd been my best friend, my support, and my encourager throughout this entire ordeal. I even teased that, although she deserved someone special in her life, I hoped she would remain single. Of course, it was selfish of me to think that way, but I couldn't fathom the thought of another man having her full attention. Tiffany was a special woman and needed someone just as special in her life. I only hoped that man could very well be me.

As I grabbed a bag of chips and a soda pop and stood in line to check out, I noticed the guy in front of me looked a little familiar. I couldn't seem to place him, but I'd seen his face before. I decided to tap him on the shoulder to see if he knew me. Maybe we'd gone to school together or something.

"Hey, my man, what's good?" I greeted him.

"Hey, what's up," he said quickly with a nod and turned back around.

"I'm sorry, I didn't mean to bother you, just wondering if we may have gone to high school or college or something together, because you look very familiar."

"Oh, well, I don't know. You don't look very familiar to me, but who knows, maybe we did go to high school together. I never went to college."

"Well, I'm Terrence. Terrence Montgomery. Does my name ring a bell?"

"No, I can't say that it does. It might hit me later though. Anyway, take care of yourself," he said as he stepped to the counter to check out.

I wasn't sure why it continued to bother me, but I really didn't think I knew the guy from school. I checked out my items, played a couple of lottery numbers, and started to walk back to my truck when it finally hit me. "David?"

That was Tiffany's David, who I'd seen on a picture from her Facebook page. "But what are you doing over here?" I sat in my truck with my eyes beamed in on his car. I wasn't sure why, but I had the strangest feeling about him being this close to Tiffany's home. Maybe he'd watched or possibly stalked her even. Thinking of how to handle this, I watched him closely as he pulled out of the gas station lot. He made a turn as if he were headed in Tiffany's direction, but I knew that couldn't be possible. I hurried to start my ignition, and I followed him, keeping a good distance so he wouldn't notice me. My heart pumped faster and faster as I continued to watch him go in the very direction of her home.

"What the hell is going on, Tiff? I know you couldn't be back with him. There's no way." Sure enough, moments later, I watched him pull his car into her driveway and get out. My eyes were glued to his every move as I saw him grab a couple of bags out of the trunk of his car.

"What the hell is he doing? Is he staying here?"

As I watched him ring the bell, I saw a shadow of her come to the door. Without any hesitation, he walked right in, which told me she'd already planned this. I wanted to hop out of my truck and go right up to her front door, but that would make me look crazy. Then I started to call her again, but she wouldn't answer with him being there. The crap just didn't make plausible sense to me after all he'd done to her.

"No, Tiff, damn. What are you thinking? How could you even be entertaining this jokester?"

I sat there in my truck completely clueless. I didn't want to admit it, but I was bothered by it. Just the thought of her being back anywhere near this man made me sick to my stomach. I didn't know whether to be more upset with her for taking him back, with him for playing with her heart, or with myself for believing in her.

Here I was ready to divorce Patricia! Here I was wondering if maybe there could actually be a future with us, and you're back with this jerk? Really, Tiffany?

The next thing I knew, I started my engine and sped off as quickly as I could. Anger burned inside of me as I replayed all our conversations. I'd listened to her all this time as she told me how I deserved true happiness. I believed her when she said Patricia didn't realize the man she had in me. She'd told me that if I ever left this situation, I would make the right woman extremely happy. Foolish of me for thinking that woman might be her. Here I thought we were getting closer when all along she'd still been playing around with this lame fool. I was hurt more than anything and didn't plan on letting her get away with this nonsense.

"Well, if you're going on with your life with him, I guess I have no choice but to go on with mine."

I couldn't drive my truck fast enough heading back in the direction of my house. But I didn't want to be there or with Patricia, either. Tiffany controlled my mind, and no matter how I wanted to rid myself of these feelings, it seemed damn near impossible. My pride was shot and my ego bruised, but I had to find a way to deal with it. The only way I could actually foresee that was removing Tiffany completely from my life. The thought of that alone scared me, but it would be best for everyone involved. She could go on with her life with David, and maybe this was actually my answer with regard to me and Patricia. I'd asked for a clear answer on what to do about my marriage, and I guessed this was it. Patricia and all of her family and friends would be happy. Unfortunately, though, I would be the one missing out on true happiness.

There was only one other place I could think of that would soothe my pain. I quickly stopped at the nearest ATM and withdrew as much money as I could from my account. Then I headed in the direction of the casino, my old home away from home. Nothing would cheer me up more than to win some cash, and I planned to play every nickel I had in order to win big or make this pain go away, whichever came first.

I walked in and immediately inhaled. I hadn't been here in months, and now that I was, I felt like a drug addict about to get a much-needed fix. To my surprise, not much had changed. If I didn't already know for myself, I would swear I'd just been there yesterday. Everything was the same, including some of the people who looked like fixtures. Spotting my favorite dealer at her table, I headed right over. There were only two other men sitting there.

"Hey, Jasmine."

I saw her same pleasant smile immediately cross her face when her eyes met mine. "Aren't you a sight for sore eyes."

"Yeah, I had to take a little break for a while and regroup, but here I am. I'm back."

"Well, I'm glad you're back, and you look great as always."

"Thanks. Now c'mon and deal me in, and let's get this party started," I said, patting the table while hoping this would be my cure for tonight's events.

I thought it would take me a while to get into a real groove, but that wasn't the case at all. Jasmine dealt hand after hand, and each one was a winner. I was slowly beginning to feel better, although I still couldn't seem to pull my thoughts away from Tiffany. I wanted so badly to call her to see if he was still there. Deep down inside, though, I felt that I already knew the answer to that. That nauseated feeling started to kick in again, so I tried harder to focus on my winnings. At least that was until I began to get a whiff of a very familiar scent.

"I missed you," she whispered over my shoulder.

I saw Jasmine look at the woman and frown when I lost my last hand she dealt. On one hand, I hated that I was being distracted, but on the other, I was glad she was there. I could use a familiar face, so I pleasantly welcomed the distraction. Lisa was just as beautiful as I could remember.

"Hey, you."

"It's been quite a while. I thought I would never see you again."

"I needed to take a break. That's all."

No longer interested in the game, but instead focused on Lisa, I asked Jasmine to cash me out. She didn't seem happy at all but granted my request anyway. I'd only won about $250 over what I'd already played, but the night was still young. It didn't matter to me if I was there until sunrise. I had someone to keep my mind away from Tiffany and David.

Lisa and I walked over to the bar, and I ordered us two cocktails each. My eyes scanned up and down her curvaceous body as she sat down. I didn't know what was wrong with me, because any other man would have killed to be in my seat at that moment, but nothing could pull me away from Tiffany.

"How have you been, stranger?"

"I can't complain. How about you? I must say that you are looking gorgeous as usual."

"Why thank you. You're not looking bad yourself. So where have you been? What's kept you away?"

I heard her question, but my eyes were drawn to her full lips. They were so sexy just like Tiffany's. I was actually tempted to kiss them.

"Terrence, did you hear me?" she called out as I downed both of the double scotches I ordered in a matter of seconds.

"Uh, yeah, I heard you," I said, summoning the bartender for another round. "But do we have to talk about me?"

"No, we don't. What would you like to talk about?"

"Why not you and me?"

She gave me an odd look when the bartender brought my third, fourth, and fifth rounds of scotches, but who was counting? All I knew was that my pain was beginning to slowly fade away.

"I'm sorry, Terrence, but don't you think you might be drinking a little too much too fast?"

"Nope. I can handle it," I said as I looked at her. She started to resemble Tiffany more and more. In fact, I couldn't seem to help myself when I slowly reached in and tried to kiss her.

"Terrence, what are you doing? What's going on with you?"

"What do you mean what am I doing? I thought . . . I thought this was what you wanted. I mean, all the flirting and everything we did. Last time you even wanted to come back to my room with me."

"Look, I'm sorry to have given you the wrong impression. I thought that after all this time maybe she came clean, but I guess that's not the case."

I tried my best to snap out of my slightly intoxicated state and listen closely to what she said. However, she had me totally confused. "Lisa, what are you talking about? Who is she?"

"Your wife."

I shook my head in confusion, because no matter how much alcohol I'd consumed, I knew I'd never revealed to Lisa that I was married. And what did Patricia need to come clean about? None of this made any sense to me, and I waited for her to explain.

"Terrence, there's a lot you don't know that you really need to know."

"Okay, well, tell me then. What are you talking about?"

"Well, I hope you don't get upset with me for going along with things, but I'm not just some woman you casually bumped into here. Our meeting one another was actually arranged by Patricia."

"Arranged? By Patricia?"

"Yes. I'm a friend, or at least we were friends at one point. Anyway, she paid me back then to come on to you to see if you would cheat on her. When I told her that you wouldn't accept my advances, she didn't believe me. We actually got into a terrible argument, and she said some very cruel things to me. I called the deal off and haven't spoken to her since. I still came here from time to time hoping to tell you the truth, but it was like you just up and disappeared. It's crazy that I bumped into you tonight."

I couldn't believe my ears as Lisa continued to spill every little detail regarding her interaction with my wife. I was furious, to say the least. Patricia had pulled a lot of stunts during our time together, but this was the icing on the cake. She'd set me up and, once again, proved she couldn't be trusted. I wondered if this was what marriage was really supposed to be about—lies, no trust, calling the police, and setting up your spouse. Was this what I actually signed up for? Was I really supposed to spend the rest of my life like this?

"I'm sorry, Lisa, but I have to go."

I didn't give her the chance to say anything else. I simply threw some cash on the bar and left. I got to my truck and put my head in my hands. Here I was, practically stuck in a miserable marriage with someone I didn't love or trust, while the woman I was in love with had betrayed me with her ex. I was so enraged that I wanted to destroy something or someone.

Actually, I had the right mind to have it out with David. He had to have lied his way back into Tiffany's life, and I wouldn't let him take advantage of her. I also wanted to make him pay for all the hurt and pain he'd caused her in the first place. Starting my truck, I prayed that Tiffany would forgive me and understand that what I was about to do would only be because I loved her.

"I love you, Tiffany, and tonight, I hope you'll realize just how much."

Chapter 54

Tiffany

To my surprise, my meeting with David wasn't so bad after all. I was extremely cautious at first, so much so that I almost called and asked him not to come right before he got here, but something kept telling me that I had to do it. I had to face him and get off my chest everything that I'd held in for the past several months. I also wanted him to see that he hadn't left me a bitter woman. I was better in every way possible despite the foolishness I'd endured.

When he got here, he didn't hesitate to ask me for a hug. I had to think for a second if that was something I wanted to do. People normally hugged when they missed each other or wanted to show love and affection. It was neither for me, yet I decided to go along with the pleasantries for general purposes. I remembered the pastor's sermon on forgiveness and how he'd stated that you don't forgive others for their sake, but instead for your own. That had stayed with me ever since he said it, and as I looked at David, I knew it was time to practice what I'd learned.

I offered him a seat on my living room sofa and then sat in my chair directly across from him. Waiting for him to say something, I watched his eyes dance around as if he were searching for the right words to say. Then I relieved him of his stress and started first. As I spoke, I reminded myself to stay calm, cool, and collected.

"David, I have to admit that I almost feel foolish for even entertaining you after what you did. But I guess in some ways this needed to happen."

"Yes, this did need to happen. I can't begin to tell you how much of a mistake I made with everything."

"Mistake? Really? A mistake? No, honey, a mistake is putting too much sugar in your iced tea or taking a wrong turn when driving or misdialing a phone number. Those are mistakes. What you did was lie, cheat, and manipulate all the women in your life, especially me. So please, since I've given you a small fraction of my time tonight, don't waste it by lying to me and making light of what happened."

He threw both his hands up as if he surrendered. "You know what? You're right. I need to be completely honest. Tiffany, three months ago, I never wanted to get married. There, I said it."

"Then why on earth would you ask me? Why would you have me change my whole life around for nothing more than a pipe dream?"

"I don't know." He shrugged his shoulders as if that answer would suffice.

"See, here you go again with the lies, and since it seems like you don't know how to tell the truth, then you should leave."

"No, no, please. All right, I do know. I guess you could say I just wanted my cake and to eat it, too. I felt like things were going great between us and that we could have had a future together. But you kept talking about marriage, and so I thought I could keep you quiet by simply proposing."

"Oh, okay, so you only wanted to shut me up, huh? But not once did you think about the fact that you would have to make good on your proposal? But wait, there was no way you could actually do that because you were already engaged to the woman you were living with, or should I say your sister? By the way, how is Leslie? Is she still pointing guns at people?"

"Guns? What are talking about?"

"You didn't know I had a gun pointed at my head because you had me living in her house for Christ's sake?"

He put his head down in shame. "I'm so sorry. I had no idea that things went that far. I'm truly sorry, and if I could say it a million times, I would if that meant you would forgive me."

"David, listen, I forgave you long ago. I had to in order to regain my sanity. But forgiving you does not mean I have to entertain you. I allowed this meeting tonight for closure, and that's it. Whatever we had in the past is long gone."

"But you don't understand. I've changed so much, and I realize the mistakes I've made. I was foolish, and I want to make things up to you. If you let me that is. I've really missed you."

As I sat there and listened to David pour out his heart to me, he explained his history with Leslie. He shared with me why he thought it was so hard to settle down. He tried to explain why he lied about his mother being deceased. He even said how he loved me, still did, and would like to start over. I listened to him very closely, but still there were no feelings there as he spoke. All I thought about as I sat through this tale of excuses was having a glass of my wine, reading the next chapter in my book, and Terrence—the things I'd wanted to do before meeting Monica, Todd, and Andre, who'd just shot me a good night text.

Either way, my mind stayed on Terrence as I wondered what he was doing at the very moment and how I couldn't wait to tell him about all this nonsense with David. Of course, he wouldn't be happy that I allowed him to come here, but I hoped he would understand how much I needed this for me and no one else.

I'd missed the last few things that David said when I suggested we call it a night. All the apologies in the world wouldn't make me change my mind on how I felt, so there was no reason to continue. "David, look, I think this was good for the both of us, but the point is what's done is done."

"It doesn't have to be though, Tiff. Like I said, I still love you very much. Can't you at least consider us becoming friends again and starting over and allowing nature to take its course?" he asked, grabbing my hands and holding them.

"I'm not so sure about that. I've moved on," I answered, pulling my hands back to let him know he could forget whatever he had in mind.

"What do you mean you've moved on? With someone else?"

"David—"

"You know what? All right, don't answer that. I have no right to dig into your personal life. All I know is that I haven't moved on, and I want you back in my life. I need you back in it."

I looked at him and didn't know what to say. I thought about how much I cared for him at one point, although I knew for sure I didn't love him. I thought about how I'd spent three whole years with this man and had invested so much time and energy into him. I also knew that people could change, and I wondered if this entire situation brought that change within him.

"I don't know about that. I mean, I don't even trust you the way I once did."

"I know, but as I said, I'm not that same man anymore. I can make you trust me again." He got down on his knees in front of me with puppy dog eyes. "I can make you love me if you just give me a chance. And you don't have to make a decision about all of this tonight, but at least say you'll think about it please?"

I made him get up and we both stood. "Yeah, sure," was all I had left in me to say. I didn't feel like arguing about a decision I'd made months ago. No matter how much he said he changed, I didn't want to waste any more time finding out. David and I were done. He was nothing more than a part of my past, and that was where he would remain regardless of how much he pled his case.

"Hey, before I go, I have some bags for you. Leslie left them at Mrs. Smith's house in case either of us ever decided to come by. It looks like it's all your things." He gave me the bags when we headed to the door. He stood there for a moment staring at me.

"David, what's wrong?"

"You're just as beautiful as ever. That's all. Looking at you now, I can't believe how much of a jerk I've been."

Again, I was at a loss for words. Then he reached in for one final hug. It lasted much longer than the first. As I allowed him to hold me, it made me wonder why I was ever with him. I didn't feel a thing within our embrace, and I still couldn't pull my mind away from Terrence. I finally pulled away from him and we said our goodbyes. I could tell that he may have felt this would be the first encounter of many, but for me, it was definitely our last. From that point on, it would be like I never knew Mr. David Allen.

Now relieved that my time with David was over and done with, I closed my door and locked it behind him. I took the bags he'd given me, peeked inside, and dropped them in the middle of my living room floor as I prepared to take a shower. All I wanted to do was wash away the last hour's existence and then go to bed. Only three months ago, I wished I could have turned the gun on David that Leslie pointed at me. Then I thought about her and her lack of compassion for both of our situations. It was all a huge mess that I was more than happy to be out of. I had to look on the bright side of things though. If all of that nonsense hadn't taken place, I wouldn't have the life I was living now. I wouldn't have my job, my home, or Terrence for that matter.

My mind couldn't escape thoughts of him, and I hated the desires that I had, but they just wouldn't leave no matter how I tried to fight them. I wanted Terrence and only Terrence, not David not Andre nor anyone else for that matter. But then again, I also hated feeling like I was the one possibly destroying his marriage.

I tried to shake all these crazy thoughts as soon as they popped into my mind. Monica was right. As long as Terrence couldn't make some type of decision when it came to me and him, then I had to forget about him and any thoughts of a future with him. No matter what he and his wife went through, the point was he was still married to her, and I had to respect that. Maybe Monica and Keisha were right. I needed to start dating again. That was the only way I could actually let go of these feelings for him.

As I thought about Andre, I shot him a text back saying good night and that we would definitely get together soon. I went back into the living room to set the alarm before I headed to bed. That's when I saw those black bags again. "Wow, poor Leslie. I can only imagine how you feel."

After considering all that David did to me, I never thought about how much she had to be destroyed by his actions too. There she was living with him and planned on marrying this man, only to find he moved another woman into her home. Just the thought of it all was completely absurd. Though I was also a victim of David's deceit and betrayal, it didn't minimize that I aided in Leslie's heartbreak, so I decided that I would do whatever it took to make amends with her for my part in all of this. I hadn't done anything purposefully to her, but I still felt it was only right. There was no reason that either of us should hate one another. Besides, I was grateful that she was kind enough to return my things, and I had to return the gesture in some way.

After I turned off all the lights in the kitchen and living room, I decided to go to bed and read some more. Slipping off my black silk robe, I slid onto my bed. However, instead of Eric Jerome Dickey's book, I took my Bible from my nightstand and turned to Proverbs. It was the book we were studying in our Wednesday night Bible class, and I wanted to be prepared for this week's lesson. I got comfortable and started to read when I was startled by a sudden knock at my door.

"Oh, my goodness, who could this be? Lord, I hope David didn't come back over here," I said aloud as I sat up.

I jumped up, slipped my robe back on, and grabbed the bat that I kept underneath my bed for emergencies such as this. An anxious feeling crept up on me as I walked slowly back into the living room. It was probably only David again, and now I regretted my whole decision of letting him know where I lived. My heart slowed down, and I took a nice deep breath when I finally looked out and saw that it was Terrence who stood there.

Turning off my alarm, I asked, "Terrence?" as I opened the door. "It's late. What are you doing here?" He didn't say anything at all but instead pushed his way inside. I looked at him long and hard, noticing he didn't quite seem like himself. "Is everything all right? Did something happen with Patricia again?"

He still said nothing, but instead pulled me close to him and kissed me. I wanted to pull away so I could understand fully what was going on, but things were too intense. My heart raced at an abnormal rate as I could practically feel the fire burning between us. Finally, he pulled back and stared deep into my eyes. I had no idea what was going on with this man, but there was a sadness, a pain behind his eyes that couldn't be hidden. I held his face in my hands.

"Terrence, tell me what's wrong. What's going on?"

The next thing I knew he picked me up and carried me into my bedroom. I was afraid of the mere thought of what was about to take place, but still I let him lead the way. Terrence slipped my robe off my shoulders, and as it fell to the floor, it exposed my nakedness. I watched him crack a smile as he looked me up and down from head to toe. Then he placed me on the bed and positioned himself on top of me. He still never said a word, and the way he continued to look at me excited every part of my body more and more.

Then Terrence kissed me again. It was unlike any kiss I'd ever experienced with a man before. He kissed me slowly and passionately. At times, he sucked my tongue, showing me how good he was with his mouth. Then he made his way to my breasts, taking in all their fullness, first the left one, then the right, then both, as he kissed and sucked them and even bit my nipples. I squirmed around and tried my best not to orgasm that very second, but Terrence made me want to scream. He kissed his way down between my thighs, and instantly I was reminded of that night in the hotel room. I was in some kind of heaven and thanked the heavens above that this wasn't a dream. I liked it. In fact, I loved it all.

After tasting my sweet goodness, Terrence turned me on my stomach. I was extremely excited with anticipation and couldn't help but wonder what was next when I heard his voice speak.

"Get on your knees and spread your legs."

Those were the very first words from his lips since he'd arrived, and I happily and eagerly did as instructed. I loved the way he took complete control of my body. Terrence pushed my upper torso down toward the bed to put the perfect arch in my back, just the way he wanted it. I wiggled around with pure joy waiting for him to enter me, and when he did, I exhaled with such a loud scream of passion that it assured him he'd hit my spot. My body hit against his with every insertion, and I simply wanted to explode. But then he had yet another surprise in store for me.

This time he turned me back over. "Put your arms around my neck and hold on real tight."

He picked me up by my plump rear, put me against the wall, and had his way with me right there. Our bodies dripped with sweat, but Terrence didn't miss a beat as he hit deep with every stroke. I enjoyed our escapade so much that I'd let the truth of what was happening escape me. He was once again cheating on his wife, and I was sleeping with a married man. Although I surely wanted all that Terrence had to offer, I didn't want it like this. With that, the reality of our actions crashed down on me, and all the pleasurable feelings I was experiencing turned horrific.

"Terrence, stop, please. Please just stop. We can't do this," I said as a single tear fell down my cheek.

He gazed into my eyes in the most perplexed manner, and then wiped away my tears. The house was extremely quiet, but you could still hear the heaviness of our breathing.

As his breathing slowly found its way back to its resting point, he softly said, "I love you, Tiffany."

The tears started to flow freely from my eyes at that point because it reminded of that day when he first said those words to me. I wanted desperately to say it back to him. Hell, I wanted to scream it to the world, but if I had, it would only make matters worse. If he truly loved me, then he would make a decision, and that was it. There was no way I could continue to be intimate with him while he was married to another woman.

"Terrence, this should not have happened," I said as I started to pace back and forth. He only continued to look at me in a confused state. "Would you say something, please? Tell me why you did this."

He grabbed my arm and pulled my body close to his again. Terrence held me as tight as he could, and although I was afraid of going even further than we already had, I didn't want to let go.

"Tiffany, I love you," he said again.

I pulled away from him and freed myself from all my inhibitions. This would be the first time in my life that I was totally and completely vulnerable to anyone. I couldn't hold back my feelings any longer.

"Terrence, I love you too, you know that. But the truth is I love myself more than this. I told you that I've been there and done the whole married man thing before, and that's no longer where I am in my life. I realized how wrong it was, and I don't want karma coming back on me in that way. I don't want another woman's blessing. I feel like I deserve so much more than that. I want a man who's going to love and adore me and only me. I believe I'm worth that much. So the fact that you haven't started your divorce says it for me, and this can never happen again."

He looked away and then started to pick up his clothes from the floor and put them back on. I didn't know if he'd heard me, understood me, or what because he still didn't say anything. After getting dressed, he walked back to the front door while I followed right behind him, grasping for anything that he was willing to give.

"Terrence, say something . . . please."

He opened the door, turned around, and gently kissed my lips. "Thank you, Tiffany. For the first time in the longest time, everything seems perfectly clear to me. I know now what needs to be done."

That was all he said before he turned to walk out my door. I had no idea on earth what he meant or what that meant for him and me. All I was sure of was that things could never go back to what they were between us after tonight. The thought of that alone frightened me even more. There was no way I could look at him day in and day out when I knew how we felt for one another, and then have to watch him go back to her. I had to remove myself completely from this equation for both our good, no matter how much it hurt.

Chapter 55

Patricia

I'd glanced over at my clock a couple of times already to look at the time. Last night after Terrence left, I had a strange feeling that he wasn't going to return, so I decided to stay the night in my house, in my bed. I couldn't help but wonder where he might be. Actually, I had a gut feeling that he more than likely ran to her. My stomach was in knots from trying to think of what to do. Although I could see from the look in his eyes when he left that our marriage was completely over, I still didn't want it to be. Maybe I had a horrible way of showing it, but I loved my husband and couldn't imagine life without him. I also wasn't about to let him run off and be happy with her. There was no way I would ever allow that to happen.

Lying there in our bed, I took in his scent from his pillow. Finally, I decided to do the one thing that had never crossed my mind. I got out of bed, got down on my knees, and prayed to God to heal my marriage. I told God how I vowed to stay with Terrence for better or for worse, and I meant it. After my prayer, I got back into the bed and decided I would do what I hadn't done. I would give him the space that he needed to think things through. I wouldn't call or text or demand to know his whereabouts. And I surely wouldn't pop up here at the house anymore half dressed. Instead, I would wait for him to come to his senses and choose his wife and children again.

Chapter 56

Tiffany

I hadn't slept a wink the rest of the night when I finally got up to face my decision. Deep down it wasn't what I wanted, but I knew it was what had to be done. All things considered, after Terrence left, I immediately called Keisha. I hated waking her at that hour, but she was the only one I could turn to. At first I wasn't sure if the girl heard anything I'd said from being in and out of her sleep. But then I realized she woke up the minute I told her what happened between me and Terrence last night.

"What? It finally happened, huh? Girl, how was it?"

I realized from her reaction that I'd never disclosed to her our night at the hotel. Maybe that was because we'd both vowed that what happened would remain there. But this time, I needed to confide in my best friend. "Keisha, now you know I'm not going to discuss the details, and what do you mean, 'finally happened'? You act like this is something you've been waiting for."

"Girl, are you serious? From what you've shared with me, it sounds like you two are crazy over each other, so it was bound to happen eventually, that's all."

"Well, I never planned on this happening over and over again while he's still married to her, and now I have no other choice but to—"

"But to what?" she cut me off.

"Keisha, this was a huge, huge mistake. There's no way I can be here after this."

"Wait, so you're questioning the whole life you're building there because you finally had sex with the man you love? Oh, and the man loves you back? Are you for real?"

"He's a married man. You know I already did that with Chris for way too many years of my life. I don't want another situation like that, and I won't play second to any other woman, not at this point in my life."

"Look, this seems different to me from what happened with Chris. I mean, Terrence is married, but something makes me feel like the two of you really belong together. Haven't you been the one telling me that you just never know what the future holds? What if this is the love you've been waiting for all your life? What if this was the entire reason you moved to Texas in the first place, to meet him?"

"All of that sounds great, and I probably believed that myself once, but the point is that the man hasn't made a single step toward getting divorced. Besides, the more I think about it, God is not going to give me someone else's husband."

"But what if God wasn't the one who brought them together in the first place," she mumbled under her breath.

"What did you say?"

"Nothing, girl. Nothing at all."

Keisha felt I was making the biggest mistake of my life, but she finally backed down and didn't pressure me any further. I assumed she could hear the pain in my voice with how distraught I was and simply wanted to be my friend.

"I just need to come back for a little while to clear my mind. So if you don't mind, I need to stay at the house with you."

"Now you know you don't need to ask me that. If it's up to me, you never have to leave."

"Thank you. But I promise I won't be there long. I'm going to clear my head and put a little distance between Terrence and me so that we can both put things back into perspective. Anyway, I love you, girl."

"Hey, I got you. You're my sis for life."

After I received the green light from Keisha, we hung up so I could begin my plans for leaving Texas for a little while. It amazed me how much she'd changed over these past few months. When I first relocated, she was the one rooting for me and David, although she wasn't fully happy about the move itself. Now she was completely in Terrence's corner. I heard her when she said that we belonged together, and even if I agreed with that, I wasn't sure it could happen. That would ultimately mean I'd destroyed another woman's family. The more I thought about things, I couldn't do that, especially not with my desire for a husband and family of my own one day. Keisha seemed to think that Patricia was the one who destroyed her own family. If that was true, only time would tell. For now, I knew exactly what I had to do.

Next, I shot Monica a text and asked to meet with her before school started. She wouldn't be happy about this, but I at least hoped she would understand. Shortly after, I sat in her office fidgeting around as I waited for her to finish a phone call with Todd.

"Okay, girl, I'm sorry about that. Todd isn't feeling well today, and you know how men can act like big babies when they're sick. But anyway, what's up with you? What's so important? And did you happen to speak with Andre anymore last night after leaving?"

"We sent good night texts to one another, but that was it. But, Monica, I'm here because I just wanted to thank you for not only being an amazing boss but also an even better friend. I can't thank you enough for everything you've done for me."

"Oh, well, you are more than welcome, Tiffany, but why are you talking like you're leaving or something?"

I didn't say anything at first, but then the words spilled out at a hundred miles per hour. "I need to take a leave of absence for a little while. I'm going back home to St. Louis."

She came from behind her desk and sat on the edge of it directly in front of me. "What is this about? Is everything all right? What's going on?"

I had no idea it would be this difficult, and I couldn't look directly into her eyes. Instead, I kept my head down. "It's just what I need to do for the good of everyone involved right now."

"What does that mean? Is there something you're not telling me? You can talk to me, Tiff."

"I know, but I can't talk about it right now. I promise to call and tell you everything when I make it back to St. Louis. Please believe me, though, that this is for the best right now."

"I don't understand, especially since I thought things were going extremely well for you here in Texas, but I guess I have to accept your decision. Only you know what's truly best for you. And if you need to hear me say it, your position will be waiting for you whenever you return."

"Thank you, Monica," I struggled to get out, although I had no idea when I planned on returning. The only thing I did know at the moment was that it wouldn't be anytime soon.

"Before you go, can we pray together?" She stood up, taking my hands in hers without actually giving me a chance to answer.

My eyes were so filled with tears when we both hung our heads and Monica began to pray. That was what I would miss most about her. She always encouraged me and had a prayer ready at any given moment. It was then that I realized how blessed I was and that I had the best of both worlds when it came to my friends. Keisha was my hood, ride-or-die type of friend while Monica was my refined, spiritual type of friend. I loved and needed them both in different ways, and I thanked God for them.

When Monica finished praying, she hugged me as tight as she could. She whispered in my ear that she loved me, and I told her the same. I walked out of her office and headed toward Terrence's. Luckily, I had the key, so I didn't need security to let me in. As I looked around the room, every conversation, every laugh, every hug we'd shared played in my mind.

I'd written Terrence a letter that I needed him to have before I left. I walked over to his desk and was immediately struck by his wedding band lying right there. That was the final confirmation I needed that what I was doing was right for us all. Feeling as if I were about to burst at any second, I placed the letter on his desk, said my goodbye, and quickly left.

Chapter 57

Terrence

After leaving Tiffany's, I knew exactly what had to take place. There was no more dragging my feet with this or asking myself should I or shouldn't I stay or go. I now had a clear decision and direction regarding my life, no matter who was hurt in the end.

When I arrived home, I found it strange seeing Patricia's car still there. I was sure she would have gone back to her father's by now. But since she hadn't, this was the perfect time for me to say what I needed to say.

I'd decided to go upstairs and sit in the chair in our bedroom. Patricia was sound asleep in our king-sized bed and never heard me come in, but I wanted to be there the minute she woke up. I knew I probably shouldn't say everything I had on my mind, but after what Lisa told me, I had very little care or concern for Patricia's feelings.

I kept a close eye on her as she tossed and turned in the bed. I wondered if she was having a bad dream. If so, it served her devious ass right. A second later, when she snapped her eyes open as if she'd been scared straight, I was right there, watching her every move. Looking at her made me wonder what I ever saw in this woman in the first place. She rubbed her eyes and then jumped out of her skin when she looked over at me as if she'd seen a ghost.

"Terrence, what are you doing?" She grabbed her chest. "You damn near scared the living daylights out of me."

"Good morning, Patricia," I said in a very calm and monotone voice. "I'm not sure why you're here, but I hope you had your last good night's sleep in that bed."

"I'm here because despite what happened last night, this is still my home too, and I can sleep here if I want.

I ignored her words and continued with my mission. "We need to talk."

She got out of the bed and moved around the room as if I hadn't said anything.

"Did you hear me? We need to talk."

"Yeah, I heard you," she responded nonchalantly, like she couldn't care less about what I said.

She moved from the bedroom to our master bathroom going about her normal morning ritual. I calmly sat right there and continued to speak because I knew she could still hear every single word. She could try to ignore me all she wanted, but I had just the thing to say that would get her full attention. The minute she walked back into the bedroom with her toothbrush dangling from her mouth, I said it.

"Patricia, I've put this divorce off long enough, trying to spare your feelings. It's time that I move forward with this, so we need to talk about the house, kids, finances, and everything else."

It all came out matter-of-factly, and I watched her as she stopped dead in her tracks and turned to face me. I knew then that she'd heard me loud and clear.

"What did you just say?"

I looked her directly in her eyes and repeated myself loudly and firmly. "I'm moving forward with the divorce, and it shouldn't take long because the house is going into foreclosure and the boys are not biologically mine. Everything should be cut and dried."

She began to laugh hysterically as if I'd told some amazing joke. "Cut and dried, huh?"

"Yes, and I'm absolutely serious. I don't think I've ever been so serious about anything in my entire life."

"So you really plan on following through with a divorce? You actually think I'm about to allow some other woman to step in and destroy my family?"

"What are you talking about?"

"You know good and well what I'm talking about. Ever since you met that coworker of yours, she's had your nose wide open. I've dealt with you coming home talking about her and that damn soul food restaurant she's hyping you up about. I've put up with you going out to dinner with her and your boss. And if you can remember, you even called out her damn name while inside of my mouth. I put up with it all, Terrence. But what I won't let happen is for that woman to completely destroy my family and home."

"Tiffany is not the issue here. If you want to see who has destroyed this marriage, then you need to take a good look in the mirror."

"Here you go blaming everything on me as usual when I've done nothing but try to love you. I've had my father call, my friends, even the pastor, and you didn't respond to me or anyone—only that woman."

"Wait, did you really say that you've tried to love me? Do you actually call this love? How can you say you love me when you don't even trust me? You always accuse me of cheating, you hacked my social media accounts, you called the police on me, and to top everything off, I just found out that you paid Lisa to set me up. Yeah, paid her with my money, not yours."

Her eyes darted around at the sound of Lisa's name, and she didn't open her mouth to say a word. Not one peep.

"Yeah, I guess you never thought I would find out about your dealings with Lisa, huh?"

She sighed and waved me off with her hand. "I don't care that you know. I did exactly what I had to do at that moment to find out what was going on with you, because you sure wouldn't tell me. That should show you the lengths I would go to for you. That should show you how much I love you."

"You know what? The sad part is that you honestly believe what you're saying right now."

She looked away almost in shame.

"Listen, I'm sorry to say this, Pat, but I don't love you. At least not in the way I should as your husband. I truly believe you are a good person. I even believe you would make a wonderful wife to the right man. But you and I, we're just not good for each other. That's as clear as I can make it. And I'm not trying to hurt you, but I refuse to live the second half of my life unhappily. I'm just not happy. I haven't been for quite a long time."

She went back to her routine still as if I hadn't said anything.

"I know you heard me. And just so you'll know, I'm having my attorney draw up the paperwork in the morning. This way there won't be any surprises when you're served."

"Do what you must, but just so *you* know, I'm not signing anything. If you press the issue, then I'll have no choice but to make this divorce a living hell for you. You will pay me every single penny I'm worth. My children and I have gotten used to a certain lifestyle, and it's going to stay that way. So it's your choice—either her or your family."

I paid no attention to Patricia's threats, and I didn't plan on changing my mind. This divorce would happen whether she liked it or not.

She went back into the bathroom and I started to get ready for the day. A moment later, I noticed that a text had come through on my cell phone. It was Monica asking me to call her as soon as possible. I had no idea what she could want, but if she was contacting me this early, then it had to be something urgent.

I dialed her number, and she picked up immediately. "Hey, Monica, what's up?"

"What's up is I need someone to explain to me what's going on."

"What are you talking about? What's going on with what?" I questioned her.

"Coach, are you really trying to act as if you have absolutely no idea what I'm referring to?"

"If I did, then I wouldn't be asking. Now what's up? What's so urgent?"

"It's Tiffany. She's gone. You didn't know?"

There was no way I could have heard her correctly. My heart began to feel like it pounded straight through my chest. I didn't know exactly what she meant by "gone," and I hesitated in asking her, fearing what might come from her lips. I spoke slowly. "Please try to calm down and tell me exactly what you are talking about."

"All right. Well, first she texted me early this morning and asked if we could meet before school. When she got here, she didn't seem like herself. Then out of nowhere, she told me she needed to take a leave of absence, saying something about going back to St. Louis for a little while to clear her head. She wouldn't go into details as to why though."

My mind went back to last night. She was distraught over what took place between us, but never did I think she would just up and leave. I didn't know whether to be more upset or hurt by this news. I also thought I'd made myself clear that I finally knew exactly what I needed to do for both of us. That was when I recalled my exact words.

"Damn, maybe I was a bit vague," I said aloud.

"Vague about what, Coach? What are you talking about?"

Before I answered her, I suddenly remembered David. Last night before I arrived at her house, I had every intention to catch him, and I planned on making it absolutely clear to him that he was not welcome in her home or better yet her life. But once I got there, my focus was no longer on him. I remembered her standing there in the doorway in a black silk robe. She looked beautiful, innocent, and pure even. I had to be with her at that moment, and any thoughts of David were totally dismissed from my mind. But now I wondered if he'd played a part in her decision to leave. What was he doing at her house in the first place? Was she now torn between me and him? I needed answers, but I could only get them from one person.

"Monica, I'll try to explain everything later. Did she happen to say when she was leaving?"

"Not outright, but I assumed it would be immediate. She even gave me her keys and asked me to keep an eye on the house. Please tell me what's going on. Tiffany has become a dear friend to me, not just my employee. If something happened, then I would really like to know."

"Look, I can't get into it now, but I promise to call you back and explain later."

I hung up without giving her a chance to ask any more questions. I had to get to Tiffany before she headed back to St. Louis. Grabbing my keys, I ran out of the house as if my whole life depended on it. I drove as fast as I could while I dialed her cell phone over and over again, only to continually receive her voicemail.

"Dammit, Tiff!" I yelled, pounding the steering wheel with my fist.

If only she would talk to me and give me the opportunity to fix things. I called a few more times but received the same outcome. I drove in complete silence while I prayed to myself that I could stop her. She had become such a huge part of me. She was everything I could have hoped for or imagined in a woman. She had become my support, my confidante, and overall my best friend. I needed her and simply couldn't picture my life without her in it.

Moments later, I slowly pulled up to her home. Tiffany's truck was nowhere in sight. I hoped that maybe it was parked in the garage. I hopped out of my truck without even stopping it completely and ran up the driveway.

"Sir. Sir," her neighbor called out to me. "There's nobody home."

I stopped dead in my tracks and turned to face him. "What do you mean nobody's home?" I asked, knowing exactly what he meant.

"The owner is gone, sir. Taking a little trip back home was all she told me. I told her I'd watch the house until she returned."

There was that word again—gone. My heart sank as his words hit me like a ton of bricks. I didn't even know what to do at that point. I thought about going to St. Louis after her, but I wouldn't even know the first place to find her. She still hadn't answered her cell phone either. It seemed like in a matter of a few hours, Tiffany was out of my life just as quickly as she walked into it.

With the wind knocked out of me, I took a seat on the porch. I was sick about it and couldn't seem to force myself to leave. Then I figured I would head over to the school and hit the gym until it was time for the boys' practice. That way I could take out my frustration on the field.

That was until I saw him pull up.

Any pain I felt suddenly turned to rage, and all I could see was red in front of me. My eyes watched as he parked his car and got out of it, strutting as if he belonged there. His eyes caught mine, and I couldn't fully seem to remember what happened from that point on.

I wasn't quite sure how much time passed or exactly what transpired. When I partially came to my senses, I had David hemmed up by his collar against his car as the neighbor and two other gentlemen tried to pull me off him.

"Get off me," he yelled over and over. "What the hell is wrong with you?"

I didn't even know myself what was wrong with me. All I knew was that I needed someone to pay for Tiffany being gone, and he happened to be the opportune person.

"I said get off," he yelled once again.

Her neighbor yanked me off, and you could practically see the anger as it flowed through the both of us.

"What the hell are you doing here?" I shouted as I watched him standing there and trying to gather his composure while he smoothed his clothing. We stared each other down as I wondered what Tiffany ever saw in this guy in the first place.

"Wait a minute, you're that guy from the gas station last night. What the hell are you doing, stalking me or something?" David asked accusingly.

"All you need to know is that I'm a close friend of Tiffany's and it would be in your best interest to stay far away from her."

"Oh, really? Says who?"

"Yes, really. Says me," I shouted, walking toward him again.

The way I felt, if her neighbors weren't there, I would have torn him apart limb by limb. And I thought he knew it, too, because I could see the fear in his eyes as they danced around. I literally wanted to put my hands around the man's neck for what he'd done, but I tried to let my guard down and back away.

"Look, I don't know what's up with you, but I didn't come over here to be harassed or threatened. I'm here for Tiffany."

At that point, it dawned on me that he had no knowledge that she'd left. That in itself made me feel like I had some type of advantage over him, because I knew her whereabouts and he didn't.

"Where is she anyway?" he questioned.

"She's gone," was all that I offered up. I wasn't about to tell him where, when, why, or any of that. I simply left him standing right there. Besides that, I didn't want to focus any more energy on him. I wanted to go over to the school. I needed to speak with Monica and try to get to the bottom of things.

Chapter 58

Terrence

An hour later, after crawling through Texas traffic, I finally sat in Monica's office trying to explain everything that happened last night.

"You're really trying to tell me that she had David at her home last night, and he had overnight bags?"

"Monica, I wouldn't have believed it myself if I hadn't seen it with my own eyes."

She stood from behind her desk and began to walk around her office. "Maybe that was why she was so persistent about leaving the restaurant last night," she said out loud. "But I wonder what would possibly make her let him back into her life."

"I've been beating myself in the head trying to figure that out too. Especially after seeing how bold and care-free he was with stopping by today. But you were with Tiffany last night?"

"We only grabbed a bite to eat. But there has to be some reasonable explanation for all of this, especially if David is involved. I just wish she had talked to me or you first."

"Yeah, me too."

"How are you doing?"

"Not great. I have my issues at home, and now all of this. And in some ways, I feel like a lot of this is my fault. At least, her leaving is."

"Now you can't go blaming yourself."

"Yes, I can, and I do. See, there's a lot you don't know."

I didn't want to outright share my and Tiffany's intimate details. However, I needed someone neutral to confide in. I was positive that Monica would be the perfect person. Besides, she was already so invested in both of us. Monica and I immediately became friends when I started working here. I'd already shared so much with her regarding my marriage. Plus, she and Tiffany had become close as well. It made sense to talk to her.

"As I told you, I went over there to share something that happened between Patricia and me, and that's when I saw David. I got so upset that I left and ended up at the casino. That's when I found out more disturbing news about Patricia. And well, somehow I found my way back at Tiffany's. Initially, I went back to have it out with him and tell him to stay away from her, but that time he wasn't there. That's when I invited myself into her home . . . and into her bed."

The shocked and unpleased expression on her face told me that she was not only surprised by my actions but disappointed in them as well. "It wasn't right, but I also thought it was what both of us wanted. Anyway, she became extremely paranoid about it happening because I'm still married and haven't gotten divorced yet. That's where things must have gotten complicated for her. But I never thought she'd go to this extreme, especially because I tried to assure her that now I know what needs to happen."

Monica placed her hands on her hips with her head tilted to the side. "Really? And what's that, Coach? Because I can't blame her for feeling uneasy about all of this. As much as I know what a good guy you are, you're still a legally married man, and that's not fair to her."

I got up, walked over to her picture window, and looked out almost as if I were searching for Tiffany as my heart longed for her. "Monica, I know that I've been unfair, actually to Tiffany and Patricia both. That's why this morning I told Pat I'm moving full steam ahead with the divorce process. I've already made a call to my lawyer to get things rolling."

Once again shock filled her voice. "You're kidding. Are you serious? Are you really sure this time? I mean, you've mentioned divorce before, but you've never gone through with it."

"This time is different. It finally hit me that there's no possible way I can keep on in this charade of a marriage. I refuse to live out the second half of my life like this."

"Well, I can't say I don't agree with you, but I guess I'm only trying to make sure it's what you want and what's best for everyone involved. Divorce is a huge decision and shouldn't be taken lightly or made because someone else is in the picture."

"You're right. But staying in a marriage that I'm not happy in or that does more harm than good is not right either. And believe me, I've tried to hang in there and stick it out. I tried the whole counseling thing. I've tried it all, you know that."

"I'm going to ask you something that I never asked before. Did you pray about your marriage?"

I took a deep breath in and exhaled before I answered as best I could. "Monica, you know I believe in God, and I know the power of prayer. I also know that God honors marriage. But in all realness, what if He wasn't the one that brought me and Patricia together? What if this was all our doing for all the wrong reasons? Do I still pray and ask Him to keep us in something that was doomed from the start? When I don't love her?"

She put her hands up. "Hey, don't beat me up about this. I'm only playing devil's advocate and making sure you've exhausted all of your options."

"In my heart and soul, I have. This is something I've been torn over for a long time. But it's like last night everything suddenly came clear for me."

"Because of Tiffany?"

"In some ways, yes. She was not the reason for my decision though. When I found out that Patricia actually paid someone to seduce me in order to catch me cheating, well, that was basically the final straw. There's no love, trust, or honesty between us if she could do something like that. There's nothing that this marriage is built on except for lies and deceit on her behalf. And don't get me wrong, I'm not placing all the blame on her. There's probably a lot I could have done differently, like made her feel more secure for one, but I can't put my all into something that my heart is not in."

"What did she have to say?"

"She's upset of course. She even threatened to fight me tooth and nail on this, but I don't care. I just want out."

"I won't say I'm not happy about your decision. I've told you before that I think your wife has insecurities that you can't fix. And you're right. No one should live their life in misery. My only question now is, what does this mean for you and Tiffany?"

"You know, the funny thing is, had you asked me this last night, you would have had a completely different answer. At this point though, nothing. She's gone, and neither of us knows when she's coming back. I have no way of reaching her, and she's not answering my calls. So what am I supposed to do? Then there's this whole thing with David that I still don't understand. I feel like maybe it wasn't meant for her and me to be together."

"Well, I don't know if that's true, but I still think there's more to this thing with David and her sudden leaving than either of us know. I'm sure she'll contact me though, and I could—"

I cut her off before she finished because I knew exactly where she was headed. However, I'd already made my decision. Tiffany had walked away from me without a word. She'd allowed someone back into her life who was nothing less than toxic. I couldn't handle that. I needed to give up any hopes of being with her. Maybe we both needed time away from one another. With that in mind, my only priority was to get this divorce over with as quickly and painlessly as possible and somehow find peace again.

"No, Monica. I appreciate it, but I think I need to be alone for a while."

She walked over to me and looked me in the eyes. "All I'm saying is please do not let true love slip by. Sometimes people on the outside can see things better than those inside the situation. I strongly feel that you and Tiffany both are running from the truth instead of to one another, where you both want to be. But I'll stay out of this until you want me involved. Just know that I'm here in whatever way you need me."

I hugged Monica long and tight. I was thankful for her friendship and all that she'd offered me over time. I also agreed with her. Tiffany and I were running from the truth. I was in love with her, and I knew she loved me. Yet I was also beginning to see that sometimes love just wasn't enough.

I left Monica's office and headed to mine. Going straight to my desk, I saw my wedding ring lying there. Before I knew it, tears crept down my face. I'd never been one to cry, but I couldn't seem to help myself. I felt like a failure once again knowing I was about to go through another long, drawn-out divorce process.

Then, as I stood there, I noticed a small white envelope sitting on the desk beside my ring. It was in her handwriting with my name on the front. Part of me wanted to rip it open to see if she left me an address or something where I could find her, but then I also didn't want to be let down if she hadn't. She could very well be saying that she decided to give David another chance. I wasn't in the mood for any more disappointment. So I put the envelope in my pocket and left. I hadn't made up my mind if or when I ever planned to read it.

Chapter 59

David

Things couldn't have been going worse for me, and now on top of that, I had to deal with some maniac who had his eyes set on Tiffany. Who did he think he was anyway to come at me like at? If I hadn't been fearful of catching some type of criminal charges, I would have surely beat the jerk to a point where he wouldn't have been able to recognize himself. With my blood still boiling, I got in my car and started dialing Tiffany's number.

"Dammit. Voicemail. What the hell am I supposed to do now?"

When I left Tiffany's house last night and got back to Sonya's, she'd locked both her front and back screen doors so that I was unable to get in. I'd called her over and over again on both her cell and house phones only to receive her voicemail message on both. I even thought about trying to break in through one of her bedroom windows but decided against it. I knew she was still upset with me for suggesting an abortion. Since I was already down on my luck, I didn't want to find myself arrested and hauled to jail for breaking and entering. With no other choice for the night, I decided to keep my car parked in her driveway and sleep there. I laid my seat back in my car, closed my eyes, and tried to think of a surefire plan to get Tiffany back once I found her. She was my only hope now.

First, however, I planned to attempt to talk with Sonya again once daylight hit. If I could somehow talk her into terminating this pregnancy, then we could both call it fair and go our separate ways. Things didn't go as planned, though, when I woke up to someone banging a flashlight on my car window.

"Excuse me, sir, excuse me."

Peeking out of the corner of one eye while the other was still shut, all I could see was a man in blue waving a damn flashlight around. What the hell were the police doing here? I slowly let my window down while I kept my other hand in view. I didn't want any unforeseen problems to arise.

"Uh, hello, Officer. How can I help you?"

"May I see your driver's license and registration, sir?"

Without asking him what I'd done, I went ahead and gave him what he'd asked for. It took a little while, but he finally came back to my car after running my name.

"Sir, we got a call from the owner of the house that someone was trespassing on her property. I'm going to have to ask you to leave the premises immediately."

"Trespassing? She's damn near my baby momma," I yelled.

"Sir, I don't know the extent of your relationship. All I know is that the owner says this is her home and that you are trespassing on her property. So unless you can show some sort of paperwork that says you reside here too, I'm going to have to ask you again to leave."

"Yeah, yeah, all right. I hear you, Officer."

He gave me back my license and registration. *This heffa had the audacity to call the damn police on me?* He sat there and watched as I started my car and pulled out of her driveway. She must have been watching too, because the second I pulled off, she had the nerve to text me to never show up at her house again. She also threatened that I'd better reconsider getting a job because I would have child support to pay for the next twenty-one years.

Sonya had to be insane if she actually thought that was going to happen though. I could have knocked her door down and strangled the life out of her, but I decided to take a different tack. To my surprise, when the officer asked for my identification, I came across her debit card in my wallet. She must have forgotten that she gave it to me last week when I needed some gas in my car, because I surely did until now. She'd given me the PIN and everything, so I figured I'd actually give her a reason to call the police on me.

First I stopped by the bank and withdrew some of the cash to have as pocket change. Then, after filling my tank up and grabbing a bite to eat, I really set my thoughts more on thinking of the best way to win Tiffany back. She was my only hope now of all three women I'd dealt with because she was the only one who might have an ounce of compassion for me. At least, I hoped that would be true. It might be if I came up with the best plan. And now with close to $50,000 from Sonya's checking account at my disposal, that wouldn't be hard to do.

All I needed to do was play Tiffany's emotional side to my advantage and have her let down her guard with me. I had already played the pitiful "woe is me" hand last night, but she had been a lot stronger than I'd thought she'd be. As I sat at the red light in front of me, it finally hit me smack dab in the face. I could tell her I was sick and battling some deadly disease. That way, I was sure to win her over and get back into her good graces. She would feel so sorry for me and would probably break her neck to do everything in her power to help me. Then I would tell her that my only dying wish was to spend the rest of my life with her. I knew in my gut that she would forget about every single thing that happened and take me back then. That was my entire plan. Now all I had to do was find her.

How the hell could you just up and leave, and where did you go, Tiffany?

All types of things began to run through my mind, but something told me for sure that this Terrence guy had something to do with her decision. Maybe she was moving in with him. I dismissed that theory, though, because something told me he didn't know any more about her whereabouts than I did. Then St. Louis crossed my mind, but I couldn't imagine her doing that either with all the progress she'd made here, especially now that she had a home. I didn't know what to think, but I had to find her. If hunting her down to express my undying love for her didn't make me seem totally sincere and committed this time around, I didn't know what would.

Once again, I began dialing Tiffany's phone over and over, but it didn't even ring. It went straight to voicemail each time, so I knew she'd turned it off. I thought about calling her best friend, Keisha, but Tiffany more than likely had told her everything that'd happened between us, and she wouldn't have anything to do with me either. With nowhere else to go until I located Tiffany, I decided to use Sonya's card some more.

I went to a top-notch hotel and paid for a suite for the next few days. That would give me more than enough time to wipe out Sonya's account, try to find Tiffany, and begin my mission to win her back. I could picture it all, especially the look on that punk's face when he found out that we were back together. That would serve him right for ever putting his damn hands on me.

One Month Later

Chapter 60

Patricia

One whole month later, he still hadn't attempted to call off this foolishness of a divorce. I'd come here to the house and started throwing the rest of my clothing in a suitcase piece by piece. Terrence had been living here, and I'd been in and out since both of our names were on this house and the divorce wasn't final yet. Actually, it hadn't even begun because I refused to sign the papers. I just knew that he would eventually come to his senses by calling this whole thing off and trying to fix our marriage. But I'd forgotten how stubborn my husband could be. Whenever he set his mind to something, he always prepared himself to see it all the way through. That was why I came by this morning and decided it was finally time to take a different approach. I was tired of playing the nice wife.

I still didn't plan on signing any papers, but I would give him a taste of how miserable he would be without me. All of the utilities were still on in the house because of me since everything was in my name. Well, once I got the rest of my and the boys' things out of this house, I was having everything shut off. If he wanted to live the single life, he was going to be single and broke. Little did he know I'd been checking our joint bank account, which didn't have anywhere near what it had before, and I was about to wipe that out, too. Not to mention, more letters regarding foreclosure had been piling up inside the mailbox. I'd been making a point to come by and get the letters out of the box without bothering to tell him about them. If he was dead set on this divorce, then I was surely about to give him a run for his money.

"What are doing?" he asked, walking into the bedroom like it was all his territory and not mine.

"I'm packing. What does it look like I'm doing?"

"Are you going on a trip somewhere?"

"No."

"So where are you headed?"

"Look, why all the questioning? Me and the boys don't live here anymore, so there's no point in any of our belongings being here either. Why are you acting so concerned now?"

"I was only asking."

"Well, if I need to say it, you will have the house all to yourself now. I won't be in and out any more like I have been."

"Pat, you really don't have to leave. I can go ahead and find somewhere to stay, and you and the boys can move back in. I mean, I know how cramped you all must be at your father's place."

"Like you really care. Anyway, I'm doing what's best for everyone involved. Oh, and you can even go ahead and move your little girlfriend in here, too, if you like."

"I've told you a million times that I don't have a girlfriend. And I don't see why we aren't able to sit down like two adults and decide how to split our belongings."

"No, we're not going to split our belongings. If this is what you truly want, then I'm telling you now that you'd better be more than prepared to purchase a home twice this size. Besides, there's no way I could ever stay here. There are far too many memories."

"All right then, why don't we just let the courts decide all the details instead? I see now that there's no sense in trying to be reasonable with you. But just so you know, this divorce really doesn't have to be an ugly one unless you make it that way."

I turned up my nose because he continued to talk as if he were sure I would allow the divorce to happen.

"Anyway, I didn't come up here for all of that. I wanted to tell you that I'm going away for a couple of days. My pops is sick. Actually, he is very sick. He's in ICU, and it's not looking good for him at all."

I didn't say anything. I didn't get that warm and fuzzy feeling where his father was concerned because of our last encounter. Of course, I didn't hate the man or anything, and I wanted him to be in good health. But I'd never forgive him for the way he came here and practically turned my husband against me and had him stay at a hotel with him.

"Patricia, did you hear me?"

"Yes."

"So what? You have anything at all to say? No apologies for his illness or well-wishes for him to get better?"

"What do you want me to say? It's not like your father, or any of your family for that matter, ever really liked me. Now you want me to feel sorry for the man?"

"Trust me, he doesn't need your pity. I just thought that since you are so against this divorce, you could at least try to be a supportive and loving wife."

"I can do that when you call the divorce off. I can instantly become the perfect wife for you when that happens."

"You know what? Never mind. I simply thought that out of respect you should know that I'll be gone for a few days if you came by the house."

"Sure, whatever."

His cell phone rang, and it almost seemed like he got a little nervous as he looked at the name of who called.

"Hey, I need to take this, but do whatever you feel is necessary, Pat."

He answered his phone as he walked out of the room and headed back downstairs. He was exactly right. I would do what was necessary by listening to his phone call, because his reaction to whoever it was didn't seem right by a long shot. I could tell he definitely didn't want to talk to them in front of me. So I stood on the stairs where he couldn't see me while he talked to the person in the kitchen a few feet away.

"Yeah, Randle, so like I said on your voicemail, my father is very sick, and it's not looking good. Actually, his doctor is not giving him much longer to live. That's why I thought it was necessary to call you. See, the thing is, I need to speed up this whole divorce as quickly as possible. I need you to do whatever you can to get this done within the next week or even days. I know it's a lot to ask, but I'm going to inherit a million dollars from my father's estate if something happens to him, and I want to make damn sure that my wife will never benefit from it. There is no way I can give her half his money when she doesn't even like the man."

He was still talking to his attorney, but I'd already heard more than enough when I ran back upstairs and did my happy dance all around our bedroom floor.

A million dollars. $1 million. There's no way in hell I'm divorcing you now, Mr. Montgomery. I will get my half if not all of it.

All I needed to do was keep us legally married until the old man croaked. That wouldn't be hard. I could buy some time by not signing the paperwork. Although, knowing my husband and his connections, he could easily get around that minor factor. I paced the floor and bit my nails trying to think of a surefire way to get half the money, when suddenly it came to me.

My worst enemy was now my good luck charm. At the very last minute, when my husband would think that everything was going his way, I would let my attorney know that he went against our prenuptial agreement by having an affair with little Ms. Tiffany Tate. He may have thought he'd gotten around that clause in the prenuptial agreement because I didn't have proof, but he'd better think again. With that amount of money involved, I could make the proof somehow fall from the sky. Now that I had that golden nugget in my back pocket, Terrence would have no choice but to call everything off and share the wealth with his dear wife, or he'd be forking over at least half of that million if not most of it.

A sense of relief started to come over me when I pictured myself rolling around in our king-sized bed over all that money. Of course, he would probably be angry with me in the beginning, but I was sure he would get over it when he saw how nice and pleasing I'd suddenly become if he stayed in the marriage. All I wanted was for him to get rid of her and go back to being a husband and father to me and the kids. Then and only then would I be the wife he'd always dreamed of.

I thought how Tiffany Tate was the reason for all of this divorce talk anyway. She was the whole reason my family was falling apart. With that in mind, I started to devise a plan that guaranteed she would be completely out of the picture for good. Then he would have no choice but to stay with me. Either way, whether it was proving he had an affair with her or getting her out of his life, it all boiled down to getting rid of her or handing over his father's money. It would ultimately be his choice.

I didn't have everything completely figured out, but ideas came to me slowly and surely. If I was going to prove an affair and mess up their little relationship at the same time, there was no way I could do it all on my own. I needed some help, and like magic, I knew just the person I wanted to use. Once I waved around the idea of getting a portion of $1 million, I was positive I would have his total cooperation.

I hopped on my old laptop in our bedroom and went straight to Tiffany's Facebook page. I remembered that I'd seen a picture of her and her ex with their names tagged on it. Once I got on, I noticed that it looked as if she hadn't logged on in a while. That in itself made me wonder if she purposely tried to hide something by not posting anything. However, I tried not to get too far off-track and stay focused on my task at hand. I scrolled through most of her pictures when I finally came upon the exact picture I was looking for.

"David Allen. Just the man I need."

I clicked on his name, and it took me over to his personal Facebook page. He didn't have his blocked either, so I decided to scroll through his recent posts to find out all I could about him. There wasn't really much to look at because it appeared he didn't have a lot going on. Figuring I could come back and be nosy another day, I decided to get right down to business. I clicked on the option to send him a private inbox message.

Hello, Mr. David Allen. We don't know one another personally, but I got your name from a friend, Ms. Tiffany Tate. I have a proposition for you that would be worth your time financially if you're interested. It's way too much to go into detail here on social media, so I'm hoping that we could meet sometime soon, very soon. Please respond at your earliest convenience. Thanks a bunch! Pat.

I was nervous when I pressed send, but I did it anyway. I knew deep down that this could possibly go all wrong or all right, and I prayed for the latter. If nothing else, I was sure I would hear back from him with two questions: what was the proposition, and how much was involved? Just the thought of getting her completely out of my husband's life while I became $1 million richer made me inhale and exhale a huge sigh of relief. Once again, I smiled.

Chapter 61

Tiffany

"Listen, you have been moping around this house for the past month now, and I'm sick of it. I really think you should just call him," Keisha hounded me.

"Call who? And no one is moping."

"Yes, you have been, and you already know who I'm referring to. Remember? The person's name you don't want to be mentioned in this house? Tiff, I'm sure he's missing you just as much as you miss him."

I hated to admit it, but I did wonder if Terrence missed me. I missed him desperately, but I refused to tell Keisha or anyone else that. I'd made up my mind to remove Terrence from my life when I came back a month ago, and I planned on sticking with my decision. He was married, and until he was completely divorced, we both needed to respect that fact. So as hard as it was, I needed to go on with my life, and so did he. My only problem was whether I could keep that promise to myself once I returned to Texas.

"Keisha, can we please talk about something else?"

"All right, all right, but I'm only saying that you haven't been yourself since you came back, and I think it has a lot to do with Terrence. Oops, I mean 'him.'"

"It doesn't and I'm fine. If anything, I'm just a little frustrated because I haven't decided when I'm going back home."

"Seems to me that someone is running from something or someone."

"Leave it alone already."

"Okay," she said, waving me off and walking into the kitchen.

She was right about one thing, though. Maybe I was running. I had created the perfect life for myself in Texas, and I hated being back in St. Louis. I felt like I'd outgrown everything here and Texas had become my home, and I was happy there. Yet I was here. I immediately thought about the school and Monica, the church I'd been attending, and everything else I'd fallen in love with. It had all become so much a part of me. Even he had become a huge part of me. It was strange, because although I said I wanted nothing to do with Terrence, I was shocked I hadn't heard any more from him. At first I'd gotten call after call, I assumed when he first found I was gone. I'd let them all go to my voicemail. But there had been nothing since, which left me dumbfounded, especially after the letter I wrote. I guessed I shouldn't have expected the man to come looking for me all the way in St. Louis, but part of me wished he had tried a little harder.

Every time I thought about it, it made me upset that I'd allowed myself to be so vulnerable and transparent. I'd poured my freaking heart and soul out to him, and he ignored me like it was nothing. I knew at that point that I had made the right decision for both of us. Besides, he was probably trying to work things out with her, and I was totally fine with that.

What was even stranger, though, was that I'd been hearing from David when I thought I'd made myself perfectly clear to him about where he and I stood that night I allowed him to stop by. For the first couple of weeks or so that I'd been gone, he'd left me a voicemail daily saying he needed to talk to me and wanted to see me. But then suddenly his calls came to a halt, and I hadn't heard from him since. I actually forced myself to call once or twice, but I only received his voicemail. I prayed that he was all right and made a mental note to call again once Keisha left. There was no way I could let her find out that I'd contacted him, especially instead of reaching out to Terrence. She would have a crazy fit about it, and I would never hear the end of it.

If the roles were reversed, I would have felt the same as she did. But she just didn't understand where I was spiritually in my life. In my heart of hearts, I only wanted to make sure he was all right, and that was it. No matter how much of a jerk he'd been to me, I couldn't allow myself to hate the man forever like she wanted me to.

Chapter 62

David

"Thank heavens for daylight."

I walked out of the police station once again a free man. I'd sat in that jail cell for the past fifteen days because Sonya called the police on me. Lucky for me, the judge dismissed her case due to a lack of evidence that I'd stolen her debit card. She had no way to prove that the reason I had her card wasn't because she'd given it to me as a gift during our relationship. I'd pleaded with them to just check the paperwork at the bank when she'd added me to her account. I went on to explain that instead of having my own card, I simply used hers. The judge found it fair to have all charges dropped against me and set me free.

I immediately inhaled the fresh air and stretched my arms and legs as I looked around my surroundings like it was my first time fresh out of the womb. That moment helped me realize how much we took the simple things in life, like our freedom, for granted.

Looking inside of the big yellow envelope marked "Property" they'd given me before my release, I tried to make sure all of my belongings were there. Instantly I felt deflated because, just as I'd suspected, they'd seized any cash I had on me for evidence. So now I was stuck at a police station with no money or transportation, because my car had also been impounded when I was arrested. I also found that the only thing I did have left of any value, a ring I'd purchased for Tiffany, was also gone. I'd purchased it right before they arrested me as a way to possibly win back Tiffany's affection. They'd actually pulled up on me when I left the jewelry store. I figured the owner must have alerted them when I made such a big purchase with what I said was my sister's card. They'd given the ring to Sonya since they said it was ultimately hers from being purchased with her money. I couldn't focus on all of that, though, because right now I was desperate for cash. Any amount given to me at that point would do.

First, I planned to sweet talk my mother into allowing me back into her home. It might be difficult with her new live-in boyfriend there, but there was no way she could deny her one and only son. Once there, I could regroup and gather my thoughts on some other way to get back into Tiffany's life. I had already come up with the idea of faking an illness, but I was leery about it. I wasn't sure that it would work, and it would be just my luck if I wound up sick in reality.

Pulling my cell phone out of the envelope, I powered it on while thinking about the best way to approach my mother. I wasn't sure it would have any juice, but I prayed I would at least have enough for one call. Once I turned it on, it lit up and alerted me that I had voicemails, texts, and Facebook messages that awaited me. It also flashed a warning that it only had about 10 percent of its power left, so I hurried to check my voicemails. I was positive they were only from my concerned mother since she hadn't heard from me in so long. Just as I figured, most of the messages were from her. Then there were several from Sonya threatening me over her money and child support. I purposely saved those just in case I needed them for some reason in the future.

Then, to my surprise, there was a couple from Tiffany. She'd said she only called to make sure I was all right. Just hearing her concern for me made me smile, though. It was the first time I'd genuinely smiled in the last couple of months. I was thrilled that she felt the need to check on me, because that meant she really didn't hate me as much as I thought she did. It also showed me that I still had a slight chance of getting back in her good graces if I played my cards right.

Before I returned her call, I decided to check the texts first. There were numerous texts from an unknown number, all making threats against my life. They said things like, "Karma is a bitch," and "You'll get what's coming to you." After giving it a little thought, I narrowed it down to either Sonya or Leslie. However, I had to admit that there might be other women out there I wasn't completely honest with either. Trying not to let it shake me, I figured I'd check the Facebook message I'd received. It had me pretty curious since I really wasn't a social media junkie like most. In fact, I only had a Facebook account because Tiffany encouraged it, and I didn't have many followers, so I couldn't think who would have contacted me.

My eyes went directly to the sender's name before I opened the message. It was from someone named Pat. I opened the message, and after the third or fourth time reading it, I was stunned and wondered if this was some type of practical joke or spam. But then I thought how it couldn't have been because she'd said she got my name from Tiffany. Suddenly, that amazing feeling I'd felt a second earlier quickly vanished as I now knew this, and not so much my well-being, was probably the reason for Tiffany's calls. I read the line over and over again that there could be some type of financial gain involved, so I thought it was definitely worth looking into, especially under my financial circumstances. I left the woman my name and number, and in a matter of minutes, I'd received a text message from an unknown number. I assumed it was her.

Moments later, I sat at a small table in the back corner of the Starbucks directly across from the police station. She'd said in her text that it would take her less than an hour to get here. I sipped my glass of water and charged up my phone as I patiently waited for this mysterious Pat lady to arrive. Something in my gut told me that there was more to this offer than she let on, but she'd mentioned money, and I was desperate enough to hear her out.

After sitting there awhile, I figured I would finally call my mother so I would have a place to sleep for the night besides my car.

She answered with a bit of both panic and anger in her voice. "David, honey, where are you? Are you all right? And what the hell were you arrested for?"

"Mom, calm down, please. I'm fine. How did you know I'd been arrested?"

"I'm a mother. After I didn't hear from you for a few days, I knew that something was wrong. I think I called around to every hospital and jail in the city. That's when I found out you'd been arrested. Those good-for-nothing police wouldn't even let me see you. They only told me that you would be released soon."

"Well, it's all right. It was just a misunderstanding with a female, that's all."

"Now don't tell me it was that young girl Tiffany who came by here that night. I told you I felt something wasn't right with her just popping up over here."

"No, Mom, it wasn't Tiffany."

"Well, who in the world have you gotten yourself mixed up with now who would call the police on you? I told you if you had your own stuff and stopped depending on these women, then you wouldn't be going through any of this."

"Momma, please, I really didn't call for all of that right now. I need to know if you mind me coming over to the house for a couple of days until I get everything back in order."

"Oh, I don't know, honey. You're a grown man, and you know I have my friend here and—"

"Wait a minute. Ain't that the pot calling the kettle black? You fuss at me for lying up on women, but you can have some man lying up on you?"

"He's not some man. Jeffrey is my man. Believe it or not, I can have whoever I want in my house!"

I missed the whole rant my mother was starting when I looked up and saw a tall, slender woman with a fair complexion walk in the door and look around. She actually looked a lot like Tiffany from a distance with her haircut. I wondered if this was Pat.

"Mom, look, I have to go, but I'll see you tonight. I promise it will only be for a few days."

I hung up before she had a chance to debate it, and I stood up when I saw the woman walking toward me. She smiled from ear to ear like she'd struck gold, yet I couldn't shake the strange feeling I had.

Approaching the table, she stuck her hand out and introduced herself. "Hi, David, I'm Patricia. How are you?"

I hesitated as I stuck my hand out and tried to figure out what her deal was. "Hello, uh, how are you?"

"I'm great. I can call you David, right?"

"Uh, yeah, sure."

"Is that all you're having? Water? Because I'm famished. I think I'm going to order a salad."

I didn't want to tell her that water was all I could afford at the moment. Besides, I only wanted to get right down to business and get out of there. "I'm fine actually."

Everything was silent after she ordered her food. We both kind of looked around, waiting for the other to speak. Finally, she said, "I guess I should tell you why we're here."

"Uh, yeah, you said something about a proposition that I would be paid for?"

"Yes. You will be paid very nicely if you can help me with something."

"And what exactly is it and how much are you talking?"

"Listen, I know you're concerned about the money, so let's go ahead and get that out of the way. I'm about to inherit one million dollars."

"One million dollars?"

"Please calm down and lower you voice. I am willing to pay you a very nice sum from my inheritance if you can get rid of someone for me."

"Oh, wait, wait. I'm not that kind of guy. I'm not killing nobody off, lady. You got the wrong one for that."

She laughed as if I'd told some hilarious joke. "Would you calm down, please? David, I'm not asking you to kill anyone."

I took a deep breath of relief, but I wasn't sure if I wanted to know any more of what she had to say. She continued anyway.

"Look, what I'm asking is that you keep Ms. Tiffany Tate away from my husband. I promise if you can do that, you'll come out very well off financially."

Now I was completely confused because I thought Tiffany was where she'd gotten my name. "But I thought you and Tiffany were friends."

"I only mentioned her name to get you here. I believe she's been involved with my husband, and I need her out of his life. Since you are her ex, I figured you could help me out with that."

"Let me get this straight. You're saying that Tiffany is having an affair with your husband and you want to pay me to keep her away from him?"

"Yep, exactly. Look, David, my husband and I are having a few problems, nothing we can't fix though. Now he is asking me for a divorce, but I feel that's only because of her."

Tears started to slide down her face as her tone softened a bit. I could see the pain within her, and she was a totally different person from when she first walked in.

"Listen, I'm sorry about your marital problems, but I know Tiffany, and she's no home-wrecker."

"Well, I know my husband Terrence, and he wouldn't walk away from his responsibilities as a husband and father if he weren't being influenced by her."

She said the name "Terrence," and suddenly my mind went right back to a month ago. I still fumed over the way he'd thrown me up against my car that day at her house. Not to mention, I didn't want him anywhere near her. Instantly, I knew that my chance for revenge had come.

I rubbed Patricia's hand to try to soothe her pain. I hated the thought of doing anything to hurt Tiffany, but retaliating against Terrence while getting paid to do it was a win-win situation for me.

"Patricia, what exactly do you want me to do?"

Her tears dried up quickly as she looked into my eyes. "I really don't care how you do it. You can come up with that part yourself. Just keep her away from my husband, and I promise you won't have to worry about anything financially ever."

My phone rang. I was amazed at the way this day was going—it was Tiffany. Patricia and I both were stunned.

Chapter 63

Tiffany

I'd dozed off across the couch when Keisha came out of the kitchen and grabbed her purse and keys from the sofa where she'd left them. "Hey, I need to run and get something from the grocery store for the chili I'm making tonight. Did you need anything while I'm out?"

"Nope, I think I'm good."

"Okay, then I'll be back in a minute."

I thought it was the perfect time for me to reach out to David again. Praying he was all right, I listened to his phone ring three times with no answer. I was about to hang up when the ringing suddenly stopped and his groggy voice said my name. "Tiffany?"

"David. How are you? Is everything all right with you?"

There was a pause until his voice slowly made out his next words. "Uh, actually, no. Everything is not all right. I'm sick. I . . . I have cancer."

"Oh, goodness, David, no."

"Yeah, honestly I've known since that night I came to your house. That's why I was so desperate to see you."

"But why didn't you say anything then?"

"I don't know. I was prepared to at first, but then seeing how happy you were with your life, I didn't want to lay my problems on you."

"Look, we've been through a lot, but I still have your best interest at heart. I don't wish any negativity on you, especially not this. You really should have told me so I could be there for you."

"You mean, even after all I did and all that's happened? You would really still be there for me?"

"Of course."

"See, that right there is exactly why I fell in love with you in the first place, and why I still love you."

I tried to let his last statement go in one ear and out the other. He was probably very sincere in his feelings, but I felt bad that I couldn't return the sentiment. I cared for him dearly as a friend and always would, but nothing more than that.

"Well, is there anything I can do for you? Anything that you need? Just say it."

"Honestly, this might be a huge request, but is it possible that I can come and see you? I mean, seeing you would make me feel a million times better just like it did that night."

"Oh, I, uh, I don't know about that. I'm not even in Texas right now."

"But I can come to you wherever you are. Please just say you'll think about it. It's just that this sickness has had me thinking about life overall lately, and I would hate for anything to happen without getting the chance to say what I need to say to you face-to-face."

"Please don't talk like that, David. Nothing is going to happen to you. Just let me think about it, and I'll get back in touch. Okay?"

"Okay, that's fair. That's all I'm asking, and I love you, Tiffany."

I hung up without saying another word. I felt extremely bad for his condition. However, instead of having the desire to see him, I longed for Terrence even more. David's condition made me realize how short life was and how much I truly needed Terrence back in mine. I looked at my phone and thought about dialing his number but quickly changed my mind.

"He is married, Tiffany, and you have to respect that," I told myself, although it didn't make things any easier.

Chapter 64

David

I hung up with Tiffany and looked at Patricia, who stared at me with the biggest smile plastered across her face. She'd encouraged me to answer the call, although I was somewhat cautious. I really didn't want to hurt Tiffany, but right now I had to do what I had to do. I played the only hand I had and went along with the whole illness idea I'd come up with previously. I assured Patricia that I could make her feel sorry for me and this would keep her out of Terrence's life. I was positive that Tiffany would grant any final wishes I had under the circumstances.

We sat there and went over a few more minor details before she pulled out $1,000. She'd said it was all she had to offer until the inheritance from Terrence's father came in. I didn't debate it because it was much more than what I had in my pockets. We shook hands on our deal, and Patricia walked out a very happy woman. I, on the other hand, still felt a slight uneasiness about it all. I couldn't let myself focus on it, though, because I had to make arrangements to head to St. Louis. Although Tiffany only said she would think about it, I was absolutely sure I would hear back from her sooner rather than later.

Chapter 65

Terrence

Although I wasn't looking forward to the trip ahead of me, I was thankful to finally board the plane. I couldn't wait to lay my head back and shut my eyes for some peace and relaxation. Patricia had me so mentally drained with all of her antics for the past few months that this was very much needed. It was unbelievable, the lengths she went to in order to have me call off the divorce. She'd tried sex, she used the kids, she whined and begged, and now she'd threatened to take me for everything I had. I would be completely shocked if that actually happened though. After everything Pat had been up to to destroy this marriage, a judge was sure to be on my side.

I wondered, however, why she just couldn't let things be between us. Why wouldn't she simply find another man who would love her the way she needed to be loved? I'd almost allowed myself to feel bad for not being that man for her. That was until her reaction to my father's illness. It was so disrespectful and the worst display of the so-called love she professed to have for me. It practically made me sick to my stomach, and I couldn't have been happier to have left for a few days. The sight of her alone repulsed me from that point on, and it was best to be hundreds of miles away from her, or there'd be no telling what I would do.

I drifted away into my thoughts and found myself in thoughts of Tiffany again, which seemed to happen quite often. I wondered what she may have been doing at the moment and if she thought of me the way I did her. I hadn't heard from her since that night at her home, which surprised me the most. Although I figured it was for the best. There was still way too much going on in my life, and I wouldn't want to put her through any of it. I did wish I could tell her about my father though. When she was here, she'd always made sure to ask about my parents and their well-being. She'd even spoken to both of them over the phone, and it became a routine for her and my mother. They enjoyed talking to one another, and they likely would have been friends for a long time. I loved the bond they were building, which was nothing like the nonexistent relationship between my mom and Patricia. Actually, my mother only called Pat whenever she couldn't get in contact with me. I thought it all had to do with the whole wedding on both their parts. My mother felt a way about not being invited, and Patricia felt some type of way about the fact that they wanted us to hold off on things.

It all had me thinking about why things turned out the way they had. I wondered if everything in life was based solely on our choices or if things were destined to be the way they were. I tried never to regret anything in life, but I wished I could somehow turn back the hands of time. I never would have married Patricia. I probably would have done things right with my children's mother, and we would have had the life we'd always dreamed of. That was only wishful thinking though. Everything happened for a reason.

Fidgeting around in my seat, it was hard for me to fall asleep, so I decided I'd try to read a book for the remainder of the flight. I was exhausted, but I'd never been able to sleep among strangers. I pulled out the latest book by T.D. Jakes from my carry-on bag. Lately, I found myself trying to deepen my relationship with God. It was something Tiffany suggested I do, and she'd bought the book for me one day as a surprise. I wasn't into reading the way she was, but I found that I enjoyed the wisdom and knowledge that Jakes poured into his teachings.

Turning to the last chapter I'd ended on, I suddenly came across that white envelope with my name written across the front. Picking it up, I began to look at it in my hands. I remembered sticking it inside the book one day as I contemplated reading it. Now there it was in front of me. It had been a whole month, and I still struggled to open it. In fact, I almost tore it up and left well enough alone, but curiosity kept eating away at me. I wanted to know—actually, I needed to know—what she'd said and whether it was good or bad. I pulled on the corners of the envelope and ran my finger under the flap. Then I pulled out the ivory-colored stationery. I was amazed that after all the time that had passed, it still carried her scent. Holding it up to my nose, I inhaled her beautiful aroma. Then slowly, I unfolded the letter and started to read.

Dear Terrence,

By the time you read this letter, I will be on my way back to St. Louis. I'm sure things seem confusing, which is why I felt you were owed an explanation of why I left so abruptly. For the longest time, I prayed for very specific things in a man. Then when I didn't get those things in the men I dealt with, I thought that God hadn't heard my prayers, or if He had, that I wasn't worthy of receiving what I asked for because of the mistakes I'd made in the past. Then you showed up out of nowhere, and you are everything I could have hoped for, prayed for, and imagined. I didn't think someone like you even existed. You are living proof to me that God is so real, so amazing, and that He still hears and answers prayers, not in our time, but His. However, I also know that sometimes the right people can meet one another at the very wrong time in life.

What happened between us last night and at the hotel was beyond special to me. It was what I longed for, desired, and needed from you in so many ways. It confirmed for me what I've already known deep in my heart for quite some time now: that I am totally and completely in love with you. But we were also wrong for allowing either time to take place. You are a married man, and no matter how much I wish that things were different, they're just not.

See, the thing is, I've told you before that I've been there and done that with the whole relationship with a married man, but I never went into detail. He and I were coworkers who became very close friends, kind of like you and me. Then, in our vulnerability and immaturity, we crossed the line. We promised each other that it would only be that once, but it wasn't. Before we realized it, years had passed, and I didn't know how to let go of what I'd allowed myself to become so comfortable with. I used to be one of those women who would say I would never be with a married man. What I learned is that we just never know the cards that we're going to be dealt in life and to never say never.

Terrence, that relationship had a hold on me that I couldn't seem to let go of. I knew it was wrong, but I couldn't remove myself from it. After a while, it was no longer about sex, love, or any of that. I wanted out but somehow felt stuck in it. I tried everything: crying it away, eating it away, and even drinking it away. Nothing helped. That was until I finally became real with myself. I prayed night and day for God to give me the strength to let go, no matter what it took or no matter how it hurt. And I promised Him that if He did, I would not allow myself to enter into another relationship of that manner again.

That's why I had to leave. I needed to clear my head and heart of you and this entire situation we have. I made a vow to God, and I fully intend to keep it even if it means losing you, because I just want who He has for me. I just want that one man who will love me and only me. The one who will give his all only to make me happy and see a smile on my face. That man who is willing to love, protect, and cherish my heart. That's all I want. I know that if I just stop, wait, and trust in Him, God will one day send that man into my life and he won't belong to someone else. So my leaving was not about me and not about you, but about my promise to God. I hope you can understand this.

I love you with all my heart, Terrence Montgomery, and maybe, just maybe, our hearts will meet again . . . at the right time.

Tiffany

I took a moment to let the words from her letter sink in. My mind raced at a million miles per hour as I thought about all she'd said. She'd poured her heart out to me, and I knew how difficult that had to be for her. All I wanted to do was hold her in my arms. That was where I wanted her to be forever. I could have kicked myself for not reading the letter sooner. I was sure that things would have turned out much different than they were now. Finally, I knew that it was time to stop playing games and take matters into my own hands. If there was one thing I'd realized through my father's illness, as well as with this situation with Patricia, it was that life was short. And it was way too short to be anything but completely happy. With that said, I knew that for me, true happiness meant being with Tiffany. I loved her and no longer wanted to be without her. It was about time that she knew that.

I couldn't power up my cell phone fast enough when the plane came to its landing. The first person I called was Monica, and she answered immediately.

"Hey, Coach, how are things? How's your dad? Is he doing any better?"

"Hey, Monica. I'm just getting off the plane and heading over to the hospital as we speak. I can tell you more about my father when I get there. But actually I'm calling about something else."

"Oh, okay. What's up?"

"I'm going to need a few more days off work if that's all right with you. I'm taking another trip."

"Another trip? Where?"

"St. Louis."

At first I heard a bit of hesitation then suddenly sheer excitement in her voice. "Oh, my God. Terrence Montgomery, what are you up to?"

"Trust me, Monica, you'll find out everything soon enough."

Monica's reaction assured me even more that I was doing the right thing when I hung up the phone with her. I couldn't help but smile as I thought how possibly my and Tiffany's whole lives would change in a day or two after I made this trip. I grabbed my bags to head over to see my pops when my cell phone rang. My eyes grew large when the name flashed across the front of it. It was Tiffany.

Chapter 66

Keisha

There was no way I would let Tiffany make the biggest mistake of her life. I'd been her friend for a long time and knew her like a book and also what was best for her. She might very well be a little upset initially with what I had in mind. But I was sure she would quickly get over it.

Coming back in from the grocery store, I called out to her when I didn't see her in the living room. Her keys and phone were still lying on the coffee table, so wherever she was, it wasn't far.

"Tiffany? Tiffany?" I called out once again before I noticed the note lying on the kitchen counter. She'd let me know that she went for a few laps around the track to get some exercise in. I hated when she didn't take her keys and phone with her, though. I would always tell her that just about anything could happen, but she could be so stubborn sometimes.

I looked out the window to make sure I didn't see her walking up the street before I picked up her cell phone. I only wanted to sneak and get Terrence's number to call him later. However, my mouth dropped when I saw the very last call she'd made.

"David? What in the world are you doing talking to him?"

I scrolled through the text messages to see if there had been any communication between the two, but there wasn't. Then I looked out the window one more time before I pressed send to dial Terrence. I was so nervous that my hand holding the phone practically shook the entire time. I didn't want Tiffany to be upset with me, but this was for her own good. After several rings, I finally heard the connection.

"Tiffany?"

"No, Terrence, this is Keisha, Tiffany's best friend. We haven't officially met, but I needed to talk to you. Do you have a sec?"

"Uh, yeah, sure. Is everything all right? Is Tiffany all right?"

"Well, yes and no. I really don't have long before she returns from her walk, but whether Tiffany wants to admit it or not, she's in love with you and needs you in her life. Now I may be overstepping my bounds, but I felt this was necessary. She's been miserable ever since she came back to St. Louis. Not only that, but I just saw that she's been in contact with her ex, who I know means her absolutely no good. I'm not totally aware of the status of your situation, but if you truly love her, then please do something. I mean, call her, text her, come here, but please do something."

"Keisha, Keisha, slow down. I'm actually two steps ahead of you. Right now, I'm out of town seeing my father, but I plan to come to St. Louis tomorrow. I love that woman just as much as she does me, and I refuse to let another day go by without expressing that to her. I have a plan, but I'm going to need your help to pull it all off."

"Yes, yes, whatever it is, just tell me and I'll do it. I'll text you my number so that we can communicate more, but I gotta go because I think I hear her coming."

I hung up with Terrence, deleted his call from her call log, and threw her phone back down on the coffee table. I still had the most unsettling feeling after finding out that she'd been in contact with David, but I was also extremely excited about whatever Terrence had in store. I smiled at the thought of finally seeing the two of them together.

"Hey, what are you sitting up here smiling at?" she said, walking in out of breath and all sweaty.

"Girl, nothing, just remembered a joke someone told me."

"Well, you'll have to tell me the joke after I shower."

I heard her talking, but I wasn't listening. Instead, I shot Terrence a quick text so that he would have my number. He sent a text back to inform me of the first thing he wanted me to do. I was about to burst with anticipation for tomorrow, and I prayed that this would be the beginning of all her dreams coming true—as well as having that creep David out of her life for good.

Chapter 67

Tiffany

Today started as any other day did. After I enjoyed the chili that Keisha made for dinner last night, I'd fallen asleep on the couch with a bottle of wine and a book. As usual, Keisha must have made sure I'd gotten into bed, because I didn't remember a thing after. Stretching and yawning, I squinted from the bright sunshine that peered through the windows, and I listened to the birds chirp a melodic tune. Already this let me know that it was going to be a beautiful day, and I couldn't wait to get up and get started. I already had my entire day planned with a little retail therapy and a much-needed trip to the spa. That was until I heard a knock on the door. Seconds after, Keisha peeked in.

"Hey, girl, I thought I heard you moving around in here. Hurry up and get dressed. I want to go and have breakfast."

"Breakfast? After the dinner we had last night? Keisha, I can't. All I would focus on are the extra miles I would need to run to keep all this food off."

"Would you stop it? You have the perfect figure and don't need to focus on any extra anything. Besides, I wanted to do a little something to cheer you up. I know things have been difficult for you, and I don't want you getting discouraged about it all. I've got a funny feeling anyway that all your luck is about to change, my dear."

"Well, I sure hope you're right about that."

"I am, so hurry up and get dressed already."

She left with this huge smile on her face. I wasn't sure why, but I sensed something strange going on. Keisha was never this giddy about anything, so that alone made me curious as to what her deal was. Then again, maybe it was only my need to control everything, so I tried to ease up a bit. Besides, Keisha was right. My situation had become a bit depressing, and a good breakfast with my friend would definitely cheer me up.

Looking in my closet to find an outfit for the day, I thought back to the very day I'd met David. I'd needed a little cheering up back then, too, and that was when Keisha and I went to Sweetie Pies. That was also the day my life changed for me. I immediately told myself that this breakfast wouldn't be a repeat of that day. Any random man who sat alone this time would definitely stay alone.

An hour later, Keisha and I pulled up to Goody Goody, one of our favorite St. Louis restaurants to have breakfast. The entire ride there it seemed like we were both in our own worlds. She'd been communicating with someone on her phone, mainly listening and responding yes or no whenever she talked. What was even more strange was her constant giggling with whoever it was. I started to wonder if maybe there was some mystery man in her life she hadn't told me about. Maybe that was what all this sudden niceness was about. Maybe she was going to drop some bomb on me like she was moving out of the house to be with this person. It wouldn't be that far-fetched, because Keisha was beautiful and could have had just about any guy she wanted. Maybe she was trying to soften the blow because things hadn't turned out right in my own love life.

Those thoughts of her brought me right back to thinking of David. Maybe he hadn't turned out to be my happily ever after, but I hated the thought of him being sick. I'd made a vow to myself to be there for him in any possible way I could. I would need to keep my dealings with him totally quiet though, especially from Keisha. She would never understand my compassion for David.

I tried to snap out of my thoughts as we headed inside. I was starving and couldn't wait to indulge. Besides, Keisha finally took a breather from her phone, and I wanted to get to the bottom of all the suspicions I had. We sat down and ordered mimosas along with their chicken, waffles, and scrambled eggs. After the waiter walked away, I started right in on her.

"All right, that's it, Keisha. Fess up already! What's going on with you? And don't go giving me any crap, either."

"Tiffany—"

"No, stop bull-crapping me. What gives? Do you have a new friend you haven't told me about?"

"What? Girl, no, it's nothing like that at all. You know without a doubt that if I'd met someone, you would be the first to know. I can't keep a secret like that."

"Okay, then what's up?"

She put her head down for a moment, then looked back up at me. "Look, I can't actually say right now, so I'm asking you to please don't make me tell you."

"Tell me what?"

"I told you I can't say. Please just trust me on this, and relax and enjoy this moment, all right?"

I really didn't have any idea what she meant by relax and enjoy the moment. What moment was she even referring to? I wanted to press the issue further and make her come clean. But I knew Keisha all too well, and the girl couldn't hold water. She would let whatever was going on slip out sooner or later. With that in mind, I tried to just go with the flow, although it took everything in me not to ask her more questions.

Shortly after, the waitress brought our food out, and the table became quiet as we enjoyed everything sitting before us. The only sound was that of the clicking and clacking of our forks as they scraped the plates. Soon, though, I looked up and noticed Keisha right back on her cell phone. This time she mainly texted instead of talked.

With the lingering silence, so many things started to go through my head. I still missed my life in Texas and needed to hurry back there. I wanted to get back to work, the church, and simply the life I'd started to create, minus Terrence. Then there was this whole thing with David that I needed to figure out. And on top of it all, as much as I hated to admit it, my heart missed Terrence something crazy. I wanted to talk to him, smell his scent, and look into his dark eyes. It killed me inside not to reach out, but I had to stick to my guns.

Suddenly, Keisha interrupted my thoughts. She placed her phone on the table and looked at me in the strangest way. There she sat with the same smile on her face from earlier.

"Girl, what is wrong with you? What's all this smiling and grinning about?"

"Okay, so, I know things have seemed a little odd and that you've had a million and one questions."

"Yes, I have."

"Well, I just sent you a text message with instructions to follow. Again, I'm asking you to trust me on this, and I promise if you do what it says, everything will be revealed to you by the end of the day."

"Will you please stop playing around already and tell me the deal? This is crazy."

"Please, Tiffany? Trust me."

Keisha was absolutely right. I did have a million questions, but I realized at that point she wasn't going to say a word. So instead, I looked at the text that flashed across my cell phone and hoped to get some answers. I read it a couple of times, then looked at her with curiosity.

Suddenly, I realized that this was the doing of Mr. Terrence Montgomery. I wasn't exactly sure how he and Keisha had connected, but I wasn't upset about it in the least. In fact, there was a small hint of excitement that rushed through me. My heart began to beat faster as I read the text over for the third time and again the fourth.

Come to the Ritz-Carlton Hotel at seven. Thirteenth floor. Room 1307.

Tears immediately flowed heavily down my face as this was the same floor and suite number we'd had that very first night together. Keisha must have sensed that I'd started to put two and two together.

"Now do you understand why I couldn't say anything?"

I only shook my head yes because I was unable to speak.

She handed me a note across the table. "All right, so I had to write this for Terrence, but they're all his words. I just wrote exactly what he told me, okay?"

I shook my head yes, wiped my tears the best I could, and started to read.

Tiffany,
I don't know about you, but this past month has been the worst for me. I've had trouble eating, sleeping, and even thinking about anything else other than you. All this time, I thought that maybe we'd done the right thing by giving us time away from one another. Then yesterday when I read your letter for the very first time, everything became clear to me. Tiff, baby, I need you. In such a short amount

of time, you have helped me become a better me.
You have given my life meaning and purpose. You
have shown me what real, true, and unconditional
love is. You're my reason, you are my peace, you are
my air, and I don't want to go another day without
you in my life.
   Terrence

I tried to speak, but nothing seemed to come out. I still had so many questions. I wondered why he just read my letter yesterday. I especially wondered what was going on between him and Patricia now. Although I wanted to believe otherwise, I knew there was no way she would ever let go of their marriage. So I wondered what he was up to. Terrence had to know that I wouldn't have any dealings with him if he hadn't had that part of his life resolved. He knew how I felt about it.

Keisha spoke, "Here is the key to the suite, honey. Now the rest is totally up to you."

My hand shook as I reached to take it from her. I still couldn't believe that all of this was happening. Keisha came over to my side of the table and hugged me tight as she tried to wipe away my tears.

"Listen, by now you should realize how much this man loves you. Please just try to remove everything else from your mind and enjoy this moment with him. This is finally the beginning of all your dreams coming true."

"But what about his wife? What about—"

"Stop it already, all right? Let Terrence explain everything to you. Just enjoy the moment."

I tried my best to do exactly what Keisha said and forget everything else and focus solely on me and him. There was still the matter of David and his illness that weighed heavily on my mind, but I dismissed it quickly. I wasn't about to allow him to ruin this moment for me.

Keisha continued, "Hey, since we have some time to kill, I was thinking that we could swing by the nail salon and get manicures and pedicures, my treat. I want you to relax, feel your best, and enjoy this as much as possible. Oh, and I need you to do be a huge, huge favor."

"What's that?"

"Forget that you ever met David Allen."

I had no clue what made her say that, but even if I wanted to, I wasn't sure that was possible. If I'd never met David, then I wouldn't have had my life in Texas that I loved so much. I also would have never met Terrence. I wished I could forget, but if only she knew that was now much easier said than done.

Chapter 68

Terrence

I was mentally and emotionally drained after my visitation with Pops. I tried to remain hopeful that he would somehow pull through, despite the way things looked. He was his normal joking self, which was good to see. He also tried his best to discuss his estate, but I reassured him that no amount of money meant anything to me compared to his life. My only goal was to ensure I kept it far away from Patricia if it ever came to that point.

Luckily, on the ride home, I contacted my attorney, who had some welcome news for me. I wasn't sure if I would be able to get this pulled off, especially since she was so against it. However, he told me that he'd pulled some major strings for me with the judge to try to speed up the process. He said if all went well, I would be a legally divorced man much sooner rather than later. I was completely relieved and ecstatic about the news. Even if that hadn't been the outcome though, I'd already made up in my mind that nothing would stop me from being with Tiffany—not Patricia, not this nonsense of marriage, not David, not anything.

Thinking of her brought a huge smile to my face. I wished I could have seen her face when she received the text. I started to laugh to myself. Knowing that Tiffany was such a sensitive person, I was sure she cried a river's worth of tears. I was truly thankful that I had Monica's and Keisha's help in all of this so far, but now the rest was up to me. I prayed she would be overjoyed over the suite, and I couldn't wait to get there with her.

First things first, I thought as I finally arrived back home. I wanted to check on the house, grab a couple more items to throw in my bag, and even see what Patricia was up to before my flight. She'd been extremely quiet, no calls, texts, or anything. Since that was highly unlike her, I became nervous about the unknown.

I took a deep breath and exhaled as I put my key into the keyhole. I'd already prepared myself for any drama she threw my way, but I was totally stunned when I opened my door and saw my house completely empty. I walked in and went from room to room only to see nothing at all inside. She'd even had all the utilities turned off. I'd told her that it didn't matter to me if she and the boys weren't there, but I'd never thought she would do it like this. She took everything without so much as leaving me a shower curtain in the bathroom.

Once again, she showed no thought or concern for me. I wondered why she couldn't just talk to me. Why couldn't we just amicably go our separate ways and try to even salvage some type of friendship between us? This didn't have to be ugly, but clearly she wanted it to be. I wasn't about to give her that satisfaction though. I knew she was somewhere patiently waiting for me to call and act a complete fool with her. That was why she'd been so quiet. I wouldn't do it.

My clothing and other personal belongings were still inside the guest bedroom I'd slept in from time to time, and that was all I was concerned about. As I moved closer toward my belongings, I saw envelopes on top of envelopes from our mortgage company. It appeared that our beautiful home was heading toward foreclosure sooner than I imagined, and Pat never said a word. Of course,

I knew I'd fallen behind a few months on the payments, but I hadn't realized it had come to this.

I struggled to put my focus back on Tiffany and not Patricia and this whole situation. Now I definitely needed to get to her as quickly as possible. She was my only solace, and I needed her desperately before I did something to Pat that I would surely regret.

Chapter 69

Patricia

Nothing had gone the way I planned, and I became frustrated, to say the least. The minute Terrence left to see his father, I had a moving crew pack up everything in the house and put it in storage while the kids and I were still at my father's home. I was sure I would have heard from Terrence by now begging me to return home with all of our belongings, but I hadn't heard one single peep out of him. I wanted to call and go in hard, but I had to keep this ball in my court. I needed him to be the one chasing me, and I needed him to do it quickly, because there was no way I planned to stay in my father's cramped space much longer.

Yeah, true enough, I shouldn't have left in the first place, but I had to do something to show Terrence that I meant serious business about him calling off this divorce. If he wanted to keep playing games with me, this was just the beginning. I'd show him exactly what he'd lose, including half of his father's estate.

Speaking of which, I'd also called the hospital several times to find out if his old man had croaked. They would only say that, due to privacy regulations, they couldn't provide certain information over the phone. However, after enough tears and with the right nurse willing to break the rules, I got exactly what I needed. She told me that he was still in stable condition and even offered to contact me should anything change. She just didn't know how badly I needed that to happen before Terrence found a way around this whole divorce thing.

What really had me heated more than anything, though, was now staring me directly in my face. Since I hadn't noticed activity on his social media, I had to find out what he was up to. Suddenly, I remembered that his cell phone was under a family plan with mine and the children's. I had total access to his calls, texts, and everything. From the looks of it, he'd definitely been in touch with someone with a St. Louis area code. In fact, it looked like my dear old husband had taken a trip there. He'd sent a text to someone to meet him at a hotel in suite 1307. That immediately made me think of my new friend. I'd already made sure he was headed to St. Louis and ready to do whatever necessary to keep that woman away from my husband. *I spent damn good money for his help, so he'd better be ready to keep his end of the deal.*

With that in mind, I dialed David's number to give him the hotel information. Whatever was supposed to take place between Tiffany and Terrence was surely not about to happen. *Over my dead body.*

"Hello?"

"Where are you?"

"Hello to you too, Patricia. I'm just arriving in St. Louis. I'm about to get an Uber to my hotel. What's up?"

"It looks like we're going to be upgrading your stay while you're there. I need you to reserve a suite at the Ritz-Carlton. Try to see if there's any way you can get on the thirteenth floor."

"Wait, did you say a suite at the Ritz? Do you know how much a night's stay there would cost? Why there anyway?"

"Look, will you calm down, please? I mean, the last I checked, you weren't paying for any of this anyway.

Besides, I thought you might actually be happy about the upgrade."

"I am. I just don't see the need to waste money on some fancy suite. I'm not that type of guy. I don't need all of that."

I wanted to tell him how well I could see he wasn't that type of man. However, I didn't have time for all that. "Listen, your little girlfriend and my husband are supposed to meet there at seven in room 1307. I need you to make sure that the meeting doesn't happen by any means necessary."

"How in the world am I supposed to do that? Break into her room and kidnap her or something?"

"If that's what it takes, then hell yes, David. Do whatever's necessary to make sure they don't meet, especially if you want to see any piece of the million dollars."

The phone became strangely silent, and I knew his thoughts were on that money.

"Are you still in? Because if not—"

"Yes, Patricia. I'm in, okay?"

"Good. I'll get some more cash for you. But you need to call me the minute you get there."

I hung up without giving him a chance to say another word. All I knew was that he'd better make damn sure my husband and that woman had no contact with each other.

Chapter 70

David

People never talked to or handled me the way Patricia had, and I wasn't used to it. If it had not been for the money involved, I surely wouldn't have any further dealings with her. I was kind of having a change of heart about following through with any of this. I knew deep down that Tiffany didn't deserve any of this. She didn't deserve my lying to her about being sick. She didn't deserve for me to come between her and someone she obviously cared a lot about. Not to mention I had already taken her through so much. I wondered if the money was even worth it anymore.

But then I kept thinking about that jerk Terrence. Call it a man's pride perhaps, but I just couldn't seem to let go of him putting his hands on me. In addition, part of me couldn't wait to see the look on his face when he saw Tiffany with me and not him. That thought plus the money kept me involved, but with the way I felt, there was no telling what I might do come this evening. *Patricia just might be in for a very rude awakening.*

Chapter 71

Tiffany

It was now a few minutes after five, and I'd just arrived at the hotel. I'd enjoyed an absolutely beautiful day with Keisha so far. After breakfast, we went to my favorite spa and got full-body massages. Then from there we went to the nail salon. She said she wanted me to look and feel my best, which I did. I wished, however, that I'd had the time to get my hair and makeup done, but this would simply have to do.

I'd sat here in my truck for at least five or ten minutes in deep contemplation. Once I exited this vehicle and went inside, my whole life would change in a matter of minutes. I wasn't sure if I was actually ready for that, but something made me feel like I was. This just felt right. Terrence felt right. Then finally I found the nerve. I grabbed my overnight bag and headed inside.

The elevator ride up to the thirteenth floor seemed like the longest ever. My heart skipped a beat as I thought about seeing him again. It had been so long, and I couldn't wait to be in his presence. Now as I stood in front of the suite door, I looked at the large numbers plastered on it: 1307. My mind traveled back to that night with Terrence and what had taken place. It was beautiful, and I wanted more beautiful nights with him.

I opened the door, and the suite was amazing. It was adorned with crystals and red roses throughout. Even on the bed were rose petals that spelled out "I love you." There was a wet bar with champagne already chilling. On the coffee table were various platters of fruit, veggies, and cold shrimp. The lighting was dim with a hint of red in it, I was sure because Terrence knew that was my favorite color. It was all carefully thought out, and I was amazed that he and Keisha were able to pull all of this off. Walking from room to room, I almost felt like I was going to pass out from it all. Then I opened the door to the bathroom, where there was a Jacuzzi filled with rose petals and bubbles. There were also candles, a glass of champagne, and a tray filled with chocolate-covered strawberries sitting on the edge of the Jacuzzi. All I heard was Keisha in my ear continually telling me to enjoy the moment. That was exactly what I planned to do until Terrence arrived and especially after. I was going to enjoy every single moment of it all.

I was so relaxed after I soaked in the Jacuzzi for an hour and then applied my lavender oils to my body. I lay across the king-sized bed with yet another glass of champagne. I entertained myself by trying to find the sexiest position for whenever he walked in. I almost wanted to call Keisha, but I promised her I wouldn't. She wanted me to focus on nothing else but me and him. So I played with ideas in my head of what to do first, whether I wanted to hug him, kiss him, gaze into his eyes, or simply talk. I was so anxious and fidgety and unsure of how to respond. That was when I heard a soft knock at the door. My nipples instantly stood at attention while my clit turned flips inside of my black lace thong. I jumped out of the bed, stood up, and ran over to the door, flinging it open, prepared to embrace him. That was when I got the shock of my life. I damn near fainted.

"David?"

He stood there and looked at me with the most dumbfounded expression on his face. I had the same one. Although he'd seen my body before, I hurried to grab my robe and cover myself in my see-through negligee.

"What are you doing here? How did you even know—"

"Tiff, look, I only have a short amount of time to say what I need to say. We both know that."

He walked closer to me and took my hands. "First, I need to apologize to you again for everything that I did. There's no excuse for any of it, and I can't say I'm sorry enough."

"Please don't do this. Not now. You have to leave."

"I still love you, and I keep kicking myself every day for messing up with you." A tear started to crawl slowly down the left side of his face. "But I'm a sick man now. I realize that I probably brought this on myself. I deserve this for how I did you, Leslie, and even other women."

His tears became stronger as I embraced him and held him in my arms. Then he pulled away and knelt down on one knee. I couldn't believe this was all happening, especially now.

"Tiffany, please allow me to make it all up to you. Please let me be the man I should have been to you back then. If I'm going to die, please let me die trying to do everything I possibly can to make you happy."

I didn't know what the hell to say. One part of me hated him for doing this right now, but then the other part of me truly felt his pain. I almost wanted to grant his request. However, I didn't love him and never would. I didn't want to sacrifice another minute without Terrence for something I knew could never make me happy.

I made David stand up, and I took him into my arms, preparing myself to let him down in the most gentle and respectful way that I could.

Chapter 72

Terrence

There it was in front of me: suite 1307. Once I crossed to the other side of that door, my entire life would change. I smoothed down my clothing, checked my breath to make sure it was still fresh, and put my key into the door as quietly as I could. I wanted to catch her totally by surprise hopefully naked and waiting for me. But when I opened the door, I heard noises that just didn't sound right. Actually, it sounded as if someone was crying, and not Tiffany. I slowly crept inside and peeked around the corner of the entryway.

There they were, standing there, embracing one another. She didn't even see me because her back was to me. Yet I saw them. I stood there completely motionless as I watched the two of them together. He held her tight, his eyes closed, and she gently rubbed the back of his head. I didn't know what the hell was going on and felt like this had to be some type of joke. I wanted to yell out to her, but nothing seemed to come out. That was when he opened his eyes, looked dead into mine, then smiled and winked at me. Before I knew it, I ran up to him, snatched Tiffany away from his embrace, and pushed her onto the bed. Then I grabbed him by the collar and threw him up against the wall.

"What the hell are you doing here?"

"Get off me, you maniac."

"Terrence, David, please stop. Break it up," she screamed. I felt her grab my arm. "Terrence, please, calm down. The man is sick for heaven's sake."

I dropped him and turned my attention to her. "Sick? Do you think I give a damn about that, Tiff? What the hell is he doing here?"

"Terrence, please, would you just give me a second to handle this?"

"I'm calling the police on you for assault. This will be the last time you put your hands on me," he yelled.

"David, stop it."

"Either he leaves or I do," I yelled at her.

The room suddenly became quiet as we both put our attention on her. I looked at her, then him, then back at her. He looked at me with the same damn smirk as before, but what bothered me most was the look in her eyes. They pretty much said everything I needed to know at that moment.

"Forget it. If this is who you want, then fine." I started to walk out of the room.

"Please wait," she called after me. "It's not what you think."

She'd followed me into the hallway by the elevator as I pressed the buttons nonstop.

"Tiffany, go back inside the room."

"Please just listen to me. I can explain all of this."

I didn't hear her because my phone started to ring in my hand. I looked at the number, and it was my stepmother. I tried hard to prepare myself for whatever she was about to say, but as I put the phone to my ear and heard her whimpering, I got the news that damn near destroyed me.

"He's gone, Terrence. Pops is gone."

I looked at Tiffany standing there, then at him standing in the doorway of the room. "I can't do this with you right now. I just can't."

As I got into the elevator, we took one final look at one another. As the doors closed, I prepared myself to never speak with Tiffany again. Instantly I figured that maybe this was yet another sign from God that I needed to stay and fix my marriage with Patricia.

Study Questions

Tiffany

1. In the beginning, Tiffany prayed and asked God if David was the man for her. He gave her a clear answer, yet she still went beyond His will. Have you ever received an answer from God but still chose a different direction? Could she (or you) have saved herself (yourself) heartache and pain by listening to God from the very start? Why is it so hard to do this?
2. Do you think it's harder for a single person to be patient and wait for God for their mate when everyone else around them is married and has families?
3. Do you think Tiffany ignored the warning signs with David because of her desire to be married?
4. Do you think it was destined for Tiffany to relocate to Texas and meet Terrence? Do you believe in fate? Have you or would you ever relocate for love?
5. As a single woman, should she have cut all interaction with Terrence from the very start once she found out he was married? Can a single woman be friends with a married man, even if she's not friends with the spouse?

David

1. David had ill intentions from the very start with Tiffany and found it difficult to be totally honest

with her. Are a lot of men today like David or does it depend on the man?

2. Do you think David was less likely to settle down because of his age and being set in his ways or because of his overall financial situation?
3. David honestly had nothing to offer any of the women he was involved with. Do you think they settled for him because he was single and available?
4. Do you blame his mother at all for continually pacifying him, or was she simply helping her son?

Terrence

1. Terrence stated from the beginning of his marriage that he believed he and Patricia loved each other but were never in love with each other. He married her out of obligation while she married for help with her children. Do you think people marry for reasons other than love? If so, can these types of marriages ever work? Can they eventually fall in love with each other?
2. Do you feel Terrence was well within his rights? Did Patricia's behavior contribute to his feelings?
3. Terrence was highly attracted to Tiffany from the start of meeting her and vice versa. Do you blame Terrence, Tiffany, or both for his failed marriage?
4. Do you think Terrence made Patricia insecure because of his dealings with other women?
5. Should he have tried harder to work out his marriage because of the vows they took before God, even if there was no love there?

Patricia

1. Patricia was labeled as insecure. Did you feel she was really insecure, or had Terrence's actions made her that way? If he'd actually given her the love and attention she desired, do you think she would have been a better wife?
2. What are your thoughts on Patricia choosing her son over Terrence when he wanted to put him out? Who do you feel was wrong in this situation?
3. Do you think Patricia was well within her rights to not want Terrence's father staying there seeing that they he'd never met her or her children?

Overall

1. Who do you think will end up together in the sequel, *I Didn't Think You Existed: Fool for Love?*

   - Tiffany and David
   - Terrence and Patricia
   - Tiffany and Terrence
   - Patricia and David

Readers' Responses

"Wow . . . *I Didn't Think You Existed!* The storyline was well written and captivating making it a page turner. The plot was also relatable, and the food references especially gives it a homey feel!"
—Katrina Clark

"*I Didn't Think You Existed* had me deep in my feelings. I was for real, for real mad. I cursed all of the characters more than once, maybe because each of them reminded me of someone I know. Nonetheless, it's a good read, thought provoking, and a real page turner!"
—Doris Redmond

"*I Didn't Think You Existed* will take you on a roller coaster of emotions. You will definitely relate to at least one of the characters and find yourself imagining if you were in the story!"
—Chasity Wilson

The Author

After attempting several different career paths, author Hazel Ro embraced and followed her passion and God-given talent as a fiction romance author and entrepreneur.

Her love for writing started at an early age when she found release in journaling her thoughts. Hazel Ro would take whatever negativity from her reality and build her own world by drawing from her imagination and creativity.

However, never in a million years did she imagine her writing manifesting into her first published novel, *I Didn't Think You Existed*. Its story line uses an entertaining yet effective way of dealing with real-life issues such as cheating and adultery, betrayal, lies, broken relationships, spirituality, and so much more. Hazel Ro's ultimate objective through this first piece and others is to promote and encourage healthy African American relationships.

Aside from writing novels, Hazel Ro is passionate about anything of the arts. She coproduced her first stage play *For Better or For Worse* in 2012 and loves music, poetry, and singing.

Hazel Ro is a graduate of Lindenwood University, where she earned her MA in mass communications. She has her BA in sports and entertainment management from Fontbonne University.

Hazel Ro is originally from St. Louis, Missouri, but has found her home in Chicago, Illinois, since April 2015.
—Ro Chamberlain—

Find *I Didn't Think You Existed* and other novels by Hazel Ro by visiting www.hazel-ro.com.

There, the author can be contacted for discounted book purchases for large orders, group discussions with book clubs, speaking engagements, and more!

Thank you again for your support!
Hazel Ro

Acknowledgments

As much as I love to write, I still find it extremely difficult when it comes to thanking those that have supported me in this journey. There are so many, from family, friends and supporters, that have encouraged and assisted me in this process, that there are no amount of words that can truly convey my overall thankfulness and gratefulness.

First and foremost, I thank God, our Father and Creator for giving me the gift of writing. This entire process has truly been a dream come true from beginning to end, but I am seeing for myself that it has always been a part of Your master plan for my life. You said in Your word, "For I know the plans I have for you...plans to prosper you and not to harm you, plans to give you hope and a future." I have believed and stood firmly on this one verse from the very start, and I am witnessing Your holy word come to pass. Thank You, Father!

Of course, I owe a huge thank you to one of the best literary agents in the business, N'Tyse. You believed in me and my writing from a simple meeting over social media. You went out of your way to get me the best deal possible with the publisher of my dreams, and you have done it all with elegance and class. I can only hope that we will have many successes to share from this point forward. Thank you for all that you do.

Also, to the entire publishing team with Urban Books, I truly appreciate each and every one of you, especially Mr.

Acknowledgments

Carl Weber. I cannot begin to thank you enough for taking a chance on me. I hope this book and future releases make you proud for giving me this opportunity. Thank you from the very bottom of my heart. I couldn't imagine being a part of a better publishing house for my literary career.

Thank you again to my family and friends. It's far too many to name, but please know that each and every one of you hold a very special place in my heart.

It goes without saying, thank you to all of my readers and supporters! With this being my first published release, I can only hope and pray that I have presented a quality read that captures your hearts, minds, and souls. I wanted to offer something that was relatable to anyone who reads it, and I believe I did just that. I hope that you all feel the same. Thank you from my heart for allowing a new author like myself a moment into your worlds.

Last, but not least, I give a special thank you to a very special friend. You know who you are. Just a simple reminder: what's understood between us will never have to be explained to anyone else. Thank you.

With all the love in my heart,
Hazel Ro